"This is my home. I will never leave it."

Her eyes flared in challenge. "Even if you burn Brambly to the ground to force me away, I'll erect a tent in the ashes and keep warm sleeping on the embers!"

His body drew up tight and tall in response to the fight in her. She had been right about him. He wasn't used to being contradicted, certainly not by a woman.

But this hellcat was no ordinary woman. Even now, instead of being intimidated and frightened, she stared boldly back, her hands clenched into fists, those full lips of hers pressed together stubbornly. Aggravation at him gripped her enough that she panted with it, her breasts rising and falling tantalizingly beneath her coat with each quick, shallow breath, and he could feel the heat of her body through his jacket and along his legs where his thigh pressed against hers.

"And you will stop ordering me about!" She smacked his hand away from her face. "I am not one of your men, Colonel."

He clasped her chin again. "Trust me, angel," he rasped, his voice husky as he tilted her face upward, "of that I am well aware."

His mouth swooped down and captured hers.

DUKES
ARE
FOREVER

ANNA
HARRINGTON

FOREVER

NEW YORK   BOSTON

Forever
Hachette Book Group
1290 Avenue of the Americas
New York, NY 10104

HachetteBookGroup.com

Printed in the United States of America

First Edition: November 2015
10 9 8 7 6 5 4 3 2 1

OPM

Forever is an imprint of Grand Central Publishing.
The Forever name and logo are trademarks of Hachette Book Group, Inc.

The Hachette Speakers Bureau provides a wide range of authors for speaking events. To find out more, go to www.hachettespeakersbureau.com or call (866) 376-6591.

The publisher is not responsible for websites (or their content) that are not owned by the publisher.

ATTENTION CORPORATIONS AND ORGANIZATIONS:

Most Hachette Book Group books are available at quantity discounts with bulk purchase for educational, business, or sales promotional use. For information, please call or write:

Special Markets Department, Hachette Book Group
1290 Avenue of the Americas, New York, NY 10104
Telephone: 1-800-222-6747 Fax: 1-800-477-5925

To Pam Xanthopoulos, Kim Warren-Cox, and Billie Gateley for all the dinners, bottles of wine, tears, and laughter we've shared over the years. My love and friendship to you always.

A very special thank-you to Michele Bidelspach, the best editor I could have hoped to work with, to Angelina Krahn and Mari Okuda for your attention to detail, and to Sarah Younger, the most patient agent in the world.

PROLOGUE

On the Battlefield in San Cristobal, Spain
November 1813

"Forward!" Colonel Edward Westover yelled above the cracking gunfire and the clashing steel bayonets as he raised his saber into the air.

He dug in his heels, and his horse leapt toward the melee of blue and red uniforms on the field where until just hours ago sunflowers bloomed. The yellow petals now stained red with blood lay crushed beneath pounding hooves as the British cavalry charged the end of the enemy's cannon line. Known as the Scarlet Scoundrels for their red uniforms on the field and their roguish actions off it, the dragoons were ordered to stop the barrage of artillery for the infantry's advance, but Edward's personal mission was to protect as many of his men as possible.

His two most trusted captains flanked him as they charged together into battle, shooting and slashing without pause, both prepared to give their lives to win the battle for the allied forces.

"To the right!" Edward shouted, setting his horse toward a gap in the line.

Nathaniel Grey shouted in answer as he struck his saber at a Frenchman who had advanced farther than the infantry should have allowed. Beside him, Thomas Matteson pushed through the gap, firing his pistols and reloading on horseback while never breaking stride.

As the French infantry gave way against the onrushing cavalry, the three men galloped to the right flank of the cannon. The enemy line broke into a confused scurry, with men succumbing to the horses bearing down on them.

Within two hours, the allied forces had routed the enemy and sent them fleeing in a disorganized retreat. The French cannon line abandoned, the British infantry pushed forward to secure the village. By the time the cavalry returned behind their line, they were exhausted, their mounts' heads hanging low and the men slipping gratefully from their backs.

"Westover!"

Edward turned. "Here!"

His shout split the noise of the line as the men reorganized around him by tending to the wounded, capturing loose horses whose riders had been knocked from their backs, and collecting weapons they'd captured from the enemy.

Leaving Lieutenant Reed still on horseback, the man having solemnly volunteered for the dangerous mission of being the line messenger for the battle, Nathaniel Grey walked slowly toward Edward, his spine straight with solemn determination.

As he approached, Edward saw the hard lines of his face and the harsh set of his jaw. His friend's normally bright eyes were somber.

It was the look of death.

He steeled himself. The battle had been horrific, and he was certain several good men perished in their charge. He'd grown used to the terror and fury of battle, but the aftermath never grew easier.

"Grey," he said soberly as the captain stopped in front of him, then glanced over at Thomas to indicate with a nod that the other man should remain. The three men had been through hell together during the past few years, and they would face together whatever was in the message that made Nathaniel Grey suddenly so grim.

"Colonel, there's news from England." Meeting Edward's gaze, Grey hesitated, then drew a shaking breath. "Your brother is dead."

CHAPTER ONE

London, March 1815

Edward Westover stared across the card table at the man he was about to destroy.

The balding, paunchy gambler dabbed at his sweaty forehead with a handkerchief, then tugged at his cravat as if it choked him. The man's gaze lifted to meet his, and a jolt of satisfaction pulsed through him at the fear on the man's face.

Let the bastard be afraid. Let him get exactly what he deserves.

During the past year, Edward had thought of little else than the satisfaction he'd feel when this moment arrived, when he'd finally receive the justice that the English courts had denied him. Nearly every moment since he returned from Spain had been focused on ruining this man's life, and even now, beneath the stoic expression he carefully showed the room, he burned with hatred and a driving need for retribution.

In a matter of seconds, Phillip Benton would lose his last hand, and with that, his life as he knew it would be over. Edward watched the man closely and waited, counting off each heartbeat, and the only outward sign of his anticipation was a slight quickening of his breath. This must be how the devil felt when he took a man's soul, Edward decided, except that Benton had no soul to take.

The dealer turned the last card.

Benton gaped at it, unable to believe he'd lost. As Edward watched him blanch, a flash of satisfaction shot through him.

"The game's finished, Benton." *And so are you.* "Now, I'll take what you owe me." Welcoming the pleasure of the man's destruction, Edward reached for the marker and tossed it to him. "*Everything* you owe."

Benton forced a pacifying smile. "I haven't got it all with me tonight, of course."

Edward glared at him. From his arrogant demeanor, it was clear Benton still had no idea who he was or realized the tragedy connecting them. But he would learn soon enough, and then Edward planned on making him regret for the rest of his life the actions that brought them together.

Benton motioned the gambling hell manager to the table. "Thompson, I've gotten myself into a spot again." With a forced laugh, Benton's jocular tone belied the desperation of his situation. "Would you assist me with my friend here"—but the scornful glower Edward shot him was far from friendly—"by advancing me enough to pay off my losses?"

Thompson coughed nervously, his eyes darting to Edward. "'Fraid I can't do that."

"Thompson!" he cried incredulously, loud enough that the men at the surrounding tables glanced up. He lowered his voice. "Have I ever failed to repay you? Have I ever forfeited so much as a pence?"

"You've always been a good customer."

Benton beamed. "Hand me a paper, then, and I'll swear out a note. My word's good."

Thompson turned awkwardly toward Edward. "What would you have me do, sir?"

"Why are you asking him?" Benton demanded.

"Because I hold your notes," Edward drawled, taking immense pleasure in the confusion that flashed across the man's face.

Benton snorted. "Thompson holds them."

"I bought them from Thompson," Edward explained, summarizing in a few words the time-consuming work of the past twelve months leading up to this moment, "just as I bought up all your debts. All the credit you owe the merchants, the lease on your rooms, your stable bills, and every pound of your gambling debt in every hell across London."

Benton turned scarlet. "What in God's name is going on here? Thompson!"

The manager shook his head. "You had too many notes, Phillip. You still owe me from last autumn. When I received the offer to purchase your debts—"

"Purchase my debts?" His voice rang loudly through the hell, stopping the play at all the tables. The men paused to stare, and hushed whispers rose throughout the room. "Sir, I demand an explanation!"

"I purchased your debts," Edward answered coldly, hating the man more with each passing heartbeat, "and now I demand repayment on them. *All* of them."

"You cannot demand such a thing."

"The law gives me the right to reclaim them with a fortnight's notice. Consider this your notice." Edward knew the answer, yet he took a perverse pleasure in asking, "Unless you can't pay?"

"Of course, I can pay!" His indignation sounded loud enough that everyone in the room heard it, but as he sank down in his chair, his shoulders sagging, he lowered his voice. "But not in a fortnight."

"Not at all," Edward corrected, relishing the man's defeat. "Even if you sold every possession you own, you would still be in my debt." *Exactly where the bastard deserves to be.*

Despite the heat of the crowded gambling hell, Benton shivered. He looked at the marker on the table as if staring at his own grave.

"You'd send me to debtor's prison?" Benton's voice strangled in his throat.

Edward had considered doing just that many times during the past year—thrusting him into a cold, windowless prison to let the man rot away in his own filth behind stone walls.

"No." He wanted a public revenge with absolute control of every aspect of the man's life. If he couldn't hang the bastard, he'd at least make the man wish he were dead. There was no mercy in him tonight. That died a year ago with Stephen and Jane. "But I will take your house, all its furnishings, your horse, your clothes…" He venomously bit out each harsh promise and signaled to a distinguished-looking man standing awkwardly by the hall's entrance. "Every last pence."

"I'll be left with nothing." He dabbed at his forehead with the handkerchief, then croaked out a pathetic laugh. "Nothing except my daughter."

"Then I'll take her, too," Edward said with an icy facetiousness. "And every last ribbon on her head."

"Who are you?" Benton demanded again, furious at being publicly humiliated.

The man reached their table. "Yes, Your Grace?"

Benton blinked, then bellowed, "*Your Grace?*"

"This is William Meacham." Edward calmly nodded toward his family's longtime attorney. "He'll inform you of the arrangements."

"Go to hell!" Benton clenched his fists. "I'm not agreeing to anything."

Benton swung his gaze to Meacham, and Edward could see the frantic thoughts spinning through the man's head. He'd seen that same angry desperation on the faces of defeated enemies when the battle was over and the terms of surrender negotiated. How little men changed from battlefield to barroom. And for this man, surrender was unconditional.

He'd give no quarter of any kind to this enemy.

"If you refuse my terms, Benton," Edward promised, "then I *will* throw you into prison."

Benton's face darkened with fury. "You would do that— you would ruin my life?"

"Yes."

"Why?"

"Because you ruined mine."

Benton caught his breath. "Who *are* you?"

"Don't you recognize me?" Edward rose from his chair, drawing up to his full six-foot height. This was the moment he'd planned for during the past year with an almost blind relentlessness, and as he'd expected, with it came a sweet flash of shattering satisfaction. "Edward Westover."

"Westover..." The name struck Benton with a violent shudder. "You're *Colonel Westover*?"

As he stared at Benton, the full force of his hatred and revenge rose in him and vanquished whatever brief satisfaction and pleasure he'd felt only moments earlier. Edward leaned over the table to gaze mercilessly at him. "I am the brother of the man you murdered."

He spun away from the table and stalked through the gambling hell toward the front door, putting the length of the room between them before he strangled Benton with his bare hands. Lost in the wrathful thoughts of his vengeance, he was oblivious to the presence of the man standing in the corner, who had watched tonight's events unfold and fell into step behind him.

His carriage waited at the front entrance, and he climbed inside. The tiger closed the door.

Shutting his eyes, Edward took a deep breath and waited for the peace that should have been his, the relief and happiness at finally making the bastard pay. But it didn't come, and even the flash of exquisite satisfaction he'd felt when Benton realized his identity was now gone. He felt only the same need to destroy Benton that he'd carried for the past year, tempered by the deep emptiness he'd felt since the moment in San Cristobal when he learned of Stephen's death.

The door flung open, and the man who had watched him from the shadows jumped inside. He pounded his fist against the roof, signaling to the coachman to send the team forward into the night.

"Colonel Westover." Thomas Matteson gave a short salute as the carriage lurched into motion. "Interesting evening."

"Captain Matteson." Edward glared at the old friend who had become like a brother to him while fighting together in Spain. And whom he now wanted to throttle for interfering in his life. "Get the hell out."

Ignoring that, Thomas relaxed against the squabs as casually as if he'd been invited into the carriage rather than flinging himself inside.

"We're in London. It's Lord Chesney here, if you don't mind." Thomas flashed a charming grin, the same one that had attracted the hearts of women across the Continent. Edward had lost count of the number of times he'd rescued the man from angry Spanish fathers. "I'm a marquess now, I daresay."

"So I'd heard."

Shortly after the battle at San Cristobal, Thomas's father inherited as Duke of Chatham, which meant this fearless former captain was now Marquess of Chesney and heir to a duchy. Which meant his life was too important to risk in the army. Dying in battle was fine for second sons but never for peers or heirs, a lesson that Edward knew only too well.

"I've proven you wrong." Thomas angled out his long legs. "You said I'd never make anything of myself."

"I said you were reckless and would get yourself killed," he corrected solemnly, unable to keep his concern from his voice. He was afraid his friend might yet prove him right.

"We're both headed for the Lords now." Thomas grinned at him. "Say a prayer for Parliament."

But Edward was in no mood for teasing around tonight, especially given the way fate had thrust the peerage upon both of them. The irony was humorless.

"Where's Grey?" Edward wouldn't have put it past the man not to be outside hanging off the carriage at that very moment.

"Somewhere in England."

Thomas's answer wasn't facetious. After he was wounded in the war, Grey's connections to the underbelly of society made him valuable enough that Lord Bathurst, Secretary of War and the Colonies, insisted he join the War Office. Grey was one of their best agents, and "somewhere in England" was as close as anyone could know.

Edward reached toward the door with the full intent of shoving Thomas out into the night. "I suggest you join him."

The marquess clucked his tongue. "Becoming a duke has made you rather testy, Colonel. I prefer the man who used to set enemy tents on fire. He was more reasonable."

"You have no idea," he muttered. Then he exhaled a ragged breath, knowing the tenacious man wouldn't leave him alone until he had what he came for. No matter how damnably irritating the trait, Edward couldn't begrudge him. It was the same tenacity that had kept the former captain alive in Spain. "Why are you here?"

"I need your help," Thomas answered solemnly. "I have a friend who needs me to save him from himself."

Edward glared at him through the shadows. He trusted Thomas with his life, but in this, he was overstepping.

"If I wanted your help," he growled, "I would have asked for it a year ago."

"You weren't ready for it then."

Edward gave a derisive snort. "You think I'm ready for it now?"

"I think you're just as bullheaded as you've always been," Thomas answered, affection clear in his voice despite his words, "but I am not going to let you ruin a life without trying to stop you."

"Benton's, you mean."

"Yours."

Edward clenched his teeth, but even that small show of outrage was forced. He wasn't angry at Thomas as much as at what he represented—his old life, the one he'd been forced to leave behind. But that life was gone forever.

"How do you know about my plans for Benton?" he demanded.

"Your aunt Augusta. She asked me to talk you out of this scheme of yours."

"Then you can tell her it's too late," he assured him. "Meacham is settling the agreement now."

"You can still let Benton go." Thomas met Edward's gaze with deep sympathy. "What happened to your brother was unforgivable, and Benton deserved to hang for it. But he didn't. The magistrates let him go, and now you need to let him go, too, before he destroys your life as well."

Edward stared at him blankly, saying nothing.

There was a time when he would have sought out Grey's and Thomas's counsel and most likely taken their advice just as he would have his own brother's, but that was before his world changed. The Colonel Westover whom Thomas had ridden beside in the fires of war was gone. He might as well have died on the battlefield.

"You saved my life, Colonel, many times." Thomas leaned forward, his face intense in the dim shadows cast by the swinging carriage lamps. "And I will not let you ruin your life now."

Edward almost laughed. There was nothing Thomas could do to either stop him or help him. Except… "Can you watch Benton? I need someone I can trust to keep an eye on him until everything is settled."

Apparently realizing it was time to surrender the battle in hopes of eventually winning the war, Thomas grudgingly agreed. "I'll contact Grey to see if he has men to spare. But promise me you'll consider letting Benton go."

The hell I will. Edward held his gaze and lied, "I'll consider it."

But he would never change his mind. Benton was his prisoner now, as surely as if he'd chained him to the walls of Newgate himself. He might be free to come and go as he pleased, but he'd be living in rooms Edward chose for him. His every move would be watched, his every activity and choice would be Edward's to make, and never again would he have so much as a halfpenny to his name. There was nothing that would ever make him set that bastard free when his own brother lay dead in the churchyard.

"Good night, then, Colonel. And give my best to Aunt Augusta." Thomas opened the carriage door and swung outside, to drop away onto the street and disappear into the darkness.

Blowing out an irritated breath, Edward slammed the door shut.

Thomas was wrong. Revenge had proven easy. He didn't have to hang Benton; he didn't even have to give the man enough rope to hang himself. All he'd had to do was follow along behind and pick up the pieces. It had been that simple.

He'd won. He'd attained his revenge and received every capitulation he'd wanted, giving Benton exactly the punishment he deserved—the loss of everything he held dear. At the card table, when Benton realized who he was and what he'd done, an intense satisfaction struck him unlike anything he'd ever experienced before in his life.

But the sensation faded, and quickly, until all that was left was the same emptiness as before. Instead of the happiness and relief he expected, he felt hollow, as if he were missing half his life, with no idea where to find it.

*　*　*

Katherine Benton pushed back the hood of her cloak as she entered the blacksmith's house, her leather bag gripped tightly in her other hand.

"Forgive us, miss," Mrs. Dobson greeted her, "for fetchin' ye in the midst o' th' night like this."

She smiled reassuringly. "You did the right thing in sending for me."

The worried mother moved the toddler in her arms to the other hip as another child wailed from somewhere upstairs and two boys chased each other through the rooms. There were now ten children in the small but well-kept house, with Kate delivering the last baby herself.

"Bless ye, miss," Mrs. Dobson sighed gratefully, and for a moment, Kate saw the glisten of fatigued tears in her eyes, "you comin' to help us, an' you wit' all yer own troubles."

Your own troubles. Ignoring the prickle of humiliation, knowing the woman meant well, Kate placed a comforting hand on her arm before Mrs. Dobson could go into detail about those troubles or remind her of how Mr. Dobson had been kind enough to buy her horse last year when she needed money. "Where's Tom?"

She pointed toward the stairs, then shooed away two youngsters at her skirts.

"Would you bring up a kettle of hot water and a mug, please?"

The woman nodded, and Kate hurried upstairs. Tom must have truly been ill tonight to have all the household in such an uproar, the children out of their beds and running wild, from the oldest at fourteen right down to the baby. Stomach trouble, the boy who had been sent to fetch her reported. *Please, God, let it be something I can fix.*

Taking a deep breath to steady herself, she stepped into the little room beneath the eaves that served as the bedroom for all six of the Dobson boys, with the three girls and the baby sharing a room downstairs. A young boy lay scrunched up on the cot in the corner, his father trying uselessly to comfort him as he grasped at his abdomen and groaned in pain.

Kate gently elbowed Mr. Dobson away, set her bag on the edge of the bed and opened it, then looked down at the boy. "Hello, Tom."

"Hello, miss," he returned, forcing the greeting out through gritted teeth. Sweat beaded on his forehead. His face was pale, and his arms never released their hold over his middle.

She frowned. "James said your stomach hurts."

"Somethin' awful, miss." He swallowed down another groan.

"Show me exactly where."

The boy glanced uncertainly at his father, who nodded

his permission, and Tom pushed the blanket down to his hips with one hand while pulling up his nightshirt with the other, baring his little, flat belly.

Kate touched his stomach carefully, starting with his lower left side and working her way across. "Here?"

He shook his head. Moaning, he placed his fingers over a spot high in the middle just under his sternum.

"Here?" Kate pushed into his abdomen, and he cried out. Her eyes narrowed, and from what she knew about this particular boy, she suspected... "Open your mouth for me, Tom."

He opened wide, and when she looked inside, she scowled, all worry inside her vanishing.

Now, she *knew*. "You sneaked out of bed tonight, didn't you?"

His eyes widened—he'd been caught. "Miss?"

"And judging by the pains, I'd guess most likely around midnight. Isn't that so?"

With competing looks of suffering and guilt flitting over his young face, he nodded.

She sat back on the bed and raised a sharp brow. "You got into your papa's tobacco."

He shot a worried glance at his father and moaned. Being caught—and fear of the punishment to come—only made his bellyache even worse.

"Your son has an upset stomach," Kate informed both husband and wife, who had remained in the doorway, the baby still in her arms and a tenacious toddler clinging to her skirts. "He'll be better by morning." She cast a sideways glance at the boy. "And I have a feeling that after tonight, he'll never touch your stash again. Will you, Tom?"

The boy glumly shook his head.

"Good. This should help." She pulled a bottle of white powder from her bag and poured some into the cup Mrs. Dobson handed her when Kate signaled for both it and the kettle. She poured in hot water, then stirred it. "Drink this." When the boy frowned warily into the bubbling mixture, she explained, "It's saleratus. The bubbles will help settle your stomach. Go on—drink it up."

Making a face as if being tortured, Tom gulped it down, then gasped in distaste.

"You'll be better in a few hours." Kate stole a glance at the mother and father, obviously overwhelmed by their brood. "How old are you, Tom—nine or ten?"

"Eleven, miss."

Even better. "Old enough for a job, then. Come visit me at Brambly tomorrow. We could use a boy for the stables."

That was a lie. Brambly had no need of stable boys, because Brambly had no stables. Because Brambly no longer had any horses except for an old swayback no one would take off her hands if she paid them. But she also knew that one less child to worry about would help ease the burden of the Dobson household, even if she wasn't certain how she'd manage to feed one more mouth in hers. But she would. Somehow, she always managed to find a way.

She closed her bag and stood to leave.

"Miss, are ye certain 'bout Tom goin' to work fer ye?" Mrs. Dobson pressed as she followed Kate downstairs. The couple wasn't poor but neither were they wealthy, and although sending Tom to work for Kate meant less money spent on him, more importantly it meant one less child to supervise.

"We could use the extra hands."

From the twitch of the woman's lips, she clearly didn't believe Kate, but she didn't challenge her. "T'would be a great help, miss. It's always somethin' wi' children, ain't it?"

As if on cue, the baby wailed. The woman sighed and opened the door.

Kate stepped outside into the darkness and cold, not looking forward to the miles she'd have to walk home through the darkness.

"Ye should count yerself fortunate, miss, that ye don't have no children t' constantly scold an' fuss over."

Kate forced her smile not to waver despite the stab of jealousy. No, she had no children of her own and most likely never would. To make the sacrifices necessary to have a husband and family...She simply couldn't bring herself to do it.

"Yes." She drew her hood down over her face. "How very fortunate I am."

* * *

Inside his study, Edward poured himself a whiskey. Taking a gasping swallow and welcoming the burn, he turned toward the fireplace, where dying embers still glowed. He jabbed at them with the brass poker until he'd sparked a weak flame, more to physically expel the pent-up frustrations inside him than to stir up a fire. Around him, the town house was dark and quiet, with Aunt Augusta and the servants catching the last few hours of sleep before dawn.

He envied them. He'd hadn't slept well in over a year. And he knew he wouldn't tonight, either.

He was simply tired. That's why he didn't feel the lasting happiness he'd expected at bringing Benton to justice and why he let Thomas's words prickle him. In the morning, once he'd slept and the success of his revenge settled over him, the joy of vindication would come. He would feel happy then.

Happy? *Christ.* He'd be glad if he could feel anything.

With a curse, he tossed back the remaining whiskey and stared at the fire.

"Your Grace?"

He glanced up as Meacham paused in the doorway. Edward signaled his permission to enter, glad for the man's arrival. The sooner they settled everything regarding Benton's situation, the better.

Meacham nodded politely. The Westover family attorney for nearly thirty years, William Meacham had proven himself time and again to be a superior lawyer and a dedicated employee. Occasionally over the years, even a friend. When Edward's father died and Stephen inherited, with the two brothers just twenty and nineteen, Meacham had been an invaluable advisor, and Edward owed him more gratitude than he could admit or the man would accept.

For all the history between them, however, Meacham would never assume familiarity, and he would never cross any lines of decorum, not even at four in the morning. As the new duke, Edward should have been pleased by the deference paid to him, but it rankled. Since he'd inherited, no one was open and honest with him anymore.

His lips twisted. Apparently, except for Thomas Matteson.

"My apologies for the late hour," Edward said quietly.

"None necessary, Your Grace." Meacham reached inside his coat and withdrew the papers he'd prepared.

"Benton agreed to your terms and in exchange signed over all his possessions, just as you demanded. He is bankrupt and in your debt." Then he added quietly, "Congratulations, sir."

Edward glanced at the papers only long enough to make certain Benton's signature crossed the bottom of each, then turned back to the fire.

It was done, then. Phillip Benton was now penniless, his life completely and publicly ruined. He would live in the small room in Cheapside that Edward provided, on a single pound's allowance that Edward gave him, watched at every moment and unable to make a move without permission—he had become a prisoner, or as close to one as he could be without being put into chains. His life had become Edward's to ruin, just as Benton had ruined his.

So why wasn't he happy?

"Thank you, Meacham. We're done for tonight."

The attorney hesitated. "There is one more item, Your Grace."

"What is that?"

"He has a daughter."

Edward frowned into the fire. Benton mentioned a daughter, but he hadn't thought the man was serious. In the months since he'd been having Benton trailed, his investigators hadn't seen nor heard any mention of a child.

He shouldn't be surprised, though, to learn Benton had a daughter who meant so little to him that he never went to see her or contacted her. The bastard had destroyed his own life through gambling, whoring, and drinking, and ruined the girl's life right along with his by denying her the care she deserved. A man like that didn't have the heart to love a child.

Meacham continued cautiously, "He requested that you become her guardian."

"No."

"If I may, sir, I think you should reconsider. Her mother is dead, and now with her father's situation—" A sharp glance from Edward made him censor himself. *Good.* Meacham and Thomas could both keep their bloody opinions about Benton to themselves. "You have your reputation to consid—"

"Damn my reputation," he muttered.

Meacham stiffened. "Your Grace, I do not believe you mean that."

Edward narrowed his eyes on him. This was as close as the man had ever come to overstepping between them, of being so familiar as to attempt to chastise. But Meacham wasn't wrong. Edward couldn't have cared less what happened to his own reputation, but now as the duke, he held the responsibility for the reputation of the Westover family and the title, whether he wanted it or not.

"Sir, you have made it so her father is no longer able to financially support her. Morally, she has become your responsibility. Best to make it legal as well." The attorney added plainly, his expression as paternal as Edward had ever seen it, "If you do not provide for her, and her situation becomes common knowledge, you will become a social pariah."

And Augusta right along with him. His aunt was his only family now, and he would never do anything to hurt her. "Fine." He turned dismissively back to the fire. "Write the contract."

"This is the right decision, sir," Meacham assured him. "It would have been regrettable to you if an innocent had been hurt."

Edward said nothing, not able to summon enough guilt to care. He'd seen hundreds of innocents hurt during the atrocities of war. What was one child's lack of ribbons compared to that?

"Someone should also travel to her home to ensure the suitability of her situation. I'll arrange for one of my assistants to leave next week—"

"No," Edward interrupted. "I'll go."

Meacham paused in surprise. "Pardon?"

"I'll go myself." Not that he truly cared about the little girl's feelings, but a legal clerk swooping down on her and frightening her was the last complication he needed when he wanted everything settled with Benton's situation as quickly and easily as possible. Screaming children and angry nannies would only add to his headaches.

He had another reason for going as well. After the ordeals of the past year, it would do him good to spend a few days alone in the countryside, riding and hunting, far from the family seat at Hartsfield Park and all the memories there. He wanted to go someplace where he could forget, if only for a few days, and where he wouldn't have the constant reminder of Stephen and Jane.

So he would meet the child, determine her living situation was satisfactory, then be on his way. Most likely, he'd be gone by teatime.

"If there's anything else," Edward instructed, "see me in the morning. Good night, Meacham."

"Your Grace." With a shallow bow, Meacham retreated from the study.

Edward refilled his glass and swirled the golden liquid thoughtfully. *So Benton has a daughter.*

Had.

She belonged to him now, as close to being his own daughter as possible without sharing his blood, and she'd become his responsibility to raise, educate, and eventually marry off when she came of age. Rather, that is, she'd become Meacham's responsibility, as he planned on never directly concerning himself with the child again after his visit to Sussex.

He hadn't planned on this, but now that she was part of the battle's aftermath, the guardianship would only make his revenge that much sweeter. She was a spoil of war he had no intention of ever letting Benton see again.

A daughter's life for a brother's. Fair retribution.

"Strathmore?"

Aunt Augusta appeared in the doorway. Despite the late hour, she held her head regally, every inch of her a countess.

He returned his tired gaze to the fire. *Good God*, he was exhausted . . . "No, just Edward."

"*Just* Edward?"

He rolled his eyes at the oncoming onslaught from Augusta and her fierce dedication to social position. Childless herself, his widowed aunt raised him and Stephen after their mother died when they were just boys, her duty as the duke's sister to keep them in line and away from scandal. They'd been a handful for her, but she'd corralled them with a stern command and a sharp glance. One of the few people in the world able to reprimand him, she still possessed the ability to shake him with a single look.

Such as the one she now leveled at him. "You are the Duke—"

"It is what I desire tonight." Forced decorum was the last thing he wanted to deal with, all those reminders of how much his life had changed. Tonight, he wanted to be just Edward again. "Please, for tonight, let it be."

She drew up her shoulders in that posture of grudging surrender she assumed when she knew she'd pressed as far as possible but wouldn't win.

"I apologize for waking you," Edward offered, hoping to mollify her and avoid further argument.

"I heard the door."

"It was Meacham," he told her gently. "You should go back to bed and get a good night's rest. I'll join you for breakfast."

"Do you need anything? Should I call for Huddleston?"

He shook his head. Huddleston was a good valet, always eager to assist and please, but Edward found the attention cloying. He preferred to dress himself, just as he had in Spain despite having an aide-de-camp at his disposal, preferring his privacy. He would gladly do without a man completely if he could, but as a duke, that was impossible, and because Huddleston had been Stephen's valet, Edward kept him on.

"Sleep well, then." As she turned to leave, she rested a hand against his arm.

But he shifted away. He didn't want her motherly concern tonight, preferring to be left alone in his misery. Or it would have been misery, had he been able to feel even that.

Her face softened. "The title does not rest easy on you, does it, Edward?"

With a sag of his shoulders, he looked away, not wanting her to see the grief in his eyes. "It was Stephen's burden to bear, not mine."

"Your brother never considered it a burden. He saw it as his heritage."

"I'm a soldier." He shook his head. "This life was not meant for me."

"But it *is* your life now. Dear boy, you can spend all your time trying to convince yourself that you are still an army colonel, but you are not." A deep sigh escaped her, not of pity or mourning, but one borne of a wish that he could accept his new place as she had. "And you will never be *just* Edward."

With a soft kiss to his cheek, she left the room.

For several moments, Edward simply stared after her, unable to gather enough emotion inside him to be angry or hurt at her words. But he felt nothing. He leaned a tired arm across the mantel, too apathetic even to refill his glass and drink himself into oblivion.

As the second son, he was raised to make his own way in the world, and he had gladly done just that by purchasing an officer's commission when he finished university. On the battlefield, it mattered nothing that his family was one of the most powerful in England. What signified was character. His ability to carry out orders with an unfailing dedication to his men set him apart. And he excelled at it, earning himself four field promotions.

Then, in a cruel twist, fate stripped away all he'd worked so hard to achieve. The moment he inherited, his life as Colonel Westover disappeared, as if he had also died that day in the carriage accident that killed his brother and sister-in-law. He had been forced to step into his brother's life and carry on. As if his own existence up to that point hadn't mattered.

Legally, he was now Duke of Strathmore with titles and properties scattered across England, but he deserved none of it. By rights, he should still be fighting on the Continent, and Stephen should still be alive.

With Jane.

Even now, his chest tightened at the thought of her. The night Edward met her, when she'd entered the ballroom for her debut, he'd been mesmerized. With her dark hair and brown eyes, she wasn't a typical English beauty, but she had a vitality that drew him, a charm that the stiff rules of English society hadn't yet forced from her. He'd somehow managed to secure a waltz, and by the time the orchestra sent up its final flourishes and he whirled her to a stop, laughing in his arms, he was lost, despite knowing she wasn't meant for him.

The daughter of an earl, she was born to be the wife of a peer, and her future—and choice in husbands—had never been her own. And in truth, she'd never made any commitment to him.

Still, he pursued her in that reckless manner he possessed when he was younger, with the devil and his consequences both be damned. But he'd been too young, too inexperienced with women and the world, and far too arrogant to realize there were some things he'd never be able to have. No matter how much he wanted them. And he'd wanted her, not just for an affair but for the rest of his life, yet he never suspected she didn't share the same desires for a future together. So one warm afternoon as they lay tangled in the sheets of an unused guestroom at Hartsfield Park, he told her he loved her.

His eyes pressed shut against the memory. From ten years away, he could hear the sound of her nervous laughter and stunned voice as clearly as if she were still in the room with him...

Love? At least she'd had the decency to cover her mouth with her hand in apologetic shame as she murmured,

Surely, you cannot seriously think that I could ever marry an army officer—oh, Edward, no... Her wide-eyed disbelief melted into a soft expression of pity. *I thought you understood*...

Apparently, he hadn't understood at all.

One week after that, he left for war, to put as many miles as possible between them, with no intention of ever returning.

And two months later, his brother Stephen, Duke of Strathmore, announced his engagement. To Jane.

Despite the fires of war and his anger at her betrayal in marrying his brother, it took several years to purge her from his mind. He'd led reckless charges into battle and offered to take the place of men of lesser rank in dangerous missions, not because he had a death wish but simply because he no longer cared what became of him, if he lived or died. Eventually, he purged her from his body, too, with a string of nameless women.

All of this he kept from his brother, who had once been his best friend and closest confidant. At first, he was too ashamed to share with Stephen how he'd fallen for a woman he should have realized all along could never be his. Then, when he learned of the engagement, this second, deeper humiliation by the woman who became his sister-in-law changed everything between the two men, and Edward knew he would never be able to tell him. The confidence they'd shared in each other since they were boys had been irrevocably destroyed, costing him not only his heart but also his brother.

The result, he calculated, was a distinguished military career and an immeasurable distrust of women. He would allow himself to enjoy their flirtations and attentions and gladly take whatever pleasures they willingly gave, but he would never again trust one with his heart.

Then, in an instant, his world ended.

Stephen and Jane had gone to London to celebrate the long-awaited news that she was with child. But drunk and angry from a night losing money at cards, Phillip Benton raced his phaeton through the narrow streets, blindly speeding around a corner and into the oncoming carriage. The two teams collided in a mangle of wood and metal, blood and flesh. Stephen and Jane were cut down in the prime of their lives, while Benton walked away without a scratch.

Edward had been a country away when it happened, oblivious to the horrific and monstrous changes that fate had flung at his family.

The full weight of the Strathmore legacy descended upon him like an avalanche, ripping him from his command and forcing him back to England and into a life he'd never known nor wanted. Overnight, he'd become one of the most powerful men in the kingdom, responsible for estates and all their tenants and employees, bank accounts worth small fortunes, a seat in Parliament, and the private confidences of the Prince Regent himself.

His brother and Jane had been killed, but Edward had been sent to hell.

CHAPTER TWO

Brambly House
Sussex, England

Katherine Benton slowly reached the spoon toward the bowl poised precariously over the lamp, careful not to jostle the contraption as she gently stirred—

"Miss Kate!"

Her hand jerked. A gasp tore from her throat as she helplessly watched the tripod tumble over, smash against the stone floor, and splatter the dish's contents down the front of her dress in a brown, stinking mess.

"Blast it!" The unladylike curse flew out before she could stop it.

She blew out a frustrated breath, then bent to pick up the pieces of her ruined experiment. Her entire day's work, wasted.

Sunlight slanted through the window into the laboratory

she'd created in the old smokehouse where she worked her experiments and mixed her medicines, and as a bonus— *usually*—where she had a quiet place to work, keep her most important books and notes, and tend to the villagers' minor wounds. For graver injuries, she went to them, usually on foot because Brutus, the last of the farm's horses, never moved faster than a spine-jarring walk.

As she reached for the leather-bound journal where she recorded her notes, she wiped away a clinging glob of goop from her forehead.

First attempt unsuccessful, she scratched out, then wiped a glob of brown goop from the page and flicked it onto the floor. *Will make second attempt tomorrow under more controlled circumstances.*

"Miss, come quick!" Dorrie's shrill voice pierced the quiet afternoon. The cook, whom Kate kept on at Brambly because she could barely boil water and so couldn't find employment anyplace else, was better than a church bell when it came to getting attention. "A visitor! An *important* visitor!"

"Coming." With a sag of her shoulders, she extinguished the lamp, closed her journal, and headed across the yard toward the house.

Brambly House was beautiful in the afternoon, especially on early spring days like this when the sunlight shined golden and warm on its walls. Its façade marked five expansions in the past, each a different size, so the house appeared more like a series of interlocking blocks positioned randomly next to each other rather than a house with a planned architectural footprint.

But its asymmetry only added to its charm as far as Kate was concerned. She loved every mismatched inch of it.

It wasn't only the house that gave her a sense of pride. Brambly's owners had also earned a respectable reputation over the years as caretakers for the village, and Kate hoped to do the same. The village did not have a doctor; the nearest man who could claim any sort of medical training lived ten miles away in Oxbridge, and she wouldn't have trusted that incompetent drunkard with a dead cat. So when she'd been just seventeen, she stepped in with her homemade medicines and bandages to do the best she could. It was a calling borne of need, but in it, she'd found a purpose for her life and a deep love of medicine, right down to the tiny bottles in her laboratory that held her most precious mixtures.

Further, the villagers all knew her and trusted her. She'd practically grown up in the village lanes, a child who was more than a handful for Mrs. Elston, the woman who had been hired as her governess when Kate unexpectedly lost her mother when she was only twelve. Likewise, they all knew that Brambly had fallen on uncertain economic times and that she'd done what she could to cut expenses.

But these days, she worried even that might not be enough.

While the land generated revenue, there was never enough to pay for repairs, restock the barnyard, pay the servants' wages...the expenses never ended. So she fixed the worst of the buildings, kept a handful of animals, and maintained a subsisting, if sparse, existence in the home she loved with the servants who had become her family.

All of it was hers alone to manage. Sometimes, the responsibility worried her into sleepless nights, but she would never part with the farm. She held Brambly in her own right, by special entailment from her maternal grandparents to keep it out of their son-in-law's hands. Phillip Benton had never won over their hearts the way he'd won their daughter's. Her grandparents were right to worry, and Kate agreed with their caution. Although it broke her heart to acknowledge it, her father had never been dependable. His selfishness had led to angry arguments and harsh accusations against her mother, and later, when Kate took over the farm, to more hard times and tears than she wanted to admit.

But the problem her grandparents hadn't foreseen was her mother's death before Kate could marry and Brambly could come under the protection of her husband.

Because Kate was an unmarried woman, her father held all responsibility for her under the law. So while the land belonged to her, the meager profits it generated belonged to her father, along with the household furnishings, farm tools, and livestock, right down to the last little piggy. Whenever Papa visited, some of it always left with him...ivory candlestick holders, a silver teapot, a keepsake box—all carried back to London and sold. Even now a pang of bitter sadness rushed through her at the thought of all she'd lost since her mother's death. And along with the anguish came helpless anger that Papa kept putting worthless business schemes above his family's security.

There had been some awful arguments between them since her mother's death, in which he'd demanded the property outright, but she'd always refused and always would. Brambly was her home, and she would never part with it.

But she did help him however she could. Oh, Phillip Benton certainly wasn't a saint, but he was still her father and the only relative she had left, so she couldn't simply abandon him, even if she rarely saw him. And a part of her still clung to the hope, however small, that someday he would find the right business investment and earn enough money to take care of her and Brambly.

Although—she bit her lip as she thought sadly of the empty larders and barren rooms—if she had to wait much longer, would there be anything left to save?

"Miss Kate!"

She rolled her eyes. "Coming!"

Kate hurried around the garden wall and saw Dorrie waving impatiently from the doorway.

"What is it?" she asked as she stepped inside the house. "Who's here?"

"In there." The cook nodded toward the room that had once served as the formal drawing room when her mother had been alive.

"Who?"

"Edward Westover."

But Kate knew no Westovers, and a quick look around the foyer told her he hadn't bothered with the formality of presenting either a calling card or a letter of introduction.

Dorrie's eyes shined. "A *duke*!"

She caught her breath, surprised and puzzled. Why on earth would a duke come to Brambly?

"The Duke of Strathmore," Dorrie added with an impressed air, as if the full title made a difference. But Kate wasn't the kind of person to catch the attention of any peer, for any reason. "He asked specifically for Mrs. Elston, but the ol' busybody's gone off t' the village."

"Well, then he'll have to meet with me instead." Kate reached for the drawing room door. "Let's not keep His Grace waiting."

Dorrie shot her a warning look, which Kate promptly brushed away, the same way she'd dismissed the woman's motherly concerns since she was twelve. Still, she paused for a moment, then threw caution to the wind as she forced a welcoming smile and flung open the door.

The man waiting inside turned toward her, and she froze. Her heart stopped.

Dark eyes landed on her, so dark they reminded her of black velvet, and for a moment, she could only stare back, captured. An unexpected tingle curled down her spine and heated her clear through to her toes. She swallowed. Hard.

This was a duke? Trim and muscular, tall and darkly handsome, with a firm jaw and broad shoulders stretching beneath his jacket... *Oh my*. Perhaps she'd wrongly underrated dukes.

He frowned, and with horror, she realized she was staring. Dear Lord, she was *staring*!—and shamelessly.

Before she could tear her gaze away, the careful façade on his face slipped and revealed an expression somewhere between amusement and puzzled surprise. Yet in an instant, the inscrutable mask returned.

"Colonel Edward Westover," he introduced himself. Then added almost in afterthought, "Duke of Strathmore."

She gave him a flustered curtsy. "Welcome to Brambly House, Your Grace."

"Thank you." He paused, frowning at her. "Are you all right?"

She blinked. "Pardon?"

"Are you all right?" he repeated, loudly and slowly. Definitely more impatiently.

"I'm fine." When his gaze moved to the large, brown

splatter across the front of her dress, she realized what he meant. "Oh! I accidentally spilled on myself."

His frown deepened. "How many times?"

"Just—never mind." Her cheeks flushed, mortified.

He said nothing, but she could sense the disapproval in him. It was palpable.

Irritation instantly replaced her embarrassment, and she indignantly raised her chin. "My apologies for not being prepared for your *unexpected* arrival, Your Grace." She didn't bother hiding her annoyance. "What brings you to Brambly?"

"Business," he answered simply.

"Business?" She puzzled at his casual dress of a maroon jacket over a white shirt, tan breeches and matching waistcoat, and worn black boots. He was dressed for a day of riding or hunting, not of conducting business. He wasn't even wearing a neck cloth, for goodness' sake! And she certainly couldn't think of any business that would bring a duke to Brambly.

Then he confused her even more by holding up a doll. "I'm the new guardian of Katherine Benton."

"What?" she choked. *What* had he just said?

He stared at her as if she were a bedlamite, then blew out an exasperated breath at having to repeat everything. "I am Miss Benton's new guardian."

For a beat, Kate froze in stunned disbelief. Then she laughed, at first the giggles just sputtering from her, then growing until her shoulders shook, her hands trembling so hard she could barely take the doll from his hand.

"I'm sorry," she apologized, checking her laughter. "It's all just a little...absurd!"

His jaw tightened. "I assure you, Mrs. Elston, my presence here is not absurd."

"No, you're correct about that. You are..." Her head tilted curiously as she studied him. "Definitely not someone I would consider absurd."

Her green eyes swept over him, blatantly scrutinizing the breadth of his shoulders, his chest, which narrowed to a lean waist, the muscular thighs beneath his tan breeches. Wavy, thick black hair accentuated mercilessly dark eyes, so dark they were almost as black as his hair. He was obviously a man used to physical work and outdoor pursuits, nothing at all like the other men of the aristocracy she'd seen, those paunchy fops who flaunted fashion and behaved like spoiled children.

But this one—well, there was nothing soft nor spoiled about this man who filled the room with his presence and wasn't regal so much as proud, confident...

Dangerous.

She swallowed hard, her earlier amusement evaporating beneath those hard eyes. "I'm afraid there's been a mistake." She held out the doll to return it. "I'm Katherine."

"You're Katherine Benton?" His face darkened as he bit out through gritted teeth, *"You're* Phillip Benton's daughter?"

"Yes." It was her turn to stare as he repeated himself.

"How old are you?" he demanded.

Taken aback by his sudden ire, she wisely decided this wasn't the time to tell him his question was rude. "Nearly one-and-twenty. And as you can see, I have no need of a guardian."

Accepting her words as an invitation, his gaze roamed over her, and she shivered, goose bumps forming on her skin everywhere he looked.

"Has my father fallen ill, Your Grace?" she asked with

a flash of guilt that she hadn't thought to ask immediately about Papa, and also with the hope of distracting his roaming gaze away from her.

His eyes flickered coldly back to hers. "No."

"Then my apologies, sir, but someone is playing a joke."

"Whose joke, Miss Benton—yours or your father's?"

She caught her breath. The icy edge to his voice was even more alarming than his fury had been only moments before. Who *was* this man? And he was certain he'd been named her guardian—oh, good Lord, what was Papa up to now?

She had no idea, but it was time this man left, handsome duke or not.

She started toward the door to show him out. "I apologize, truly, that you came all the way here on a wild-goose chase—"

Stopping to glance back, she'd noticed with aggravation that he hadn't moved an inch even though she clearly wanted him gone. Oh, this man was as arrogant as his title!

Holding her gaze, he wordlessly reached into his jacket pocket and withdrew a piece of paper, then held it toward her.

"What's that?" she asked warily.

"The guardianship agreement."

Hesitantly, she took it. In legalese, complete with official wax seals and signatures, the agreement was clear—Phillip Benton had signed away all rights and responsibilities to his daughter, Katherine Anne Benton, *to be placed into the guardianship of His Grace, Edward Westover, Duke of Strathmore, Earl of Hampstead, Viscount Loudon, until such time as she marries and transfers all responsibility for her care to her husband.*

Kate's mouth fell open in disbelief. No, this couldn't be! Her father was selfish and irresponsible, but he would never simply hand her over to a stranger as if he were selling livestock. And he certainly wouldn't give up the tangential claim he had to Brambly.

But he had. His signature covered the bottom of the page.

She glanced up and caught the duke's gaze on her, watching her reaction closely. Those black eyes...she'd never seen anything like them, or the man behind them, and she trembled.

"It's not true," she whispered.

"I assure you it is," he stated evenly. "Apparently, Miss Benton, we have a lot to discuss."

His grim expression sent an icy chill cascading through her. Whatever her father had done, it was deadly serious if it involved a man like this. "Yes." She felt the blood drain from her cheeks. "Apparently."

As he took the contract from her, she was unable to read the emotions behind his inscrutable expression, but she knew he was studying her, contemplating her. Like some problem he needed to solve. Her stomach knotted with confusion and sudden worry in warning not to trust him.

"If you don't mind," he proposed evenly, "I'd like to remain here for a few days. I want to make certain everything is settled properly before I leave."

Remain here? *Oh no...No, no!* But even as dread sickened her, she knew she had no choice. She couldn't refuse a duke, especially one with a legal document naming him as her guardian, no matter how badly she wanted to toss him right out on his aristocratic backside. And a very fine backside, too, she thought with chagrin.

"Very well," she acquiesced grudgingly, then said as politely as she could between clenched teeth, "I would be honored to have you as my guest. Why don't you wait here while I have refreshments prepared?"

He raised a quizzical brow, his eyes sweeping around the empty room. "Wait...where?"

Oh, curse Dorrie for not putting him into the sitting room! Taking a patient breath, she forced a sickeningly saccharine smile. "May I suggest London, Your Grace?"

With that, she spun on her heels and stormed from the room, her hands clenched into fists at her sides.

* * *

Edward frowned after her. This chit was a handful.

Provoking, strong willed, with an irreverence for authority—he didn't know whether to laugh at her or throttle her. Standing there in front of him as she'd done, so primly with her hands folded and the sunlight falling onto her shoulders, she could have passed for an angel. But while her body might have been divinely crafted, that personality belonged solely to the devil.

Yet something about her puzzled him, and he glanced around the empty room. There was more going on here than just a guardianship agreement. No horses or grooms in the stable, few barnyard animals, fewer household furnishings—what exactly *was* her situation here?

Apparently, nothing in Phillip Benton's life was as it seemed.

Including his daughter.

She wasn't a child, yet Benton signed her over. But why? Did he simply want to cause trouble, his own petty revenge? Or was something more despicable at play? Even though she'd not batted an eye in recognition when he'd spoken his name and her reaction to the agreement seemed too startled, too earnest to be faked, could he trust the daughter any more than he could the father?

No matter Benton's motivation, Edward wouldn't protest the guardianship. Releasing her from their agreement when he didn't know Benton's endgame was unthinkable. What was that saying from his days when he'd served as an aide to General Hollingsworth?—keep friends close and enemies closer. At this point, there was no telling if Katherine Benton were friend or enemy, and he doubted as he caught the lingering scent of honeysuckle that he could keep her any closer without ruining her.

He knew one thing for certain, however. He wasn't leaving until he had answers.

If she were truly innocent and knew nothing of the guardianship, he would give her whatever help he could. But if she were trying to deceive him, then God help her.

Because he would destroy her.

* * *

As she raced upstairs, Kate struggled in her panic to catch her breath and slow her pounding heart. She felt as if the rug had been ripped out from under her. A rug? Oh, it was so much worse than that—her life had been upended. And she had no idea what to do.

She hurried into her room and caught her reflection in her dressing table mirror, halting in mid-step. A look of horror reflected back as she glimpsed the full extent of the splattered mixture stained down her dress and smeared across her forehead. She was a complete fright, her dress filthy and stinking, and her unruly red hair falling loose from its braid. *Good Lord*, she looked like a street urchin. Who had been rolling in the mud. For days.

Well, that certainly explained why he'd stared at her like that.

But the guardianship agreement, could anything explain *that*? Or why her father would sign such a thing? Lately, on those rare occasions when he visited, it seemed Papa did nothing but argue with her about ownership of Brambly. Yet he was still her father, and he would never sign her away as if she were nothing more than a knickknack to be sold for his convenience…wouldn't he?

No. That would be going too far, even for Papa.

The guardianship was obviously a mistake, except that Edward Westover didn't seem the kind of man who made mistakes. Duke or not, he was unlike anyone she'd ever met. And there wasn't an inch of him she trusted.

But if the guardianship was legally binding, if her life was truly at his mercy—

She shuddered. She'd seen how miserable and anguished life had been for her mother under her father's control, her freedom and choices dependent upon a man who did not love her and regarded her only as a burden. Mama had surrendered everything for love and suffered horribly because of it. Her father never loved her mother, yet he'd made her regret every day of their marriage that she loved him. Only in death did she finally escape his control.

No, living her life bent beneath another's will was *not* an option.

Mrs. Elston knocked at her door, but the plump woman

didn't wait for an answer before huffing and puffing inside, struggling to catch her breath from hurrying up the stairs.

"I just arrived...from the village." The words emerged in wheezing bursts. "Saw Dorrie...A duke?...What on earth?"

"Thank goodness you're here." Kate hurried to her writing desk. "I need you to go back to the village—"

"*Back* to the village?" she gasped.

"Yes." She scribbled out a letter, then folded it carefully before sealing it with a drop of wax and handing it to Mrs. Elston. "This has to go to my father on today's mail coach."

Mrs. Elson shook her head adamantly, already exhausted from the first trip to the village. "No, not unless it's a matter of life and death—"

"It might very well be," Kate assured her gravely. "Please, go. I'll tell you everything once you're back."

With a sigh, the old governess took the letter and headed heavily toward the door.

CHAPTER THREE

$\mathscr{I}$f she isn't downstairs in five minutes," Edward warned Mrs. Elston through gritted teeth, "I will go up to her room and drag her down myself!"

The old governess bristled. "As I told you, Miss Kate is feeling unwell—"

A sharp curse exploded from him, telling her exactly what he thought of Miss Kate's sudden illness.

"*Your Grace.*" Her brows shot up, offended. "With all due respect—"

He rolled his eyes, knowing that whatever she was about to say would lack all respect.

"—you have swept into our home without warning, upset both my little Katie and the entire household, and are now making demands as if you own the place."

"I do own it," he drawled.

"Brambly House is entailed," she informed him pointedly. "It is owned solely by Miss Kate to be relinquished only to the *gentleman* she marries." Her emphasis clearly implied that despite his title, she found him to be no gentleman. "If she wishes to forgo your company, you should have the decency to give her peace!"

She stood squarely in front of him and blocked the stairs like a bulldog guarding its dinner. While ordinarily he would have found that loyalty admirable, tonight he was ready to throttle her for it.

"Mrs. Elston," he growled, tired from a long day of traveling and now hungry since dinner was over an hour late, "if Miss Benton doesn't come downstairs, I swear I'll—"

"You will do what, Your Grace?" a soft voice challenged from the landing.

He glanced up, and when he saw her, the rest of the threat vanished from his lips. *Sweet Lucifer*, she was a vision. Although a decade out of fashion, the ice-blue silk gown she wore was cut just carefully enough to tantalize without being improper, with its fitted bodice accentuating her slender waist and its neckline revealing a hint of firm breasts beneath. As she descended toward him, her upswept red hair shining like fire, the dress shimmered enticingly over her curves with each move.

She stopped two steps from the bottom, her eyes level with his and just the hint of a self-assured smile at her lips. The sweet scent of honeysuckle wafted down to him like a cloud, and his gut clenched with unbidden arousal.

The disheveled woman who greeted him earlier had transformed into a beautiful woman, like a caterpillar into a butterfly. And left him speechless.

"You'll do what?" she pressed.

His lips twisted impishly at his now-empty threat. "Throw you over my knee and spank you."

"Your Grace!" Mrs. Elston swung her gaze at him, appalled that he would even suggest such a thing.

Kate raised her head defiantly, her green eyes blazing. "I'd like to see you try."

Good God. His cock twitched at the temptation.

"Miss Kate!" Mrs. Elston blurted out, aghast at her charge's scandalous behavior.

Ignoring the old governess and fighting back an amused chuckle, Edward held out his hand. "Truce?"

She hesitated, clearly not trusting him.

"Until dessert at least?"

She placed her gloved hand into his and allowed him to help her down the last two steps and toward the dining room as she conceded, "Until dessert, Your Grace."

"Edward, please," he corrected. Given their odd situation, such formality seemed inappropriate.

"Then you must call me Kate," she insisted, a mischievous glint in her eyes. "All my guardians do."

"You have a lot of guardians, do you?" he asked dryly.

"Oh yes." She gave a flippant wave of her hand, the mocking gesture indicating how ludicrous she found their situation and her desire to be free of it. "Lately, it seems there's a new one dropping by every day."

He paused in mid-step, then slid her an irritated sideways glance as she continued on, slipping her hand away from his arm to precede him into the room. As his gaze roamed down her backside, the curves beneath the gown and the soft sashay of her hips once again reminded him that this was no child in need of a guardian. This was a woman.

Worse, he thought grimly as the man now responsible for guarding her reputation, she was beautiful. The moment she debuted, every man would set his sights on her. And it wouldn't be with the intention of marrying her.

Heaven help him, he was in serious trouble.

An old servant in a worn butler's uniform stood beside the doorway and bowed from the waist. Edward grimaced at the formality. All he wanted was a quiet country dinner.

"Your Grace." Kate lightly touched his arm. "It is my pleasure to introduce you to Arthur, Brambly's butler. He has been employed by my family for over forty years. Isn't that so, Arthur?"

"Yes, miss." The man proudly inclined his head.

"Arthur, this is His Grace, the Duke of Strathmore."

Edward frowned, taken aback at the introduction. Why on earth would she introduce him to a servant?

Yet she smiled adoringly at the old butler. "Would you attend His Grace while he's here? He has no valet."

"I would be honored, Your Grace."

"Not necessary." He didn't need a valet, and even so, he doubted that Arthur's arthritic hands would be much help. Besides, he suspected that the old butler was up well past his normal bedtime now, and they hadn't even sat for dinner. By the time they finished, Edward wouldn't be surprised if the man had nodded off.

"Your Grace," Kate admonished softly.

He glanced between her and the butler, a look of disappointment flashing over Arthur's wrinkled face and her cheeks darkening. Then he realized—the formality surrounding his visit wasn't for him, it was for the servants. Most likely, none of them had been in the same house with a duke before, and the old butler would be pensioned being able to say that he had once personally attended the Duke of Strathmore.

But Edward had unwittingly denied him that honor, and he felt the heat of Kate's ire as her eyes narrowed.

"I meant that I would like port by the fire before retiring," Edward amended quickly. "Of course, I want Arthur for my valet." He kept his face carefully blank to hide the lie told only to please Kate. And perhaps keep the truce beyond dessert.

Another bow, this one so low that Edward thought the old man might teeter over. "You are too kind, Your Grace."

"Yes," he sighed, "apparently."

Seeming mollified, Kate proceeded toward the table.

As he followed, Edward glanced around the dining room, which was just as bare as the rest of the house, right down to the missing draperies in two of the four windows. The table extended the length of the room, but where there should have been chairs enough for sixteen guests, only five remained, and all the sideboards were gone. He said nothing about the room's missing furnishings as he helped her into her chair, noting that kitchen dishes and mismatched silver set the table.

Something was definitely wrong here, and as he took his place, he was determined to find out what.

Arthur brought in dinner. As with everything else, the food wasn't as expected. There should have been three times as many courses, cheese plates, bottles of white and red wines for each course, and bowls of fruits and nuts served between. But this meal lacked all of that. The roasted hen was small and simple, the wine watered down, and there were no footmen to serve and clear except for Arthur, whose gnarled hands shook so much as he ladled the soup that Edward feared he would end up with more of it on the tablecloth than in the bowls.

Yet Kate beamed at the butler with open affection.

"You're quite fond of him," Edward commented when Arthur left for the kitchen.

"Very." Her smile faded as her attention returned to him and to their conversation, and he suspected that she was considering just exactly how far she could trust him. "He was employed by my grandparents as a footman, and when my parents married, Grandpapa insisted Arthur accompany Mama to Brambly. He's been here ever since."

"He's dedicated to you."

"As I am to him," she admitted quietly, fondness lacing her voice.

His lips twitched at that. No lady of the *ton* would ever make such a comment and certainly not during dinner when servants weren't discussed unless to complain about them. Just another reminder of how different Kate was from the quality. It was a difference he would have found refreshing except that she reminded him of Jane.

Physically, the two women were nothing alike—Jane was tall and dark-featured, but Kate's red head barely came to his shoulder. Jane was fashionable, slender, urbane, and always aware of propriety even when she didn't follow it, but Kate... well, she'd greeted him wearing a stained dress. Their appearance might be opposite, but both women had the same outgoing and vivacious personalities that lit up a room the moment they entered it, the same quick wit and bright smiles.

And both had fathers who attempted to control their daughters' lives.

Edward studied her over his wineglass, his eyes narrowing. Jane had succumbed to her father's manipulations. Would Kate do the same?

As they ate, he questioned her about the history of Brambly, and as hostess, she obliged by telling about the small farm and the handful of tenants and servants, its gardens, and the village. She caught his interest when she explained how she took care of the sick villagers, and he was fascinated by the way her eyes grew bright when she described the self-taught medical studies she'd undertaken, her laboratory, and experiments.

"But they sometimes go wrong," she admitted after a moment's hesitation.

So that explained her appearance that afternoon. "Is that how you stained your dress?"

"Unfortunately," she divulged with a self-deprecating sigh, "it went awry just as you arrived."

"Still, I'm impressed." And at the way her cheeks pinked prettily at the compliment, he was glad he'd mentioned it. "And at all you do for the villagers."

"It's the responsibility I bear for being fortunate enough to live here," she explained guilelessly.

Edward watched her with wonder. His aunt would have been appalled at her charitable attitude. No, he mused, Augusta would have already suffered apoplexy from being introduced to the butler.

But ignorant of society rules, Kate was simply intriguing.

With Arthur absent from the room, Edward took the liberty of refilling their wineglasses. "Tell me more about the farm."

She looked at him warily. "What do you want to know?"

He shrugged to deflect her suspicions. "You grew up here. What was that like?"

She hesitated, then apparently deciding that chatting about her childhood on the farm posed no threat, she told him about the household staff, her late mother, the villagers...everything except her father.

Phillip Benton's absence in the conversation was curious. Surely she knew about her father's involvement in Jane and Stephen's deaths. How could she not, given the severity of the accident? Yet she'd given no indication she even knew who he was. Her life at Brambly would have to be so isolated, so insular—

But it was. One glance at the farm proved that. No newspapers, no close neighbors, little contact with anyone except a handful of local villagers and the physicians scattered across England with whom she communicated by post.

Perhaps she knew nothing about his true connection to her father after all. And *that* would be more than curious. It would be a bloody relief. Not just that she was innocent in the agreement but also because it made his role of guardian easier. True, he had limited knowledge of how guardianships worked, but he assumed one was much more enjoyable when the ward didn't despise her guardian for seeking revenge against her father.

By the time dessert was finished, their attempt at polite conversation had dissipated into an uneasy silence. Dinner was now officially over, and so was their truce.

"Thank you for an enjoyable dinner, Your Grace." Kate folded her serviette next to her plate. "Arthur will show you to the sitting room, then assist you upstairs. Good evening."

As she rose from her chair, Edward stood. "Miss Benton, a moment."

She stopped.

His eyes darted toward Arthur, who waited patiently by the doorway. "May we speak privately?"

"Could it wait until tomorrow?" A nervous wariness edged her voice. "I'm quite tired."

"It won't take long." If they settled everything tonight, he could leave first thing in the morning and not have to give another thought to what she knew about her father. Or him.

"Very well." With an apprehensive expression, she led him into the sitting room.

Unlike the other rooms, this one was still furnished, complete with worn but comfortable pieces of furniture arranged around a fireplace, where a small fire heated away the nighttime chill. The draperies were drawn against the cool night, and piles of books sat stacked haphazardly on tables next to small porcelain statuettes, carved wooden boxes, and delicate flower vases.

But it was the painting over the fireplace that seized his attention and brought him to a standstill, a portrait of a beautiful woman nearly identical to Kate. The same oval-shaped face and pert nose, the same elegant neck, spirited emerald eyes, red hair like flames—right down to the same ice-blue dress.

"My mother," Kate explained. "She was very beautiful, wasn't she?"

When he tore his eyes away and glanced down at her as she stood beside the fireplace, he saw double. The resemblance was uncanny. "Very," he murmured.

"Mama was just two years older than I am now when she sat for that portrait. My father commissioned it as an anniversary gift."

He stiffened at her mention of her father, the first one

all evening. "That was thoughtful," he drawled. "He must have loved her very much."

"No," she answered softly, honestly, not hearing the sarcastic edge he was unable to keep from his voice at the thought of Phillip Benton having enough heart to love anyone, "but she loved him." Her gaze never left her mother's portrait.

And his gaze never left her. "And you?" He closely gauged her reaction. "Does he love you?"

"Of course, he does."

"How do you know?" he challenged.

She slid a taunting glance in his direction. "Because he sends guardians to take care of me."

Sharp-tongued chit. "Then by all means." He gestured toward the sofa. "Let's discuss the guardianship."

She hesitated, then settled stiffly onto the cushions. "There is nothing to discuss as I do not need a guardian." Her hands folded delicately in her lap. "Clearly, there has been a mistake."

Edward knew better. There was no mistake. Phillip Benton's full intent was to make him her guardian. What he didn't know was why.

"My attorney spoke directly to your father regarding the agreement," he explained. "It's a binding contract placing you under my care."

"Why would my father give me a guardian—now, at my age?" She tilted her head as she looked at him, as if he were an object in a curio cabinet. "And why would he pick you?"

He folded his arms indignantly. "What's wrong with me?"

"Nothing as far as I can see."

Her green gaze drifted over him, and he stayed perfectly

still as she studied him, down his tall body, back up... thighs, chest, shoulders, mouth—when her gaze met his, she paused to stare, and in response, he arched an amused brow.

Caught, her eyes widened in embarrassment and she glanced away.

Edward smiled with devilish enjoyment at her discomfort, even feeling slightly flattered at the innocent attention. Since last year, women openly scrutinized him all the time, not bothering to hide the lust on her faces. Women who wouldn't have given him a second glance before threw themselves at him now. It was amazing what inheriting a duchy could do for a man's popularity.

But he'd never experienced such critical appraisal from someone like Kate before, someone who couldn't have cared less what titles he possessed. Someone so innocent yet bold. A virginal devil. The experience was...not unpleasant.

She cleared her throat. "You're a complete stranger and, well, not in the same social circle that my father occupies."

She was right about that. He was a duke, albeit a reluctant one; her father was the poorest of gentlemen. And Edward did his best not to occupy *any* social circle.

"Your father and I entered into a business arrangement." Not a complete lie, although the arrangement was forced and the business revenge. But he had no intention of sharing that, not when he still didn't know if he could trust her. If she were innocent of her father's machinations, the truth would only hurt her. And if she were complicit, he wanted no more ammunition placed within her reach.

She rose to her feet, asking carefully, "What kind of arrangement?"

His chest tightened. Judging from her hopeful expression, she knew nothing about the situation he'd forced onto her father or how deep her father's debts ran, how very close he'd come to being locked up in debtor's prison or killed by one of the men he'd cheated.

"I've become your father's executor," he explained, carefully choosing his words and conveniently glossing over the ugly details. "I've assumed his obligations."

"So *you* are managing his business affairs now?"

Her question hinted at gratitude rather than accusation. As he nodded, an unexpected stab of guilt struck in his gut.

She beamed and tossed up her hands. "Well, that explains it!"

"Explains what?"

"Papa's been trying for a successful business venture for so long…" A laugh of relief escaped her. "When he signed the guardianship contract, he must have thought he was signing just another business document."

Unexpectedly, she threw her arms around his neck and hugged him, laughing happily as she buried her face against his neck.

"Oh, thank you!"

For a moment, he let her press herself against him, taking shameless pleasure in her softness, in the honeysuckle scent and warmth of her. Then he took her shoulders and set her away before he forgot she was his virginal ward. And the daughter of his enemy.

"Thank me for what?" he asked cautiously. It was quite a leap to go from thinking the guardianship was a mistake to thanking him with such unabashed gratefulness.

"I've been so worried." The words poured from her in a wave of relief. "Papa's had nothing but one failed venture after another, companies that went bankrupt, shares in trading companies that came to nothing. And Brambly—I don't think there's anything left to sell. Thank you!"

She laughed again, then rose up on tiptoes to cup his face between her hands, her green eyes sparkling with happiness. His gaze dropped to her full mouth, thinking she might kiss him in her excitement. And very much wanting her to do just that.

"Thank you, Edward, so much!"

For the first time, she spoke his given name, and he cringed. She stared up at him as if he were a knight in shining armor when in reality he was the furthest thing from it.

"Katherine," he admitted somberly, gently pulling her hands away from his face, "you were one of the obligations."

Her expression melted into confusion. "What do you mean?"

"When he asked for the guardianship, he implied you were just a child."

"You're wrong." She tugged her hands free from his, her face darkening. "You must have misunderstood."

Edward's throat tightened with sympathy. Her father obviously didn't love her as she believed, and he'd signed her away as easily as all his other possessions, without a second thought of what would become of her. For all the man knew, Edward could have turned her out on the street, forced her into marriage, or shipped her off to Australia. As her guardian, he had the legal right to do any of that, and as a duke, he could take advantage of her in so many other ways to which the law would simply turn a blind eye.

If he didn't hate the bastard before, he certainly did now.

"I am sorry, Katherine," he said gently, truly apologetic, "but your father knew exactly what he was doing."

CHAPTER FOUR

$\mathcal{K}$ate stared at Edward, stunned, her eyes stinging. She refused to believe him. He was wrong. Simply *wrong*!

She wasn't naïve. As a father, Phillip Benton had always been more absent than present in her life. He rarely visited, even when her mother was still alive, staying only long enough to collect his allowance before galloping back to London. From her earliest memories, Kate couldn't remember a time when he'd ever kissed her cheek or told her he was proud of her. And none of that changed after her mother died except that his visits came even less frequently, and not at all once she adamantly refused to give him Brambly last year. It hurt to realize the kind of father she had—absent, lacking in affection, more concerned with money than his family. And it utterly wrenched her heart to know that he'd never wanted her, that he'd married her mother only because she'd gotten with child and because he'd wrongly assumed Brambly would be his.

Yet he'd never abused her, which was more than could be said of some fathers, and only when they argued about Brambly did he raise his voice. When her mother died he'd allowed her to stay on at the farm, where she was happy, instead of making her live with him in London. She would always be grateful for that. He hadn't taken her independence away then, and she refused to believe he'd do so now.

Especially, she grudgingly admitted, if it meant giving up his connection to Brambly when he thought there was still money to be had from it.

She lifted her chin, uncertain if she were more frustrated with her father or Edward. "Papa would never sign me over to be rid of me."

His dark eyes grew solemn. "If he cares about you, as you claim—"

"He does." Certainly, he loved her. He simply *had* to. He was her father and the only blood family she had left, and the alternative was unbearable. "My father loves me."

There! She saw it again, that hard narrowing of his eyes for just an instant whenever she mentioned Papa. She frowned. "Why do you—"

"*If* he cares about you," he repeated, "perhaps he felt the best situation was to make you my ward. You fall under my protection now, which means I am responsible for you and Brambly."

Her chest clenched, and for a panicked moment, she couldn't breathe. "Brambly is a freehold," she explained slowly, carefully, so there would be no mistake, "owned in my name by special entailment. Under the law, neither you nor my father can sell or mortgage it."

"True," he agreed, in the same careful tone, "but under the law, you own only the land. As your guardian, I hold the responsibility for managing the estate." His quiet words sliced into her like daggers. "Technically, then, Brambly's mine."

She shook her head, beating back the waking nightmare engulfing her. "I run Brambly." Her heart thumped with alarm. "I've taken care of the house and the servants since my mother died. And I will not let you take it away from me."

"I'm not taking it away from you. Your father did." His jaw clenched against her accusation. "Phillip Benton went bankrupt less than a fortnight ago and signed over all his obligations to me, including you."

Oh God, no. Her stomach sickened. *Bankrupt*, and not enough money left to pay his debts. Even if she sold every last piece of furniture in the house... "But he cannot repay you—" She choked, her hand going to her throat as it tightened. "Why would you do such a thing?"

The black flicker in his eyes told her he had no intention of answering that. "Why do you keep defending him?" he accused instead.

"Because he's my father. He's protected me fro—"

"He left you alone in an empty house with servants too old to take care of themselves let alone watch over you," he countered. "He isolated you and forced you to fend for yourself. That's not protection, Katherine. That's rejection."

She stared at him, and in her stunned confusion, she was unable to prevent a single tear of frustration from sliding down her cheek.

His broad shoulders softened. "My apologies for upsetting you." A touch of regret tinged his voice.

When he reached up to brush the tear from her cheek,

she swiped angrily at his hand and shoved it away to wipe at her own tears herself. *Blasted man!* Why wouldn't he just leave, and leave her alone?

He grimaced. "But I swear to you that I *will* protect you."

He reached for her arm, and she jerked back, gritting her teeth. "And who protects me from *you*?"

As soon as the words flew from her mouth, she regretted them.

White anger flashed across his face, and there were such shadows behind his eyes it seemed as if a black place had taken his soul. She shivered, unable to break her gaze from his dark eyes and the spell they cast over her even as he took a single step toward her, closing the distance between them.

"Until last year, I was a colonel on the Peninsula." Each word snapped out in anger. "I pledged my life to protect those of my men."

With a soft gasp, she retreated a step, but Edward advanced again, once more closing the distance. Her heart pounded so hard that the sound filled her ears.

"In battles so fierce the horses were bloody up to their fetlocks, soldiers deaf from cannon fire, riders so tired they could barely hold their sabers—I fought to keep them alive. And afterward, when they lay dying on the field, I still fought to save as many as I could."

She felt the blood drain from her face as she pictured him in the midst of battle, surrounded by suffering and death, by the confusion and cruelty of war. Those eyes, what horrors they must have witnessed, what hell...

"Why—" Around the choking knot of sudden fear in her throat, she breathed out, "Why are you telling me this?"

"Because I protected my men, and I'll damned well protect you." He leaned toward her, bringing his face level with hers, his eyes blazing like brimstone. "I took responsibility for every death under my command, and for your sake, Miss Benton, you'd best remember that."

His words weren't a threat but a warning, an explanation of the man he believed himself to be, and she had the undeniable feeling he'd told her to keep her away.

But she refused to be cowed, certainly not in her own home. Despite the racing of her heart and shortness of breath, she forced herself to ask as evenly as possible, "Is that all you wanted to discuss with me, then, Your Grace?"

He lifted his brow, silently asking, *Isn't that enough?*

Scowling in vexation, she clenched her hands into fists, biting back the urge to ask how many men had tried to kill *him*. She'd never meet a more infuriating, aggravating man, and she couldn't wait for morning, when he would be gone from her home and, hopefully, from her life.

"Well, then." She turned toward the door, praying he couldn't see how her hands trembled. "Good night, Your Grace. As I'm certain you'll be off before I've risen—"

"I am not leaving."

She froze, her foot stopping in mid-step, her hand on the door. Slowly, she faced him. "There isn't any point in staying." She wanted to be very clear that he was no longer wanted here. "That guardianship agreement is a mistake. I will not give up control of my life and home to you or anyone, so there is nothing left to discuss."

"Oh, we've only begun to discuss this," he drawled. "I'm responsible for ensuring the quality of your living, and I'm not leaving until I'm absolutely certain you're safe and sound here."

He stalked toward her, each step fluid and silent, and

she was struck by how much he reminded her of a panther, gracefully hunting. Which meant, she realized with a hard swallow, that she was his prey.

He stopped in front of her and folded his arms across his broad chest. "Even if it takes weeks."

"Weeks?" she squeaked.

"Weeks," he repeated firmly as fire glowed in the black depths of his eyes. "Like it or not, angel, thanks to your father, we're stuck with each other."

Without waiting for a reply, he reached around her for the door, shoved it open, and strode out.

* * *

Edward stood with tried patience while Arthur undressed him. As he'd anticipated, the old man was more bother than help as he removed the jacket from Edward's shoulders, brushed it off, then discovered that there was nowhere to place it in the sparsely furnished bedroom. No armoire, no adjoining dressing room—not even a hook.

"Just hang it on the bedpost," Edward offered at the butler's befuddlement, doing his best to muffle his exasperation.

"Yes, Your Grace." Arthur hung the jacket. "You'll forgive us, sir, for not having a proper room for you. We weren't expecting guests."

"It's fine." During his army days, he'd slept in much worse. This empty room was a luxury compared to nights sleeping among rats in the mud.

Arthur tried to unbutton the waistcoat next, but the old butler's arthritic hands shook so badly that he could barely grasp the buttons.

"I can get that," Edward assured him, but when he saw a dejected look cross the gray brows, he added, "but I need help with my boots."

"Certainly, sir."

Edward sat on the bed and yanked off his boots before the butler could make a grab for them and potentially knock him to the floor, then handed them over. "Shine them for me?"

"They'll be ready in the morning, sir."

"Actually, I was hoping you could sit there"—Edward nodded toward a wooden stool positioned near the fire—"and shine them for me now so they're ready when I wake."

It was a silly notion, that his evening dress boots should be ready at dawn, but the old butler didn't so much as blink at the oddity of it. "Of course, sir."

As Arthur sank onto the stool and began to wipe at the boots, Edward fought not to breathe an audible sigh of relief. He didn't want to keep the man awake shining boots that didn't need polishing, but the act was self-defense.

He unbuttoned his waistcoat and removed his cravat. "Is she always so stubborn, Arthur?"

"Miss Kate? Aye, sir. Always willful, even as a child."

"She must be insufferable to work for," he said tightly.

"Not at all. She's an absolute gift!" With a crooked smile, he jabbed the boot into the air to punctuate his point. "Don't know what would've become of me if not for her—or the lot of us, for that matter."

"You would have found employment elsewhere."

"Beggin' your pardon, but no, sir—there isn't a household twixt here and London that would hire us. And Miss Kate knows that. Even wit' her own troubles, she takes care of us."

Even with her own troubles. Edward frowned. The stubborn woman was certainly frustrating, but she didn't deserve to have problems.

"That's why I'm happy you're here, sir." He paused, as if weighing not only how much he could trust Edward but how much he was overstepping his station, then boldly continued, "It's time someone looked after Katie for a change."

Edward turned away dismissively. "She has her father."

"That good-for-nothing wastrel? *Bah!*" With a scowl, Arthur attacked the boot with the polishing cloth. "Never cared about her mama nor Katie, nor anything 'cept the farm itself, and only for the money he could steal from it. Hasn't been here for over a year. Even then he left mighty quick when he found out the miller was demanding real payment."

"Real payment?" Something about the way Arthur said that tingled the hairs on his neck.

"Aye. Last year, Miss Kate arranged to barter for th' cost of grinding flour with fruits an' vegetables. But come spring, t'weren't no more to exchange, and the miller asked for money to clear the rest o' the bill."

"So her father was forced to pay the debt."

Arthur scoffed. "*Miss Kate* paid the debt."

"How?"

"Why, she sold her horse! Loved that little mare, too, she did. Cried for weeks o'er it, though she thought none of us know'd it."

That, Edward realized coldly, was why Brambly's stables were empty, except for the ancient swayback in the barnyard. "And her father?"

"Rode off in the middle o' the night with the last piece of th' good silver." Arthur rubbed at the leather until it shined. "That's the way it is with him. He arrives out of the blue—sometimes he'll bring little gifts of ribbons, combs, that sort of thing—always bribes, if ye ask me."

Edward thought of the doll he'd brought for the child he expected to find, a gift to a little girl who might be frightened to meet him. He hoped Kate had seen it as just that, not as a continuation of her father's bribes. Although why it mattered what she thought, he couldn't say.

"Then he's gone in a day or two. And always, somethin' from Brambly goes with him."

"Brambly's entailed," he corrected, pulling his shirt free from his trousers. "She owns it, not her father."

"Aye, Your Grace. Katie owns the house." He raised a gnarled finger into the air to capture Edward's attention. "But her father owns everythin' *inside* it. An' what he hasn't managed to steal away, she's had to sell."

Edward's brows drew together. Arthur confirmed what he'd suspected. Benton cared nothing for his daughter nor her desperate situation here. In fact, he was complicit in it, stealing it from her piece by piece until nothing was left.

Arthur finished the boots and stood stiffly, then placed them at the foot of the bed. "Anything else, sir?"

"No, that will be all." His tone was sincere as he added, "You were quite helpful."

"Sleep well, then, Your Grace." Arthur closed the door. "I'll be back in the mornin' to help you dress."

Edward froze. Back in the morning? *Good God.*

Exhaling a long breath, he crossed to the window to stare out at the chilly night and the crisp moon, which lit the countryside in a silver-white glow. Below him, the front lawn of Brambly swept down to the lane in one direction and to the ribbon of river beyond the orchards in the other.

Beautiful, peaceful... he easily saw why Kate loved living here.

She was innocent in the guardianship her father had tricked from him, he was certain of that now. Such a proud, independent woman would never have allowed anyone to take control over her, and she clearly wanted him gone, both from Brambly and from her life.

Yet he couldn't just ignore her situation and leave her here to fend for herself. Given what he knew about her father and what he had seen of the farm, she needed him more than she realized.

Except that she despised him.

He opened the window to let in the night air and leaned on his palms against the casement. He shouldn't care what she thought about him. After all, she was nothing but an unforeseen complication.

But she also didn't deserve to suffer because of her father's sins.

Bloody hell. He rubbed his forehead. What was he going to do with her? Until she married and the burden passed to some other unfortunate man, he was legally responsible for her and the farm.

He supposed he should give her an allowance, let her remain at Brambly, and not give his little flame-haired angel a second thought.

But he couldn't. By leaving her here without assistance or protection, he would only be extending the same rejection and isolation thrust onto her by her father.

And he was *nothing* like Phillip Benton.

Running a hand through his hair, he blew out a harsh breath. *Christ.* He had no business speaking to her like that tonight, trying to threaten and intimidate. Behaving like an absolute villain. But she had gotten under his skin, and so he'd lashed out. The woman could drive a saint to fury.

Yet it was more than just the way she looked. It was her independence, confidence, self-reliance. That easy laughter, her bright smiles. Most of all, it was the way she fearlessly stood up to him. Most men weren't that brave in his presence, but this slip of a country gel looked him directly in the eyes and fiercely stood her ground.

True, she pricked at him. But oddly enough, he also found himself wanting to protect her. Now that he knew what she'd gone through to save the farm and the handful of servants employed on it, he wanted to safeguard her even more.

He caught his reflection in the window, and his gaze dropped to his left shoulder, to the place where seven years ago a bullet ripped through his flesh and muscle.

Anyone looking at him now would never have suspected that the wound had nearly killed him. But it also ultimately saved his life. When he first arrived in Spain, before he'd met Grey and Thomas and still felt the sharp torment of Jane's betrayal, he'd been rash and reckless, charging into battle at every opportunity. Until the bullet found him. It had taken a ball in the shoulder and nearly losing his life in order for him to move on from Jane.

God only knew what it would take to untangle Kate Benton and her guardianship from his life.

* * *

In her room, Kate, stared at her reflection in the mirror, and with a soft sigh, she wondered again what her mother would think of the woman she'd become.

"It's peculiar, that's what." Mrs. Elston unfastened the tiny buttons down the back of Kate's dress, slipped it from her slender shoulders, and helped her step out of it. "No good will come of this, mark my words."

Normally, Kate would have undressed herself, and Mrs. Elston would already be in her own room, the covers pulled up to her chin and snoring loudly. But tonight, Kate craved the comfort of the woman's motherly attentions. Edward's arrival had shaken her world, and with the veiled threat he'd given her before he'd stormed from the drawing room, he'd also shaken her nerves.

"He can repair Brambly," Kate reminded her quietly.

The guardianship was a mistake. Even if he'd gone bankrupt, her father would never have given up his claim to the farm. But having the duke's help might just bring Brambly back to the splendor she remembered from her childhood, long before her mother died and her father left it in the hands of unscrupulous agents who stole from the accounts and let it fall to ruin.

Mrs. Elston snorted as she placed the dress into the armoire. "We don't need any help from the likes of him."

Guiltily, she lowered her eyes. "If the agreement is true, I'll ask him to pension Arthur and Dorrie."

"Oh." The old governess paused, then closed the armoire. "Well, there is *that*, I suppose."

Kate bit her bottom lip. She planned on asking Edward to pension Mrs. Elston, too. All of them deserved quiet retirements, even if Kate didn't want them to ever leave Brambly. She wanted them to stay right there, continuing to take care of each other as they had since her mother died.

Her chest panged, and she briefly closed her eyes against the fear and worry swirling inside her. Her life was spinning out of control, all because of a piece of paper. Edward promised her his protection, and for that, she should have been grateful. But at what cost—the surrender of Brambly and her own freedom?

"And all the accounts can finally be paid in full." She forced a lightness into her voice she certainly didn't feel. "Hopefully, I can convince him to expand the orchards to increase Brambly's value."

"Is that what he plans on doing with you?" Mrs. Elston removed the pins from Kate's hair. "Increase your value?"

Kate frowned. "What do you mean?"

"Dress you up, debut you into society." She shrugged. "Parade you through London to attract a husband so he can wash his hands of you."

"His Grace wouldn't do that." But her denial was unconvincing even to her own ears. He wouldn't...or would he? Edward was practically a stranger, after all.

As if reading her thoughts, Mrs. Elston continued, "He may be a duke, but he's no gentleman."

Saying nothing to that, she let Mrs. Elston brush out her hair, something the old governess hadn't done since she was a little girl, but tonight, it brought both of them solace. Yet she wasn't a child anymore. In fact, she was now as old as her mother when she married her father.

Kate turned away from the mirror, unable to tolerate tonight the memories of her mother's unhappy marriage. Mrs. Elston was wrong. Edward could dress her up and parade her down the promenade all he wanted, but she would never subject herself to the same misery as her mother. She would never give up her medicine, Brambly, her freedom...her heart. She may look identical to her mother, but she would never make the same mistake of marrying a man who did not love her.

Mrs. Elston laid out her night rail. "I want you to get a good night's rest. You'll straighten out this whole mistake in the morning."

But Kate was beginning to think that the agreement wasn't a mistake. She had seen her father's signature right there on the document—Edward Westover *was* her guardian.

The old governess squeezed her hand reassuringly, then excused herself for the night. It had been an exhausting and nerve-wracking day for her, too. The entire household had been turned inside out by the duke's arrival.

She slipped into her nightgown, turned toward the bed, and stopped. The doll that Edward had given her that morning sat propped against her pillow.

With a soft sigh, she traced her fingertip over the silky blond hair and lacy pink dress. Her shoulders sagged. How could someone so cold and controlling also be thoughtful enough to bring a doll for a child he'd never met?

She crawled into bed, pulled the duvet up to her neck, and stared at the canopy above her. When she was child, if anyone had brought her such a lovely gift, she would have been certain he would be kind to her. But now . . . Well, she simply wasn't certain of anything anymore.

CHAPTER FIVE

$\mathcal{I}$n the early morning sunlight, Kate slipped from her room and made her way through the silent house with every intention of dealing with Edward Westover in the only way she knew how.

She was going to hide.

Oh, she was such a coward! And prowling through her own home like a thief, no less. But it was better to simply hide than risk saying more things she would regret and make her situation worse, so she planned on being long gone before the sun inched any higher and not returning until after dark, when she hoped he would have already retired to his room. To fill her time while she hid, she'd busy herself by thinking up the next excuse to avoid him tomorrow. And the day after that, and the one after that...until he gave up this silly notion of being her guardian and left.

She couldn't risk another argument like last night's. The last person she needed as an enemy was the Duke of Strathmore, yet she'd never been good at holding her tongue. So the best course of action was simply to avoid him.

She moved silently downstairs to the study, to leave a note for Mrs. Elston so she wouldn't worry about her. With its cherry furnishings and brilliant white trim, the study was her favorite room, and the place her mother had preferred to work. Kate used to play for hours with her dolls in front of the fire while Mama sat behind the desk and tallied the estate's books. Oh, how she missed those carefree days! When her mother was still alive, Brambly possessed funds for properly—if frugally—being self-sufficient, and her mother managed it brilliantly. Even then, Papa rarely visited, gladly leaving the farm to his wife's oversight as long as she paid his allowance. Business, whether foreign or domestic, had never been Phillip Benton's strong suit.

Since her mother's death, though, the study had suffered the same thinning of furnishings as the rest of the house. The rug she'd played on was gone, along with the draperies, the paintings...Only the desk remained, which was too big to fit through the doorway, along with the books, which her father thought held no value. Yet Kate still enjoyed spending time here even though it now meant sitting in the room alone, juggling the dwindling figures herself.

As she slipped inside, she glanced over her shoulder to make certain no one saw her, then closed the door, turned—

And gasped.

"Good morning, Katherine."

Edward sat behind the desk with a quill in his hand,

making notations in a small notebook. Gone were his formal evening clothes from the night before, replaced by a plain white shirt with a black waistcoat and tan breeches. Scandalously without cravat and coat, his shirtsleeves rolled up to reveal muscular forearms, he seemed dressed more for a day of outside chores than business work, but judging from the stacks of books on the desk, he planned to do exactly that all day. A half-eaten breakfast sitting nearby proved that he'd already been there for quite some time.

She rolled her eyes. The man was an early riser. *Wonderful.*

"Your Grace." Her shoulders sagged as her plan to hide dissolved away. Gathering what was left of her shredded courage, she stepped forward. "My apologies for disturbing you."

"Not at all." He stood graciously and moved out from behind the desk to greet her. "Did you need me?"

She bristled at the man's audacity. No, she most certainly did not *need* him. "I came for a book."

Not strictly a lie. She often took a book with her when she went walking, and if that was the excuse she needed to hide from him for the rest of the day, then she'd gladly take an entire shelf of volumes and haul them on her back like a beggar woman if necessary.

But a different set of books drew her attention, the red leather bindings of those stacked at his elbow. Brambly's account books, the detailed ledgers where she so carefully recorded every one of the farm's transactions and jotted down notes on strategies to pay for repairs and replace the household goods even as they'd disappeared around her.

She pointed at them. "Those are the estate books." Hot

humiliation rose in her cheeks at what he must have seen there. She jabbed her finger accusingly. "You were looking through Brambly's accounts?"

"Yes."

"How *dare* you!" She snatched up the books and cradled them against her chest. "You have no right—"

"I have every right," he countered evenly. "The farm is now under my oversight, and I cannot make arrangements until I know exactly where it stands financially."

Where it stood financially was deeply in trouble. She raised her gaze until it locked with his. "How much did you see?"

"Enough," he answered solemnly.

Sliding the books back into their proper place on the shelf, she raised her chin. "So now you know."

"Yes," he answered simply, as if not wanting to worsen her humiliation. Or her ire.

But it was too late for that. She pulled her shoulders back in preparation for battle, then faced him, not bothering to hide her irritation. "And what *arrangements* have you decided to make?"

For a moment, Edward said nothing as he stared at her, as if carefully considering what he should tell her. Then he offered, "Building repairs and supplies, livestock, new servants to hire and others pensioned, replacement of all the missing household items and furniture." Each item he ticked off sent a fleeting panic skittering through her. Then he paused, "And you."

"Me?" she squeaked, wondering how on earth she had been added to a list of farm repairs.

"You need a lady's maid, a new wardrobe, horses and carriage—"

"*No.*"

He was visibly surprised at that. "No?"

"No," she repeated firmly, crossing her arms over her chest. "Undoubtedly, Your Grace, you are not used to being told no."

He arched a brow.

"And certainly not by a woman."

His brow rose impossibly higher.

"That is not what I meant!" Her face flushed hot with quick embarrassment. Oh, she wanted to crawl under the desk and hide! Nothing was innocent around this man, not even casual comments. He twisted *everything* around. Including her insides. "I *meant* that anyone who looked at you would see that you're obviously not the kind of man whom women tell no—"

When he grinned rakishly at her, she snapped her mouth closed, mortified. In trying to explain, she was only digging the hole deeper.

"I think I might find your observations fascinating," he drawled, his voice nearly a low purr as it fell softly over her like velvet. *Good Lord*, his voice was velvet... How could something so soft be so torturous? "Go on, then." He gestured with a wave of his hand as he leaned back against the desk in utter amusement. "Explain to me why women never tell me no."

She raised her chin, but beneath her indignant scowl, she was deeply unsettled by the intimate turn of the conversation. "I have no idea what other women have told you, Your Grace, but from me, you will only hear *no*, on every occasion."

"Miss Benton," he sighed resignedly, "I truly believe that."

Kate stared at him, speechless, not knowing whether to be insulted or pleased. Or disappointed.

"So you will be relieved to learn that I've also sent for Michael Brannigan, the son of my agent at Hartsfield Park. He's a good man, and he'll do a capable job here." His eyes shined devilishly. "And you can tell him *no* all you'd like."

She ignored that barb, if not the quick ire it shot through her. "The farm doesn't need an agent," she protested. "I'm responsible for Brambly."

He sized her up with a glance. "Know how to judge and purchase quality cows and sheep, do you?"

"No," she replied with a raise of her brow, mockingly sizing him up the way he had just done her. "Do you?"

"No." When she began to smile in smug victory at his answer, he added, "That's why I employ Brannigan. He'll be here within the fortnight."

Her mouth slapped shut with an audible *Humph!*

With a grin of amusement at her expense, he circled behind her and pulled the last account book down from the shelf where she had just placed it, then returned to the desk and reached for the quill.

Oh, he was the most infuriating man!

"I want your word to recompense for any salary Brannigan accrues or anything he purchases," she pressed, "even if the guardianship is proven invalid."

"You have it," he agreed, although she saw his jaw tighten at her hope that the agreement was still a mistake.

"I also want final approval of all major decisions regarding the farm."

He nodded. "As long as they don't contradict mine."

Kate clenched her hands into fists. Oh, his arrogance!

To persist in looking through the books, to hire an estate agent without her consent—

But as a sickening, inky black sensation of frustrated defeat sank through her, she knew he was right, drat him. If he wanted to take over Brambly and make changes, it was his legal right. There was nothing she could do to stop him.

Feeling the sharp throb of a headache behind her eyes, she spun on her heels to leave. She needed air to clear her head, space to think of what to do next in this battle, and time to slow her pounding heart, which she was beginning to think had nothing to do with her situation and everything to do with the man now responsible for it.

"Katherine."

She stopped. Steeling herself for whatever new torment he planned on aiming at her, she took a deep breath and faced him. "Yes?"

He rose slowly. "I want to apologize for last night." He stepped to the front of the desk to lean back against it and bring his dark eyes level with hers. "Those things I told you about the war... Gentlemen should never speak about that, not to a lady."

Her chest tightened as she caught a glimpse of something softer beneath his hard surface, a refinement beneath the sharp steel. The gentleman beneath the soldier.

Apologizing must have cost him a great deal, even though she suspected it wasn't the warning he regretted but the way he'd delivered it. He'd wanted her to keep her distance, and judging from the way his arms now crossed his chest, he still did.

Yet he was apologizing, and for the first time since he appeared on her doorstep, she felt hope. For him.

She took a hesitant step toward him. "Actually, I'm glad you told me."

He snorted a disbelieving laugh.

Approaching him slowly, she maintained a façade far braver than she actually felt. She was certain he wanted to intimidate her, but if he thought she'd back down, well, he was dearly mistaken. She'd seen enough hurt villagers to recognize suffering, including emotional suffering that never healed. Her medical work had made her an expert in reading pain in the depths of their eyes, and this man was wounded. Deeply.

Compelled by the urge to help him, the healer inside her unable to deny comfort even to him, she lifted her palm against his cheek.

He flinched but didn't pull away, instead remaining as still as a statue beneath her touch, his entire body tense like a taut rope ready to snap.

"Please believe me," she admitted in carefully chosen words, "that I am relieved you felt the need to reassure me about yourself."

"I didn't tell you that to reassure you," he corrected tightly.

"No, you did it to warn me away." His eyes flickered, and she knew she was right. "Nevertheless, *I* found it reassuring." Her fingertips warmed against his cheek. "It was war, but commanding your men wisely, training them well... How many men did you save, Edward?"

"Not nearly enough."

"Every man you could," she countered gently. The horrors he must have seen, the guilt he must be carrying inside him even now...

Imperceptibly, she felt him turn his face into her hand, just a small increase of pressure and warmth against her palm, as if seeking consolation in her touch. Her heart skipped. Perhaps he wasn't the belligerent tyrant he'd tried so hard to portray, after all.

Emboldened, she traced her fingertips across his smooth, freshly shaven face, along the high cheekbone that looked chiseled from marble but felt soft and warm. Did he feel like this everywhere on his body, so smooth and soft on the surface, so hard beneath—

His hand clamped over hers, and she startled with a soft gasp, her heart leaping into her throat.

"And if I had a choice?" he demanded.

"What?" She tugged her hand to free herself, but his fingers held hers so tightly it was impossible to pull away.

"If I killed without remorse?" His eyes locked onto hers. "I'd be a common murderer, deserving of the worst punishment in the world."

Suspecting they were no longer speaking of the war, but for the life of her unable to fathom his true meaning, she breathed, "Yes."

"Would I deserve your compassion then?"

"Even more so." She refused to look away.

He clenched his jaw. "You're wrong. Some acts can never be forgiven."

"I never said forgiveness."

His eyes flickered in incredulousness. "You can be compassionate but not forgive?"

"Yes." She suspected that the question was some kind of test, and his unyielding expression told her that he didn't trust her answer.

"Be careful to whom you show compassion, Kate." His voice lowered to a warning. "You don't know the extent of the evil that men are capable of committing."

Her heart thudded, so hard she was certain he must be able to feel it through her fingertips held in his. But shamefully, it wasn't fear that sent the blood rushing through her ears but dark attraction, and she trembled. "Are you speaking in generalities, Edward? Or do you mean yourself?" She hesitated. "Is that why you shared what you did, to warn me? Well, I simply don't believe that of you."

"You should." He released her hand.

Although she pulled away from him, she remained close enough to catch his scent of leather and soap.

"You're not capable of it," she said quietly but confidently, instinctively knowing he was not the kind of man to hurt anyone unprovoked. Not the man who brought a doll to a little girl he'd never met just to reassure her. "To be evil, you'd have to be set on deliberately destroying a man's life out of pure maliciousness, on taking pleasure in it. You would never do that."

He narrowed his eyes. "What makes you think you know what I'm capable of doing?"

* * *

Edward watched her as she stared back, her lips parted delicately in surprise. He'd flustered her again. *Good.* He liked putting her off-balance, because the more he could unsettle her, the farther away from him she'd stay.

Oh, she was an intriguing enigma. Young, kindhearted to a fault, and financially on the brink of bankruptcy, she desperately needed funds and an estate agent to manage them, but she was too stubborn to admit it. He'd spent the past two hours combing over Brambly's books, and the ledgers revealed her situation to be even more dire than he'd assumed. In six months, he calculated, she'd be up against a wall, unable to recover. True, her father was stripping away the household goods one at a time, but only before the creditors could storm the place and do it themselves.

Whether she liked it or not, the guardianship was the only hope she had of saving Brambly. Yet at every step she fought his attempts to help her when as her guardian he could have easily thrown her to the wolves. Instead of being furious, the damned woman should have been grateful.

He would die a very old man before he understood women.

"Building repairs, livestock, and servants," she answered confidently, as if it were obvious.

He blinked, doubting he would ever understand *this* one.

"You just took it upon yourself to make Brambly a proper farm again," she insisted. "I don't like that you did it without consulting me, but a truly evil man would never even consider doing that."

"Unless that's what I want you to believe."

She scoffed, "Spending thousands of pounds for farm improvements?"

He'd done far more than arrange for farm improvements. He'd arranged to take care of her for the rest of her life, only she didn't know that yet. So many lives had been ruined the night of the accident. The least he could do was save one innocent from the wreckage. Even this muleheaded one.

"If that's your diabolical plan, then you're doing a very poor job of being evil. Unless, of course, you'd like to prove exactly how terrible you are by canceling every arrangement you've made and letting me return to my normal life." With a rebellious lift of her chin, she reached around him to snatch the ledger from the desk, then slipped the book back into its place on the shelf. "In which case, I will gladly agree that you are wholly wicked, worse than Lucifer himself."

As she faced him, she arched a brow as if daring him to challenge her and make good on her offer to rescind all his arrangements and go on his way. After all, he knew she'd wanted exactly that since the moment he arrived.

But he didn't rise to the bait, instead choosing to stare at her silently as he realized exactly what kind of trap he'd stumbled into. Agree or disagree, either way she'd won, and he was intelligent enough to know to keep quiet.

"Good day, then." She left before he could stop her again.

Shoving himself away from the desk, Edward cursed and crossed to the window overlooking the lawn. She was wrong about him. So very wrong...and the sooner she realized that, the better off they'd both be.

Of course he was capable of committing evil. Hadn't he spent the past ten years proving that? And he had been very, very good at it. Coldly cutting down men in battle, coveting his brother's wife, ruining Phillip Benton's life to secure his revenge—

And now Kate.

Blowing out a harsh breath, he ran his hand through his hair, noting with self-recrimination that his fingers shook. Unbidden dreams came last night of having her naked and eager beneath him, and with the guardianship giving him ultimate power over her, didn't the damned woman realize just how capable he was of ruining her? And in that sin, he would take immense pleasure.

He saw her emerge from the house into the sunshine of the side garden. With a wide-brimmed hat flopping around her face, she held her skirts hitched so she could walk quickly away from the house and from him. With every other stride, he glimpsed a flash of shapely calf and the cold glint of the hand trowel she grasped like a sword.

"Like an avenging angel," he muttered, smiling grimly at the perfect picture of female contradiction.

Katherine Benton surprised him. He wasn't certain why he'd felt the need last night to warn her about himself or why he felt it necessary to apologize this morning, but he hadn't scared her off. She was tougher than she appeared, and he supposed he had Phillip Benton to thank for that—years of neglecting his daughter had made her independent and strong, in both mind and spirit, and she certainly wasn't going to be easily cowed.

Still, he'd tried to warn her, to keep her away and prepare her for the truth about him and her father when it did eventually emerge. Instead of taking the warning, though, she'd tried to console *him*, as if he weren't already beyond redemption. As if he could still be saved.

For a brief moment when she was touching him, he almost felt as if he could be. His chest warmed from the soft caress of her hand on his cheek, and he craved her forgiveness and consolation even as he tried to convince her he didn't deserve salvation. He could almost believe—

No.

Her touch had been arousing, he'd admit that, especially since he hadn't been inside a woman in over a year. Especially since he found the verbal sparring and her quick mind as equally arousing as her body. And especially since he was finding it harder and harder to remember that she was his enemy's daughter and his virginal ward. That was all.

"You don't want to know what I'm capable of doing, angel," he murmured as she vanished from sight behind a stone wall. "And God help you if you try."

CHAPTER SIX

In her laboratory, Kate rolled the bandage around Mr. Putnam's forearm where a large splinter from an accident at the mill had pierced his skin. He'd come to her to have the dressing changed, and she'd cleaned it carefully, applied a fresh salve, and was now carefully securing a new bandage. As she worked, he related the latest village gossip, although most of the tongues were wagging about her and the duke.

Wonderful. That was the last thing she needed, to be placed at the center of local gossip. Wasn't it already bad enough that the villagers snickered about how she broke all propriety by trying to be a woman doctor? And yet, she mused as she tied off the bandage, whenever any of them were hurt, she was the first person they sought out.

"Come back in five days, and I'll change it again," she told Mr. Putnam as she washed her hands.

Five days. Exactly how long it had been since Edward arrived at Brambly and turned her life upside down.

For the first three days, she'd successfully avoided him by visiting the village, keeping to the woods, and even hiding in the dusty hayloft of the old barn, which seemed like a good idea until she'd let loose a sneezing fit that led him right to her. On the fourth day, he'd insisted she spend the morning showing him the property, so she'd insisted they bring Tom Dobson, the blacksmith's son she'd hired to tend to the horses she didn't own. They'd ended up at the river, where Edward showed the boy how to fish while she watched them from a blanket under the tree and grudgingly accepted that perhaps—just *perhaps*—spending the day with Edward hadn't been so awful after all.

But today, she had to get back to her work.

"Thank you, miss." Mr. Putnam slid off the stool and held his hat a bit sheepishly in his hands as he approached her. "Me an' my wife agreed—yer to have this."

He reached into the hat and withdrew a coin, then held it out toward her.

"Thank you, but I cannot accept it," she refused gently. She never accepted money for her medical work. It would be an affront to God if only those who could afford medicine and care had access to it while the poorest were left to suffer.

"You saved my arm, Miss Kate. The red streaks were already startin' up t' the elbow when ye tended it."

She grimaced. When he finally found the courage to come for help, that is. It had almost been too late, and cleaning out the infection had been more painful than it needed to be precisely because he'd waited so long. "Mr. Putnam, I cannot—"

"Please. The missus would have a fit if'n I came home wit' it." He set the coin down on her table and moved toward the door before she could return it, doffing his hat. "Good day t' ye, miss."

"And to you—and back in five days, you hear?"

"Aye, miss!"

With a frustrated sigh, she snatched up the coin and shoved it into her table drawer. Two other coins were tucked inside from payments made to her last week by other villagers who'd been hurt in the same accident as Mr. Putnam. She scowled. Apparently, no one was willing to follow her wishes these days, especially men who thought they had the right to—

"So this is where you do your medical work." The smooth, masculine voice curled through her.

With a shiver, she glanced up and caught Edward leaning casually against the doorway, his tall body filling the frame. He glanced around the laboratory, taking in all her equipment, the rows of little bottles on the shelves, the herbs hanging from the ceiling. Then his gaze landed on her, and her body heated as his dark eyes took her in, too, lingering on her far longer than they had on the medicines.

"For what it is," she answered, suddenly nervous. Being in here alone with men from the village had never bothered her, but being alone anywhere with Edward unsettled her through to her toes.

"It's remarkable," he acknowledged.

He stepped inside, and a disconcerted twitter pulsed through her at the way his large body dominated the little space. Funny how the laboratory had never seemed so small before until he was there, when she couldn't put more than a few feet between them. He stepped forward and turned his attention to the bottles on the shelves next to her shoulder... A *very* small laboratory.

She moved back and bumped against her table, with no place to escape unless she wanted to run out the door. And *that* would be an even harder act to explain than nearly falling out of the hayloft.

"I'll introduce you to Dr. Brandon, our family physician in London. He's very progressive." Edward threw her a sideways glance. "I think he might enjoy discussing medicine with you."

Her chest warmed at his generosity. "Thank you."

"We can add that to our list of changes, too."

She eyed him warily. "What's that?" He'd made enough changes already, thank you very much. She wasn't certain she wanted any more.

"A doctor for the village. Mrs. Elston says the nearest one is ten miles away. Apparently, that's why you've had to step in."

She frowned. Apparently, Mrs. Elston was spending too much time chatting with the duke. "I do what I can."

"A real doctor would be able to assist you." He turned his attention back to the shelf of medicine. "Then you wouldn't have to help the villagers all alone."

He reached past her to pick up one of the bottles, his arm brushing against her shoulder and sending another shiver through her. Taking a deep breath, she found her voice and asked as steadily as possible given the inexplicable trembling in her knees, "What can I do for you, Your Grace?"

He slid the bottle back into its place, and she swallowed

hard, wishing he would move away from her and return to the house. Better yet, that he would return to the city and stop disconcerting her like this.

"This arrived for you." He reached beneath his jacket and removed a letter. "From London."

Her heart skipped with both hope and dread. She knew without having to look—her father's letter about the guardianship. Whatever the answer, she knew her life would change once again, and she didn't know if she had the strength to endure another upheaval.

He frowned. "It's from your father, isn't it?"

"I don't know—" His eyes narrowed, and Kate had the sinking feeling he suspected she would lie to him. Instead, she answered truthfully, "But I hope so."

He gave a slow nod, and she felt a pulse of relief that she'd apparently given the right answer. "You contacted him."

"Yes, the day you arrived. I had to be certain the guardianship wasn't a mistake." Drawing on all her resolve, she held out her hand. "May I?"

Slowly, he placed the letter on her palm, but he didn't leave to give her privacy to read it. Instead, he leaned back against her worktable and watched her closely as she popped open the wax seal and unfolded the letter. Her eyes darted across the few lines of scrawled handwriting, and her chest sank—

"It's true," she whispered, blinking hard to clear the blurriness from her eyes as she read it again, not believing that her father had willingly handed over control of her life to a stranger. "He agreed—he made you my guardian...But why?" She choked back the tears as her fingers tightened around the letter. "Why would he do this?"

He tensed. "He doesn't say?"

"No." She swiped at her eyes and crumpled the letter in her fist, not knowing whether to be hurt or angry, to cry or scream, and wanting desperately to do both. Instead, a bitter laugh tore from her, "But he asked for money!"

"Kate." Tenderness softened his face. "I'm sorry."

She shook her head, the desolate heartbreak rising inside her, and she felt broken, like a glass shattering from the inside out.

"You were right," she rasped and pressed the letter to her chest as if she could physically keep back the despair of what her father had done to her. *Oh God*, how much it hurt! So much she could hardly breathe. "He doesn't love me. He signed me away…He signed me away…" A drop of water landed on the letter, smearing the ink, and only then did she realize she was crying.

"Katherine." Edward pulled her into his arms, holding her close.

But she couldn't stop. All the emotion she'd kept locked inside poured from her now, from all the years when she'd wanted so desperately to believe her father loved her, all the lies she'd told herself about how he would someday take care of her as a good father should. All of it ashes now, all her memories of him and all her hopes for the future crumbled into dust. She wept for the loss, grieving nearly as hard as when she'd lost her mother.

"Kate, please, don't cry," Edward murmured achingly as the sobs overtook her, his hands soothingly stroking her back. She buried her face against his neck, and her hot tears soaked into his shirt as she cried so inconsolably that her entire body shook against his. "I'll take care of you, I promise."

But she'd had enough of empty promises from her father, and she wanted none from Edward. How could she trust him? "Why?" She gulped for breath to force out the words through her cries. "Why *you*?"

When he hesitated, she suspected he wouldn't tell her. But then, quietly, "Because I bought up all his debts," he explained solemnly.

"What do you mean?" She raised her head to stare up at him, her hands clenched around his lapels. She barely knew him; she'd never even heard of him until he arrived on her doorstep. How could Papa have known he would care for her?

He wiped the tears off her cheeks, his touch surprisingly tender. "Your father asked me for the guardianship as part of the debt arrangements. I think he wanted me as your guardian because he wanted me to spend my money on you and Brambly." His mouth drew down into a frown. "His form of petty revenge."

Her puzzled eyes searched his face. That sounded exactly like something her father would do, and yet... "You agreed willingly?"

"Yes."

Her throat tightened. Behind the stoic mask he showed the world, there lurked a kindness in him that he would take on such a burden. But she could see more in his eyes, on his face—*guilt*. What was he hiding from her? He wanted to comfort her, and even now he ran his hands up and down her arms to console her. Yet there was so much more he wasn't confiding, she could sense it.

"Of course, when I agreed..." He blew out a deep breath and admitted, "I thought you were five."

Despite the tears still clinging to her lashes, she gave a

small bubble of laughter and pressed her hand against her mouth, her suspicions easing. "I'm not a child."

His lips twisted grimly. "I know that *now*."

She sniffed. "That's why you brought the doll?"

"Bribery," he admitted, tucking a stray curl behind her ear and caressing her cheek as he drew back. "I've never known what to do when children cry."

But the way his fingertips trailed over her cheek and the responding shiver that swept through her told her that he very much knew what to do with grown women, and heat stirred low in her belly. The amusement dissolved from her, replaced by a warm yearning. "Well, you don't bribe them with gifts."

"Then what do you do?" Another slow caress of her cheek…

And another tingling shiver. "You hold them," she whispered. "And you tell them they're safe, that everything is going to be all right."

His dark eyes stared deeply into hers. "You're safe, Katherine," he murmured as his arms tightened around her and drew her against him, "and everything is going to be all right."

"But I'm not a child," she protested softly, although she desperately wanted him to keep holding her, despite knowing no good could come of it. And he wasn't comforting her as much as making her nervous. *Very* nervous. Shaking her head, she released her hold on his lapels. "And you don't know that it's going to be all right."

Then she stepped back from him, sliding away along the table to put the length of the laboratory between them. And thank goodness, he let her go.

Her heart sped from just the caress of his fingers across

her cheek. If she stayed in his arms a moment longer, she would be just weak enough to kiss him. And *that* she simply couldn't do. She'd already lost control of Brambly to this man. If she lost control of her body to him, too, then...then she would lose everything. Just as her mother had.

"No, I don't," he agreed, running a hand through his hair as if he didn't know what to do with it now that he couldn't touch her.

"And Papa...he'll never be able to repay you—"

"I know."

His eyes turned cold, the heat she'd seen in their depths just moments before disappearing at her concern about her father, and her breath hitched as a warning prickled up her spine.

He reached down to pick up the letter she'd dropped at his feet. "I want him indebted to me."

"Why?" she whispered as worry swelled inside her chest. Oh heavens, what had Papa done now?

"So I can keep him in London under my watch." With a grim look of determination, he held out the letter to her.

But she stayed right where she was, not daring to come close enough to take it. If she did, she might very well find herself right back in his arms. "Edward, what aren't you telling me?"

His face was somber and harsh, and the way he looked at her made her stomach knot with dread. "Your father is dangerous, Katherine," he told her quietly. "He's hurt people, and I don't want him anywhere near you, not even at the other end of a letter."

Her eyes widened in disbelief as she stared at him. *Dangerous?* Impossible! Edward was wrong. Her father wasn't a criminal. He could be emotionally cruel, she'd seen that with her own eyes, but he would never physically harm her. "He wouldn't hurt anyone, not like you're suggesting."

His eyes flashed black, and she gasped at the icy intensity in him. "More than you know," he bit out coldly. "He hurt my family, and now that you're part of all this, I won't let him harm you, either."

Hurt his family? But that . . . that couldn't be! She felt the blood drain from her face, and her hand reached out for the table to steady herself. Her throat tightened. Dear God, had he hurt Edward? "What did—"

"You are not to contact him without my permission, understand?"

"He's my father, Edward. If he's in trouble, I have to help—"

"You can't help him now, Kate. It's too late." When she refused to accept the letter, he set it down on the table beside her, then reached to take her chin and hold her still as he stared into her eyes. "I want your word that you'll not contact him without my permission and that you'll tell me if he tries to contact you again."

She wouldn't agree to that. Edward was her guardian, but he didn't have the right to control her like this. No right to tell her whom she could or could not contact, especially when it came to her father. Papa had never cared for her, she knew that now, but he was still her only living relative and the man her mother loved. There should be some loyalty in that, in her duty as a daughter . . . shouldn't there?

If she refused to help him when he needed her most, then wouldn't that make her as hardhearted and indifferent as he was?

"I want to be able to trust you, Katherine." At her answering silence, Edward added quietly, "And I want you to trust me."

But it was mistrust that swirled through her. And confusion. How could she trust a man she didn't know, when she no longer trusted even her father?

"Do not contact Phillip Benton," he ordered quietly. "Nothing good will come of it."

With no other choice but to do as he said, she nodded, turning her face away at the stab of guilt that sickened her.

"Good." He moved toward the door. "I'm going for a walk to assess the boundary fences. I'll see you at dinner, then." He paused to glance back at her with a look of patient consternation. "And please don't make me climb into the hayloft again to fetch you."

Then he was gone, and she sagged back against the table, hanging her head in her hands. Her entire body trembled. How had it happened so quickly? In just five days, her life had been upended, and she was now clinging to control by her fingertips.

She'd lost control of Brambly, yet Edward promised to help her repair and restore it. She'd lost her father, too, with that letter, although she knew it was the loss of the dream of having a loving father in her life that she'd wept over. And when Edward held her in his arms to comfort her, she'd nearly lost her mind.

Her shoulders slumped in hopelessness. She didn't know whom to trust or what to believe anymore.

Edward claimed her father was dangerous, that he hurt people, but how could that be? Phillip Benton was a bad father and husband, for all accounts utterly unsuccessful in everything he'd attempted. But to maliciously hurt someone... He simply didn't have the spine for it.

But she'd come to know Edward fairly well during the past week since his arrival at her doorstep and his intrusion into her life, and what she'd learned was that he was not the kind of man who entered battle lightly. If he believed her father had hurt his family, then...oh, God help him!

She pushed herself away from the table and began to pace, chewing on her thumbnail as she circled the small room and tried to figure out what to think, what to do...

Her father had signed her away, she had proof of it. But he'd also asked for the guardianship. Even if Edward was correct—and she wouldn't have put it past Papa to suggest such a thing merely out of spite and his own gain—he'd still had the presence of mind to think of her at his lowest point. There had to be some kind of affection for her in that, no matter how perverse his rationale. There *had* to be! Because the alternative was that Papa not only cared nothing for her but also thought of her only as a pawn to be played. And that was simply unbearable.

Biting her bottom lip, she glanced at the letter. He wanted money, and she'd always given it to him in the past. What difference would it make this time to give him what little she had left?

Except that Edward had forbidden it.

He'd wanted her to have no contact at all with Papa without his permission, and she knew he'd never agree to let her send even this last bit of money, certain that he believed her father had already taken enough from her, mistakenly believing he would hurt her. But he needed her now, and for the first time in her life, she could make a difference to him.

She rubbed at her temples, not knowing what to do. To which man did she owe her loyalty?

Her gaze drifted from the letter to the table drawer where she'd hidden the three coins. Edward didn't know about those. She'd earned them herself; they didn't come from Brambly, so they were hers to do with as she pleased. Including sending them to her father in one last attempt to help him.

Her heartbeat sped. If she sent the coins, then she could let her father go from her life forever, without feeling any guilt. She would know that she had made her best, last attempt to love him as a daughter should. And Edward would never discover what she'd done.

She hurried to the journal and tore out a blank page, then took her pen and scribbled, *Papa, here is what little money I have to give you.*

She hesitated with the coins resting in her hand. It was more money than Arthur, Dorrie, and Mrs. Elston would have earned in a month, and she closed her eyes tightly against the pang of guilt at sending the money to her father rather than paying it to them. But at that moment, he needed it more than they did, and it would be the last she would ever give him. Three little coins... Not exactly twelve pieces of silver, yet she couldn't shake the notion Papa had betrayed her by signing her away.

She paused, the pen tip poised just above the paper— then impulsively dashed out, unable to completely banish the desire to make him love her, even now, *What else can I do to help? Your loving daughter, Kate.*

She folded the letter, carefully sealing the coins inside, then hurried to the door and called for Tom. The boy trotted out from the stable where he was undoubtedly once more brushing Edward's horse. For the past few weeks, he'd been a stable boy for a barn without any horses, and now that one was finally stabled there, he didn't want to leave the colt alone. If that horse wasn't bald by the time Edward finally left for London, it would be a miracle.

She pulled him into the laboratory, just out of sight of any prying eyes, and placed the letter in his hand. "Take this to Mr. Guerson at the posting inn and tell him to send it to London right away."

The boy nodded and hurried away. "Yes, miss!"

* * *

Damn that letter! Edward grabbed up a rock from the river-bank and heaved it as hard as he could. *And damn Phillip Benton!*

Even in this last letter to his daughter, when the man admitted he cared so little for her that he was willing to sign her over to a stranger to get her off his hands, the bastard had the gall to ask for money. But then, Edward shouldn't have been surprised, because Kate had been trying to buy her father's love for years. He would have admired her loyalty if it wasn't so deeply misplaced.

From the top of the riverbank, he could see the old brick smokehouse in the distance that she used as her laboratory. Even from his short visit inside, he could still smell the herbs and chemicals of her medicines, just as he could smell the faint scent of honeysuckle, which still clung to him from holding her while she cried, harder than he'd ever seen any woman cry. So hard he thought she might just break. He'd felt helpless to console her.

Then, suddenly, the embrace changed, and consoling wasn't what he wanted to do to her. *Sweet Lucifer*, he wanted to ravish her. He wanted to shove her across the table and plunge between her thighs until her cries of heartache became cries of passion. And for a moment, when he felt her pulse race beneath his fingertips, he was certain she wanted that, too.

Until she had the good sense to step out of his arms.

And thank God she had. Their situation was already tenuous at best, downright confrontational at worst now that she knew how he'd come to be her guardian, and the complications that would follow from seducing his virginal ward... *Good Lord*.

There was also the matter of trust. He'd learned the hard way that people couldn't be trusted, especially women. But he wanted to trust in Kate, and he wanted to believe that, for once, a woman could give him the peace he craved.

But thoughts like those were dangerous. They implied an importance in his life that he wasn't willing to give to any woman, least of all to Benton's daughter. He might as well sacrifice himself to the flames right now.

But her fire would taste exquisite.

With a curse of frustration, he plunged down the bank and dove fully clothed into the cold river.

CHAPTER SEVEN

Nine Days Later

"Oh, drat it!" Kate rolled her eyes at the perfectly good lavender plant she held in her hand. Then she looked down at the patch of garden she'd been weeding, and her shoulders sagged with self-reproach at the yard-long stretch of soil where she'd thoroughly plucked every plant and left standing a row of weeds.

Digging a hole with her fingers to replant the lavender, she cursed herself for ruining yet another chore. Just as when she'd tried to sort a box of bandages earlier and nearly tossed out the good ones and left the bad, everything she'd attempted to do today had gone wrong. And she knew why.

Him.

Edward Westover, she decided as she sighed with cha-

grin, overwhelmed her. If it were only the way he looked—
with those broad shoulders and muscular arms, that charming grin, which could turn into a rakish smile in a heartbeat,
and those eyes, the same ones whose blackness once frightened her but now reminded her of velvet—she could ignore
him and go on with the normal activities of her everyday
life.

But it was more than just how attractive he was. Good
Lord, she actually found herself starting to . . . *like* him.

During the fortnight he'd been at Brambly, she hadn't
minded spending time with him during the lingering con-
versations they shared over dinners. Or the long walks
they took through the fields. The chess games they played
in the evenings. The stories he shared about army life,
the descriptions of Spain and Portugal. Even his kind re-
marks when she told stories of her medical work, despite
his obvious bafflement that a woman would want to be a
scientist. And she certainly didn't mind the way he stared
at her whenever he thought she wasn't looking.

Oh, they still sparred at every opportunity, but she'd
begun to find him delightfully challenging in a way that
completely unsettled her. He'd turned her world on end
and stolen away her ability to concentrate on anything. But
him.

Which was why she now found herself kneeling in the
middle of a weed patch, thinking not about her herbs and
medicines but about him, and beginning to wonder if perhaps, just *perhaps*, he also wondered about her.

"Miss Kate!" Mrs. Elston leaned heavily against the
garden wall and struggled for breath from hurrying from
the house.

Her chest tightened with fledging dread as she looked

up from beneath the large brim of her floppy hat. Mrs. Elston running from the house always sent up a warning inside her because it so rarely occurred. "What is it?"

"The duke...wants to ride this afternoon...insists you accompany him. And," she panted, "he's refusing to...let you decline."

"Ride?" Kate puzzled, confused. "But I don't have a horse." Except for Brutus, and she doubted the old sway-back could even fit beneath a saddle.

"Those were his words. *Ride*. And to be ready within the hour."

She wanted to refuse. She should refuse. She rolled her eyes in surrender—she *couldn't* refuse. Not one of his direct orders. So, heaving a sigh, she removed her gardening gloves as she climbed to her feet to return to the house and dress for an afternoon outing with a duke who insisted they go riding, apparently on a magic carpet.

An hour later, she was clean, dressed in an old forest-green riding coat and matching hat that had once belonged to her mother, and ready *not* to ride anywhere. With a breath of determination—and deciding to leave her riding crop behind for fear she might crack it over Edward's head before the outing was over—she grabbed her gloves and went downstairs.

He waited in the foyer, dressed casually in the same maroon jacket and tan waistcoat and breeches he wore the afternoon he had arrived. The same afternoon two weeks ago, she recollected, when he thought he would only be at Brambly for a few hours before riding off and never bothering with her again.

She frowned. Hers wasn't the only life her father had upended.

He sketched a bow over her hand. "Katherine, you look lovely."

She fought down a blush. "Thank you."

"And thank you for joining me."

She pulled her hand free with a bit of pique. "I don't believe I had a choice, Your Grace."

"You can't blame me." He smiled at her irritation, and in response, a slow heat crept into her limbs. "A beautiful companion improves any activity."

She caught her breath. Was he...*flirting*? If it had been anyone else, she might have allowed herself to believe... But certainly not him.

As she narrowed her eyes, quick suspicion curled through her. Oh, this man could be very charming when he wanted to be, which left her wondering exactly what he was up to now.

He offered his arm. "Shall we?"

He led her outside to the barn, where his chestnut colt waited, saddled and ready. She stopped, eyeing the horse and its owner equally suspiciously. "You said we were going riding."

"We are."

"I thought, perhaps, you meant..." A carriage, actually. Or even old Brutus. But she hadn't expected this, or the pang of odd disappointment. Her shoulders sagged. "Two of us on one horse?"

"Why not?" But he glanced away, his lips tightening oddly.

"It's unseemly, and you know it." She removed her hand from his arm and from the hard muscles her fingertips felt beneath his sleeve. "Good afternoon, Your Grace."

She scowled as she turned back toward the house. He'd

interrupted her work and made her change—for *this*? Obviously, he was playing some kind of joke on her, but she wasn't at all amused.

"So you don't want your gift, then?" His hand closed over her elbow from behind, stopping her.

Swallowing down the flutter in her somersaulting stomach at his touch, she glanced dubiously over her shoulder at him. However much she distrusted this charming side of him, he'd still managed to raise her curiosity and draw her to him. "Gift?"

Smiling devilishly, knowing he'd caught her like a fish on a line, he let loose a sharp whistle, and Tom emerged from the barn, leading a horse behind him.

Kate blinked. It *couldn't* be . . . "Misty?"

She couldn't believe her eyes. Her horse! The one she'd raised from a foal but had to sell to pay the miller. Beneath the new sidesaddle and bridle, the mare's black coat had been brushed until it shined like polished ebony, and beside the mare, Tom grinned.

Rubbing her hand down the soft muzzle, Kate stared incredulously at Edward. "You did this—you brought her home."

He shrugged at her surprised accusation, a smile tugging at his lips, his velvet eyes not leaving hers.

"I never thought I'd see her again," she whispered, unable to speak any louder through the sudden tightening of her chest. This was the best surprise she'd ever been given. She blinked again, this time to hold back the tears of happiness threatening at her lashes. "I don't know how to thank you."

"Brambly needed a saddle horse," he replied casually as if the difficulty of tracking down her horse and buying it back took no effort. "You can't very well go bouncing around the countryside on an old plow horse." He leaned toward her, amusement shining in his eyes. "It's unseemly."

She laughed and threw her arms around his neck to hug him tightly. "Thank you!"

"Katherine." Surprise sounded in his voice as his hands lifted to her back in a loose embrace.

She froze. He was . . . hugging her back? For a heartbeat, she felt the strength of his hard body held against hers, and heat blossomed everywhere they touched.

Then his head lowered to brush his lips across her temple, and he murmured, "Kate."

Startled, she jumped away but not before she caught the heated look in his eyes. It fell over her like a warm summer rain, and she trembled at what she saw in his gaze. It wasn't appreciation for her gratitude, although from the way he stared at her, she suspected he wouldn't mind if she launched herself into his arms to hug him again—she saw arousal.

"We should go." Her voice was far huskier than she intended as she stared at him, her eyes never leaving his for fear he might just pounce if she glanced away.

"Then come here," he ordered gently.

Her heart skittered as she glanced around. There was no block nearby, nothing to use to mount her mare. Which meant . . .

He held out his hand.

Realizing what he intended, she fidgeted with her gloves. "I can mount on my own, Your Grace."

His lips curling into a grin, he ignored her and clasped her around the waist, turning her around and pulling her back against him. It was only for a moment but long enough for her to feel the muscles of his legs pressed against the backs of her thighs, his hard chest against her back. Then he lifted her. As she settled gently onto the saddle, his hands slid down from her waist to take a surreptitious touch of her leg.

He hadn't meant it as a caress. She knew he was only helping her onto the horse. Yet heat flared where he'd touched her, and she shivered.

Appearing oblivious to the tingle of longing he stirred inside her, he handed her the reins, then swung up onto his colt in an easy, fluid motion. He set the horse forward, only to pull up short when she hadn't moved and glance back at her.

She arched a brow. "Is Tom joining us on foot, then, or will he ride behind you?"

He glanced down dismissingly at the boy. "Neither."

"We need a chaperone, Your Grace." Good Lord—*a* chaperone? With the way her body pulsed from even such a fleeting caress, she feared they might need two.

"Unnecessary." He circled his horse back to hers. "You don't need a chaperone." He slapped the mare across the hindquarters and sent her trotting down the drive. "Not when you're with your guardian."

"How convenient," she muttered, his horse settling in beside hers.

"I don't make the rules," he drawled with a teasing gleam in his eyes. "I just enjoy them."

When he leaned out of his saddle and placed his gloved hand over hers, ostensibly to adjust her grip on the reins, her heart fluttered. Oh, they were going to need a dozen chaperones...

"And for some reason, Kate, I find myself enjoying your company." His voice softened with an undertone of curiosity, as if he couldn't quite believe it himself. "Very much."

And then her heart completely stopped. She had to swallow before her mouth found the words to stammer, "But all we do is argue!"

A slow grin drew her attention to his sensuous mouth. "I know."

Then he pulled his hand away from hers and eased back in his saddle.

She stared in blinking disbelief, trying to comprehend what had just happened. True, his smile was full of arrogance, as if both daring her to contradict him and secure in the knowledge that she wouldn't. But with the sunlight shining on his black hair and broad shoulders, his muscular thighs hugging the saddle beneath his tight breeches, he looked so incredibly *male*, so masculine she couldn't help but stare and for so long that after several moments he arched a brow.

Turning away to cover the burst of red heat across her cheeks, she deftly threw the conversation back at him, forcing a light tease into her voice as she asked, "What else do guardians do, then, besides force their wards into scandalous afternoon rides?"

"Well," he replied slowly as if he'd given considerable thought to that question himself, "normally, they provide a quality education."

"Too late, I'm afraid. I already have Mrs. Elston."

She saw his lips twitch at Mrs. Elston's expense. "Well, then, perhaps I can provide a respectable governess for *her*."

The unguarded amusement she glimpsed in him made her chest lift, and she laughed. It was so nice to see a lightness in him for once, rather than the dark brooding that seemed permanently fixed to his brow. Although she hated to admit it, Edward could be quite amusing. When he wasn't making her furious.

"I suppose there's always boarding school," he added.

Her laughter choked. There was nothing amusing about *that*. "So you intend to send me away?" Despite her playful tone, she remembered Mrs. Elston's warning that he wanted to improve her value in order to marry her off.

"Would that work?" he inquired impishly with a sly glance in her direction. "Because I'm certain we could find one in far northern Scotland that—"

"No."

It was his turn to laugh, this time at the fierce scowl she shot him for suggesting such a thing.

"I thought you'd like that." Another grin, more proof that he was enjoying himself by baiting her so mercilessly. "Learning all the important things in life, such as how to pour a proper cup of tea, speak French badly, make seating arrangements for boring dinner parties—"

Kate nearly laughed at his list of necessary skills. "I'd enjoy remaining at Brambly."

She liked her life just as it was, happy and safe at home with her medical work and the servants. It was a small but important life, one she would never willingly surrender.

"It seems, Your Grace," she commented as she turned the mare down the lane skirting the river, "there isn't much a guardian can do for me, so you'd best release me from that contract."

Ignoring her blatant attempt to get him to tear up the

agreement, he instead said so quietly, so seriously, that he immediately drew her undivided attention, "Actually, there is something I can do."

She held her breath warily.

"I can sponsor your debut." He kept his gaze firmly focused on his colt's flickering ears. "And secure your presentation at court."

"You're mad!" She sharply drew up her horse, gaping at him as if he'd sprouted a second head. "Absolutely not!"

He shot her a puzzled look, clearly not expecting that. "As the ward of a duke, you'll be one of the most sought-after ladies—"

"To what end?" she demanded, suddenly irked.

"Marriage, of course," he replied as if the answer were obvious.

"*Marriage?*" she choked out, frightened to within an inch of her life. Her guardian, discussing marriage plans— he was the only person in the world who now held the power to force her into such imprisonment. Marriage would be the end of her. "Never!"

That pulled him up straight. "You have no intention of marrying?"

"No."

He blinked. "Whyever not?"

"Because I don't need a husband."

"Need aside, you might enjoy being married."

She arched a brow in challenge and pinned him beneath her narrowed gaze. "Are you married, Edward?"

"No."

"Whyever not?"

"Because I don't need a husband," he answered, deadpan.

He pressed his colt into a gentle gallop, ending the conversation and leaving her no choice but to follow.

Turning away from the river, they cut across the open fields and slowed only to splash through a shallow creek. Her mare took the water without pausing, but Edward's colt hesitated. Just a moment's pause, but enough for her to race several lengths ahead.

"First one back to Brambly wins!" she challenged, urging her mare into a run.

Giving a shout, he gave chase.

His horse's giant strides ate up the distance until he caught her at the edge of the woods, yet she charged fearlessly on. Her hat flew off into the field behind her and her hair streamed loose, but she didn't care. The race was exhilarating! She couldn't remember the last time she felt this free, this *alive*.

Beaming with happiness, she pressed herself lower over the mare's neck and urged her faster.

"Surrender!" Edward shouted as he moved his horse even with hers.

"Never!"

"You can't outrun me."

She didn't have to outrun him, only outsmart him.

She pulled the reins sharply to the right, and her little mare darted down a narrow trail into the woods.

Edward jerked back in surprise at her quick maneuver, but his large horse was slower than hers to turn, its stride too powerful to stop quickly. With a laugh at her cunning, he expertly spun the colt into a tight circle and charged after her. He caught up with her easily, but the trail wasn't wide enough to overtake her.

"I'll pass you in the open fields," he warned from behind, and she felt her pulse speed from the thrill of the chase and from the smooth sound of his deep voice swirling through her.

"Probably," she called out over her shoulder, flashing him a mischievous smile.

"I'll win!"

"Oh no, you won't!"

When they broke out of the woods and the trail spilled into the open field, he dug his heels into his horse's sides, and it surged forward, its hooves pounding into the turf as it flew past her black mare.

From her vantage point, she saw his hard muscles ripple beneath the jacket as it drew taut across his shoulders and his thighs tightly hug the saddle. He mesmerized her. He was utterly fluid on horseback, as if he'd been born in the saddle, and she'd never seen a better horseman in her life. She could have watched him ride like that for hours.

But she wanted to win the race even more. She leaned low in the saddle and urged her mare on.

They galloped in the open now with only a short stone wall and a field of a few hundred yards between them and the barnyard. There were no more narrow trails or trees for her to duck into, but her mare was small and quick. She could easily win over the fences—

"That way!" he shouted and pointed down the field to send her away from the wall.

His colt wanted to jump the wall and head straight back to the stable, tossing its head and fighting for the rein, but she knew from the way his strong hands expertly kept the horse in check that Edward didn't think she could safely make the jump and that instead they should take the long route back to Brambly. But if they did that, he would win.

"I can make it!" she yelled.

"Go around!" he ordered.

Letting him get a few yards ahead, she pulled up her horse, changed directions, and headed straight for the wall.

"Kate, no!"

Just as she set the mare for the jump, out of the corner of her eye she saw his horse rear into the air and spin on its hind legs, then charge after her. He was bearing down on her, the large colt's strides eliminating the distance between them before the mare's hooves even left the earth. Landing easily on the other side, she heard the loud pounding of Edward's horse at her shoulder, the beast not even pausing in its stride as it took the jump.

Edward snatched the mare's bridle into his fist and pulled both horses to a stop. A sharp curse exploding from him, he swung to the ground. He clamped his arm around her waist and jerked her from the horse, slamming her back into his chest with a teeth-jarring thud.

For a moment, he held her suspended against him, her feet dangling in midair.

"Edward?" she whispered fearfully.

In answer, he carried her to the wall and dropped her onto it, her bottom bouncing on the stones and making her wince. Then he placed his palms flat on both sides of her and leaned in to trap her with his body.

She shivered as she stared up at him. The look on his face was murderous.

*   *   *

Damned woman! Gritting his teeth, Edward shook both from anger and from the terror that stabbed him when he saw her turn for the wall. Foolish, reckless—did she want to break her damned little neck?

He clenched his jaw so hard that the muscle in his cheek twitched. "What the *hell* do you think you were doing?"

With a frown of confused irritation, she pushed against his shoulders to move him away, but he wasn't about to budge. "I took a jump."

"In a new saddle on a horse you haven't ridden in months—you could have been killed." He'd seen it happen too many times during the war, when green horses threw their riders or fell jumping barriers, when new saddle straps simply snapped. Even good riders were killed falling beneath their horses, trampled by pounding hooves, their necks and backs broken when they hit the ground. And the thought of Kate falling...His hands shook from imagining it, his heart thudding painfully against his ribs.

"I was fine."

"I told you to go around," he snapped.

Another futile push, another irritated scowl. "We were racing, and I couldn't win if I didn't take the jump—"

He grabbed her shoulders and shook her once. Hard. Her eyes flew open wide. *Good.* Now he had her attention.

"I'm responsible for protecting you. If you'd fallen, if you'd been hurt—" His hands tightened on her arms. "Christ, Kate!"

She gasped as he took her chin and forced her to look at him. Reflexively, her hands reached for his shoulders to keep herself from tumbling backward off the wall, and her fingertips dug into the muscles beneath his jacket.

"Do not *ever* defy my orders again," he warned.

Her chin jutted up the way it did whenever he upset her. Which seemed to be all the blasted time. "I took a jump—"

"If you do, I swear," he seethed, "I will send you away."

Her breath hitched, her mouth falling open as she gaped at him. "You wouldn't dare!"

But he would do exactly that—he'd send her away and never let her return. He'd done it to his men in Spain when they defied his orders, and he'd certainly do it to her, too, if it meant protecting her and saving her life. "I will."

"This is my home. I will never leave it." Her eyes flared in challenge. "Even if you burn Brambly to the ground to force me away, I'll erect a tent in the ashes and keep warm sleeping on the embers!"

His body drew up tight and tall in response to the fight in her. She had been right about him. He wasn't used to being contradicted, certainly not by a woman.

But this hellcat was no ordinary woman. Even now, instead of being intimidated and frightened, she stared boldly back, her hands clenched into fists, those full lips of hers pressed together stubbornly. Aggravation at him gripped her enough that she panted with it, her breasts rising and falling tantalizingly beneath her coat with each quick, shallow breath, and he could feel the heat of her body through his jacket and along his legs where his thigh pressed against hers.

"And you will stop ordering me about!" She smacked his hand away from her face. "I am not one of your men, Colonel."

He clasped her chin again. "Trust me, angel," he rasped, his voice husky as he tilted her face upward, "of that I am well aware."

His mouth swooped down and captured hers.

The kiss was so sudden, so predatory, that she gasped beneath his lips and her body stiffened in his arms, but she made no move to push him away, and so he made no move to temper the onslaught of his mouth as it ravished hers.

Then she softened against him with a trembling whimper of surrender, her body arching up from the wall to press against his as she returned the kiss. Her hands at his shoulders no longer clung to him to keep from falling away but to keep him pulled close. The tip of her tongue darted out hesitantly to touch his—

He groaned and shoved his fingers deep into her tumbled hair, not to stroke through her loosened curls but to cup her head against his palm, to keep her mouth molded against his.

His tongue pushed her lips apart to thrust inside and claim her in the kiss he'd wanted to take since the moment he saw her glide down the stairs that first night at Brambly, appearing both so desirable yet so unobtainable. Her kiss was just as wonderful as he'd imagined. Spicy and sweet, moist and hot—she tasted of honeysuckle and woman, unbelievably delectable.

"Edward," she moaned, his name a plea against his lips that shivered all the way through him to the tip of his cock.

He ached to touch her, and his hand at her hip drifted slowly up toward her breast—

"Miss Kate! Your Grace!" Mrs. Elston's shrill shout echoed across the countryside. "Where are you?"

He pulled back, breaking the kiss but not releasing her from his arms. Just far enough away to glance over her shoulder and see in the distance that Tom had captured both horses as they ran back to the barn and that Mrs. Elston stood on the front portico of the house, glancing frantically around, trying to spot them.

"Let me go," she whispered.

"It's all right." His voice came hot and ragged against her ear. "She can't see us from there."

But her hands shoved at him, slapping against his shoulders and chest. "Let me go!"

Immediately releasing her, he caught her hand. "It's all right," he repeated calmly, trying to make her understand that her reputation was safe. "She's too far—"

"Why did you kiss me like that?" she demanded, her face flushing bright red, although he couldn't have said whether from anger or embarrassment.

"Because I wanted to." Such a childish thing to say, yet true. He'd wanted to kiss her. Desperately. "And so did you."

She didn't deny it—*couldn't* deny it, not with the way she'd responded to his kiss. But a look of heated confusion crossed her face, a fierce bewilderment and self-recrimination evident in her flaring eyes.

"Good Lord, chit," he muttered in surprise, "it was just a kiss."

Her hand rose to touch her lips, still red and moist from his. "No." She turned her face away. "It wasn't just a kiss."

Not just a kiss? Of course, it was. It was nothing more than . . . *Oh Lord.*

Her *first* kiss.

Trying not to let the surprise and guilt register on his face, not wanting to make her embarrassment any worse than it already was, he slowly released her hand. "My apologies, Kate," he said gently. "I didn't realize—"

"Don't," she whispered. "Edward, please—don't say anything."

And for once, without argument, he did exactly as she asked.

CHAPTER EIGHT

$\mathcal{K}$ate stood in front of her bedroom window, staring out at the rainy night. The room was cold, the fireplace dark, but she didn't have the energy or will to light a fire. Anyway, she didn't want to face the light, not tonight. Tonight, she wanted to hide.

She hung her head in her hands, guilt and shame clenching in her belly. What had she done? Her first kiss, her *very* first kiss...*oh God!*—why did it have to be with him? The man who was ruining her life. The man who wrenched control of Brambly away from her. How could she be so weak and foolish? Of all men, *him*!

When Edward pulled her from her horse and admonished her like a child, she had been furious with him. How dare he speak to her like that! Her control of Brambly had been snatched away, her life upended—and he was angry because she'd dared to take a *jump*? But she'd gone too far in arguing and pushed him. And he pushed back. Deliciously.

Demanding and fierce, his kiss tasted of man and fire, and she'd lost herself in the sensation of him, shamelessly moaning against his mouth as the white-hot fury she'd felt pulse through him just moments before was instantly replaced by something just as hot, something just as barely restrained...something she desperately wanted to push to the limits, then follow willingly over the edge.

But then, the way he'd looked at her afterward, as if it had all been a horrible mistake— *Blasted man!*

The worst part was she didn't know if she should be furious at him or ashamed at herself, because she'd liked it. Very much. And very much wanted to do it again.

Wringing her hands, she restlessly paced her room, as if pacing could calm her racing heart and squelch the memory of that kiss. But it wouldn't. She needed air and space, needed to be someplace where she could think and figure out what to do about him.

Silently, she left her room and made her way downstairs in the dark to the sitting room.

As she stood in front of the fireplace and stared up at her mother's portrait, hot tears of confusion and frustration burned her eyes. She'd lost control of Brambly and her life, with no idea how to get it back.

"What am I going to do?" she whispered to her mother.

"To begin with," Edward answered quietly from across the room, "I'd demand an apology for my behavior this afternoon."

Startled, she spun around, swiping at her eyes with the back of her hand. Thank God the darkness hid the scarlet flush of her cheeks at her embarrassment of being caught seeking out her dead mother for solace, and the quick suspicion flared that he'd been spying on her. She clenched her fists. If he said one word to her about that—just *one word*—oh, she'd make him regret it!

Instead, he pushed himself out of the chair and asked quietly as he approached, "Are you all right?"

Her shoulders sagged. However much she wanted to believe he was just despicable enough to be spying on her tonight, his casual state of undress told her otherwise. His shirt hung untucked around his hips, with his cravat already removed and his unbuttoned waistcoat dangling open across his chest. All of it denoted his expectation of being alone. So did the glass of port in his hand.

In the shadows, he looked dark, dangerous, and incredibly masculine. So much so that she shivered as she remembered the way that same tall, lean body had pressed against hers that afternoon. How that same mouth, which now pulled down into a concerned frown, had tasted on her lips.

"I'm fine," she answered. But she was so very far from fine.

Believing her with a slow nod, he set his drink aside to start a fire in the cold hearth. The flames gradually took hold in a small fire, but large enough to cast a warm light into the night-chilled room.

"When I was a child, I was afraid of the dark," he admitted, rocking back onto his heels to stare into the flames. "I used to keep candles burning all night. After Nanny tucked us into bed, I'd crawl from beneath the covers and light one."

She hesitated . . . then, her curiosity about him simply too strong to ignore, asked, "Did you ever get caught?"

"Eventually."

"When?"

"The night I nearly burned down Hartsfield Park."

Despite herself, she bit back a bubble of laughter. "I found you sitting in a dark room, so you must have overcome that fear."

He nodded. "I found something even more frightening."

"What?"

"War," he commented dryly. Brushing off his hands on his thighs as he straightened, he glanced at her. "I don't recommend it as a cure for children."

"I should think not."

A wry smile twisted at his mouth, then faded into a grimace. He took a deep breath. "Katherine, it's obvious that we've been at cross-purposes since my arrival."

She stiffened, steeling herself. His voice assumed a formal tone, as if reciting a practiced speech, and with each word, her stomach pinched harder in warning.

"I had no intention of causing problems," he continued apologetically. "I came here because I thought you were just a child, to make certain you had a proper home and staff to care for you. When I learned the truth, the circumstances were such that I felt I had to remain longer than expected. But now, I've seen all I need to." He reached for his glass and swallowed down the remaining port, signaling the end of his speech. "I'm leaving in the morning."

Her throat tightened. Edward was leaving. That was what she'd wanted, wasn't it? For him to go away, for her life to return to the way it was before he arrived . . . *Wasn't it?*

"Then I wish you safe travels," she murmured, too stunned to know what else to say, except . . . "I hope you're able to visit us again soon."

He studied her over the rim of his glass, his lips twitching. "Why do I doubt your sincerity?" When she opened her mouth for a cutting retort, he interrupted, "Apologies. You have every right to be angry with me. This afternoon, I forgot who you were."

She frowned, puzzled. "You forg—"

"Brannigan will arrive in a few days, and you're quite capable of taking care of yourself until then. If you need anything Brannigan can't handle, I'll send my attorney." Then he added with a wry smile at some private joke she didn't understand, "In the future, I'm certain Meacham will feel the need to oversee all matters concerning you himself."

Folding her arms, she lifted her chin. "So for the rest of my life, I'm to live as a guest in my own home?"

"Until you marry."

"Then it *is* for the rest of my life." Grimly, she shook her head. "Shackled forever to a man who isn't even my husband."

His jaw tightened as if insulted. "Dozens of young ladies in London wish for nothing more than to be attached to me for the rest of their lives."

"Then, by all means, you should ask one of them to be your ward."

He arched a brow and drawled, "Being my ward isn't the position they want to occupy."

She gaped at him, shocked at such a brazen innuendo. He'd meant...oh, the devil take the man!

"Don't worry, Kate. You won't be under my care long," he assured dryly. "Some brave man will come along and offer for you. For all that you're stubborn, challenging, sharp-tongued—"

Her lips pressed into an irritated line. "Why, thank you."

"—you're also quite beautiful."

Her breath caught. *Beautiful.* The word hung in the silence between them until it dissolved beneath the rain striking against the windows. In the flickering shadows of the firelight, they stared at each other, neither moving, neither looking away.

Finally, she replied, "So I've been told." She arched a dubious brow. "And what good is it?"

* * *

Well, Edward thought, *that* was unexpected.

Knowing the benefits of flattery, he'd complimented countless women over the years, and their reactions had always been the same. A thank-you, an innocent blush, a flirtatious smile that sometimes led to more-intimate flattery, sometimes to intimacy itself. Since he'd inherited, the women he encountered had practically thrown themselves at him, hoping for a chance to become the next Duchess of Strathmore or, failing that, his mistress.

But none had ever dismissed a compliment so out of hand before, the way Kate did. Ironic, that for once he'd meant it.

He watched her pick up his empty glass and reach for the bottle of port on the mantel. "Insects still eat the crops, sick children still suffer in the village…" She smiled mockingly, an expression aimed more at herself than him. "And my gardens still insist I tend them with my hands rather than burst into blooms simply because I've graced them with my presence."

Taking the liberty, she refilled the glass and held it out

toward him. He received it grimly, feeling duly chastised for forgetting she was an ordinary woman, just as he'd forgotten that afternoon that she was his ward. And he could never let that happen again.

"What do you do to make the world a better place, Edward? Surely, even your handsome presence cannot cause spontaneous change."

Handsome presence. He bit back the impulse to ask if she'd poisoned the port. "I've done my duty to my country." Enough for two lifetimes, in fact.

"Of course." She nodded sincerely. "You won the war, but what do you do now?"

"I manage my estates."

"To what end?"

The question lacked malice, but he found it irritating, nonetheless. Mostly because he'd been asking himself the same question for the past year. In the army, his life possessed purpose, until his brother's death changed everything. The heat of Spain suddenly replaced by the cold damps of England, spicy foods replaced by bland English meals, a day of physical work replaced by ... what? Hours spent sitting at a desk, balancing ledgers and reading reports.

His jaw tightened. "I have my responsibilities."

"Such as?"

"Property oversight, investments, expansions—"

She rested her hand gently on his arm, her green eyes sparkling mischievously. "And what good is it?"

So his little hellcat was baring her claws again. "Careful, Katherine," he warned, "that future husband might find you rather difficult."

"So I've been told." With a sigh, she turned toward the dark window to gaze out at the night.

His lips curled into a private smile. Standing there in bare feet and what he assumed to be a plain night rail beneath her robe, wild hair hanging loose around her shoulders like silk flames, she was guileless and completely unconcerned about the impropriety of the two of them being alone in a dark room, half-undressed. And any duenna worth her salt would have been horrified at the way she'd spoken to him.

But no other woman had ever challenged him like this. And inexplicably, he found himself liking it.

Self-reliant and independent, she possessed a quick intelligence that the restraints of proper society drove out of most women. Outspoken, bullheaded, and impertinent beyond belief, but also with a vulnerability and gentleness that not even her father's abandonment could destroy. All of it had him wanting to help her. Yet he also knew the best thing he could do was leave her alone.

Starting first thing in the morning.

He stepped up behind her, confused by his own desire to be near her. "Why don't you want to marry?"

"And give up my lifelong attachment to you? When so many women in London want nothing more than to be—"

"Katherine." A quiet warning. The time for verbal sparring had passed.

She sighed. "I'm not against marriage. It's a perfectly fine decision for most women."

But you are definitely not most women. "And for you?"

"Marriage means losing."

"Brambly, you mean."

"Yes—and my medical work. My work matters." With a glance, she dared him to challenge her, although he wouldn't have dreamt of ruining the tender trust she was finally showing him. "I'm the closest person to a doctor this village has. Still not much of one, I'll admit, but better than nothing."

"And marriage?"

"No man wants a doctor for a wife."

Edward couldn't disagree. Being a leech was a questionable profession even for a man. For a woman, unthinkable. No medical school would admit her, no doctor would practice with her, not even with female patients. No husband would want his wife in contact with sickness and disease, filth and contagion, or the scandal of physical examinations. The best she could hope for was to be a midwife, and only then if she married a farmer or a smith. Or became a spinster.

For some reason he couldn't explain, he wanted so much more for her.

"And you?" she prompted, turning the conversation onto him. "A man of your age and rank, surely you should have a wife by now. Someone to host your parties and give you an heir."

"I've put myself on the shelf," he quipped, deadpan.

"Edward," she chastised.

He grimaced. She sounded exactly like Aunt Augusta. "Until last year, I was an army colonel, and being a soldier's wife is always a grim prospect. Then, once I was back in England, other business distracted me, and parties and heirs held little concern."

"And now?"

"Now," he commented dryly, "I have my hands full with flippant, ungrateful wards who don't realize when they're overstepping boundaries of privacy."

A knowing smile played lightly at the corners of her

mouth, and he felt that smile warm into his chest. Boldly, she took the glass from his hand and drank the last of the port.

As he watched the soft undulation of her elegant throat, his cock flexed. He'd been semihard since she stepped into the room, all night-mussed in that thin robe, her hair wild and loose. Now, standing close enough to smell her honey-suckle scent, he wondered if she'd taste like port if he kissed her.

She licked a drop of the sweet liquid from her lips with the tip of her tongue—

He went completely hard. *Sweet Lucifer.*

"I'm not ungrateful to you, Edward." She set the empty glass aside. "But I don't want to be controlled. I'm doing something that matters, and I don't want a husband who thinks he has the right to take that away." She raised her gaze to his. "Or a guardian."

"I don't want to control you, Kate."

"Yes, you do," she countered. "Since you've been here, you've taken it upon yourself to hire an agent, fill the larders, buy livestock—" Her lips pressed together grimly with a loud sigh. "Edward, you bought me a horse."

"All with your best interests in mind." And he had. There was something about this woman that had him want-ing to protect her. To spoil her. He found himself not only wanting her but wanting to spend time with her, enjoying her smiles and laughter, her quick wit, the way her eyes shined so mischievously when she thought he wasn't look-ing at her. But he'd found himself doing almost nothing except looking at her.

She shook her head. "All without my consent. And this afternoon in the field, you were very controlling then."

Understanding dawned on him. So *that* was it. It wasn't the kiss she objected to, but the way it was done.

And knowing that... "I sincerely apologize," he offered earnestly.

"Well, then." Her shoulders visibly relaxed. "I'm glad you realize you were wrong—"

"You misunderstand."

Touching her chin, he tipped her face to catch the firelight dancing in the green depths of her emerald eyes.

"I am not apologizing for kissing you."

Her breath hitched, and the soft gasp rushed through him, straight down to the throbbing tip of his cock. Thank God he was just cad enough to leave his shirt untucked when she entered the room.

"Then why are you apologizing?" she whispered.

"Because I didn't know it was your first kiss."

A blush instantly heated her cheeks.

"If I had known," he continued, his gaze settling on her sensuous mouth, "I would have made certain that it was soft, sweet... I would have been gentle."

She batted his hand away and stepped back. "There's nothing gentle about you!" She laughed, unaware of the way her description pricked at him. "You might be a duke, but in your bones, you're a colonel who's used to giving orders, and I doubt you could ever be soft or sweet—"

Without warning, he swept her up into his arms.

She gasped. "Edward, put me down!"

"All right," he agreed tersely. He sat down in the chair beside the fire, bringing her down with him on his lap.

Her face level with his, she sat across his thighs with one hand behind his neck and her bare feet dangling in the air. She struggled in his arms, off-balance and unable to jump down, and clearly unaware of what her wiggling bottom was doing to him.

"I meant—on the *floor!*"

Oh, he'd gladly lay her on the floor, in a heartbeat.

She slapped at his shoulder, but he easily caught her wrist.

"Be still," he ordered gently, and immediately she stopped moving.

A warm pleasure surged through him as he felt her racing pulse beneath his fingertips at her wrist, saw the quick rise and fall of her breasts as her breath grew shallow. She wanted his kiss, he could see it in her eyes. But she was too inexperienced to know how to ask for it.

So he would gladly teach her. "It's time for a lesson, Katherine."

She trembled but didn't resist as he brought her hand to his mouth. "What kind of lesson?"

"This kind." His lips caressed the tender skin of her wrist, then down her forearm, leaving a trail of moist warmth across her flesh.

Goose bumps rose instantly in his wake. Like magic. She stared at him incredulously, and in those emerald-green pools he saw uncertainty...and dark arousal. Heat gathered low in his gut at the way she looked at him through lowered lashes, in half innocence, half anticipation. And wholly desirable.

"Would you like me to show you how gentle I can be?" he murmured against her wrist.

Her answer came as nothing more than a breath, so low he almost didn't hear... "Yes."

His chest squeezed with hard arousal at her answer, a feeling he certainly didn't deserve but couldn't resist.

"Then, lesson one." As he placed a kiss in the delicate angle of her elbow, he pointedly arched a brow to reinforce the lesson. "Gentle."

Her body trembling, she closed her eyes and shifted closer.

The corners of his mouth tugged upward in wonder. If she reacted like this to such an innocent caress, how would she react when he touched her more intimately, to cup her breast in his hand or stroke up her inner thigh? And he desperately wanted to find out.

Pressing his advantage, he brushed his knuckles across her cheek, contenting himself with this small touch. For now. "Soft." His thumb traced across her lips, over each tantalizing rise and dip of her sensuous mouth. "So sweet..."

With a breathless sigh, her lips parted in invitation, and he bit back his responding groan.

He should release her. He had no business touching her like this, but she had dared him, once again completely wrong about him. When it came to women, he knew exactly how to caress them softly and gently until they moaned, until they whimpered beneath him with a burning desire to slide him inside, just as he knew when they wanted to be taken rough, hard, fast.

A demanding urge deep inside him wanted to prove all that to this infuriating, frustrating woman and make her finally realize she knew nothing about what he was capable of doing. And the last thing he wanted to do at that moment was release her. With Kate, he felt alive for the first time in a year, and the blood pumping through his veins pulsed hot, each heartbeat electric.

Why this slip of a woman who irritated him beyond reason should affect him like this made no sense. Or that she could confuse him so much by both arousing and comforting at the same time. Impossibly innocent and wholly inexperienced, she drew him until the pull of her was undeniable, the aching of his hard cock impossible to ignore, and he recklessly sought the peace he instinctively knew he'd find with her.

His arm slid behind her, to encircle her waist and draw her closer. "Gentle."

She stiffened, her hands flattening against his chest, as if she didn't know whether to clasp him tighter or push him away. And if she knew what was good for her, she'd be shoving with every ounce of her strength.

But she didn't fight him, not even when he sifted his fingers through her fiery waves the way he'd yearned to do since he first laid eyes on her. The strands curled provocatively around his fingers. He'd lost count of the number of women whose hair he'd touched in his life, but none of those had ever felt like this.

Her face was even with his, his mouth so close to hers that he felt her catch her breath when he whispered, "Soft…"

When he cupped her face in his hand, she leaned into his touch and nuzzled her cheek against his rough palm. Silent consent.

Aching to kiss her, he tilted her face upward and touched his lips to hers.

"Sweet." His mouth swept back and forth across hers with a hushed groan. *So unbelievably sweet…* There was none of the physical demand of that afternoon's embrace, none of its urgency or desperation. Instead, his lips delicately caressed hers in a tantalizingly innocent kiss. Nothing more than a featherlight tease, the kiss stirred a warmth inside him and gave an unexpected lift of the weight from his shoulders.

But when her hand slid up his chest to tangle into his shirt and tug him closer, he forced himself to pull away. Not because he wanted to stop—he ached for her, and if she shifted just an inch in his lap, she'd immediately discover exactly how much—but because he could very easily continue.

If he did that, the kissing lesson would turn into something much less innocent, something demanding and controlling, just as she'd accused him of being that afternoon.

Her eyes fluttered open, her hooded gaze fogged with arousal. When her lips parted in confusion—

"*That* was how your first kiss should have been," he murmured, his voice husky.

"Oh." She shivered, and he couldn't help but smile, more pleased than he had a right to be, more relieved than he wanted to admit that she hadn't tried to slap him. Again.

When she didn't say anything more, he brushed his thumb across her bottom lip, still hot and moist from his mouth. "What are you thinking?"

Her brows knit together. "That I'm...confused."

"Good."

"Good?" she puzzled.

He nodded, reluctantly pulling his hand away from her lips before he let it drift elsewhere over her body. "I'm feeling a bit confused myself, and I'd hate to be the only one."

That must have been the right thing to say, because he saw the tension in her shoulders loosen as the nervousness left her. When she smiled at him, the heat of it stirred something deep in his gut. It wasn't just lust. His little angel was doing all kinds of things to his insides, chasing away the darkness and making him feel alive, raising emotions he hadn't felt for a woman in years.

And *that* was the problem. This beautiful, intelligent, independent woman who made his heart race and his gut burn in ways no one else ever had was also Benton's daughter. And now his ward.

She buried her face against his neck, her warm lips brushing against his bare skin as she relaxed against him. "You're not alone, Edward."

His breath hitched at her soft words.

He wanted her.

Dear God, how much he wanted her! To bury himself inside her warmth, find comfort in her arms, and forget the past year and every change fate cruelly thrust onto him...Judging from the trembling arousal he felt in her, he knew she'd give herself to him.

But he didn't deserve to be redeemed. Certainly not by someone as selfless and good as Kate, certainly not when all he could do was take...her body, her innocence, the solace of being in her arms.

However much he wanted to stay, remaining here was madness. No one would fault him for fleeing back to London and letting Meacham sort out the rest of this mess.

Which was exactly what he needed to do.

"I'll leave in the morning," he informed her again, more to convince himself than her.

She rested her palm lightly against his chest, his heart beating fast beneath her fingertips. "You can stay a few more days, until Brannigan arrives." It was not a question.

He said quietly, "I thought you wanted me to leave."

"So did I," she admitted, and his chest warmed undeservedly at the trust she showed him with her honest answer. "But I think I've changed my mind about you."

He wanted to know exactly what she meant by that, but now was not the moment to press, not when she was being friendlier to him than she'd been since he arrived. Not when he was feeling at peace for the first time in well over a year. Perhaps in a decade.

"You truly want me to stay?" he murmured into her soft hair.

She nodded silently, her cheek rubbing against his shoulder.

So do I.

Chapter Nine

Katherine.

Through the night's stormy darkness, Kate saw Edward approach.

The dark shadows highlighted his chiseled cheekbones, and in the flashes of lightning, she saw his eyes stare at her wickedly, blazing desire in their black depths. Each step brought him closer as if he were stalking her like a wolf coming to devour her. She shuddered against the overwhelming arousal flaming inside her, her breathing fast and shallow.

He leaned over her, his hands reaching for her shoulders. His warm touch radiated from everywhere, even inside her own body, and prickled heatedly across her arms, her face, her neck, over her breasts and down to that aching place between her legs. She throbbed, all the blood in her body pooling right there, and everything swirled around her, all inverted—up was down, rough was sweet, pleasure was agony.

Dear God, how she wanted the agony of his pleasure!

Katherine . . . Kate.

Her body trembled, her heart pounded, but she wasn't afraid. She wanted him in bed with her, their arms and legs entwined until it was impossible to tell where she ended and he began, his weight pressing her down—

He grabbed her shoulders and shook hard. "Kate!"

She startled, her eyes flying open.

"Miss Kate—wake up!" Dorrie shook her again.

In a fleeting moment of panic, her heart racing, she sat up and glanced around. The rain pounded down against the window and broke the stillness of the dark, cold bedroom. But Edward wasn't there. She'd only been dreaming of him. Again.

Kate stifled a yawn. "What time is it?"

"Almost midnight."

"What's the matter?"

"Emma Mulderry's son came to fetch you—"

"The baby!" Instantly awake, Kate flew out of bed and hurried to her dressing table. "Run down to the kitchens and wake Tom," she ordered. "Tell him to saddle Misty, then fetch my saddlebags from the laboratory. And put the bottle of port from the sitting room into the bag, too, will you?"

"Yes, miss!" She scurried from the room.

Kate scrambled into her clothes, forgoing her pretty riding coat for more study layers, and stomped into a pair of old boots. She bothered with her hair only enough to twist it into a knot at her neck, then grabbed her coat and wide-brimmed hat to keep the rain off her face. As she left, she took the pillowcase off her bed.

By the time she reached the front door, the leather bags waited for her. Filled with her medical tools and medicines, her kit wasn't much, but she kept everything ready in case of emergencies to help however she could. She mounted her mare and hurried off into the storm.

Mud and water covered the dirt road as she rode toward the village. Normally, she would have gone through the fields, fording the river where it widened just below the locks and the old lockkeeper's cottage. But tonight the river ran high and fast, swollen from the rains, so she continued on the roads and crossed over the wooden bridge north of the village.

The simple, three-room cottage where Emma Mulderry lived with her husband, John, and their five children stood on the far end of the village. Their middle son stood outside in the rain, waiting anxiously for her to arrive. Kate dismounted and handed him the reins. Without knocking, she pushed open the narrow front door.

Only two stubby candles and a weak fire lit the main room, but in the dim light, she saw the three youngest children sitting on chairs against the wall, staring toward the bedroom with worried eyes. Dim figures stirred in the bedroom beyond, with the wife lying on the bed, the husband holding her hand.

Emma Mulderry nodded at Kate's arrival, and with a moan, she dug the flat of her palms against the sides of her bulging stomach as a hard labor pain seized her.

"I came as quickly as I could," Kate apologized, then went right to work, setting her saddlebags on the plank table in the center of the main room and digging out her supplies. "How long have you been in labor?"

Dark circles framed tired eyes in the strained face, and sweat beaded on her brow. "Since early afternoon."

"How far apart are the pains?" Kate had delivered enough babies to understand the timing of the pains and how to gauge how much longer she had left.

"Close," the woman whispered, relaxing as the labor pain subsided.

Giving birth to her sixth child, Emma was more experienced at this than Kate, but she would do her best to help. She turned to the oldest of the two daughters sitting on the chairs. At eight, the girl was old enough to assist her. "Eliza, I need you to put on a kettle of water and heat it for me, all right?"

Eliza nodded and, with a hesitant look at her mother, went to the fireplace, where a copper kettle hung on a large metal hook. She took it down and carried it outside to the well.

Just as she slipped outside, the middle son scurried into the house from stabling her horse.

"Jacob," Kate ordered, nodding to the two younger children, "take your brother and sister down to Mrs. Bailey's for the night."

He nodded, obviously grateful to be sent anyplace else. "Yes, miss!" Then he herded the younger children out the door and into the rain, which now fell in hard waves across the village.

"Mr. Mulderry." Kate turned to the husband. "I need you to leave, too, please."

With a parting glance at his wife, he nodded and left without protest. A birthing room was not the place for men.

Finally alone with Emma, Kate sat down on the stool beside the bed and took her hand, feigning more bravery than she felt. "This baby is going to arrive just fine."

At that faint reassurance, the woman nodded, but her lips pressed together grimly.

Carrying the heavy kettle with both hands, Eliza waddled into the house. Kate poured some of the water into a basin, then set the kettle into the fireplace, and in a matter of minutes, the water was hot. Kate spooned an herb mixture into a mug, then filled it with hot water and handed it to Emma, ordering her softly to drink the mixture to help with the discomfort. Then she soaked a cloth in the bowl of cold water and placed it onto Emma's forehead as she eased her onto her back.

Delicately, Kate moved her hands over the bulging belly to feel for the baby's position. "Everything seems fine," she sighed with deep relief. "Now, we just have to wait."

She returned to the bed to spend the next hour holding Emma's hand through the pains.

Outside, the storm intensified. The rain poured down as thunder echoed across the village, and the wind picked up steadily. The rain and cold had driven John Mulderry back inside from the barn to pace the main room. Kate hadn't the heart to ask him to leave again.

A knock pounded at the door, but Kate ignored the interruption and kept her attention on Emma, who gripped her hand tightly for support. The baby was coming. Soon.

"I'm searching for Katherine Benton." The masculine voice carried as deeply as the thunder rolling overhead.

Edward. Her heart thudded hard in a jumble of emotions. With a quick squeeze to Emma's hand and a promise to be right back, she slipped into the main room.

He stepped in from the pouring rain, his large presence instantly filling the tiny house. Water dripped from his long coat and muddy boots, and his dark eyes, nearly hidden beneath the brim of his hat, scanned the dimly lit room.

Then he saw her. With an expression mixed of fury and relief, he crossed the room to her and took her arm to draw her aside.

"Are you mad," he demanded, keeping his voice low, "leaving the house alone in the middle of a storm?"

"I've gone out many nights in rain much harder than this."

"Tonight's rain has turned into a flood," he corrected, worried anger hardening his face. "You should have told me."

She certainly did not need *his* permission to leave *her* house. "I do not—"

"I would have come with you to make certain you were safe."

Her heart skipped. Whatever sharp retort she'd been about to deliver was lost.

To make certain she was safe . . . Was he worried about her? Her chest warmed. Perhaps she was beginning to mean more to him than just the burden of a guardianship, after all.

Her breath caught—where on earth had *that* thought come from?

True, just a few hours ago, he was teaching her how to kiss, and she'd enjoyed it. Much more than she should have. But that had only been an object lesson in how little she knew about him. And she obviously didn't know him nearly well enough to wonder whether he had come after her through the storm because she was his ward or because he cared about her.

"I didn't want to wake you," she offered instead.

"I wasn't asleep." At the sultry murmur, heat swirled down her spine. "I was still wide awake because of you."

She stared wordlessly into his face, still damp from the rain. He had ridden through a storm at night across unfamiliar countryside to find her. To protect her. No one had ever done anything like that for her before, and it made her throat tighten with emotion. So did the implication in his reply. That she bothered him enough to keep him from sleeping.

And *that* made her tremble.

He blew out a heavy breath, and sudden relief eased the tension in his broad shoulders. "Don't ever run off like that again, Katherine."

Run off? Hardly. At that moment, she wanted nothing more than to wrap her arms around his neck, press herself close, kiss him...With a hard swallow, she nodded.

To think, just days ago she had been frightened of him and wanted nothing more than for him to leave and never bother her again.

As his gaze drifted toward the bedroom, she knew there would be time later to sort out what all this meant. But now, she was needed here.

"How can I help?" he asked as if reading her thoughts.

She withdrew the port from her saddlebag and pressed the bottle into his hand. "Take Mr. Mulderry to the barn?"

He nodded his understanding.

As she turned back toward the bedroom, he stopped her with a light touch to her arm. He stole a moment from her to brush a curl from her tired forehead and tuck it behind her ear. Only a small gesture, but Kate felt her heart skip at its reassuring familiarity, at the warm comfort it stirred inside her.

"Mr. Mulderry." Edward slapped his arm around the

man's shoulder and led him toward the door. "Nothing for us men to do here. Join me in the barn for a drink."

They stepped into the howling wind and rain, closing the door behind them. And Kate returned to the bedside as the hard labor began.

Finally, after what seemed like hours, the baby emerged, and Kate's hands trembled as she lifted it into her arms, small but pink and healthy. With a hard shudder, the baby began to cry. At first a soft burbling as it struggled to fill its tiny lungs with air and breathe in its new life, then growing into a strong wail.

Kate carried the baby to the basin and gently washed warm water over it, then swaddled it in the pillowcase she'd pulled from her bed and placed the infant into Emma's arms. Tears ran down the mother's cheeks.

"It's a girl," Kate whispered, fighting the pull of emotions inside her. She was so happy for Emma, yet so sad that she would never experience being a mother herself.

"Thank you." Emma pulled the baby closer. "Oh, thank you!"

Kate's throat tightened at the scene of love in front of her. "I'll get your husband," she offered.

But she didn't have to. The baby's cries had reached the barn, even through the black rain, and Mr. Mulderry had come running. When he saw the baby, he beamed and charged through the house to his wife's side.

Kate watched in happy fascination as the giant man gently pulled the pillowcase down with his large forefinger to stare in wonder at the tiny babe.

A hand rested possessively against her lower back. "You are the most amazing woman," Edward said quietly behind her.

"I didn't do anything." She fought down the blush at his compliment.

The way Edward's eyes flickered told her he disagreed, but instead of challenging her, he lowered his head to brush his mouth against her temple. "You are beautiful."

Then she did blush, hot and scarlet and embarrassed. "I look a fright."

"I didn't mean your appearance."

In that moment, the coldness she had come to associate with him vanished, replaced by a low, smoldering heat she felt all the way down between her legs. She had no words to answer him.

"Come on," he murmured. "Let's get you home."

He helped her into her coat, then turned her to face him, and he fastened the buttons all the way up to her chin to make certain she would be safe against the storm. He was protecting her again, just as he'd already done so much to help her with Brambly.

Her throat clenched at the generosity of all he'd done for her, this man who claimed less than a fortnight ago that he was capable of evil and did not deserve her compassion. He had been so wrong.

He frowned down at her, his hands resting lightly on her shoulders. "Is something wrong?"

"Edward, I…" Blinking hard, she wanted to tell him how grateful she was that he cared about her, that having him near drove away the loneliness and fear. But all she could manage was a raspy, "Thank you."

Wrapping her hands in his coat's lapels, she tugged herself against him and touched her lips to his.

He tensed for a moment at the unexpected kiss, then he whispered her name, and his arms came up slowly across her back. When the tip of his tongue traced over her lips, tasting at the corner of her mouth, she trembled.

She lowered herself and pulled away, lingering a moment with her hands still tangled in the lapels of his greatcoat and her forehead resting against his shoulder, unable to make herself let go completely.

With a tremulous sigh, she reluctantly stepped back. "We should go now."

Nodding, he silently took her hand to lead her outside into the storm.

He lifted her onto her horse, and they rode through the cold rain pounding down upon them, drenching them clear through to their skins. Edward rode first, keeping his horse in check and the gait slow so Kate's mare could make her way more carefully across the cobblestones in the village, then over the slippery layer of mud when the road turned toward the south. His horse was steady, well trained, and walked on calmly, ignoring the storm raging around them.

But her mare was skittish, upset by the booming thunder and flashes of lightning, shying at every shadow. Kate fought to keep her seat.

Edward frowned back at her. "Do you think you can handle her if we trot?"

"Yes," she affirmed, her chattering teeth hiding her doubt. With her hands so cold she could barely close them around the reins, she simply didn't know if she could, but she refused to admit it. Chilled to her bones, she shook violently, so cold she ached, and she wanted nothing more than to get back to the warmth of Brambly as quickly as possible. He eased his horse into a trot, and she followed.

When they reached the river, she reined in beside him

and tried to peer through the darkness, but the night was too dark, the churning river too black.

"The bridge is out," he shouted above the noise of the rushing current.

He pointed into the darkness. Her eyes followed, and she saw it—at least two feet of water rushed over the bridge in a torrent.

"Is there another way?" he asked.

"We might be able to ford by the lock."

"Show me."

As Kate led him along the river, Edward rode closely at her side. The gusting winds whipped the trees, their boughs creaking and snapping loudly and adding to the noise of the rushing river beside them and the skittishness of her horse. Only when the next flash of lightning lit the black night did she realize that Edward was leaning forward in his saddle, his hand clamped firmly around the mare's bridle to keep her from dashing away.

When they reached the lock, he pulled both horses to a stop. His face was inscrutable as he scanned the wide, shallow spot in the river and contemplated how deep the water would be, how fast the current.

He shook his head. "We'll go back to the village."

She grasped his arm, her head shaking. She was beyond tired, so cold that her teeth hurt from chattering, and she couldn't bear the thought of riding all those miles back to the village when Brambly was less than two miles away on the other side of the river. "Can we try to cross?"

Even in the darkness, he frowned grimly at the way her body shuddered, and she saw his resolve melt beneath her pleading eyes.

"All right," he agreed reluctantly. "But keep your feet

out of the stirrups until we're on the other side," he ordered, "and don't wrap your hands in the reins."

She nodded anxiously.

"Follow me, and stay close."

With a tap of his heels against the colt's sides, he set the horse forward into the river.

The current ran fast, the water high. After only a few steps into the river, the water came up nearly to the little mare's belly. But as they went on, the water level stayed steady, and by the middle of the channel, Kate was already focused on the far bank.

Without warning, a large branch rose up from the black water and barreled toward Kate's mare. Twisting in the boiling current, the branches slammed against her horse's hindquarters. The mare lost her footing in the raging water and splashed down into the river, kicking and slipping, whinnying frantically.

"Edward!" Kate plunged into the icy water.

She struggled to swim, but the current was too strong for her already tired body, the struggle too hard in the freezing water, which soaked heavy into her skirts and dragged her down. Her fingers turned numb, and the muscles in her arms and legs refused to move.

With a cry, she slipped beneath the black surface.

A strong arm went around her and heaved her up from the water. She clung desperately to him, and her fingers dug into the hard muscle of his forearm as Edward dragged her toward the bank.

Holding her wet body securely in his arms, he carried her from the river and placed her gently on the muddy ground. She gasped and struggled to breathe.

He leaned on bent knees over her drenched body, then

began to rub her arms and legs hard to get the warm blood circulating through her. Her skin was cold and clammy, her lungs frozen, but she was alive. Thanks to Edward. He'd risked his life to save hers, and she knew she would never be able to repay him.

"Can you stand?" he demanded above the noise of the storm.

She nodded, and he helped her to her feet. "The horses?"

"Gone." He grimaced. "And it's too far back to the village. We'll freeze before we reach it. We have to find shelter here."

"There's an old lockkeeper's cottage up there." She pointed a shaking hand toward a narrow footpath leading up from the river. "But it's been abandoned—"

"Does it have a roof?"

She nodded, shuddering with cold.

"Then it'll do." He took her hand and led her toward the path, but her wobbly legs stumbled. He grabbed for her and held her against him until she steadied, and when they moved on, he kept his arm around her waist, drawing her close.

The cottage appeared from the blackness, hidden behind overgrown bushes and trees. Wooden shutters hung open on broken hinges, and the front step sagged nearly to the ground. The whole structure appeared as if it might tumble down on their heads at any moment. But they had no choice. They needed shelter, and already, her toes and fingers were numb.

Finding the front door locked, Edward drove his shoulder against it, pounding relentlessly into it until the rusted lock gave way. He shoved the door open and led her inside.

In the bursts of lightning flashing through the broken

shutters, she saw a few pieces of furniture covered with sheets to protect them from dust and disuse. A stairway led up to the loft, and a large fireplace took up most of the far wall. It wasn't much, but the roof was still in place, still keeping out the rain.

He drew her forward to the fireplace and searched along the mantel for the tinderbox.

She thought she heard the faint chattering of his teeth and realized he must have been as cold as she was, but he hadn't let her see that before now, fighting back his own shivers so he could appear strong and keep her from panicking. She stared at him. How on earth had she been so wrong about him? How did she ever think he was cruel and heartless?

The small fire flickered as the fingerlike flames worked to latch on to the old wood, casting a faint light into the darkness, but that was all the light necessary for Edward to find wood stacked nearby and toss it onto the fire until the flames leapt high and hot.

Kate stepped forward like a moth drawn to the warmth and light, still shaking violently. He took both her hands and rubbed them briskly between his to bring the blood back into her fingers, but his hands felt just as icy cold as hers.

"I apologize." He lifted them to his mouth to brush his lips over her knuckles. Her heart skittered. *That* did more to send heat through them than raising them to the fire.

"It's not your fault we're stranded here." She sniffed softly. "I thought we could make it across the river, too."

"No," he corrected gently, "I apologize for what I have to ask you to do."

She puzzled. "What do you—"

"Take off your clothes, Kate."

For a beat, she froze, then sputtered a fierce, "No!"

"We're both soaked," Edward explained calmly, his hands remaining clamped around hers, forcing her to listen, "and we have to get out of these clothes."

"But we've got the fire now—"

"Your clothes are wet and holding the cold against your skin. As long as you're in them, you'll never be warm."

She yanked her hands away, then grasped at the front of her coat as if he had just attempted to physically rip it from her body. "I am not taking off my clothes!"

"Not *all* your clothes," he clarified patiently, his tone growing more calm and soothing as her own voice moved closer to hysteria. "Your shift should dry quickly if you stand in front of the fire."

"And where will you stand?"

"Right beside you."

"No."

He clenched his teeth, his patience snapping. "I have never torn the clothes off an unwilling woman, but if you don't take them off right now, I will throw you to the floor and strip them off you myself."

"You wouldn't dare!"

He silently arched a brow.

Her breath hitched. He was *serious*—he wanted her to remove her clothes and stand naked in front of the fire. Right next to him. She gaped at him. "You're mad!"

"Just your outer clothes. You can keep on your shift."

"I'm not wearing a shift under my dress," she mumbled as she looked away, not wanting him to see her humiliation.

"Pardon?"

"I'm not wearing a shift!" she repeated in angry embarrassment.

At first incredulous, then darkening in disbelief, his gaze swept over her as intensely as if he were trying to see through her dress to the nonexistent shift below. Heat rose from her body everywhere he looked, swelling up inside her breasts and spilling down to her thighs. She swallowed. Hard. If he kept staring at her like that, she wouldn't need the fire to warm her.

"Well, then," he said slowly, carefully measuring each word as if he were afraid she'd slap him, "are you wearing anything beneath your dress?"

"Of course!" Then her face flushed hot as she answered, barely above a whisper, "A stay and ... breeches."

He paused, for a moment too surprised to say anything. Then, he repeated slowly, as if he hadn't quite heard her correctly, "Breeches?"

She folded her arms over her chest. "I like to wear them when I have to ride a long distance," she justified irritably, "especially in the cold."

In his silence, she didn't have to read minds to know he was probably wondering exactly how country-backward she was. *Breeches.* Oh, she was humiliated! His London society ladies would never have donned such things.

"So you ... birth babies in breeches?" he asked awkwardly, sounding just as embarrassed as she felt.

Mortified, she closed her eyes. "Yes," she ground out, "they're sturdy."

"I see." He cleared his throat. "Well, no matter. You'll be wearing something, anyway." He paused, then prompted gently, "Katherine, take off those wet clothes now."

She was aghast, even as she fought back the shaking in

her limbs from the cold. What he asked of her was wholly improper, and she would be mad to do it. Drenched or not, the last thing she wanted to do was remove any stitch of clothing in front of him. She'd rather spend the night shivering and miserable.

But she had known him long enough now to judge his moods and knew when she could push him and when she shouldn't dare. And this was not a moment to push. The best she could do was hope her dress dried as quickly as possible.

"Fine," she sighed, surrendering grudgingly. "Turn around."

* * *

Reluctantly, and calling upon every ounce of gentlemanliness he possessed, Edward turned his back to give her privacy.

But his own clothes were just as soaked as hers, so he shrugged away his greatcoat, then pulled off his boots, grimacing as water spilled out of them. Ruined. The waistcoat came next, followed by his shirt as he tugged it free of his trousers and off over his head, peeling the wet fabric from his damp skin.

Standing by the fire, he let the heat soak into his chilled muscles, bare now except for his trousers, and he contemplated removing even those. Would Kate scream in embarrassment if he did? He grinned to himself. More than likely, the little hellcat would come after him with the fireplace poker.

For a moment, though, he considered it. Seeing her reaction would be worth a stabbing.

From behind him, fabric rustled softly as she removed

her clothes, and his mind imagined the dress slipping away from her creamy skin. His cock flexed. Taking a deep breath to steady himself, he regretted that she hadn't refused one last time, just so he could have peeled her clothes from her himself.

"Do you need help unbuttoning?" he asked over his shoulder.

"No—don't turn around!"

"I'm just trying to be helpful."

"Like a wolf stalking a ewe," she muttered.

"Pardon?"

"I said, I'm almost through!"

He bit back a laugh. He couldn't remember a woman who both antagonized and amused him as much as she did. It should have infuriated him. Instead, he enjoyed it. Taking pleasure in her consternation was wrong. But it also felt so *right*.

"Finished," she finally whispered. "Turn around, if you have to."

Shaking his head at her misplaced modesty, he turned. "This is not—"

He saw her, and the argument died on his lips.

She stood shyly before him, wearing only her undergarments, and his chest tightened as his gaze moved leisurely down her body. A long corset laced up to her breasts, with two small strips of ribbon across her shoulders revealing smooth stretches of bare skin, and beneath that incredibly feminine stay, she wore a pair of boy's breeches, shortened to above the knees and buttoned snugly at the waist.

Sweet Jesus. The juxtaposition of the stay topping the breeches should have made her look absurd. Instead, she looked...delectable.

She folded her arms awkwardly across her breasts, still not daring to look at him.

He nervously cleared his throat. "Give me your dress, and I'll lay it by the fire."

Her eyes focused on the floor, she handed it to him. He pulled the sheet away from a chair beside the hearth and tossed it aside, then hung her dress over the back and his own clothes across the arms.

When he turned around, she had already grabbed the discarded sheet and wrapped it around herself like a toga. He didn't know whether to laugh at her modesty or cry with disappointment.

Instead, he frowned. She hovered at the side of the room, far from the fireplace. "Kate, come closer and warm yourself."

"I'm fine over here."

He arched a brow. "Your lips are blue."

At that, her eyes finally raised to look at him. He expected her to deny it, to protest vehemently that she wasn't cold at all. But she didn't.

Instead, she stared at him silently. Not into his eyes to show how much courage she had to stand against him, not at his mouth the way she did when she wanted him to kiss her—but at his shoulder. At the deep, jagged scar where the bullet pierced him all those years ago.

He froze. When he removed his shirt, he'd forgotten— she'd distracted him, and he'd completely forgotten...

Slowly, she stepped forward, her eyes never leaving his shoulder. "Edward?" His name was a puzzled whisper.

"I was shot," he admitted quietly, knowing what she was asking.

He heard the soft intake of air as she caught her breath,

and her eyes flickered up to his for just a moment before returning to the scar. There was neither shock nor pity in her eyes, the way other women looked at him when they first saw the scar. No, she looked at him not as a woman but as a physician, as someone who had seen such wounds before and knew that the damage went deeper than the physical evidence left behind.

As her trembling hand reached for him, he stood perfectly still, but when her fingertips brushed against his shoulder, the touch burned like fire, as though the wound were still raw. He flinched and inhaled sharply though clenched teeth.

"When you told me about the wars, you never mentioned this." He could barely hear her above the rain striking the roof. "You must have…"

Been in pain, he finished. *You must have been in terrible pain.* Or frightened. *You must have been so very frightened*… That was what every woman said when she saw the scar.

Of course he'd been in pain. Of course he'd been frightened. A bullet had ripped through his shoulder, for Christ's sake. But they'd had no idea how little they knew about the hell he'd gone through if that's all they thought upon seeing the wound that had almost claimed his life. So he'd stopped removing his shirt whenever he was with a woman.

Until tonight with Kate. When he'd grown so comfortable with her that he'd forgotten to hide the scar. But it was too late now, so he held his breath and waited for her reaction—

"You must have… felt so alone."

At her unexpected words, his gut clenched. He stared down at her in open surprise, but her attention was still focused on his shoulder. Tentatively, her fingers traced over the rough length of the ugly wound, her touch gentle and soothing, and with each featherlight brush, the old pain ebbed a little more.

"So alone, so far from home," she whispered.

Then she leaned forward and brushed her lips against the scar.

He caught his breath, steeling himself for the torment of her mouth against him, but the flinch he'd expected never came. Instead, there was only sweetness, softness, and comfort, and he remained still beneath her lips as if her kiss could reach back through time and console him from the moment the ball pierced his skin.

The sensation of her warm lips on his bare skin in featherlight kisses pulsed through him, and his desire for her grew hotter with each heartbeat, his breath coming ragged and shallow.

"Angel..." With a groan, he cupped her chin and lifted her head as his mouth came down hungrily against hers, the sheet falling to the floor at their feet.

CHAPTER TEN

$\mathcal{K}$ate moaned as his lips molded against hers, his hands sliding down to encircle her hips and pull her against him. She'd wanted this since the moment he arrived at the Mulderrys' door, this fierce and need-filled kiss, this feeling of desire and possession that only Edward could give. However delicious his kisses had been before, nothing compared to this one, to the way his mouth plundered hers and to the raw desire she felt surging within his broad shoulders and chest.

His *bare* chest.

She tried not to think about how he stood half-naked, his body pressed hard against hers, but when she'd turned around from undressing and saw him standing there, shirtless and barefooted, and the damp, sculpted muscles of his shoulders and arms glistening in the firelight from the water droplets still clinging to his skin... Well, that bare chest was all she could think about—that, and how much she wanted to run her fingertips across those muscles, to see if she could make him quiver.

She tore her mouth away to gasp for breath, but his lips went immediately to her neck, delicately placing one kiss at a time down to the hollow at the base of her throat, to flick his tongue against her racing pulse.

"Edward," she whispered and melted against him, knowing there was no hiding from him how much his kisses aroused her, how he made her blood hum and her body throb.

He rubbed his cheek against her bare shoulder, the midnight stubble scratching enticingly at her skin. "You're still cold."

"I-I'm not." But she shivered, although more from his tongue licking beneath the shoulder ribbon of her stay than from the cold she no longer noticed.

He turned her toward the fireplace, to position her directly before the flames. The fire warmed her front and Edward's body heated her back, but when he ran his hands lightly down her bare arms, her shivering only increased.

"You'll warm up soon." With the way he whispered against the back of her neck, it wasn't warmth she felt but a burning ache.

"It's you, not the cold," she admitted. "You're what's making me all shivery."

He laughed, a deep and rich sound that rumbled along her spine. He slid his arms around her waist and drew her back against him, murmuring, "You make me all shivery, too."

His dark heat curled slowly through her, all the way

down between her thighs. She swallowed, her mouth suddenly dry. "Why?"

He trailed his knuckles along the side of her face. "Because you're beautiful."

She stiffened in his arms. He'd told her before that she was beautiful, but she hadn't believed him then, either. To be that naïve, especially as she stood there in boy's breeches—no, he was a duke, and back in London, he was surrounded by women far more sophisticated and refined, far more beautiful. And surely, he had his pick of them.

"You don't believe me, Kate?"

She admitted softly, "I don't know."

"Then believe I want you," he murmured hotly, his voice ragged.

His words stole her breath away, and she felt the response deep inside her, a soft hunger that swelled and pulsed with every heartbeat, until it saturated every inch of her. She felt as if she were waking up, every nerve in her body coming alive and aware of each place his body touched against hers. And God help her, she wanted him to touch her even more.

As if sensing her desire, his hand slid up her corset, and with a tug, he untied the bow between her breasts. She froze, aware only of the movement of his fingers as excitement and anticipation ran hot through her like a fever.

"I don't know why." His thumb plucked at the string zigzagging up the front of her stay and slowly unlaced it. "And I don't know why you, why now." One by one, the string freed from the eyelets, and the corset opened. "But when I thought I'd lost you tonight, I was terrified."

When the lace slipped free of the last eyelet, he stepped back just far enough to peel the stay from her shoulders and down her back, dropping it to the floor. She closed her eyes, not because she was nervous of standing so exposed before him, but because she couldn't resist giving over to the sumptuous sensation of the soft air tingling over her bare breasts, freed from the confining stay and warmed by the fire. No longer cold as tendrils of liquid heat licked at her body, down her arms and legs, out to the ends of her fingers and toes.

"So beautiful." His voice crashed hoarse and hot through her as he placed a tender kiss at the back of her neck. Whatever doubts she had of him evaporated, all her hesitations of being alone with him inverted until she ached to be touched, kissed, caressed.

When his hands slid up to capture both breasts against his palms, the heat of his touch was unbearable, and she couldn't fight back a throaty whimper or the way she shamelessly arched against his touch until her bare back rubbed against his chest.

His thumbs languidly circled her nipples, which hardened like pebbles beneath his ministrations, the sensation tugging straight down through her to the growing ache between her legs. There was no ignoring it now, this need he created inside her that only he could satisfy, and when he splayed his fingers wide across her breasts, squeezing her nipples between his fingers—

"Edward!" she gasped and covered his hands with hers at the sudden panic to grab hold of him to keep from falling away.

He groaned and slid a hand down her front until he reached the waistband of the breeches. "An angel in boy's clothing," he murmured as he lowered his head and kissed her bare shoulder.

Embarrassment stole through her at his words, her cheeks burning with mortification that he would pick this moment to tease her when she was already uncertain and vulnerable.

"Don't make fun," she scolded, pushing his hand away from her waist.

Undeterred, he took her hand and lifted it to his lips, to flick his tongue across her palm, and the sensation shot straight down her arm into her breasts, drawing her already hard nipples into impossibly tighter points. "I am not making fun."

When he shifted his hips forward against her, his arousal pressed into her lower back, hard and large, and she shuddered at the desire in him. For her.

"Don't you realize how much I want you?"

She exhaled a shaky breath as her head spun, her world turning upside down. Just days ago, he had threatened to take control of her life, both infuriating and frightening her, the same man who was now telling her how much he wanted her. And she knew it was true. Because she burned with the same demanding need for him.

"I've never met another woman like you." His hand brushed in slow circles over her bare stomach, and she inhaled a ragged breath of anticipation each time his hand swept down closer and closer to the throbbing ache between her thighs. "I have to touch you, Kate. I need to feel you."

She thought she heard his voice tremble, but when he unfastened the breeches and slipped his hand inside across the smooth skin of her lower belly, the only thing she knew for certain was the scintillating excitement boiling just below his fingertips, how much she wanted him to touch her down *there*—

"Please," she begged, then shifted to part her legs wider in invitation.

When he finally stroked down through her curls to touch her wet heat, she shuddered. She bit back a moan as her hands grabbed for his hard thighs steadying her from behind, her fingernails digging into the sculpted muscles as his fingers teased lightly against her and increased the sweet burn flaming out from between her legs.

"That feels so good," she panted. "I never knew..."

"It gets better," he promised, then knelt behind her to peel the breeches slowly down her hips and thighs, pushing them along her calves and off, baring her body completely to the firelight.

He kissed her at that spot where her buttocks curved into her back, then flicked his tongue up along her spine as he slowly rose. Oh, sweet heavens, he was *tasting* her! Relishing her bare back the way a hungry man savored a feast. With a shudder, she moaned her pleasure, never believing that a man's mouth could feel this wicked and wonderful at the same time.

As his mouth caressed up her body, he brushed his hands tantalizingly along the back of her legs, up her thighs to her round bottom, then around her hips to her front and down through her curls. This time when his hand slipped between her legs, nothing hindered his seeking fingers from taking the long, deep caresses into her cleft that she so desperately craved. Nothing stopped him from nudging apart her legs from behind with his knee, to give him even more access to her sex, to gently part her folds and slide two fingers inside.

"Edward!" She tensed, then relaxed against him as he began to stroke gently but insistently while his other hand caressed her breasts, and the startled cry of his name on her lips melted into a whimper.

"Sweet Lord, angel," he groaned, lowering his forehead to rest a moment against her bare shoulder. "You're ready, and so soon..."

"Ready?" She quivered around his fingers, every nerve ending in her body shooting down between her thighs where his fingers continued their gentle exploration. She fought back a pleading whine for more as his thumb delved down into her folds.

"For me to be inside you."

"But you're already inside me," she panted as his swirling fingers heated her from the inside out.

"Not the way I want to be," he corrected in a hot rasp.

She knew what he meant—he wanted to take her innocence.

She should have been terrified of what he wanted from her, of the control he wanted her to surrender. But as she felt the pulsating fire swelling up to explode through her, starting from the tiny nub beneath his rubbing thumb and spreading out across her belly and breasts, she welcomed it eagerly with every inch of her existence.

Her tiny muscles clenched down around his fingers in a breathtaking spasm—she gasped, and Edward caught her in his arms as her knees buckled and she sank toward the floor, lowering her gently onto the rug before the fireplace.

As her breathing and heartbeat slowed, she sighed deeply. Pleasure unlike any she'd ever known before radiated through her, and she laughed with utter happiness. Unashamed that she was lying naked beneath his hungry gaze in the light of the fire. Unashamed that she had let him touch her so intimately. And wanted him to do so again.

When Edward slowly slid his body up the length of hers, having stripped out of his trousers and cast away the last remaining barrier between them, she wasn't ashamed then, either.

He brushed a damp lock from her forehead. "Did you like that?"

"Very much," she sighed, her body satiated.

"Good." Pleased, he kissed her tenderly. "Because it gets even better."

Kate smiled at him, even as she knew there couldn't possibly be a better feeling than the pleasure he'd just sent sweeping through her. It had been so wonderful. Simply breathtaking. Oh, she certainly wanted him to do that to her again, to feel once more the yearning ache until it burst through her in a flash of heat and light.

But to be even better? *Impossible.*

"I want you, Katherine, and I mean to have you." His dark eyes flickered in the firelight as he stared longingly down at her. "So if you want to stop, you have to tell me now."

Everywhere his body touched hers, her skin turned electric, tingling and hot, and the last thing she wanted to do was stop. She whispered breathlessly, "Kiss me."

"My pleasure." When he captured her mouth beneath his, she wasn't prepared for the intensity of him, for the rush of arousal that pulsed through her in a way that made her feel seductive, possessed, and completely desired all at once.

He had been holding back before, she realized, when he kissed her in the field and the sitting room. Even when he'd been stroking his fingers inside her and bringing her to release just moments ago, he'd carefully kept his own desire checked.

But now, no restraint remained in him. Hands stroked over her breasts and hips, teeth bit at her throat and shoulders, lips sucked hard at her nipples, the tip of his tongue traced the curve of her ear—and a low moan tore from her throat as her body pulsed hot and cold with each fierce kiss and demanding touch. Fire flashed through her at the same time goose bumps sprang up across her shivering skin, and the hot swelling between her thighs beat in rhythm with her racing pulse. Sweet torture, the most exquisite pleasure-pain she'd ever known.

Hot and openmouthed, he kissed her. His tongue pushed between her lips to ravish the moist depths of her mouth the way his hands plundered her body. The pulsing ache between her legs began to match the rhythm of the deep and insistent thrusts of his tongue until she could no longer tell if the relentless throbbing came from inside her or seeped into her from him. Nor did she care as long as he kept kissing her like this, stoking the delicious fires inside her.

She gasped for air as his mouth tore away from hers and traveled down her throat, his teeth nipping at her tender skin.

When his lips found her breast, she shuddered, panting fast and shallow with each agonizing flick of his tongue against her already sensitized nipple. Then he suckled at her, hard and long, and she writhed under him, unable to remain still beneath his wicked mouth.

"So luscious," he murmured against her as he shifted to her other breast, to swirl his tongue around the aching point there.

She arched toward him, her fingernails digging into his shoulders to bring him as close as possible, until he was lying with his full weight pressing down over her body. But even that wasn't close enough.

"Edward." His name was a confused plea. "I want…" She struggled to form the words, her lips thick with arousal. "I want…please."

"This?" One large hand pressed against her bare shoulder, pinning her to the rug to hold her still while the other stroked up between her thighs. She jumped at his touch, bucking her hips off the floor and shamelessly spreading her thighs wide beneath him.

"Yes," she panted out. She writhed against his fingers as they traced over her, carefully circling her but not touching her where she craved it most, teasing her mercilessly and keeping from her the exquisite pleasure he'd given her before. "Edward, please!"

He lowered his tall body and settled himself between her thighs. With a throaty whimper of need, she instinctively wrapped her legs around his waist to cradle his hips against hers. Then he reached down between them, this time to spread her sex gently with his fingers and open her wide to him. She felt the hot tip of his manhood touch against her, nestling down into her outer folds, poised at her entrance and ready.

Holding her breath in anxious anticipation, she closed her eyes and felt his hips press gently forward, his hard erection slide inside her.

Inch by torturously slow inch, he sank into her, and she sighed tremulously, her aroused body craving the moment when he would fill her completely. But instead of moving deeper, he retreated until only his engorged tip remained inside her.

"No!" She grasped at his shoulders and tilted up her

hips to pull him back inside her where she desperately needed him to be.

"Slowly, love," he warned, his body tense with restraint. "We have to go slowly this first time."

"I don't want to go slowly. It feels so—"

She moaned deeply as he stroked down into her again, this time an inch deeper than before, staying inside her a moment longer before withdrawing again until he had almost come completely out of her.

She whimpered in protest, her hands clenching into frustrated fists against his back.

"Trust in me, angel." He dipped his head to briefly press his lips against hers.

Another slow plunge, another answering moan...He repeated the carefully controlled movements, and she felt herself slowly expand as her body took him deeper inside her, both surrounding and surrounded at once.

Then he paused, holding himself above her on his forearms.

"It will only hurt once," he murmured, his own eyes closing in an almost pained expression. "Just this first time."

"But it doesn't hurt. You were right." She trailed a line of kisses across his shoulder, tasting the salty-sweet perspiration on his skin. "It did get bet—"

He thrust forward and plunged into her, tearing through the thin layer of resistance until he was sheathed completely inside her, his hips seated against hers.

A gasp tore from her at the sharp but fleeting pain, and she tensed, her body stiffening and her fingernails digging into his back.

He held still for a moment, kissing her forehead and

murmuring her name until her breathing steadied and her fingers loosened their hold, and then he began to move, to rock his body against hers. She relaxed beneath him, and the discomfort was replaced with a sensuous pleasure that stirred a heat from low in her belly up to her breasts.

A deep breath, a long sigh—then all she knew was the wonderful sensation of his body stroking smoothly into hers, his strong arms enveloping her and holding her close, and the weight of him pressing down. It was pure possession, and she surrendered blissfully.

"Move with me," he urged. He took her hips in his hands and showed her how to lift to meet each thrust, to unite in the primal rhythm of their joined bodies.

She moaned and buried her face against his shoulder. Amazing—she couldn't believe how good it felt to be this close to him, to have him inside her, filling her so completely. Simply heavenly! He was making it perfect for her, and she felt the tears wet at her lashes as emotion overcame her.

No one but Edward would have been this tender with her, this patient, and she would never regret giving her innocence to him tonight.

Then their rhythm changed, and his movements became more urgent and intense. Each thrust brought him harder against her, swelling the fiery throbbing inside her until flames licked at her toes. Every muscle in her body clenched and pulsed in time with the engulfing ache, with his quick and insistent thrusts inside her. Her ankles locked together at the small of his back, her arms clung around his shoulders, and she held on desperately against the sensation that she was falling over a cliff, plummeting away even as he pressed her harder into the floor beneath him.

With a swirl of his hips against her spread thighs, he growled and ground his pelvis down against her sex—

She shattered beneath him in a cascade of heat and shivers, crying out against the sound of the storm raging around them as her body shuddered violently.

Grabbing her arms and lifting them over her head, he drove fast and hard into her now, pumping furiously with need. With a last deep plunge, he groaned his release, and she gasped at the raw sensation of his liquid fire pulsing into her, of the sudden clench and release of his body around hers.

He sank down on top of her, his body spent and satiated. For a few minutes, neither moved. Then his heavy weight shifted away as he rolled onto his side beside her.

Opening her eyes, she found him watching her and reached up to brush his hair off his forehead, damp with perspiration and rain. As the dissipating waves of release dulled deliciously inside her, she felt connected to him, satisfied to simply lie there surrounded by the warmth and strength of his arms, without a single thought of the world outside the cottage. She'd shattered in his arms, and the feeling had been so amazing that she couldn't bear to think of him not feeling it, too, or that he didn't feel just as connected to her as she felt to him in this new, wonderful way.

And when he touched his lips to hers, more tenderly than she could have imagined, she knew he felt it, too. "Are you all right, angel?"

She placed her hand on his chest to feel the beating of his heart. For her. "I'm perfect."

"Oh yes," he murmured as his arms tightened around her and pulled her close, "you certainly are."

CHAPTER ELEVEN

*T*he hay cart swayed with a loud creak over a rut in the road, and Edward reached out protectively to clasp Kate's hand as she lay on the straw pile next to him. Although he reclined casually, staring up in silence at the passing tree-tops and white clouds, there was nothing casual about the thoughts spinning through his mind.

He hadn't said much to her since they'd awakened at first light, preferring contemplative silence this morning. Luckily, one of the farmers driving from Buxtonby offered them a ride in the back of his cart, which meant that he wouldn't have to break his silence. The nearness of the cart's driver prevented them from beginning the serious conversation they needed to have, which meant he had a short reprieve from considering the full ramifications of last night.

But lying together on the hay like this, with silence stretching between them, was the most awkward moment they'd shared since he'd ordered her to remove her dress. Ironic, how she was more comfortable around him when she was naked.

Well, then he would just have to make certain that getting Kate naked happened often, and for great stretches of time.

His chest swelled. At long last, he had something in his life that made him happy. And it wasn't just the sex, although that had been amazing. It was her laugh, her wit, her charity, even her stubbornness—she drew him unlike any other woman ever had.

"You're awfully quiet this morning."

The corners of his lips tugged upward. He should have known she couldn't remain silent, not her, but instead of being irritated, he found her endearing. "Just thinking."

"About what?"

In reply, he arched a brow, his silence speaking volumes.

"Oh." She blushed, and he knew it wasn't the crisp morning air that colored her cheeks. "Do you regret it?"

"Absolutely not," he answered quickly. Then hesitated, "Do you?"

"No—you made it..." She squeezed his hand. "Perfect."

More pleased by the simple compliment than he had a right to be, he tucked her hand against his chest, knowing even as he did that she could feel his heartbeat. Good Lord, how she made his pulse race last night! And the second time he'd taken her, when he woke her at dawn and slowly, tenderly, gently rocked himself into her, when she climaxed not with a shatter but a sigh—she'd sent his heart racing once more.

"I'd never done...that before," she admitted so softly he barely heard her.

He shifted toward her on the straw and lowered his mouth to her ear. "It's called making love," he murmured, unable to hold back a grin at her inexperience.

She looked at him through lowered lashes, in an expression of half innocence, half seduction, and his cock stirred. "I'd never...made love before," she whispered.

"I know." Risking that the driver might glance over his shoulder and catch them, Edward touched his lips to hers, then rolled away, putting a respectable distance between them.

"So I don't know—I mean, I'm wondering..." Another deep breath. "What next?"

He was silent for a long moment, then mumbled toward the sky, "I've been wondering the same thing myself."

"You cannot remain as my guardian now."

"Actually, I can," he answered quietly, although he knew it wasn't the answer she wanted to hear. There were no laws against a man bedding his ward, and he'd known a few men who had taken advantage of their situation to turn their wards into mistresses. However, he would not be one of them. "It's a binding contract." Which couldn't be voided. Not unless he asked for her father's consent to be released from the agreement, which he would never do. Destroying the guardianship meant returning her to her father's custody and leaving her unprotected, and he would never give her back to that bastard. Especially not after last night. "But we have a few options."

"And one is that we pretend last night never happened and go our separate ways," she whispered.

Keeping a tight hold on her fingers, he shot her a sideways glance, holding her gaze hard. "*That* is not an option."

Never seeing her again was simply out of the question now after tasting the passion inside her.

No, the problem was keeping her.

He refused to make her his mistress. True, most men of the *ton* kept mistresses, and many didn't bother to hide them. He was the Duke of Strathmore, for heaven's sake, and the gossip wouldn't be that he'd taken a mistress but wonder at why he hadn't taken one sooner.

But not Kate. He cared too much about her to make her an object of ridicule just to satisfy his own desires. Not that she would ever have agreed to the proposition in the first place. Not her. Most society ladies wore an air of propriety that was nothing but pretense—women who would cut a lady direct for daring to speak to a rake in public were the first to lift their skirts for the same scoundrel as soon as they could get him alone. But Kate's sense of propriety was real, and he found himself wanting to protect that. And her.

He supposed he should marry her. After all, that was what proper gentlemen did after ruining well-bred ladies, and he had to accept his responsibility.

Yet he hadn't planned on marrying and having a family of his own, resolved to leave Strathmore to his cousin. But that was before he met Kate. She was a woman who knew how to wield both charm and wit, who was kind to a fault, intelligent, and beautiful. And as last night proved, they were also well matched physically. Most society marriages were based on less.

But…marriage. *Good God.* Could he bring himself to do it?

Even if he were willing to wed her, Kate was very clear about *her* unwillingness to marry anyone. Society didn't let its ladies birth babies, heal sick men, or tend to contagious orphans, and she certainly couldn't continue her medical work if she were Duchess of Strathmore.

Yet he wasn't willing to let her go. She was his now; he'd claimed responsibility for her life when he arrived on her doorstep, and last night, he'd claimed her body.

He had no idea what he was going to do with her, but he knew he didn't want to be without her.

"Come back to London with me," he offered abruptly.

"London?" she squeaked, clearly not expecting that.

It wasn't a long-term solution, he knew, rather an avoidance of having to make a decision. But taking her back to London would give him time to make a proper decision and allow him to keep her close until he did.

"Aunt Augusta will be thrilled to meet you. You'll be able to get the new wardrobe you need, and you can enjoy the remainder of the season." He lifted her hand to his lips. "And you'll be with me."

"But I can't leave," she protested somberly. "I'm needed here at Brambly."

Rolling onto his side to face her, he reached to cup her cheek against his palm. Distress flickered across her face, and he felt a pang of guilt that he was forcing her away from her home for his own selfishness. But the alternative, of leaving her behind when he didn't know when he could see her again, was unbearable.

"Come with me to London," he tempted, "and I'll make certain you can visit Brambly every month until the season's over."

"You...really?" She gazed at him in wonder.

"It's not a long ride from the city, and—"

Catching him by surprise, she slipped her hand behind his neck and tugged him off-balance toward her, leaving him no choice but to roll over on top of her unless he wanted to fall off the cart. Her lips melted against his, and for a moment he was too stunned at her boldness to react. Then he responded in kind, and the sweet taste of her kiss increased greedily into full promise of more.

When his mouth opened beneath the tentative slide of her tongue across his lips, she plunged inside, and his cock stiffened instantly. He inhaled sharply. He'd never experienced such a swift reaction before, especially to a woman so unpracticed. Did she realize the effect she had on him, the power she wielded? Heaven help him if she ever figured it out.

"Keep doing that," he warned, raising his head to check that the driver was still blissfully unaware of what was happening in the hay behind him, "and we'll get caught." He cupped her breast against his palm and teased her nipple through her dress. "And then you'll have no choice but to flee for London to save your reputation."

"When do I have to decide about London?" A whimper escaped her, and she bit hard into her bottom lip, keeping the rest of the moan in check.

As she arched with arousal beneath his hand, he wanted to demand an immediate answer. Instead, he offered, "I won't leave until Brannigan arrives."

"Oh, that's good...that's *very* good," she murmured. He grinned, uncertain if she meant her compliment for having time to decide or for having his hand fondling her breast. Either way, he'd gladly take it.

He shifted away, knowing they'd already pushed their

luck too far. Damned propriety. What he wanted to do was roll her over on top of him, shove inside her, and let her ride him off right there in the hay.

With a growing frustration, he returned to his original position, his arm tucked beneath his head, staring up at the endless morning sky and already scheming for how to get her alone in the hayloft.

The cart passed along the river, and soon, the stones marking the lane leading to the house came into sight. The driver stopped the wagon.

Edward hopped down, then helped Kate to the ground, letting his hands linger around her waist longer than necessary. Kate waved good-bye to the driver, who tipped his hat, flipped the ribbons, and rolled on down the road.

Edward looped her arm around his, and together, they started up the drive. But when the path curved and the house came into view, they halted.

The house buzzed with activity. Several wagons blocked the front door where Dorrie directed the crowd of men unloading the goods and carrying them into the house. Large pieces of furniture, dozens of barrels and burlap sacks, bolts of fabric—it looked as though someone was moving into her house and bringing every one of his belongings with him. Along with the inventory of the entire British Museum. And most of Bond Street.

Old Arthur must have thought the same as he stood at the bottom of the front steps and fretted as four men passed him on their way into the foyer, carrying a tall armoire.

Even the barns were caught up in the commotion. A gray saddle horse grazed in the paddock next to his chestnut colt and Kate's black mare, which had returned home during the night, and another two black horses stood tied near a small gig. Two men unloaded a wagon heaped high with bags of oats, hay bales, and horse tack. Chickens scratched in the barnyard, milk cows drank at the trough, a sow oinked noisily over her six piglets at a brown goat—

Kate's mouth fell open. "What on earth...?"

"Brannigan's arrived," he answered blankly. With a knowing glance, he unwrapped her arm from his, then walked on alone toward the house to welcome the estate agent to his new position.

* * *

A shout went up from the front steps as Kate came into view. When Dorrie spied her, she ran from the house to throw her arms around her and hug her so tightly she nearly squeezed the air out of her. "Thank the angels in heaven, you're alive!"

Kate tried to pull Dorrie's arms away from her and catch her breath, fearing for a moment that the old cook would burst into tears. "I'm fine."

"When the horses came back last night without you, we were all so worried." She finally let Kate peel her arms away and stepped back. "Arthur was set to go after you, but Mrs. Elston put herself right in the doorway to his room to keep him home. Slept right there, she did!" Her eyes swept over her, then paused. "Are you all right?"

She forced down a blush, worrying for a moment that Dorrie had somehow learned to read minds and knew exactly what happened last night. Twice. "We lost the horses near the river and had to spend the night near the village."

Dorrie shot her a questioning look. "But—"

"Oh!—Emma Mulderry has a beautiful baby girl," Kate

interrupted, desperate to distract her. "Both mother and baby are well."

"Thank goodness." Dorrie frowned and darted her attention back to Edward. "And the duke? Where did—"

"Look!" Kate pointed at the house. "What's going on? An entire storeroom is being unloaded into the kitchens. My goodness! Is that a double armoire?"

The cook muttered in wonderment and shook her head. "Miss Kate, you simply won't believe what all's arrived."

Successfully distracted from asking any more probing questions, Dorrie linked her arm through Kate's and led her toward the house. With each step, the old cook detailed the wagonloads of goods that began to arrive just after dawn, along with a man named Brannigan who claimed to be the new estate agent.

"True," Kate admitted quietly. "His Grace hired him. But no worries." She patted her arm reassuringly. "He gave me his word that no major changes would be made without my approval."

"Did you approve that?" Dorrie scoffed and jerked her thumb toward two men carrying a blue velvet sofa hoisted over their heads. "Seems to me that promise's already been broke."

Kate frowned. Dorrie was right. She hadn't approved any of these supplies or goods, yet here they were, being unloaded into her house with the precision of an army maneuver.

"There's something more, too, miss."

"Oh?" Kate steeled herself, uncertain she could handle anything more happening to her this morning.

"When that Brannigan fellow arrived and you weren't home, me and Mrs. Elston thought maybe there were instructions 'bout him left in the study. So"—her shoulders slumped with guilt—"we went through the papers on the desk."

"I see." Now she would no longer be able to keep secret from the servants all of Edward's plans to renovate Brambly, all the disruptions to their previously quiet existence.

"We found this." Dorrie withdrew a paper from her apron pocket.

Kate glanced at the paper. Edward's handwriting, scrawled out in the same bold scratches he'd used to make notes in the estate's ledger books, detailing what conditions he wanted included in a pension agreement, and across the bottom, in a much more legible hand, *Will complete as you requested, Your Grace. Agreements sent by messenger within the sennight. Meacham.*

Kate stared at the letter as sudden tears of gratitude welled in her eyes. A pension agreement for Arthur, Mrs. Elston, and Dorrie! And quite a generous one at that, with stipulations she never would have been able to afford on her own. They were to have cottages, allowances, clothing stipends, and all well deserved for their love and service to her.

"Oh, Miss Kate—I'm so sorry!" Guilty horror flashed across Dorrie's face at the sight of her tears. "We didn't mean to cause no trouble. We thought there might be some explanation or instructions 'bout the deliveries—"

Smiling through her tears, Kate placed her hand on the cook's arm and squeezed to reassure her. She tried to read the words again but couldn't, her vision too tear-blurred by Edward's kindness and charity.

He had to have initiated the process at least a week ago,

not to garner favor with her or seduce her into his arms last night, but simply because he wanted to help her and do right by the servants. Her chest warmed with unabashed happiness that she finally knew the real man behind the hard surface he showed to the world. To her, he'd revealed his heart, and his heart was good and beneficent.

She called to one of the men carrying in a bag of corn-meal on his shoulder. "I need to speak to the duke. Do you know where he went?"

"Aye, miss, into the study."

Kate thanked him.

Walking through the house, she felt as if she were in a dream. A wondrous, happy dream! In less than twenty-four hours, everything had been turned completely on end. Brambly was becoming a real farm again, the servants had a fine retirement waiting for them, and she…well, *everything* about her was different now, too. All because of Edward.

Unable to hide the bounce in her step and her eagerness to reach him, she turned toward the study. The double doors were pushed open wide to the hall, and the bright morning sunshine flooded through the tall windows, making the white-painted trim and bookcases glow brilliantly.

Edward stood behind the cherry desk with several papers in his hands and a mountain of paperwork covering the surface before him, and she paused in the doorway, shamelessly letting her eyes linger on him. He looked as if he'd always belonged there, in charge of the house and in control of every inch of the property. Powerful. Commanding. Delectably masculine. A smile pulled at her lips. She knew now just how kind and good his heart, just how wicked his body.

Was this what it was like to have a husband's presence in the house? She couldn't imagine living under the same roof with this much strength and determination, but after spending the last few weeks with him, she couldn't imagine *not* having him here. And now, after last night, she realized with a joyful thrill, there would be no reason for her not to have him in her life.

Happiness tingled softly through her as she considered the possibilities of what that meant.

When Edward glanced up and his dark gaze heated at the sight of her, her pulse raced with instant arousal.

"Close the doors, Katherine," he ordered huskily, "and come here."

Doing as he bade her, she slid the doors shut and circled the desk until she stood next to him. Her body hummed with electric anticipation, already beginning to heat and pulse. Maybe, she considered as she breathed deep the wonderfully masculine scent of leather and soap, it wasn't so bad to be ordered about by him after all.

"You're responsible for all"—she waved her hand, indicating the chaos unfolding around them—"*this*. Aren't you?"

"I told Brannigan to order everything necessary to establish a household. He follows orders well."

"Apparently." She folded her arms in feigned annoyance, knowing if she didn't tuck her hands away she'd reach for him. And that would only lead to trouble. Wicked, wanton trouble. "A velvet sofa? Really, Edward—"

In one fluid motion, he captured her by the waist and set her on the desk.

He leaned over her, his mouth temptingly close to hers. "Angel, that sofa is the second-best piece of furniture in this house." He pulled her skirt up past her knees and hotly murmured, "After my bed."

Heat cascaded through her, pooling between her legs as she remembered the wonderful slide of him inside her, how feminine she felt when engulfed by his masculinity. She whimpered softly, desperately wanting him there again.

"You'll like it, I promise." He tucked a finger beneath the neckline of her dress, and with a gentle tug bared her shoulder. "That creamy skin of yours rubbing naked against soft velvet..."

When he lowered his mouth to lick across her shoulder, she moaned.

"Did you lock the door?"

"Yes," she breathed, shivering at the sinful implication in his voice.

"Good girl." As he nipped at her throat, his hands slipped behind her and quickly unfastened her dress. "Because I have to have you."

"*Here?*" she squeaked.

"Right here." He stepped between her thighs and leaned over her until she had no choice but to lie back across the desk, then followed down on top of her. "Right now."

CHAPTER TWELVE

*E*dward kissed her, hot and possessive, his tongue shoving apart her lips to plunge deep inside and coaxing her to return the intensity of his desire. With a shuddering sigh, she responded, invading his mouth the same way he had hers.

He groaned and captured her tongue between his lips, sucking hard and drawing her deeper into his mouth. *Sweet Lord*, she was delicious, and he thrilled at her eager response. He'd been half-hard since fondling her breast in the hay cart, and now his cock flashed instantly rigid at the way her body so quickly aroused, shivering with need for his. He tore at the pins in her hair to set her waves free so he could fist the fiery curls in his hand and hold her lips tight and still beneath his, relentlessly ravishing her kiss the same way he planned on ravishing her body.

She tore her mouth away, gasping for breath, but her panting only excited him more.

"So beautiful." He wiggled her skirt up to her waist. "So unusual . . . so unlike any other woman I've ever known."

He reached both hands beneath her skirt and stripped off the boy's breeches. Her eyes flew open.

Grinning at her from between her now-bare thighs, he held up the garment like a captured flag. Her hands flew to cover her mouth as a surprised squeal exploded from her, then she laughed with abandon as he tossed them over his shoulder.

He'd wanted her before, but after watching her eyes sparkle with laughter, he'd combust if he didn't have her now.

He slid his hands up her inner thighs and tantalizingly spread her open to him. His fingers found her center, plunging deep into her moist heat, and with soft moans and mewlings rising from her lips, she writhed against the desk beneath the sweet torture. She belonged to him now, and he planned on claiming every inch of her.

He lowered his head to nuzzle his face into her triangle of curls and breathed deep the feminine scent of her, of sweet honeysuckle and spicy sex, which had already been imprinted into his mind.

"I'm going to taste you, angel," he warned darkly, his breath hot against her.

Her fingers tightened on his shoulders. "Edward—"

He licked her, and whatever protest she'd been about to make dissolved into a throaty moan of intense pleasure. Her body relaxed beneath the feel of his mouth against her as his tongue took long, deep strokes into her succulent folds before his lips found her nub, already sensitive and swollen with arousal, and closed around it.

A gentle suck—her body spasmed, quivering against his lips.

Another suck, harder this time. Her hips lifted off the desk to grind herself against his mouth as a begging whimper of need tore from her throat.

But his hand on her thigh kept her pinned beneath him as he teased at her, his fingers swirling inside her even as his lips continued to nibble and suck, the heat of his mouth invisibly branding her as his.

He raised his head to watch her face. Her eyes were closed tightly, and her bottom lip was clenched between her teeth as she tried to fight back the growing ache inside her instead of giving over to it. He smiled wickedly at that. Her body was still too new to sex to know how to welcome release even as she craved it so desperately, and he burned with selfish pleasure at being the man to teach her.

Standing between her thighs, he unfastened his fall and freed his hard cock. Proof that she was ready for him glistened on the pink lips of her folds, and he was more than ready for her. So ready to plunge into her tight warmth that a drop of his dew already beaded at his tip.

"You're mine now." He took her waist and pulled her forward until her buttocks nearly hung off the edge of the desk, then reached down to grasp himself and press the end of his throbbing erection into the hot hollow at her core. "And I am taking what's mine."

She whimpered in anticipation, her body shaking with need.

But this wasn't about need. Need had brought her into his arms last night and given him peace and absolution. This—he tilted his hips to pop just the tip of his cock inside the tight resistance of her inner lips, but no farther—*this* was possession.

She writhed beneath him, pleading with her body to plunge inside and take all of her. "Edward, please—please now!"

He stepped forward and shoved himself inside her to the hilt.

She cried out at being filled so completely, so suddenly, but this time there was none of the pain of before, no resistance. And when he immediately began to thrust into her, her body bore down around his to welcome him.

"You're mine," he groaned as he drove into her. "Say it, Kate—say you're mine."

She moaned.

"Say it," he demanded, grabbing her hips and lifting them to meet his. "You're mine."

"I'm—I'm yours!" A shudder of surrender swept through her. Arching her back, she locked her ankles at the small of his back, because each powerful thrust against her sent her skittering up the desk, his hands on his hips pulling her toward him to pump into her again. "I'm yours, Edward . . ."

With a growl, he yanked down her bodice and tore open the stay to expose her breasts, and as his hips pounded between her thighs, his hands reached over her body to roughly squeeze her breasts and pull at her nipples.

Throaty whimpers panted from her, but the sounds were lost to his ears beneath his own animal grunts of need. Her arms flailed around her, unable to find any purchase on the smooth desktop, and their two bodies knocked the stacks of papers, files, and books to the floor in a tumbling mess.

With a fierce groan, he clasped her hips against him as

he plunged into her and held himself there, shooting himself deep inside her. His body pulsed hot with exquisite pleasure, his legs and arms shaking from exertion as he strained to empty every drop inside her.

But she wasn't finished and writhed herself against him, begging for him to give her release.

Keeping his spent cock inside her, he grabbed her ankles and lifted her legs up over his shoulders, and at the new angle of his body pressing heavily down on hers, he ground his pelvis hard against her, rubbing at her open sex and the exposed nub at her core. She gasped, and he did it again, lifting his hips to slam down and grind against her.

She shattered, her arms clutching tightly around his shoulders as her hips bucked wildly beneath him. He smothered her mouth with his to muffle the cry that tore from her, and he could feel her sex quivering around his cock still buried inside her, each wave of her climax pulsing through her and into him.

With as much tenderness as their joining had just been fierce, he slowly kissed her throat, then rested his forehead against her bare shoulder. For a long while, neither moved, lost in the racing of their pounding heartbeats and their gasping breaths.

"Edward?" she finally whispered.

He lifted his head from her bare shoulder, his chest panging with concern that he might have hurt her.

"You're mine now, too." With a smile, she touched his cheek, her voice husky with satiated desire. "Say it," she ordered softly with a very feminine sigh, her fingertip grazing over his chin.

"I'm yours, angel." He brushed his lips over hers, then reluctantly withdrew from her.

Removing his crumpled cravat, he used it to gently clean both of them, then cast it away into the fireplace flames. He took her hands and helped her slide off the desk, feeling a twinge of guilt when she winced in pain and rubbed at her backside. He'd used her roughly, but he couldn't help himself. And he realized with a tug of satisfaction that neither could she.

Unbidden, she reached down to fasten up his trousers. If she wasn't careful—he grimaced as her fingertips brushed against him—she'd find herself right back on the desk, his desire for her that insatiable.

"So," she said quietly, straightening his waistcoat, "Brannigan's arrived early."

"Yes." Following her lead, he laced up her stay, then pulled up her bodice to cover her shoulders. "I leave for London tomorrow morning." He reached around to her back to fasten her up. Odd that he found nearly as much pleasure in dressing her as he did in *un*dressing her. "And you're coming with me."

"I want to be with you, I do." She lowered her eyes as she smoothed down her skirt. "But I cannot go to London, not so soon."

"Why not?" he pressed. After the passion they'd just shared, he'd never be able to part with her.

She closed her eyes, and a flash of disappointment and unfulfilled longing crossed her face. "I need to be certain that Brannigan will work out here. Arthur, Mrs. Elston, Dorrie—they're all I have."

"You also have me now," he informed her as she stepped away from him to twist up her hair and pin it back into place.

She kept her back to him so he couldn't see her face, but

he saw clearly the trembling of her fingers as she tried un-successfully to place the last pin. "But I don't."

"That's why you're coming to London—"

She shook her head, giving up on the pin with a frus-trated sigh. "And after the season's over? What claim will I have to you then, except as a burdensome ward with an indebted farm?"

He took a deep breath to untie the knot in his gut. He'd known what he had to do since last night when he saw her standing there before the firelight in boy's breeches and a woman's stay, when he knew he could no longer keep himself away from her. And perhaps this new offer might just convince her to come to London, to give him a chance at more nights with her… "I'll change the terms of your guardianship."

She whirled around, stunned, the hairpin falling from her fingers. In the silence that followed as she stared at him, the pin pinged softly as it dropped to the floor.

A riot of emotions swept across her face, so shocked she couldn't speak and could only gape at him in disbelief.

"I won't void the guardianship, but I can give you greater independence," he explained quietly, knowing it was the right decision if he wanted to make her trust him enough to spend the season with him. "I would still remain as your guardian under the law, to ensure your protection, but you'd be given the freedom to make your own deci-sions and choices without interference from me or Phillip Benton. I'll have Meacham draw up an addendum to the agreement and ask your father to sign it."

She held her breath. "And Brambly?"

He grinned at her. "Yours to do with as you please."

Then he braced himself for her to come rushing into

his embrace and fling her arms around his neck—this was what she'd wanted since he arrived on her doorstep, her life and home under her own control to do with as she pleased.

But she didn't move except to raise a hand to wipe at her glistening eyes and to stare at him, accusingly, as if instead of giving her the farm he'd sworn to destroy it.

Confused, he reached for her. "Kate—"

"No." She pushed him back with a look of such abandonment and distress that it ripped his breath away. "You were going to save Brambly, and now—"

"I'm still going to help with Brambly, that hasn't changed. You have my word."

But she only shook her head fiercely. And then the true reason for why she didn't want to go to London hit him, and he felt like a damned fool for not realizing sooner—

"Brambly is yours, angel," he assured her. "No one's taking it away from you while you're gone."

In her eyes, then, he saw the wariness slowly change to trust and relief, and the surprising happiness swelling inside him nearly overwhelmed him. She stepped back into his arms, her warm body pressing gratefully against his.

"Thank you, Edward." She rose up on tiptoes to kiss him, her hand sliding possessively over his chest.

Slipping his arms around her, he murmured against her lips, "We're going to London." There was no dissuading him from that, but... "I can remain at Brambly a few more days, to make certain Brannigan settles in well."

She arched into his embrace, and his breath hitched at the softness of her breasts against his chest. "Thank you!"

With a groan of restraint, wanting to ravish her again right there on the floor but knowing it would be too much for her too soon, he lowered his mouth to her ear. "But

I also hope you realize," he murmured as he swirled his tongue inside her ear and was rewarded with a rapturous shiver, "I have no intention of keeping myself from you."

She breathed out a low moan. "I certainly hope not!"

He tossed back his head and laughed, at that moment happier than he'd felt in years. Ten years, in fact.

"You're going to be the death of me," he chided. "Now, away with you." He turned her toward the door, then slapped her playfully on the bottom to send her scurrying. "You've a houseful of goods to unpack, and I've a stack of paperwork to sort through."

"Hmm...I can think of more entertaining things to do than paperwork," she ventured over her shoulder, swinging her hips invitingly as she sashayed toward the door. "I'll be in the sitting room with the velvet sofa should you grow bored..."

"Wanton," he teased, his wolfish smile a hungry promise of what she could expect that evening.

With a last glance back at him, she sighed longingly and slipped from the room.

He shook his head with a happy chuckle and tried to focus on the paperwork, although it was downright impossible with the scent of her still clinging to him, the taste of her still on his lips.

Who would have thought that the little minx could have his head spinning like this? But that was exactly what this woman did to him. She had him wanting her, and not just for bed sport, although *that* was proving more special than he'd ever imagined.

No, he admitted to himself as he sorted through the papers, scanning over each one before setting it aside, she had him wanting her for her laughter and teasing flirtations, her kindness and loyalty, even for that stubborn way she jutted out her chin. And she wanted him, too, just as much.

Perhaps he'd been wrong. Perhaps marriage wasn't such an impossibility after—

A knock sounded at the door.

Edward glanced up. A stocky man with bowed legs and what little hair he had left swept across his otherwise bald head stood hesitantly in the doorway, hat in hand. He wore plain clothes and sturdy work shoes, no cravat, and a stained waistcoat, and the touch of apple red at his cheeks indicated that he'd already started drinking even so early in the morning.

"Brannigan's overseeing the deliveries," Edward informed him, dropping his attention back to the paperwork. "He should be down in the basement."

"Beggin' yer pardon, sir." The man stepped into the room. "I'm Guerson from the posting inn."

"Ah, Mr. Guerson, of course." Edward came forward with a smile, his hand extended. "My apologies. With all the activity going on here today, I thought you were one of the workers." He shook the man's hand. "What brings you to Brambly?"

"It's Miss Kate, Yer Grace."

Katherine. She'd been out of his sight for less than five minutes. Surely even that hellcat couldn't have gotten herself into trouble so soon. He frowned. "What is it?"

"Well, sir, you should know that all o' us in the village think right highly o' the lass. We'd never want t' see any harm come to her."

Sudden concern surged into his chest. "What's the matter, Guerson?"

"This, sir." He removed a letter from his jacket pocket.

"Young Tom brought this by a few days ago, said Miss Kate wanted it put into the mail. With all the storms and rain, the mail's been delayed, so I thought you might should see it first, you being her guardian now an' responsible for the lass."

Edward's face hardened as he took the letter and scanned his gaze across the address. *Phillip Benton.*

"Normally, I wouldn't bother ye none with somethin' like this. But it's to her papa, ye see. And e'eryone in the village knows the bloke's a worthless rat's ass." The words slipped out, and the man stammered in apology, "That is— I mean to say, he's not a good man."

"No," Edward agreed, his jaw clenching, "he's not."

"And I'd hate for Miss Kate to do somethin' foolish and get hurt, now she's got ye here to take care o' her."

"Thank you, Guerson. You were right to bring this to me." He nodded stiffly toward the door. "See Brannigan before you go and tell him to give you a coin for your trouble."

"Right kind o' ye, Yer Grace." He slipped his hat onto his head and quickly left, a bounce in his step as he headed toward the rear of the house and the basement stairs.

Edward broke the wax seal and opened the letter, and three coins clattered to the floor at his feet. As he stared at them, the same cold betrayal stirred in him from ten years ago, falling over him like a black fog creeping up to swirl through him and steal away his breath.

His eyes swept slowly from the coins to the letter clutched in his hand. With each word he read, his pulse banged harder, more fiercely, as if trying to prove that he still had a heart left in his blackened chest. But he knew better. He knew deceit and had experienced firsthand that black place that could take a man's soul.

Now, it descended over him again as he stared at her letter, its claws ripping into his chest to claim him—

His angel had damned him straight back to hell.

* * *

In the drawing room, Kate busied herself by arranging the newly delivered furniture and sorting through all the goods still to be unpacked in the crates. But her eyes kept straying to the velvet sofa in the corner, her mind replaying what Edward had told her about it. Although she tried to breathe normally, her heart still raced, and her body pulsed electric at the brazen way she'd given herself to him right there on the desk. The same way she planned on giving herself to him tonight on that sofa.

She laughed shamelessly, her hand flying up to her mouth. They hadn't even removed their clothes!

He'd called her wanton, and perhaps she was. But if being wanton made a woman feel this good, this happy, well, it was an absolute wonder that the entire female population of England wasn't cornering off men to demand they turn them wanton.

And it was all because of Edward. She craved him, so much so that she'd just begged him to possess her and willingly admitted to becoming his.

His. His hands on her body, his weight pressing delectably down on her, his manhood stroking inside her—she'd not only wanted to submit, she'd enjoyed the surrender. And she wanted nothing more at that moment than for him to possess her again until she was once more powerless within his arms.

Her whole life she'd never understood how her mother

could love her father so faithfully, despite the terrible way he treated her, the abuse he'd heaped upon her. Why had Mama surrendered her life's freedom to become his wife? And why had she remained faithful, even knowing he never loved her in return?

But now Kate knew. She'd experienced for herself the rush of feelings that made a woman want to sacrifice her freedom for a man.

Yet she wouldn't make the same mistake her mother had. She would never marry a man who did not love her, and she wasn't naïve enough to believe that Edward held feelings for her. The idea of marriage was terrifying enough by itself, but to add to it all she stood to lose . . . Brambly, her medicine, her heart. If her husband decided to take it from her, there would be nothing she could do to stop him.

With Edward, there had been no talk of marriage, and she was glad of it. Even if he had asked, she would have refused. But an invitation to London was a far cry from a marriage proposal, and so she would go with him because she couldn't bear the idea of denying herself that time with him, even if she could see no future for them beyond the end of the season. For all that he'd promised to protect her and made being in his arms so very special, Edward did not love her.

Her chest squeezed, hollow and desolate. But could he ever?

"Katherine."

At the sound of Edward's deep voice behind her, her heart leapt as hope surged through her. Perhaps, just perhaps, he was beginning to care after all.

She laughed happily as she turned toward him. "I think we should—"

Her laughter choked beneath the iciness of his black gaze. In a heartbeat, her happiness ripped away, replaced by sudden worry stabbing in her stomach, and dread clenched its cold fingers around her heart.

He stepped toward her, forcing her backward until she pressed against the wall, trapping her. He placed his hand on the wall at her shoulder and leaned down until his face was so close to hers that his breath stirred across her lips, until his eyes bored mercilessly into hers.

She swallowed, suddenly terrified. "Edward, what's happened?"

"I found something that belongs to you." His voice was ice. "I thought you might want it back."

"What is it?" she whispered, so unnerved at the sudden change in him that her body trembled at the reappearance of the black hardness that she remembered from the first time she met him.

His cold, controlled face belied the anger she sensed seething inside him. "Your letter."

"My letter?" she repeated warily, confusion and alarm roiling inside her.

When he answered, his cold voice lacked all emotion for her, so distant and uncaring that fear leapt into her chest. "To your father."

Her heart stopped. And when it began again, the pain was searing. He knew she'd written to her father, he *knew* she'd defied him... *Oh God*, what had she done?

Her body flashing with panic and desperation, she took a deep breath to steady herself and said as calmly as she could as her world fell away beneath her, "Edward, please let me explain—"

"I told you never to contact him." Slowly, his self-control and restrained anger only adding to her fear, he took her hand and placed the crumpled paper onto her palm. "But you wrote to him anyway."

Her eyes burned with unshed tears. "He's my *father*. He's the only blood relative I have left. I couldn't just turn my back on him when he needed me."

She expected cursing, fury—instead, his face was nothing more than a blank, emotionless mask as he stared at her. "You sent him money."

"Because he needed it. You said he was bankrupt." Each word was a desperate breath, willing him to believe her. "I am sorry, Edward, I should never have sent it. But it was only a letter—"

"It's much more than just a letter, Kate." His voice was an icy accusation. "You chose him over me."

"I didn't! I wanted to tell you about the letter, but—"

He arched a dubious brow. "But you were too busy seducing me for your own gain?"

She slapped him, her palm cracking hard against his cheek.

An excruciating feeling of loss and betrayal burned inside her, so hard and terrible that she couldn't breathe. She'd been swept into a horrible nightmare when all she wanted to do was awaken, safe in his arms, as she'd done that morning. Yet he was accusing her of such horrible, awful things—she clenched her hand into a fist, her palm still stinging from the contact with his cheek.

Edward froze, his only reaction a flickering of his cold eyes. Then his hand slowly rose to his cheek where a red mark already began to form, and she saw a mix of regret and guilt flash across his face. But he said nothing to apologize.

"I would *never* do anything like that," she forced out, her heart tearing. He had it all backward, completely *wrong*! She'd given her innocence to him because she cared about him, because she wanted to be in his arms, and for no other reason. "How can you believe—" She choked, a miserable wretchedness swirling through her.

"It's been done before," he said coldly.

"Not by me." She shoved at his shoulders to push him away, the searing torment inside her unbearable that he would think her capable of such an act. But he didn't budge, not even to shift away, and a soft cry of anguished frustration escaped her. "Edward, I would *never* do that!"

He gave her a freezing look of unrepentant contempt. "Just as you would never deceive me by contacting your father?"

Her heart shattered. In that moment, she felt the gaping distance between them, the cold apathy replacing the warm affection he'd shown her last night and this morning.

"I wanted to trust in you, Kate, you of all people." He stepped away from her, his hands dropping to his sides as if he'd completely abandoned her now, as if he couldn't bear to be anywhere near her, and each word sent a quiver of wretchedness through her. "But you destroyed that, and now I can't trust you again."

Her eyes were so blurred with tears that she could barely see the lines of his face, but she didn't blink to clear them away, because she didn't want to see the unforgiving coldness in him. There was no tenderness in him now, nothing gentle or warm, nothing of the man she loved.

Standing less than a foot away, Edward was lost to her.

* * *

The tiger opened the coach door. "We've arrived, miss." He flipped down the step. "Greymoor."

Kate peered beyond him through the drizzling rain at the house.

Large and foreboding, the gray stone façade blended into the low clouds behind it and stood isolated against the empty moors. Only a scattering of outbuildings gave any hint that this was more than just a deserted house in the wilderness. There was no sign of life, no animals in the barnyard, no servants scurrying to meet the carriage. Chimneys stabbed into the sky, but a lack of smoke trailing up from any of them made the scene feel even colder, even more dreary.

So this was to be her new home. She shuddered.

The tiger reached inside to grab her small bag and extended his hand to help her to the ground.

The trip had been a long one, nearly two full days since she'd been placed into Edward's coach at dawn per his orders and driven away from Brambly and everything she'd ever known, stopping only to change horses and switch drivers before continuing on through the night. She was cold, tired, and hungry, and more alone than she'd ever been in her life.

But most of all, she was angry. Edward had sent her away because he no longer trusted her and so delivered her halfway across the country in order to keep her away from her father...and from him. And also as punishment. That was why he couldn't let her remain at Brambly. He thought she'd deceived him in an attempt to free herself from the guardianship, and by simply riding back to London and leaving her alone on the farm, he would have given her exactly what he assumed she'd tried to manipulate from him—her old life in a newly furnished house. What he didn't realize, however, was that her real punishment was not being sent to the moors but being sent away from him.

Yet each mile that took her farther away only grew her determination to return to Brambly. She looked around at the rocky, harsh moors stretching out in every direction and bit her bottom lip. *Somehow.*

The front door swung open. A large woman in a black uniform blocked the doorway, her iron-gray hair pulled into a severe bun.

"Miss Benton?" she demanded in a thick, German accent.

"Yes."

"Lutz," she introduced herself, then took the bag from the groom.

Kate watched the tiger return to the coach. As soon as he swung into his place on top of the carriage, the driver cracked the whip, and the team rolled through the mud toward the road, leaving her behind.

She stood in the drizzling rain and watched until it disappeared, and with it, her last link to Brambly.

Mrs. Elston, Dorrie, sweet Arthur . . . *they* were why she was here, why she hadn't already executed her escape. Edward had kept his word and pensioned them, letting them stay on in the little cottages at Brambly, but he'd been very clear—if she ran away, he would revoke the pensions and strip away their allowances. Knowing the affection he'd come to feel for the servants during his stay, Kate wasn't certain he'd actually do it, but it was a threat she wasn't willing to push.

So she left her home without a struggle. Their pensions exchanged for her exile. It was a deal with the devil.

But the one thing she'd learned from watching her father's behavior all these years was that deals and contracts could always be manipulated. She'd find some way to rewrite the guardianship and free all of them, no matter what she had to do to make it happen.

"Come," Mrs. Lutz ordered.

Kate followed her into the house. Dark and uninviting, with heavy pieces of furniture scattered randomly throughout and no cushions, no pillows, no curtains to soften the rooms, the house was just as harsh as its furnishings. Despite the darkness of the gray, stormy day, there were no lit candles, and every fireplace was cold.

Mrs. Lutz led her upstairs, opened a door, and pointed inside.

Kate paused. A massive bed with heavy drapes dominated the room, with an armoire, a dressing table, and a single wooden chair the only other furniture. The walls were bare, as was the floor.

"Yes," Mrs. Lutz repeated with a nod, and Kate understood that this was to be her room. "His Grace his orders."

"Oh, I am certain of that," she muttered. When the housekeeper, who apparently spoke only a handful of words in English, stared blankly, Kate sighed. "Never mind."

Mrs. Lutz gestured toward Kate's cape and shoes. "No."

Apparently, *no* was Lutz-speak for undressing, and Kate removed her cloak and shoes and placed them into the housekeeper's waiting hands. With more pointing and more *no*'s, and no choice but to obey, Kate slowly slipped out of the muslin and stockings until she wore only her shift and handed them over.

Then she watched, stunned, as the housekeeper grabbed

her bag, shoved her clothes inside, then tossed the whole lot outside into the hall. When Kate started after them, Mrs. Lutz stopped her with a muscular arm.

"You took my clothes!" Kate cried out in disbelief.

A stinging crept behind her eyes. She'd been torn away from her home and now forced from her clothes as if to completely obliterate any last connection she had to Brambly. Forcing herself to breathe slowly, she was thankful at least that the anger inside her kept the sobs in check.

"Old clothes no good." Mrs. Lutz opened the armoire. "New clothes," the housekeeper assured her with a proud smile. "Moors clothes. *Strong* clothes."

Two dresses hung inside, all black and roughly made of worsted wool, a pair of sturdy work shoes sitting beneath. There were two sets of white shifts and gray wool stockings, along with a single night rail, but not another color, not one soft piece of sprigged muslin or satin. Moors clothes, indeed. Her new wardrobe was as harsh as the barren wilderness around her.

So that was his plan. Edward wanted to cut her off from the world and cast her from his life, right down to her clothes. After all, she thought with faint bemusement, wasn't that what prisoners of war were forced to do—strip from their uniforms and don prison garb, to rob them of the comfort of their identity and place in the world?

But he was wrong if he thought a Puritan wardrobe would break her. They were only clothes, and she'd gone without so much for so long at Brambly that she was used to extreme sparseness and utility. What were a few clothing adjustments when last spring she'd had to beg the miller for a sack of flour to feed her household?

Clothes! She nearly laughed at that. Edward was going

to have to try a lot harder than this if he truly meant to break her.

"Yes." Mrs. Lutz pointed at the black dress, then left the room.

Shooting a narrowed gaze at the door, Kate reached for the dress. She had no choice. The only way to free herself was to play along and wait for whatever bid for freedom she could seize.

"His Grace his orders," she mocked as she slipped it on.

Pulling her hair back into a bun, she gave a cursory glance in the dressing table mirror. At her appearance, a small giggle burst out.

She pressed her hand against her lips, but she couldn't stop, and the giggling turned into full-throated laughter. She knew that if she didn't laugh, she would have broken down from the hurt and outrage that tore at her. In angry resentment at herself for being so foolish as to believe her father would ever love her, and in utter wretchedness that now Edward never would.

Oh, there was nothing funny about her situation, but she couldn't help it. She was certain Edward wanted her in the black dress, with its high neck and long sleeves, to purposefully hide all her femininity, the same femininity he thought she'd used to trick him. A continuation of the punishment of her banishment from Brambly. But she didn't look sexless—she looked *ridiculous*!

She choked back the laughter and collected herself, then told her reflection, "You will not break me, Edward."

He believed she'd deceived him with her body. That she'd lied, schemed, pretended. But how on earth could she have ever pretended those wonderful sensations he created inside her when he made love to her? Or the way she gave herself over with utter abandon? Or her feelings for him, when she held him so close afterward, never wanting to let him go?

But in her desperation to find a way to make her father love her, she'd given Edward real cause to distrust her. She *had* sent money to Papa, and she *had* asked Edward to give up the guardianship after she made love to him. For goodness' sake, everything she'd said to him, everything he'd offered could all be seen as self-serving to that end. She would have laughed at that, too, if she wasn't so angry that he'd so easily believed her capable of it.

It was madness! All of it.

The only sins she'd committed were in wrongly believing in her father and in loving Edward, and for that, fate was punishing her. And in *that*, she realized ironically, she'd become exactly like her mother.

But she wouldn't surrender, and she refused to cry any more tears for him. Absolutely *refused*!

"You will *not* break me," she repeated fiercely. "And I *will* find a way from this place."

She might have lost Edward, but nothing would stop her from returning home.

CHAPTER THIRTEEN

London, Three Weeks Later

"There you are, Edward." Augusta swept into the study of Strathmore House, wearing a gold brocade dress as bright as the gray April day outside was dreary.

He rose from his mahogany desk to greet her, and she frowned at the stack of paperwork that had occupied him all afternoon. After his return from Spain, he'd thrown himself into running the family finances, at first to simply learn the extent of the family's properties and wealth. Now, however, since his recent return from the countryside, she was certain he pored over the books himself only because it gave him an afternoon's worth of distraction until he could leave for supper at White's and a night of drinking and cards.

"You employ several accountants and agents," she reminded him as she gestured at the paperwork. "It is unseemly for a man of your rank to be concerned with his own wealth."

"And how does a man remain wealthy if he's not concerned with it?" he quipped dryly, coming forward to give her a warm kiss on her proffered cheek and to help her off with her wrap. He handed it to the waiting footman.

"Well, I suppose it could be worse." She tugged off her gloves. "You could be at White's again, gambling it away."

"I do not gamble it away."

She scoffed. "Are you attempting to tell me that you do not play at cards?"

"No," he countered evenly, a faint smile on his lips that never reached his eyes, "I'm telling you that I do not lose."

But Augusta knew better.

In the past three weeks since his return from the countryside, he had been frequenting White's nearly every night. Always before, he'd found the club stifling, the level of gambling not challenging enough for his skills, the company insufferable. But now, he had been going there every night, playing cards until the wee hours of the morning, and she suspected it was because he did not want to face the nightly silence of the town house.

Further, he'd been losing.

Her heart lifted hopefully when she'd heard that juicy bit of *on-dit* last night at the opera. If her nephew was losing at cards, then even the activity of the club hadn't been sufficient to distract him enough to give him peace. Whatever had happened in Sussex still plagued him.

"What can I do for you this afternoon, Augusta?"

She withdrew a letter from her reticule and placed it on the desk. "This arrived at Meacham's office."

Edward's jaw tightened as he glanced down at the letter.

Then he leveled his cold gaze on her and demanded, "How the devil did they get Meacham's address?"

Augusta had long ago learned not to be intimidated by the Westover men's stares and arched a brow in imperturbable response. "I suppose the same way they were able to send letters to you at Hartsfield Park, then here at Strathmore House," she replied calmly, secretly admiring the perseverance of the former Brambly House servants in pleading for their mistress's return. "What does that make now, seven letters in all?"

"Ten," he corrected tightly.

So he had been paying attention. *Interesting.* "If Mrs. Elston has gone to the trouble of sending this one through your solicitor, perhaps you should read it."

Ignoring the letter, he leaned back against his desk, his arms crossed over his chest. A cold, distant expression masked the anger she knew simmered beneath.

It was the posture of a stubborn and strong-willed man, a determination she'd seen before from all the Westover men. With them, she had known better than to press, but with Edward, at that moment, she wanted to frustrate him even more.

Because anger was good. It meant he was still alive, that the nephew she loved survived somewhere inside the cold man standing before her.

She shook her head. "You cannot keep that girl locked up in the moors for the rest of her life."

"Actually, I can," he said matter-of-factly. "She has Mrs. Lutz to care for her, and in the moors, she cannot cause trouble."

Or, she thought, force him to resolve whatever unpleasantness happened between them during his visit, which was more likely the reason, knowing her nephew as well as she did. This time, he couldn't send himself into war to escape the woman who caused him problems, so he sent away the woman instead.

"You also cannot keep ignoring those letters," she added.

"I can do that, too."

"For God's sake, Edward," she sighed in exasperation, "what did that innocent child do to make you hate her so?"

"She is not a child," he reminded her in a low voice. "And she is *not* innocent."

Augusta pressed her lips together. "When you became determined to exact your revenge on Phillip Benton because the courts did nothing, I tried to change your mind," she explained quietly. "I even sent word to Thomas Matteson and Nathaniel Grey in hopes that they would be able to talk sense into you. But when it became obvious that nothing would dissuade you, I relented and let you carry out your plans because I realized something you did not."

He held his face impassive. "And what was that?"

"That by taking over Benton's life you were actually saving him from himself and giving him a chance to live."

Edward laughed dismissively.

"It is true. Had you not intervened, the man would either have drunk himself to death or crossed the wrong people, who would have killed him in the street." She paused to let her words sink in. "I let the guardianship stand without protest for the same reason. To save that girl. Becoming the ward of a duke gives her a chance at the proper life her father's gambling and drinking denied her."

His face darkened. "Augusta, it's none of your—"

She cut him off with a wave of her hand. "But now you have gone too far. You have taken her away from her home and all she loves." She shook her head. "She is not her father."

"No," he countered, with rising irritation beneath his calm façade, "she's worse. Her father is a stupid, careless drunk, but she"—he shoved himself away from the desk and circled behind it, his shoulders stiffening with smoldering resentment—"is as natural with deceit as any woman I have ever met."

"What *exactly* did she do to harm you?"

Ignoring her question, he glanced down at the unopened letter on the desk with utter contempt. Then he asked icily, his voice so cold it sent a chill down her spine, "You want me to deal with the letters?"

"Yes."

He put a finger on the letter and slid it across the desk toward her, unrepentant beneath her admonishing stare. "Then burn them. *That* will take care of them."

Augusta said nothing. Slowly, she placed the letter back inside her reticule, to return it to Meacham for safekeeping until Edward was ready to read it, along with all the others.

Three weeks ago, her nephew had returned from Sussex in such a state as she had never seen him. Always before, his anger had manifested itself as cold disdain and distance, and in the case of Phillip Benton, a calculated plan for revenge. But this was different. This time, he was openly angry. Meacham had borne the brunt of his wrath, as had the poor girl who had the misfortune of becoming his ward.

And Augusta delighted in it, because his anger meant he still had a heart left to burn.

She had no idea what set him off. Although she was beginning to suspect… "At least give her a dowry and help her find a husband to take her off your hands."

"To let her wreak havoc on some other poor man?" But the sarcastic tone in his voice was undercut by something else, something she saw flicker hot and deep in his eyes. It was possessiveness.

"It would be better for some other man to suffer her in his life than you." Then she added, watching him closely, "And in his bed."

Another hot flicker deep in his cold eyes—there was no mistaking it this time. Jealousy lurked inside him.

"What an excellent idea," he drawled. "Except that God hasn't yet created the man who could abide that hellcat."

Instead of upsetting his aunt, his words stirred an encouraging warmth inside her. If he could be that angry with Katherine Benton, then perhaps, finally, he could let himself feel other emotions as well.

He returned to his chair and turned his attention to the paperwork he'd been reading before she entered, their conversation dismissed.

She waited patiently, and after several moments of silence, she arched an imperious brow. "Edward."

"Yes?" He shuffled the papers, keeping his gaze downward.

"Katherine Benton."

"What *now*?" he demanded irritably.

"She has fallen ill."

"Ill?" He glanced up, his eyes intense, concerned. "What kind of ill?"

"Fever, chills, coughing—"

"Not stomach sickness, then?" he interrupted.

She frowned. For a moment, she thought he might turn pale. "Whyever would you think that?"

He leaned back in his chair, an odd expression passing briefly over his unguarded face. "No reason."

"She has taken to bed on several days. Mrs. Lutz has been attending her." She paused. "But I think you should go to her."

Stubbornly refusing to speak any more of his ward, he turned his attention back to his papers. "Have Mrs. Lutz send for a doctor. I'm not going there, and she's not leaving."

Knowing she would get no more from him than that, Augusta nodded. "I shall keep you informed of her condition."

He only grunted his reply.

She knew not to press. The same hardness and strong-mindedness that made her love the Westover men had also taught her when it was useless to fight against them. But the same blood ran proudly in her veins as well, and she knew this argument was far from over.

And when it was, she would be the victor.

Leaving him to his work, and letting him stew in his emotions over Katherine Benton, she swept up the curving stairs to her room on the second floor, a lightness in her step. Oh, *this* was unexpected!

In the five weeks since he'd become Katherine's guardian, Augusta had seen Edward look more alive than in the ten years since Jane betrayed him. True, most of the emotions running through him now were rancor and antagonism, but at least the gel stirred feelings of some kind. No one else had been able to do even that.

She smiled with amusement. Apparently, since Edward wanted to know if her sudden illness resembled morning sickness, the woman had stirred her nephew's passions as well.

"My, my, a country bluestocking," she chuckled to herself. "Whoever would have thought?"

* * *

Edward stared at his cards. He'd lost. Again.

Waving off the dealer, he pushed himself away from the table to make his way through the gaming room at White's and into the adjoining smoking parlor.

The club was crowded even for so late an hour as groups of well-dressed men gathered around the card tables, finishing hand after hand and drink after drink. Some carelessly tossed away hundreds of pounds on bad bets and poor cards; a few were so drunk they swayed even when sitting down. Each was considered part of the quality, the best of the English empire. But Edward despised nearly all of them.

At least most of them had the decency to leave him alone. One, though, a greasy-looking man with a balding head and paunchy gut, had been staring all night. Edward dismissed him as nothing more than an annoyance.

He signaled to the attendant to bring him a whiskey, then sank into a chair in front of the fire.

His concentration was gone, enough that tonight he couldn't even keep track of the cards put in front of him, no less keep a running tally of the ones remaining in the deck. Two months ago, he'd have been able to count his way through two decks of cards.

But two months ago, he hadn't yet met Katherine Benton.

She'd managed to legally attach herself to him, invaded his thoughts and dreams, manipulated her way into his arms...and then betrayed him.

He should have expected it. After all, she was Phillip Benton's daughter and a woman, an enemy on both fronts. But her trickery was made worse by the fact that he'd trusted her. He'd misled himself into thinking she was different from other women, and in the end, she proved to be just like the others.

Worse, he'd let himself desire her.

Christ, he *still* desired her.

During the day, he distracted himself with work and somehow managed to beat down the lingering yearning he felt for her.

But at night, when he was alone, the house silent and dark around him, he remembered in unbidden flashes how delicious she tasted, how sweet her touch, how eagerly her body welcomed his. And when she came to him in his dreams, it wasn't imaginings of sex that brought him wide awake and shaking as if from a nightmare. It was the way she simply held him in her arms and comforted him as no other woman had ever done.

So he spent his evenings at White's and gladly welcomed whatever distractions the place could give. Here, at least, he could be left alone.

"Colonel."

Damnation. He rolled his eyes, not bothering to glance at the man who sat down uninvited in the chair next to his. "Grey."

Major Nathaniel Grey stretched out his legs and kicked up his well-worn boots onto the fireplace fender, despite the frown thrown at him by the club's manager. His brown coat was coarse, the white shirt beneath just as plain as his tan breeches. Without waistcoat or cravat, he was drastically underdressed for a night at the club. Yet the scruffy man sporting two-days' growth of beard was also one of the best agents in the War Office and on the club's permanent list as a personal guest of Lord Bathurst, Secretary of War and the Colonies, which gave him the right to be in the club whenever he chose.

But even the manager of White's would never dare to criticize Grey openly for his careless attire. Not when he was with the Duke of Strathmore. Not with the reputation that followed him. And certainly not when everyone could clearly see the pistol-shaped bulge beneath his coat.

Edward accepted his drink from the attendant. Despite the interruption to his solitude, he was happy to see Grey. The man had been his best captain in Spain and along with Thomas Matteson his closest friend, and his presence tonight was a pleasant reminder of happier times. "What's a scoundrel like you doing here?" Despite his teasing words, warmth laced his voice.

"Reformed scoundrel," Grey corrected. "I'm a respectable man these days." He grinned at his former colonel, withdrew two cigars from his jacket pocket, and offered one to him as if they were once again sitting at an army campfire instead of in the most exclusive club in England. "I've been hearing rumors about you, Colonel. Had to hurry over to see for myself."

Edward laughed. "You heard rumors that Strathmore was at White's playing cards? Dull evening for you."

"No, I heard Strathmore was losing."

Edward cut off the cap of the cigar and tossed it into the fire. "I never lose."

"I once saw you lose a hundred pounds to a Spanish fla-
menco dancer," Grey reminded him.

"She cheated," Edward clarified as he lit the cigar on the
tableside oil lamp, "and I let her win."

"How do you know she cheated?"

"I found the cards she'd hidden beneath her skirts."

Grey grinned with rakish admiration at his old friend.
"You devil!"

A crooked smile pulled at Edward's lips. "Why do you
think I let her win?"

Grey gave a laugh around the cigar he held clenched
between his teeth. It was almost like old times. "But if
you're losing at cards, Colonel, something's amiss." He removed the cigar and studied the glowing tip, not meeting
Edward's gaze as he admitted, "Of course, I'm not worried
about you—"

"Of course not."

"But Thomas is."

Irritation flashed through Edward that Thomas and
Grey were interfering in his private life—but then, he
most likely wouldn't be alive today if they hadn't
watched over him while they'd been in Spain together.
He would never be able to repay them for the way they'd
saved both his life and his sanity during those dark days.

Leaning forward with elbows on his knees, Edward
blew out a breath and admitted soberly, friend to friend,
"I've lost my concentration." There was no point in denying it. Grey knew him too well to be fooled.

"The rumors are rife with explanations for that, too."
Grey settled back in his chair and chuckled. "My favorite
is that Strathmore is hunting a wife."

Edward laughed, but the guess hit far too close for comfort. "Frequenting courting parlors are you now, Grey? You're not the lemonade and petticoat type."

"Never knock the value of a good petticoat, Colonel." He grinned rakishly. "I certainly never have."

No, Grey had certainly never done that. Even on the Peninsula in the middle of a war, he'd managed to find women willing to engage in assignations without futures or consequence, charmingly moving from one to another as the whim suited him. And when the affairs were over and the regiment moved on, each woman somehow believed that *he* had done *her* a favor by convincing her to engage in a few nights' pleasures. Marriage was never a consideration.

It was ironic. Grey had spent years as a soldier and now risked his life for the War Office, and he thought nothing of riding hell-bent into cannon fire to attack the enemy head-on. But domestication terrified the daylights out of him.

Grey watched the cigar smoke rise into the air. "There are other rumors as well." His voice was still warm, but now, it took on a more serious tone. "That Strathmore has a new ward."

Edward slid him a suspicious glance. "You didn't hear that in a courting parlor."

"No."

"Are you spying on me now, Grey?" He took a large swallow of whiskey and bit out a laugh. "I'm not important enough for that."

"The Prince Regent has a parliament full of men he doesn't trust." His old friend's voice was low. "And he's very aware of what happens to rulers when the people become too powerful. And you—the new Duke of Strathmore, a former army colonel whose men would walk though fire if he asked them to, with a not-so-distant claim to the throne— your return has made Prinny very nervous. So when you do anything unexpected, it draws attention at the highest levels." Grey looked at him with concern, a subtle warning in his voice. "And your sudden guardianship has drawn attention."

Edward said nothing, forcing down his rising irritation at the mention of Kate. The last thing he wanted to talk about tonight was that damnable guardianship. And certainly not with Grey. Thomas was already driving him mad about it, still urging him to give up his revenge, and Augusta kept badgering him about returning Kate to Brambly. Neither of which he would do.

"I don't think you're doing a very good job of spying by telling me," Edward joked halfheartedly. "Bathurst should demand his promotion back."

"Oh, I'm certain he will sooner or later." With a sigh of resignation, he shook his head. "I'm not spying on you, Colonel, but as your friend, I am wondering the same thing. Why would Strathmore suddenly take a ward?"

He shrugged. "The child needed my help."

"And exactly what kind of help were you planning on giving a twenty-year-old child?"

Edward's hand froze in midair, the glass halfway to his lips. His gaze slid sideways to glare at Grey for a long moment, the aggravation inside him flashing to the surface. Instead of being cowed by his murderous look, though, the damned man only smiled more broadly.

"Her family has no political connections, no money, no title—all in all, a girl of no importance. I assured those concerned that Strathmore's interest was nothing more than charity." Grey puffed on his cigar and grinned at Edward's expense. "*Personal* charity, that is."

"Thank you," he bit out sarcastically. "How did you manage not to get shot by your own men?"

"Fast horse," Grey answered, deadpan.

The attendant handed Grey his drink, and he tossed a coin to the man. Then he flicked off the ash at the tip of his cigar, his brows drawing together.

"Of course, you and I both know that's not the real reason you became her guardian," Grey continued much more seriously. "You've never had to plot to seduce a woman. So perhaps the other rumor is actually true, that Strathmore's not only hunting a wife—" He paused pointedly. "He's found one."

"Ludicrous," he muttered, tossing back the remaining whiskey in a gasping swallow and wishing they would all just leave him alone.

With a shrug, Grey rolled the cigar thoughtfully between his fingers. "Make her the ward of a duke first, and her social worth is immediately elevated. Then, after you introduce her in silks and jewels, no one will give a second thought when you announce your engagement. You get the wife you want without the scandal. Is that your plan? If you don't deny it, that's what I'll report back."

Edward couldn't deny it. He'd once considered doing exactly that, but that was before Kate deceived him. "Since when does the War Office care about my personal life?"

"They don't. I'm here by order of a higher authority."

"Whose?" he demanded.

"The countess."

Augusta. Of course she was behind this. It wasn't enough that she insisted on pestering him about Kate herself; now she'd drafted his two closest friends to lead the charge, knowing he didn't have the heart to launch a counterattack against the two men who were like brothers to him. *Bloody hell.* The woman should have been a tactician for Wellington.

Edward clenched his jaw. "I made a mistake by taking her as my ward." He pushed himself out of the chair. "And you can tell my aunt that I have no intention of marrying anyone, least of all Katherine Benton."

Grey made no comment, but his expression declared that he clearly didn't believe him.

Thomas Matteson approached from behind and slapped him on the back. "Colonel!"

Edward rolled his eyes. "Should have known you two traveled as a pair."

"Two captains are better than one, that's what you always said," Thomas reminded him.

"Two *good* captains," Edward muttered irritably.

Which only earned him a grin from both men.

"The balding man by the door," he commented, turning their attention away from him and anxious to put an end to this conversation about Kate. "He's been watching me, too. He's one of your men, then?"

Grey's eyes settled on the man. "No."

"Never seen him before," Thomas seconded.

Instead of looking away at being caught staring, the man set his own glass aside and made his way through the crowded club toward them. Grey slowly stood, and the three men turned shoulder to shoulder, forming a solid, muscular front, just as they'd done many times before in Spain.

"Strathmore." The balding man stopped in front of Edward. "John Litchfield, baronet."

Edward's hard gaze raked coldly over him. "We have not been introduced."

Then he turned his back to the man and walked away. He didn't have the patience tonight for another pointless conversation, not with Grey and Thomas making the memory of Kate prickle beneath his skin.

"John Litchfield," the man repeated to Edward's retreating back, "the fiancé of your ward, Katherine Anne Benton."

Edward halted and slowly turned. *What the bloody hell did he say?*

A smug look registered on the man's face. "Is that enough of an introduction for you, Your Grace?"

Edward's jaw tightened, his fists clenching at his sides.

"Well, well," Grey murmured, his gaze moving back and forth between the two men.

Thomas nodded in agreement. "The evening just became interesting."

Ignoring their antics, Edward pinned Litchfield with an icy gaze. "You are mistaken. My ward has no fiancé."

"I signed a contract with her father," Litchfield announced loudly enough to draw the notice of the room, clearly enjoying having the full attention of the club focused on him at Edward's expense. "You have made a mockery of my engagement."

At that, Edward shrugged and started walking again. He'd made a mockery of lots of engagements, including his own brother's, and he couldn't care less what that bastard Benton signed—

"You have stolen what is rightfully mine!"

A collective gasp went up from the room, followed by whispers and open gaping as necks craned to watch

Edward's reaction. Everyone stared, including the staff, and waited breathlessly to see Strathmore's response.

Edward slowly faced Litchfield, his expression black. "What *exactly* is it," he asked, his voice even more threatening for all its cold control, "that you claim I've stolen from you?"

"My fiancée and her dowry."

"A stubborn woman and an indebted farm." He gave a bitter laugh. "You should consider yourself lucky in escaping."

The baronet held up a folded paper. "I have a contract that entitles me to her and her dowry. But now, you've stolen both."

Edward held out his hand, and Litchfield slapped it into his palm. He gave the document a cursory glance. "Her signature isn't on it," he drawled dismissively, handing it back.

"Her agreement isn't necessary. Her father and I made that contract five years ago before her majority."

"I refuse to honor it, and she most certainly will reject it." His gaze swept disdainfully over the paunchy, balding man. "And you."

Indignation flashed over Litchfield's face. "I say, that's insult—"

"Come now, Colonel!" Thomas positioned himself between the two men, his voice purposefully loud to draw their attention away from each other and the fisticuffs about to break out. "Haven't you figured it out yet? He doesn't want the chit. What he wants is money."

Litchfield's eyes glinted with quick fury. He opened his mouth to protest, but Thomas cut him off with a wave of his hand.

"Oh, she's pretty enough to wed, surely, but she's also in debt. And you know that, don't you, Litchfield?" Thomas slapped the man on the back, hard enough that he was forced forward a step by the blow. "She's the ward of a duke now, though, which means she's worth a lot more than the dowry you settled on. So now you're making a public row because you hope he'll void the contract and pay you to go away."

Litchfield shoved off Thomas's arm with a furious scowl that proved him correct. "Strathmore," he announced boldly, loudly enough to ensure that everyone in the club heard him, "I demand justice!"

At that, Edward's mouth curled up devilishly in a darkly amused smile. "Are you calling me out?"

Grey shook his head, silently warning the baronet to stop before he went too far, but Litchfield ignored him. "If it comes to that," he clarified, not smart enough to leave immediately. "I want justice for the wrongs you've committed against—"

"Fine!" Edward snarled. "Pistols at dawn on the green."

Litchfield sputtered, "But that's—"

"I'm the second," Thomas promptly offered.

"And me," Grey added.

"Good. At dawn then, Litchfield." Edward spun on his heels and stormed from the club.

Stares and whispers trailed in his wake, and slowly the room returned to normal, the men going back to their smoking and gambling, the staff to their duties. But the hum of excited gossip about Strathmore and the duel persisted and would do so straight on until dawn, although no one in the room seriously believed that the duke's honor was even remotely in question.

The baronet stared after him, his mouth hanging open, his eyes wide. "He—he really wants a duel?"

"The colonel's been looking for a fight for months," Thomas explained. "You just happened to be the first nodcock to give it to him."

"I didn't ask for a duel! He's the one who challenged—"

"Litchfield, I'm certain the manager will want you to settle your bill tonight." Grey popped his cigar between his teeth. "After all, you'll be dead at dawn."

"Is that supposed to frighten me?" he demanded, his indignant gaze swinging between the two men.

"Oh, definitely." Thomas slapped Litchfield on the shoulder again, once again felt him flinch. "Edward's the second-best shot in England."

The man stiffened. "Who's the first?"

"Me," both men answered at the same time, then looked at each other and grinned.

Litchfield paled.

"Either way." Grey shrugged. "Should be a good show."

Thomas trailed his gaze up and down the man, clearly sizing him up and just as clearly finding him lacking. He clucked his tongue in disappointment. "Won't last long, though."

"Pity." Grey shook his head regrettably as the two former captains walked away.

Behind them, Litchfield's knees gave out, and he sank down into the chair to keep from hitting the floor.

* * *

Dawn lightened the sky over London. Its cold, pale light created a thin haze beneath the trees framing the clearing at the edge of Hyde Park as Edward and Thomas stood waiting, shoulder to shoulder, facing in opposite directions so no one could surprise them.

"Think he'll show?" Thomas turned his coat collar against the cold.

"Yes," Edward answered quietly as he gazed across the empty stretch of green. If Litchfield possessed the audacity to challenge him in front of all of White's, he was certain to appear for the duel.

"It was Benton, you know." Thomas's breath clouded on the still air. "The reason why Litchfield pressed the contract, how he knew about the guardianship. Most likely they've agreed to split the money."

"I know." And Edward planned on making both men pay dearly for every pound.

The sound of approaching horses broke through the quiet. Thomas nodded toward the path. "Our man's arrived."

Edward's eyes narrowed as he watched Litchfield and his second dismount from their horses.

Dressed in black, with a jagged scar running the length of his cheek and disappearing beneath his cravat, his second remained behind with the horses and held on to their bridles rather than tying them. He was clearly a criminal, most likely hired by Litchfield because the man had no friends who would agree to second him.

The baronet wrung his gloved hands as he approached. "Strathmore."

"Litchfield," Edward countered coolly. "Still determined to go through with this?"

"Still determined to receive reparation for the wrongs you've done me."

"Well, then." Edward glanced up at the sky, now lightened to a golden yellow. "At least you picked a pretty morning to die."

Litchfield's face flushed. "There's no point in trying to intimidate me."

"I'm not trying." Edward looked at the man distastefully. "Who's your second?"

"Harry Pinkerton."

"How much did you pay him to be here?"

At the caught look that flashed across Litchfield's face before he gritted his teeth in contemptuous hostility, Edward knew he was right.

Thomas stepped between them. "Can we get this over with? It's damnably cold, and I have a soft bed and a warm woman waiting for me."

Movement and noise from the side of the field caught their attention. A dozen men who had been at White's last night and overheard the challenge made their way slowly up the sloping hill, still half-drunk from the night before and present for no other purpose than to gawk.

Also with them was Nathaniel Grey, who had been charged with fetching a surgeon on the unlikely chance someone was wounded. But judging from the grim looks on both their faces, neither man was happy, with the surgeon scowling in murderous resentment at having been woken so early to be present at such a ridiculous display and Grey grimacing at having been the one who roused him.

When he saw the surgeon, Litchfield's shoulders sagged. "We don't have to go through with this, I suppose."

Edward said nothing.

Thomas withdrew two pistols from beneath his greatcoat and held them out handle-first toward Pinkerton across the field, who only shook his head and looked away, not caring enough about Litchfield to even inspect the weapons. Thomas shrugged and presented the pistols to Litchfield for the man to choose his weapon.

Litchfield hesitated at the sight of the pistols. "Surely, Strathmore, you understand my situation."

Edward watched Thomas grin as he shoved the pistols toward Litchfield again, clearly enjoying the pantomime of this fiasco.

Litchfield's hand shook as he reluctantly selected one. "We don't have to—"

Edward snatched up the remaining pistol. "To the field." He removed his jacket and stalked away.

The baronet glanced hopefully at Thomas. According to the *code duello*, as the challenged man's second, he was supposed to attempt to broker an end to the duel before paces were taken and shots fired. Yet he did nothing to get apologies and find an agreement.

"Fine day to die!" Thomas declared, slapping the man on the back, then strolled away after Edward to the center of the field.

Litchfield gaped, his face paling. Pinkerton continued to stand off to the side by himself, not caring enough to try to intervene.

Litchfield had no choice but to step forward. His knees shook visibly with fear.

"You both know the code. Twelve paces, ready, then present," Thomas explained, going over the agreed-upon terms of the duel. "Called signal for firing, no rounds." Finally, he added, "Unless you're both willing to admit that this was nothing more than a misunderstanding."

"But I've been wronged," Litchfield sniveled. "My honor is at stake."

"Oh, for God's sake!" Edward reached inside his waistcoat to withdraw a bundle of banknotes. "Take the damned blunt. We'll count off twelve paces, then you'll delope. I'll accept your apology, and you'll live. And if you bother me again," he threatened, his voice ice, "I'll sink a bullet straight into your heart."

With a visible look of relief, Litchfield seized the money from his hand and shoved it into his jacket pocket. "Glad to be rid of the gel, actually. She and that worthless farm would've sucked my accounts dry." A pleased grin spread across his face. "Tupping her was the best thing you could have done for me, Strathmore. The money's just cream—"

Edward's fist slammed into the man's jaw, the force of the blow dropping him sprawling to the ground. "Don't *ever* speak of her again!"

Litchfield moaned and held his mouth as a trickle of blood spilled from his cracked lip.

Thomas grabbed Edward's arm and pushed him back, glancing over his shoulder at Litchfield while he simultaneously watched both men and prevented Edward from truly killing the baronet this morning. Across the field, Litchfield's second never moved, his presence completely mercenary.

"Feel better now?" Thomas asked sardonically.

"Much." Edward glared at Litchfield as he scrambled to his feet and swiped at his bloody lip with the back of his hand. The crowd of gawkers laughed.

"Twelve paces, then!" Thomas called out, marshaling the two men back-to-back in the center of the field to end the charade. "One, two..."

As Thomas counted off, he retreated to the side and watched the two men stalk away from each other.

"...Eleven, twelve...turn!"

The two men faced each other.

Thomas called, "Ready?"

"Ready." Edward's hard gaze never left Litchfield as his answer came loud and decisive.

"Yes...I'm ready." Even from nearly twenty-five yards away, Edward heard the nervous trembling in the man's voice.

"Present!"

Each man raised his pistol.

After a moment's pause, Edward lowered his pistol to his side and waited. Litchfield would delope by firing into the ground at the side of the field, effectively giving his apology, then Edward would do the same, accepting it. His honor would be upheld, and Litchfield would leave with his blackmail blunt. Everyone would go home as if nothing had ever happened, except for the gossip, which would linger for weeks—

The sound of a gunshot echoed through the trees, and Edward flinched.

For a moment, there was no movement on the field except for the small trail of smoke rising from the end of Litchfield's pistol as he held it, still pointed directly at Edward.

Litchfield stared at the spent pistol in his hand, eyes wide, as if he couldn't believe that he'd actually fired at the duke. Shocked whispers went up from the startled crowd.

"I didn't—I didn't mean to—I was only supposed to get the money!" Litchfield threw the pistol to the ground as if it burned him. He stared incredulously across the field at

Edward, who hadn't moved an inch. "I wasn't thinking—
the trigger just—"

Slowly, Edward raised his pistol and pointed it at Litchfield's chest. "Run," he snarled.

Litchfield raced toward his waiting horse.

Edward fired. The bullet pierced through Litchfield's
beaver hat, shooting it cleanly from his balding head. The
baronet froze in his steps as all the blood drained from his
face and a wet circle formed at the crotch of his breeches.

"The next time I see you," Edward growled, "I'll aim
lower."

Amid jeers from the crowd, Litchfield scrambled onto
his horse and galloped away, hanging half off his saddle in
his rush to flee. The onlookers roared with laughter. Litchfield had taken the shot, but his cowardice in fleeing only
bolstered Edward's honor in the eyes of the crowd.

Pinkerton doffed his hat at Thomas and Edward, then
mounted his horse and slowly trotted away across the park
in the opposite direction. The man couldn't have cared less
what happened to Litchfield.

The onlookers sent up raucous cheers for Edward and
raised in toasts to the duke the bottles of liquor they'd
brought with them. A rowdy drinking song broke through
the morning stillness.

Shaking his head at the debacle, Thomas sighed in relief
that the show was over and turned toward Edward, still
standing in the middle of the field.

"Thomas," he whispered.

Then he crumpled to the ground, blood blossoming at
his chest.

CHAPTER FOURTEEN

$\mathcal{K}$ate gave a wide yawn.

She wasn't tired, but she didn't want to subject herself to one minute more of evening embroidery than necessary, and she'd already feigned illness so many times that Mrs. Lutz had actually sent for a physician, so there was no getting out of it that way again. Yet the housekeeper seemed adamant that needlepoint was a hobby all ladies should do, apparently even those isolated away in the moors. But it bored Kate stiff, and instead of pricking her fingers, she'd rather be up in her room, plotting her escape.

She'd been at Greymoor for three weeks now, and her life had fallen into one of well-ordered regimentation. Thanks to Mrs. Lutz and "His Grace his orders."

The housekeeper woke Kate every morning at dawn for two hours of Bible study—in German, so whatever religious epiphany the woman envisioned was destined never to occur—followed by hours of cleaning, mending, and cooking. And needlepoint by the firelight before Kate was promptly sent to her room at eight o'clock.

It had been a hard three weeks under Mrs. Lutz's supervision, but Kate was more determined than ever to find a way home. And she *would* leave. Somehow.

She still had no solid strategy yet for returning to Brambly, but the planning gave her hope, and her anger at Edward kept her motivated. Where once she'd dedicated nearly every spare moment to her experiments and medicines, here in the moors, scheming to escape had become her raison d'être.

In the meantime, however, she didn't know how many more of these disciplined days with Mrs. Lutz she could endure.

When the housekeeper didn't pause in her cross-stitch, Kate yawned again, this time a loud, exaggerated noise.

Mrs. Lutz finally glanced up.

"My apologies." Kate feigned regret and another yawn. "I'll go up to bed now. And we'll do it all again tomorrow." She rose before the woman could stop her. "*Gute Nacht.*"

Mrs. Lutz began to shoot her a disapproving frown, but then the old woman's face softened with a long-suffering sigh. "*Ja, gute Nacht.*"

Well. *That* was a surprise. The strict widow was certainly not won over by her yet, but perhaps she was softening just a bit—

A clatter went up outside, followed by shouts. The sound of a horse on the cobblestones pulling up quickly from a gallop shattered the evening's stillness, and seconds later, a fist pounded against the wooden door.

"A message!" A man's voice rang out between knocks. "From London!"

Hurrying to the door, Kate yanked it open wide. A young rider stood on the steps, his hat and slicker wet from the drizzling rain. Splattered mud dirtied his boots, dark circles framed his tired eyes, and he reeked of sweat and horse.

"A message from London," he repeated, looking from one woman to the other. "Which one of you is Katherine Benton?"

"Me," Kate whispered, sudden fear knotting her throat. She trembled. Something was terribly wrong. "What is it?"

"The Countess of Tourney sent a message for you." He pulled a note from his coat and handed it to her, then his tired eyes glanced past her into the dry warmth of the house. "I've been riding hard since yesterday morning, miss. If you don't mind, I'd like to get some food and sleep before returning."

"Of course." Kate stared at the note in her trembling hand and resisted the anxious urge to rip it open. "There's stew in the kitchen and a bed for you upstairs. You can stable your horse in the barn."

"Thank you, miss." He touched the brim of his hat with a polite nod and left to tend to his horse.

Taking a deep, shaking breath, she stared down at the note, the cardstock heavy in her fingers, and her heart somersaulted with gathering dread, so hard her chest ached. What would Edward's aunt want with her? She was nothing to the woman, certainly no one who rated a special messenger.

"His Grace?" Mrs. Lutz asked nervously.

"No," she answered gravely, "her ladyship, the countess."

"Countess?" Awe laced her voice.

So, special messages from the countess rarely traveled to Greymoor, and that realization only sickened her stomach even more. Unable to resist any longer, her fingers trembling, Kate broke the seal and unfolded the paper. Her eyes scanned the short message—

Miss Benton,

My nephew, Edward Westover, your guardian, was gravely wounded this morning, shot in a duel. Dr. Brandon is attending him, but he fears there is little that can be done. I beg you to keep him in your thoughts and prayers.

Augusta Monvielle
Countess of Tourney

"Edward," she whispered, the breath ripping from her lungs and her body flashing numb.

She stared at the letter, not believing the message even as she read it over and over until the words blurred from the hot tears filling her eyes. Her heart squeezed so hard in her chest she winced at the sharp pain.

Gravely wounded...*Dear God, no*—Edward was *dying*!

Clutching the note to her breast as the room spun around her, she reached for the banister to keep from falling and forced herself to breathe. The thought of Edward wounded and covered with blood, crumpled on the ground in agony—*Breathe!* But her stomach lurched, and she pressed her hand hard to her mouth to keep from casting up her accounts as paralyzing fear and worry swirled inside her.

Oh God, please let him be all right!

And then the agony that pulsed through her so intensely she couldn't breathe for the harshness of it squeezing around her heart gave way, replaced instantly by a flash of outrage. That damnably aggravating, maddening, arrogant, controlling man! He'd believed the worst of her, and because of that he'd banished her half a country away, where now she could do nothing to help him. The tears of fear clinging to her lashes turned to hot drops of restrained fury.

"His Grace?" Mrs. Lutz prompted gently.

Kate glanced up at Mrs. Lutz and swiped her hand hard across her eyes, then nodded.

Confusion and deep worry wrinkled the old housekeeper's face, and Kate's heart panged sympathetically as she instantly realized how much Mrs. Lutz cared about Edward, how afraid she was for him. Just as much as she was.

Resting her hand on the woman's arm, Kate took a deep breath. "Edward's been hurt—shot." When the old woman only stared at her blankly, not understanding, Kate made a gun with her finger and thumb. "Edward...bang."

Mrs. Lutz crossed herself quickly. "Dead?"

"No!" Kate cried out, horrified that she'd even dare utter such a thing. "No, he's not!"

If she denied it hard enough, then it wouldn't come true—it *couldn't*! Edward couldn't die, not before she had the chance to see him again, not while he still hated her for loving him.

As the old woman frowned, struggling to understand, Kate felt sorry for her for the first time since she'd arrived at Greymoor. "He'll be fine," she declared firmly, to reassure herself as much as Mrs. Lutz. "*Good.* Yes?"

"Yes!" Mrs. Lutz squeezed her hand, and Kate gave a soft sob. The small gesture was the first friendly one she'd received from the woman, one that left Kate just as stunned as the news in the countess's note.

Then the old housekeeper returned to her chair, picked up her Bible, and began to pray for Edward.

Kate looked down at the note, still clutched so tightly in her hand that the paper had crumpled in her fist. Nothing in Augusta's message suggested that the countess wanted Kate to come to London and be by Edward's side, but that was exactly where she wanted to be. Where she *needed* to be.

She knew what she had to do.

And *nothing* was going to stop her.

Her heart racing anxiously, Kate waited just long enough to make certain that Mrs. Lutz was deep in her prayers before slipping unseen downstairs to the kitchen, where the messenger's wet slicker and hat were laid across a chair in front of the stove to dry. Without hesitating, she pulled them on, then silently slipped out the kitchen door.

Within minutes, she'd saddled the horse in the dark barn. The animal blew out a tired snort and shook at the saddle that once again weighted his back.

"I'm sorry, pretty. I know you want to rest, but I don't have a choice. You're the only horse here." Biting her lip guiltily, she brushed her hand over its soft muzzle. "If I promise not to make you gallop, will you be a good boy for me? Just a few miles to the next village, where I'll make certain you get lots of oats and hay."

The horse pawed at the ground. Taking that as much of a consent as she was going to get, she stepped into the stirrup and climbed into the saddle, sitting astride.

With a prayer, she clucked her tongue softly and sent the

horse toward the village, where she could catch the mail coach and, one way or another, eventually make her way to London.

And to Edward.

* * *

The butler frowned irritably with no intention of stepping aside to let Kate pass into the front hall of Strathmore House.

"Keep your voice down!" he scolded. "Midnight has struck."

"Please, let me in," Kate pleaded from the front portico. "I'm Katherine Benton." When his blank expression showed no recognition, she repeated slowly, "Kate Benton," adding hesitantly, "Strathmore's ward."

He scowled in disbelief. "No proper young lady would be out in the night alone at this hour, pounding on doors and demanding admittance—and certainly not looking like *that*!"

He nodded toward the messenger's rain-soaked coat and hat she still wore over the muddy shoes and dirty black dress beneath.

Oh, she knew she looked shameful—and judging from the way he wrinkled his nose, she most likely smelled even worse—but she'd been too worried to stop or freshen her appearance since leaving Greymoor two nights ago. Knowing she wouldn't have been able to sleep, not when her worried mind kept spinning back to Edward, she'd simply kept going, at first riding through the night on the horse, then as fast as the mail coach could take her when she'd finally caught up with it.

She wasn't naïve. Edward believed the worst of her, and in that Kate doubted she could ever forgive him. But she couldn't bear the thought that Edward might die still hating her.

"Please, I need to see His Grace!"

The butler began to close the door. "Good night!"

Tears of exhaustion gathered in her eyes. To come so close, knowing Edward was lying just upstairs—she might as well have still been in the middle of the moors if she let the door close on her. No, she was *not* leaving!

With a quick step forward, she jammed herself into the doorframe. The butler would have to cut her in two to seal her out now.

"Her ladyship, the countess," she blurted out frantically, "sent a message to me." Her fingers dug into her pocket after the note. "I came as quickly as I could." When he glowered at her in disbelief, she gave a soft cry of frustration and shoved the message at him. "Please! Tell her I'm here." A stab of desperate fear sickened her. "I need to see Strathmore. I *have* to…"

"Miss! Her ladyship is not receiving—"

"Kingsley," a female voice called out from the stairs. "What on earth is the matter down there?"

A slender woman in her mid-fifties appeared on the bottom step of the sweeping marble stairs. Despite the events of the past few days and the late hour, she appeared alert and imposing, impossibly regal in a dark lavender dress and matching cashmere wrap, her gold-gray hair swept up high. She stared coldly at Kate, still wedged stubbornly into the doorway. His aunt Augusta. There was no mistaking the family resemblance.

"Apologies for disturbing you, m' lady." Kingsley stepped

back from the door and inclined his head. "This woman is refusing to leave."

Kate slipped past him into the entry hall and dropped into an awkward curtsy, her body stiff and sore. "I'm sorry, my lady, but I couldn't wait until morning—"

"This house is closed to visitors." Augusta cut her off with a wave of her hand. "Show her out, Kingsley."

"Yes, ma'am." He reached for Kate's arm.

She snatched herself free. "Edward—I have to see him!" She hurried across the foyer to Augusta and stared at her pleadingly, putting her hand up frantically to stop Kingsley from physically ejecting her. "Is he—" Her voice choked, unable to force herself to utter the word *dead*. "Better?"

Augusta's eyes flickered with recognition. "You must be Miss Benton."

Kate nodded. "I came as quickly as I could."

"That message was not intended as a summons. But now that you are here..." The countess swept her gaze over Kate, wrinkling her nose at the condition of her dress and hair—and certainly at the smell. "However, given that my nephew fought that duel over you, I doubt he will be happy to see you when he wakes."

Despite his aunt's grim warning, her chest lightened with desperate hope. "Then—I'm not too late?"

"Strathmore is alive." A weary smile touched the countess's lips.

A wave of overwhelming relief swept through her, and hot tears stung at her eyes. "Oh, thank God... Is he here?" Glancing up the stairs, she hesitated only a moment before racing past Augusta. "Edward!"

Reaching the second-floor landing, Kate saw a footman standing outside one of the doors at the end of the wide hall, and she ran toward the room. He was inside, she knew it!

"Please, let me pass," she pleaded, but she was prepared to shove the man aside and charge into the room if she had to.

The footman glanced over her head at Augusta as the countess reached the top of the stairs. Augusta gave a nod of consent, and he stepped aside.

Taking a deep breath to steel herself against what she might see, she entered slowly. Her gaze swept around the large room, moving over the pieces of large, heavy furniture and the wine-colored velvet and silk fabrics. A fire burned brightly in the fireplace, and the draperies on the tall windows were pulled to seal out the damp night.

But it was the bed that commanded her attention—a massive piece, its four mahogany posts carved like grapevines spiraling toward the ceiling and reaching over twelve feet tall and nearly as wide. Gold ropes tied back the wine-colored drapes, and behind those, between black satin sheets shimmering in the firelight...

"Edward," she whispered.

He lay propped against the pillows, bare from the waist up except for the large bandage marring the sculpted muscle where his shoulder met his chest. His eyes closed, he looked as if he was sleeping peacefully, but as she approached, she saw beads of perspiration dotting his forehead, his lips dry, his face pale.

She sat on the chair beside the bed and reached for his hand. "Edward? It's Kate. I'm here." She tenderly brushed his damp hair away from his feverish forehead. "Can you hear me?"

"Miss?" A surprised voice cut through the heavy silence. "What do you think you're doing?"

She glanced up as a darkly dressed, gray-haired man rose from a chair in the corner. Obviously the physician keeping a nighttime vigil. Dismissing him quickly, her attention returned immediately to Edward.

"Who are—"

"Doctor, please." She had no patience now for questions about herself. "Tell me, how is he? Truthfully."

He glanced at the countess, and Augusta nodded.

"Not well, I'm afraid," he answered gently. "He's drifted in and out of consciousness for the past few days, and I've been doing my best to keep the fever down and his strength up."

She held her breath, needing to know the worst... "Has infection set in?"

"There was tremendous blood loss, but the wound was clean. Fortunately, the surgeon was present—"

Her eyes shot up and pinned him as dread clenched her belly. "Then you didn't remove the bullet yourself?"

His nose wrinkled in distaste at the thought of such bloody work. "I am a physician, miss!"

"And I'm certain you do a remarkable job." She smoothed his feathers with a forced smile. Her eyes dropped to Edward's shoulder. "But I was wondering about the wound... Is that the original dressing?"

"Of course," he answered, as if humoring a child. "The wound has to heal uninterrupted until the sutures are removed tomorrow."

Tomorrow. Her chest tightened with quick worry. Four days under the original bandages and sutures—the standard medical treatment for bullet wounds. But common

wisdom among country doctors said otherwise, to leave the
sutures in place longer to give the flesh time to grow into
itself.

More upsetting, though, was that the original dressing
was still in place. The wound hadn't been checked since
the ball was removed.

"May I see it?" She reached for the bandage on
Edward's chest.

The doctor grabbed her arm. "What do you think you're
doing?"

Saving his life! She inhaled a calming breath. "You
haven't looked at the wound," she explained as gently as
possible despite the anxious fear gripping her chest like a
vise. "It could be infected."

"I have been giving him medicines to keep the infec-
tions at bay."

She shook her head. "Dominique-Jean Larrey wrote in
a paper last winter that leaving on the original dressings
heightened the chances for infection—"

"A surgeon," he dismissed with a distasteful frown.
"And French!"

"Dr. Brandon," the countess interrupted quietly, "would
you give us a moment, please?"

"Yes, my lady." Despite his obvious irritation at having
his medical expertise questioned, by a woman no less, he
inclined his head politely and left the room.

Augusta nodded her consent. "You may proceed, Miss
Benton."

"Thank you," Kate whispered gratefully to the countess.

She turned back to the wound, trying to ignore the helpless way Edward looked as he lay so still. Her hands shook
as she removed the bandage, carefully freeing it from the

dried blood and flesh, which had started to congeal into the fabric. When it was finally removed it, she took a close, long look at the wound. Black sutures sewn haphazardly closed the gash where the surgeon dug to retrieve the ball, the skin bruised and swollen. Her heart burned at the sight. Such an ugly wound, so carelessly tended...

But no sign of infection, and she heaved a heavy sigh. Oh, thank God, *thank God*!

She reached for the cloth in the basin beside the bed, soaked it in the cool water, then touched it gently to the wound to cleanse it as best she could without disturbing the sutures. She wished she had a jar of her salve with her, although the sight of her country medicine might just give Dr. Brandon apoplexy.

Augusta watched her closely. "You truly know what you are doing, then?"

"Yes, I do." She reached for the fresh bandages on the bedside table, put there no doubt in anticipation of the scheduled suture removal in the morning.

"Strathmore said you kept medicines and tended to the villagers."

She carefully covered the wound. "So he spoke of me."

"Yes."

Unfavorably, Kate was certain, given the single-word response. But the countess had not yet removed her from the house, so his aunt most likely didn't know everything. There was hope in that, at least.

"When I received your note, I was so afraid..." Her voice died away. Then, physically shaking herself to fight back the exhaustion and emotion, she wrapped the shoulder to hold the new dressing in place and asked quietly, "What happened?"

"A foolish duel." Augusta scowled, her eyes glued to her nephew's sallow face. "With Baronet Litchfield."

Not recognizing the name, Kate focused her attention on Edward and dipped the cloth in the basin's cool water, then dabbed it against his feverish face. His skin was so hot, so pale, that worry churned in her gut.

"Your former fiancé."

Her hand stilled in stunned surprise against Edward's cheek. *A fiancé?* Impossible. "You're mistaken, my lady."

"Five years ago, your father contracted your engagement to Baronet Litchfield—" When Kate's mouth fell open, Augusta cut her off with a wave of her hand before she could protest her innocence. "Who accused Strathmore of thwarting your betrothal. I am certain he thought he'd be paid reparations, but the situation grew out of hand."

"I had no idea," she whispered, guilt sickening her as she stared at Edward's pale face. Anguish gripped like iron fingers around her heart that he would be hurt over her, and she forced herself to breathe. "I would never do anything to hurt him. I..." *I love him.*

"Tell me, then, Miss Benton." The countess's eyes narrowed on her. "Are you here out of concern for my nephew or out of your desire to return to Brambly House?"

Sudden outrage sparked through her. How could his aunt ask such a horrible question? "I came for Edward," she bit out, but at the countess's disbelieving expression, she shook her head and looked back at Edward. "You don't believe me. Well, I don't care one whit if you don't!"

"Miss Benton!" Augusta was aghast at her flippant boldness. "I am beginning to understand why my nephew is so preoccupied with you, because you two share the same complete disregard for manners."

"Yes, I suppose we do." A faint smile pulled at her lips at that bittersweet connection to Edward. "I know you can call for the footmen and have me physically removed. But you should know that in the past few weeks, I was sent away from my home to the moors, then forced to flee from even there in order to rush here." She rested her hand tenderly against his cheek. "So having been through all that, there is little you can do to make me fear you."

"Well, I have *never*—" Augusta stopped. Then, her expression grew curious. "Tell me," she asked, her voice unexpectedly soft, "how *did* you get here from Greymoor, Miss Benton?"

Deciding she had nothing to lose, Kate raised her chin and boldly met her gaze. "When the messenger brought your note, I took his horse and rode through the night until I caught up with the mail coach. Then I sold the horse and bought a ticket to London."

Augusta's face carefully concealed her thoughts in yet another stark resemblance to Edward. "The mail coach doesn't come into Mayfair at night."

"I know. I walked the last three miles."

Kate thought she saw something close to pleased admiration flash in the countess's eyes, but it was gone instantly. "So the Duke of Strathmore's ward is also a horse thief," Augusta commented dryly.

That thought had occurred to Kate, too, while she'd been riding across the moors. "I'll pay Edward back… somehow." She frowned at the impossibility of ever being able to do that on Brambly's meager revenues. "So now I guess you *can* do me harm. You can have me arrested."

"I shall remember that for the future should it become necessary," Augusta assured her. Her lips twitched.

"Strathmore will undoubtedly be impressed when he hears what you've done."

At that, Kate's cheeks flushed, although she very much doubted it. The moment he woke he'd most likely send her right back to Greymoor. "Thank you for letting me see him."

"I want what is best for my nephew."

Her eyes stung. "So do I."

Both women gazed at Edward then, his body so terribly still except for the slow rise and fall of his bandaged chest.

"There is nothing more you can do for him tonight," Augusta informed her quietly, placing a gentle hand on Kate's shoulder. "The housekeeper will prepare a room for you so you can rest." She scrunched her nose at the odor of horse. "And bathe."

"Let me stay with him," she pleaded. "I'll keep out of the doctor's way, I promise."

"Very well," Augusta consented with a regal lift of her brow. "Although it seems to me, Miss Benton, that Dr. Brandon would be wise to stay out of yours."

Kate looked up and pleadingly met the countess's gaze. "Please don't let them take out the sutures tomorrow. Let them stay in a few more days."

Augusta contemplated her, as if weighing the situation, then nodded. "If you feel that is the right—"

But Kate had already turned back to Edward, his hand tightly held in both of hers.

"Edward," Kate whispered, desperate to make him hear her, "please wake up."

No response. His eyes stayed closed, his body still.

"Just as stubborn as ever, I see," she chided in her best governess voice, although it trembled with worry. "Well, I'm not going anywhere, do you hear?"

She leaned forward to touch her lips to his feverish forehead, closing her eyes against the warmth, the familiar masculine scent, and the salty taste of him. So much had happened between them, such vulnerability and need, then the tenderness plunged into animosity... Yet he was alive, the blood still pulsing through him, and that was all that mattered now.

"Since I know how much you detest me," she forced out as her throat tightened, "you'd better wake up and tell me to leave if you want the torture of my presence to stop. Otherwise, my darling, you are stuck with me."

Sitting back in the chair, settling in for the night, she was determined to bring him back to her, and if he really could hear her, he was going to be furious when he woke. But if his anger made him better, then she'd gladly accept it. She would do whatever it took to nurse him to health.

And then she planned on throttling him to within an inch of his life for making her worry.

"You sent me to the moors, so I think I should reciprocate by telling you about every minute I spent at Greymoor." She paused. "Ready to wake up? No? All right then, you leave me no choice. Let's start with Bible study, in German."

She didn't see Augusta silently watching and listening from the doorway before finally leaving for her own suite of rooms, a knowing expression on her face.

* * *

Just before dawn, Edward's eyes fluttered open, blinking, and filled with confusion. His foggy brain had no idea where he was, what had happened, what time it was. His body was both pained and numb, stiff and cold, his limbs too heavy to move. He couldn't lift his head from the pillow. It took every ounce of his strength just to keep his eyelids from closing again.

But he felt a light pressure against his hand...warm, soft, secure. He glanced down—

And saw her.

She was asleep, sitting on a chair beside the bed but leaning her body forward onto the edge of the mattress, with her head resting gently on her left forearm while her right hand clasped his tightly even in her sleep, her fingers laced through his. As if she were afraid he might slip away.

"Angel," he whispered.

Then his eyes closed, and he drifted back into unconsciousness.

CHAPTER FIFTEEN

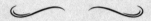

$\mathscr{A}$ugusta found Kate the next morning still sitting at Edward's side. Blinking away the foggy confusion of sleep, she sat up and stretched her aching back.

She'd stayed by his side all night, applying cold compresses to his forehead and draping damp sheets over his body until his fever broke shortly before dawn, but once it did, she still found herself mopping his brow, still brushing her fingertips across his face...anything to keep touching him and feeling the warm pulse that continued to grow stronger. When exhaustion finally overcame her, she'd slipped into a deep but troubled sleep.

"Dr. Brandon would like to examine Edward in private," Augusta informed her.

Kate glanced toward the physician as he entered, his

leather bag in his hand, then reluctantly agreed to leave, knowing she had no choice.

"Since you will be away from him for a while," Augusta explained as she linked her arm through Kate's and escorted her down the hall, "you might as well freshen up. I have had this room prepared for you." Augusta led her inside a pretty yellow-and-cream-colored bedroom, where a steaming bath already waited. "I will have a breakfast tray sent up for you."

"Thank you," Kate agreed, too tired to protest. Despite her desire to remain at Edward's side, her body ached, and a hot, soothing bath tempted her more than she wanted to admit. So did breakfast, since she couldn't remember the last time she'd eaten.

Once Augusta left, she stripped quickly and sank into the hot water, a long, grateful sigh escaping her as the heat loosened her stiff muscles. No bath in the history of the world had ever felt this marvelous.

Kate remained in the bath until the water grew tepid and the tension eased from her body, and after finally washing away the dirt and odors of her flight from the moors, she felt much, much better. But heavens, she was exhausted! A dressing robe had been left for her, so she slipped into it, and then, unable to stop herself, crawled into bed. Her heavy eyes closed, and she fell into sweet sleep.

When she woke hours later, the long-case clock on the stairway landing chimed one, and sunlight streamed through the tall windows. She climbed off the bed and stretched.

A soft knock sounded at the door.

"Yes?"

The door opened, and a maid carried in a tray. "Tea,

miss?" Smiling at Kate, she set it down on the table. "The countess requested it for you."

"Thank you." Kate warmed at Augusta's thoughtfulness when she could have ejected her from the house. Good fortune with the Westovers. For once. "How is His Grace?"

"Don't know, miss." She poured a cup and handed it to Kate. "But her ladyship did say to let her know when you were up. If you don't need me, I'll tell her."

"Thank you."

The maid nodded. "Try the lemon biscuits," she urged secretively. "They're delicious!"

Kate fought back a smile at the young maid's exuberance. Instead of taking one, she reached for the plate covered with biscuits and little iced cakes and held it out to the girl. "Please, help yourself—I won't tell."

The maid hesitated at what was clearly a breach of household etiquette, then gratefully took two lemon biscuits and slipped them into her apron pocket. "You're a kind one, miss!" Her eyes shined. "I'm Mary, one of the upstairs housemaids. But her ladyship asked that I be your lady's maid while you're here." Almost in afterthought, she gave a small curtsy, then nervously admitted, "I've never been a lady's maid before."

"Then we shall get along splendidly," Kate assured her, "because I've never had a lady's maid before."

"La! A fine lady like you?"

Kate felt a blush rise in her cheeks at the earnest compliment. She was the furthest thing from a fine lady. "Why don't you find the countess and tell her I'm awake?"

"Yes, miss!" She turned to scurry away.

"Oh, Mary?"

"Miss?"

Kate glanced around the room. "Where are my clothes?"

"Those filthy black things?" The little maid wrinkled her nose.

Kate nodded as she raised the cup to her lips and took a sip.

"Why, her ladyship burned 'em!"

She choked on her tea.

The little maid slipped away, and fighting down her amused laughter, Kate took a good look at her new room. Lace-edged velvet curtains fell from ceiling to floor, matching the drapes on the four-poster bed, and pillows sat piled high on a well-cushioned settee before a small fireplace with a carved ivory mantel. Paintings of flowers decorated the walls. The room was beautiful and feminine, filled with soft fabrics, utterly lovely, and so completely unlike her room at Greymoor.

Her throat tightened. During the past few years, even at Brambly, she'd forgotten what it was like to have such fine luxuries.

"Miss Benton, you are awake." Augusta swept regally into the room, eyeing her critically. "You are also well rested, then?"

"Yes—and His Grace? How is he?"

A faint smile of relief tugged at her lips. "Brandon thinks he is improving. His pulse is stronger, his color is better. And I have dissuaded him from removing the sutures, for now."

"Oh, thank goodness," she sighed, pressing her hand against her worried chest and deeply inhaling a great breath of relief.

Kate suspected the countess hadn't dissuaded the doctor so much as simply commanded him to leave the sutures alone, and Kate doubted anyone defied her orders. But she found herself beginning to like this woman who reminded her so much of Edward. They both possessed that hard Westover exterior that disguised a genuine warmth and humor beneath.

The countess called over her shoulder, "Mary?"

The young maid hurried into the room, a dress draped over her arm. She handed it to the countess.

Augusta held it up in front of Kate, checking the fit and length. In sage-green sprigged muslin with cream-colored lace trimming the square-cut neckline and capped sleeves, it fell gracefully to the floor from its high waist.

She nodded, pleased. "This will do nicely until your new wardrobe arrives."

"Wardrobe?" Kate repeated, not certain she'd heard correctly. "But I don't need a new wardrobe."

"My dear." Augusta's gaze leveled on her. "You are the ward of the Duke of Strathmore, and you cannot go about London looking like a German Puritan." She shook her head. "Whatever had Mrs. Lutz been thinking when she gave you that black monstrosity?"

"His Grace his orders," she mumbled.

The countess ignored that and handed the dress back to the maid, but Kate thought she saw a twitch of consternation at the woman's lips. "It is Edward's responsibility as your guardian to provide a suitable wardrobe. That," she informed her in a tone that signified she would brook no contradiction, "and all the other things I plan on informing him he will do for you."

Before she could ask what those other things were, Mary helped her into the dress and began to fasten up the row of tiny pearl buttons at her back.

"It's beautiful." Kate had never worn a dress this fashionable before. "Whose dress is it?" It was much too young in style to belong to the countess, and Edward had never mentioned a sister.

"It was one of Jane's, but she never wore it."

"It's lovely." Kate smiled at her reflection in the mirror. "Who's Jane?"

Augusta hesitated. "Edward never mentioned Jane? Nor Stephen?"

"No."

"You truly know nothing of the accident?" She stared at her disbelievingly. "Dear Lord, neither Edward nor your father ever told you..."

"No." Kate held her breath, waiting with dread, knowing something horrible was coming. Edward said her father hurt his family, but she'd always assumed it was over money. But an accident... "Tell me, please."

"Mary, give us privacy," Augusta ordered gently.

Nodding, the little maid fastened the last button, then left the room.

Augusta closed the door. She paused before turning back to Kate, as if weighing her words. "A little over a year ago, your father was gone for several weeks and was completely out of contact with you."

Kate grimaced. Papa was rarely in contact unless to ask for money or demand she give him Brambly, but the countess was correct. Last year he had been out of touch for much longer than usual. "He'd gone to Portsmouth. He'd invested in a ship that sank and had to settle the accounts." But everything she thought she knew about her father was proving to be a lie, and her chest squeezed painfully, knowing the answer even before she asked, "There was no ship, was there?"

"No."

"Then where was he?"

"In prison, awaiting trial." Her pulse pounded in her ears, so loud and violent she could barely hear as Augusta confirmed her worst fears. "For murder."

She steeled herself. "Who?"

"Edward's brother and sister-in-law."

Oh God, no... A sickening shudder convulsed through her. No—that was *impossible*! The world tilted beneath her, and she grabbed for Augusta's arm to keep from falling.

"Sit, my dear." Augusta led her to the settee.

Kate sank into the cushions and let her head fall into her hand as she fought to keep back the flood of emotions roiling inside her. And somehow remember to breathe.

"Edward had an older brother named Stephen," Augusta continued, sitting beside her and holding tightly to Kate's hand. "The two boys adored each other, and neither had a closer friend in the world. Stephen inherited Strathmore, and Edward joined the army." Her lips pressed grimly into a thin line at the memory. "Then, last year, the carriage carrying Stephen and his wife Jane was struck by a phaeton. The other driver had been drunk, racing his horses recklessly. Stephen and Jane..." Her voice choked, and she cleared her throat before continuing, "They were both killed."

Kate knew instinctively—her father was the other driver, the man who robbed Edward of his family. She pressed her hand against her stomach to keep from being sick as the nausea boiled inside her. She felt a hot, wet sensation on her cheek, and she wiped her fingers against it, not realizing in her stunned shock that she was crying.

"Edward was in Spain when it happened. He arrived

home as soon as he could, but by then, the magistrates had deemed the collision an accident. Edward was helpless to obtain justice."

Understanding fell upon her like a crushing weight. The fury she'd seen in Edward, the harshness, the coldness. Every time he looked at her, he must have been reminded of his brother and the accident, yet he'd protected her, helped her with Brambly—and through it all, she'd foolishly defended her father. Worse, she'd defied him and sent money. *Oh no . . .* Her chest clenched with guilt and remorse as she realized why he'd been so furious at her, why he'd been so upset at a single letter. Why he'd had to send her away to the moors to get her as far away from him as he could.

He thought she'd sided with the enemy.

"Edward swore to destroy your father, just as he had destroyed Stephen, so he took away his money and possessions, and then he took away as much of his freedom as he could by having him followed wherever he goes and watched at every moment." Augusta drew a regretful breath. "Phillip Benton is not a captive prisoner, but he might as well be, as his entire life is now controlled by Edward."

His entire life . . . No more of his gambling or drinking, no more reckless spending or ill-conceived business ventures, no more whoring—her father's life as he had lived it was over, and knowing Papa, he must have believed that Edward had thrust him into hell. Yet that punishment was extraordinarily merciful when Papa could have swung at the gallows for killing a peer.

But it didn't explain everything. "The guardianship—" Kate blinked her tear-blurred eyes, shaking her head. "Why would Edward agree to that?"

"Revenge."

Kate froze. Her heart stopped. "*Revenge?*"

"A life for a life. Your father took Stephen from him, so Edward took you from your father." Augusta grimaced. "Unfortunately, when Edward discovered that the child he'd expected was actually a grown woman, he was certain Benton tricked him, and I suspect Edward believes the same sort of deceit from you."

Each breath was excruciating. "But I knew nothing about the guardianship! I was just as shocked as Edward." Her hand pressed against her mouth, as if holding it could keep back the agony churning within her. "And then after we..."

She exhaled with a shudder. Oh, she *was* going to be sick!

Augusta reached for her hand and squeezed it. "After?"

"After...well," she whispered shamefully. She closed her eyes, too embarrassed to look at his aunt.

"I had my suspicions," Augusta admitted quietly.

Kate opened her eyes. The countess looked at her with a gentle, knowing expression, not surprised that her nephew had bedded his ward. Her face flushing with hot humiliation, Kate rose to her feet and turned away, afraid that if she didn't move, she'd burst into flames right there on the sofa.

"I never meant to hurt him...I was only trying to help Papa," she whispered, barely more than a breath. "Oh God, he must hate me."

"Hate you? Oh, no, my dear." Augusta tilted her head thoughtfully as she studied Kate. "I do not believe hatred is what he feels for you."

She shook her head. "He punished me by taking me away from Brambly, then banished me to the moors—"

"Because having you nearby would have kept his feelings for you fresh. The only way he knew how to protect himself was to send you out of his reach." Augusta drew a deep breath. "The problem, Miss Benton, is that you are not the first woman Edward has cared about who deceived him at the command of her father, and he believed you deserved to be punished for your deception. Your banishment to Greymoor accomplished both in his mind."

Her breath came ragged. "I didn't deceive—"

The door flung open unexpectedly, and Mary stumbled into the room, her face flushed and excited.

"His Grace," she forced out as she struggled for breath, "he's awake! Dr. Brandon—"

But the two women didn't stay to hear the rest. They were already running down the hall. Augusta hurried into Edward's bedchamber with Kate fast on her heels.

Beside the bed, Dr. Brandon glanced up at the two women. Only then did Kate hesitate, to tiptoe forward, her heart racing as her eyes fell on Edward and searched for any sign he was awake. But his eyes were still closed although his color had returned to normal, his chest now rising and falling strongly.

Tentatively, she reached for his wrist, to feel the beat of his pulse beneath her fingertips—

His eyes opened and stared mercilessly at her.

"Kate." Her name was a strangled, accusing rasp.

With a gasp, she jerked her hand away. There was no forgiveness in him, and whatever hope she'd clung to that she could find a way to make him trust her again vanished instantly beneath his cold gaze.

"Edward, thank God!" Augusta shifted to move in front of Kate, blocking his view. "Do not *ever* do anything that foolish again, or I shall kill you myself!"

But his aunt's attempt to distract him was futile. "What is she doing here?" he forced out, his voice gravelly with disuse.

The accusation in his question stirred Kate's ire, worsened by the fear and worry over him she'd carried inside her for the past three days.

"Miss Benton came as soon as she heard," Augusta interrupted. "She has been nursing you all night."

He glanced past Augusta and leveled his gaze on Kate. "Missed your chance to kill me, then?"

This was how it was going to be between them... So be it. Kate folded her arms angrily across her chest. "The hour is still early."

"Cease your squabbles," Augusta chastised quickly, although Kate had a puzzling suspicion his aunt was secretly pleased at their fighting. "Edward, do not strain yourself. You are still weak. There will be plenty of time for bickering between you two later."

"Your aunt is correct, Your Grace," Dr. Brandon interjected. "You need to rest until you've regained your strength."

"I have enough strength."

He tried to sit up, but the pain of the wound tore through him with a teeth-clenching gasp.

"Sir, the wound seam is still weak," Dr. Brandon warned. "You must not move!"

Kate rushed forward and pushed Dr. Brandon aside to take his shoulders. "Edward, please," she said softly, concern thick in her voice. "Don't hurt yourself."

He stilled immediately at her touch, but his eyes shined cold like obsidian as they rose to find hers. "Why are you here?" he asked quietly.

Not daring to answer with the truth, she avoided his gaze and eased him back against the pillows, and he went without fighting her, his strength dwindling rapidly. Of all the times and places to admit to her feelings, his sickbed surrounded by his physician and aunt was not it. And certainly not when he still mistrusted her so vehemently.

"It isn't every day a man is shot fighting a duel for me," she dodged instead. Then, because she didn't want him to see how much the duel had upset her, she forced a sardonic arch of her brow. "Although the least you could have done was win."

He laughed despite his infuriation at her, then immediately grimaced at the pain. "Sorry to disappoint you."

An unexpected stab of sorrow pierced her chest. He'd meant that tease as gallows humor, nothing more, but he'd already disappointed her by believing the worst of her, and for that, she suspected, he would never apologize.

When she reached over him to pull up the blanket, he whispered low enough so only she could hear, "I haven't forgiven you."

Despite the desolation darkening within her, she answered in the same low voice before moving away, "And I haven't forgiven *you*."

He narrowed his eyes. "Kate—"

"Rest, sir." Dr. Brandon stepped up to the bed and moved between them, gently putting Kate back, and smiled down at Edward, pleased now that his patient was cooperating. "Ladies, if you would excuse us?"

Augusta nodded and took Kate by the elbow. "Of course."

The countess led her to the connecting sitting room and

closed the doors between the rooms, and Kate gratefully sank onto the settee. Her entire body trembled as she willed herself not to cry.

Oh, they were a pair! Both of them were stubborn as mules and infuriating to the other, but even now, a connection lurked between them that couldn't be denied. He was the most aggravating yet alluring man she'd ever met, and from the moment she met him, she'd wanted her hands on him, although to both caress and throttle him in equal measure. And when they weren't at each other's throats arguing, they were tearing each other's clothes off to get closer. He wanted to control her, but she refused to surrender.

Most of all, she still loved him, despite everything, while he…did not. And now never would.

"All will be well, Katherine," Augusta assured her. She hesitated, then confided as she sat beside her and patted her hand, "He asked for you, you know. The message I sent you—he asked me to write it when the men brought him home. Perhaps he knew you would come to him when he needed you."

Kate's eyes burned with unshed tears. If he had, then it was too little, too late. She'd needed him to believe in her back at Brambly. Now, could she ever forgive him for sending her away, especially when he had yet to forgive her?

"For now, however," Augusta continued, "I think it would be best to give him distance."

But Edward's idea of distance was to send her to the moors, half a country away from her home and everyone she loved. Including him. She drew a trembling breath and resolved herself to it. "So I am to return to Greymoor, then."

"You are *not* going back to that dreadful place!" the countess corrected indignantly. "You are needed here to help salvage Strathmore's reputation." Augusta sent her a look that permitted no argument. "You will remain in London for the rest of the season, for your introduction as his ward. Because of that duel, everyone has heard of you, and now the time has arrived for them to see you for themselves. Under my careful supervision, that is."

Kate stared at her, stunned speechless. The London season? Then she remembered Mrs. Elston's warning that she would be dressed up and shown off in order to find a husband and free Edward from the guardianship. Her lips pressed into a grim line. "Are you planning on contracting me for marriage, then?"

"Heavens, no! Not after Edward nearly died to get you out of one." As Augusta considered her thoughtfully, something bright flickered deep in her eyes. "Miss Benton, I think you and I should enter into an agreement."

"What kind of agreement?" she asked warily. She'd already entered one agreement with a Westover, and she didn't know if she could survive a second.

"If you spend the season in London, allowing me to introduce you as the duke's ward and accepting invitations from potential suitors—" As Kate started to protest, Augusta cut her off with a wave. "With no expectations that you should marry any of them," she clarified, "at the end of the season you will be allowed to return to Brambly, and I will make certain Strathmore voids his guardianship." She added casually in afterthought, "Of course, should you find a suitor you wish to marry, the decision would be yours completely."

Something about the gleam in Augusta's eyes told Kate

there was nothing casual behind her comment, yet she couldn't fathom what scheme the countess had up her sleeve.

She shook her head. "Edward won't agree. He doesn't want me anywhere near him." Her heart tore as she remembered that moment in the hay cart when he'd asked her to come to London with him so he could keep her close. Since then, her world had turned inside out.

"You must trust me, my dear."

Kate *did* trust her because Edward trusted her, so she nodded grimly. "As long as I'm not forced to be courted," she repeated for emphasis.

"Oh, my dear." Augusta smiled slowly in a grin that reminded Kate of the cat who caught the canary. "What I have in mind for you is *so much* better than simply being courted."

Kate swallowed. What on earth had she gotten herself into now?

* * *

Edward blinked awake against the bright sunlight slanting through the windows. His mind was clear now, and he knew immediately where he was and what had happened to put him there. The memories of the duel and being taken home were fresh and sharp, so was the pain in his shoulder.

And so was the pain of waking to find Kate in his bedroom.

He gritted his teeth as he sat up, then sank back against the pillows. He felt better, but his body was still weak, sore, stiff. He'd been through this before, and he knew it would be quite a while before he felt normal again.

Through the set of open pocket doors separating his bedchamber from the suite's sitting room, he saw Augusta at the writing desk, penning letters in her elegant handwriting on crisp linen paper.

"Good morning," he called out to her.

She glanced up, pausing only a moment before finishing the sentence. "Good afternoon," she corrected. "You slept for nearly sixteen hours. Did you have nice dreams?"

Nice dreams? Nothing regarding his unbidden dreams about Kate was nice. Sultry, certainly, along with hot and lurid...but not *nice*.

"Yes," he lied. Then paused. "You're writing letters?"

"I am writing to our relatives and friends to inform them that despite my nephew's most recent attempt to get himself killed, it appears in all likelihood that he will survive."

He grimaced silently. Augusta loved him dearly and proved it at every opportunity by irritating the daylights out of him.

She set down her pen and turned sideways in the chair to face him. "Feeling better?"

"Much."

"You are looking better. At this rate, you will be ready to be shot again in no time."

He blew out a breath. She wasn't going to make this easy on him. "Why not?" he countered flippantly. "After all, the other shoulder is still bullet free."

Her lips pressed into a thin line, clearly not amused. "You have both shoulders bullet free for the moment." She picked up a small lead ball from the writing desk. Then, holding her arm straight out to her side, she let it fall and clank dramatically against the floor. "Thanks to the brilliant talents of the surgeon, Dr. Brandon, and Miss Benton."

"That woman was the reason I got shot in the first place," he grumbled, his shoulder aching at the thought of her.

"Your pride got you shot," she countered bluntly. Despite the well-deserved chastisement, he heard the concern for him lacing her voice. "Miss Benton saved your life. She remained at your side the entire night, tending to your wound and fever. I was afraid that if you remained unconscious much longer, Dr. Brandon would have two patients on his hands."

The entire night. That would explain the fuzzy dreams he had of her, her face floating just above his, her voice murmuring soothingly. But it didn't explain everything.

"It wasn't just her." Absently, he rubbed his sore shoulder. "There was another nurse. A German woman who read the Bible."

Augusta's lips stayed carefully still. Finally, after several seconds, she answered, "That was not a German nurse."

"Then what was it?"

"Petty vengeance."

At his puzzlement, she stood and crossed into his bedchamber. She reached for the tea service on the side table to pour him a cup.

"Special tea created by Miss Benton to help with the soreness. She's named the mixture after you."

He crooked a brow.

"*Die Auferstehung*." She held out the cup to him with a wry smile on her lips. "Resurrection tea."

Of course. Scowling, he took the cup and sipped. He wouldn't have put it past the woman to attempt to poison him, but even poison would have been welcomed to dull the pain in his chest, and not just from the bullet. "Where is she now?"

"Resting. The poor girl is exhausted. Brandon has ordered nothing but rest for the next few days for both of you."

He didn't argue. He felt better, but not nearly well enough to get out of bed. "I'll need to speak to Mrs. Lutz. We'll have to settle—"

"Mrs. Lutz is not here," she informed him. "Miss Benton traveled to London by herself."

He paused in surprise, the teacup raised halfway to his lips. "By *herself*? How?"

"You should ask her. The impropriety of it is alarming." Her normally tight lips twitched. "On the other hand, you can now have her arrested for horse theft."

He choked on the tea, coughing, then winced at the shooting pain in his shoulder. "Do I really want to know?"

"Oh yes. Quite a story, I assure you." For a fleeting moment, Edward thought he detected a hint of admiration in his aunt's voice. "But we have more pressing matters, I'm afraid."

"And what is that?"

"How to introduce her to society."

"There's a simple solution." He set the tea aside.

She blinked. "Which is?"

"We don't."

The hard-set glower she gave him told him she did not find his answer satisfactory. "That is no longer an option. That foolish duel ended any hope you had of safeguarding her guardianship. Now, everyone in London wants a glimpse of her." She paused meaningfully before adding, "The woman Strathmore was willing to die for."

He shifted against the pillows with a grimace, his shoulder throbbing with near-blinding pain now, and ground out, "I was *not* willing to die for her!"

"What you claim does not signify, dear boy, but what they believe."

"I don't give a damn what they believe," he grumbled.

"I do," she answered coolly. "The best way to silence the gossips of the *ton* is to give them access to her, let them pay calls and court her, and then, when the season ends and the rumors fade, you can send her home to Brambly."

"She'll never agree to it. She'll think you're planning to marry her off."

"Would that be such a bad thing?"

He gritted his teeth at the pain. "She'll refuse to be courted."

"Not with the right persuasion. I am certain the moment that country gel dons her first ball gown and waltzes with a handsome member of the *ton* she will fall."

"Don't count on it," he muttered. And he spoke from experience. Ball gowns and waltzing? *Good God.* She'd been naked and writhing beneath him, and the only one falling had been him.

"But that is not my primary concern," she countered evenly. "My concern is rescuing the tattered remnants of the Westover reputation."

"A bit melodramatic, don't you think?" He nearly laughed until he saw the absolute seriousness in his aunt's expression.

She fixed a stern gaze on him. "Are you not lying in bed due to a duel fought over the accusation that you voided your ward's marriage contract so you could have her for yourself?"

He stared at his aunt insolently, very much disliking her newfound impingement into his private life. "Technically, I won that duel," he reminded her.

"Which only served to make it even more believable." She shook her head, the simple gesture encapsulating how utterly foolish she found the guardianship, the duel, and all the rumors now flying through the city about him and his unknown ward. "This family has been through too much in the past year to allow its reputation to now be smirched by this."

Edward lowered his gaze. If she meant to make him feel guilty, she'd succeeded. The arrow hit straight into his heart. Augusta loved him like a mother, and he had unduly put her through fresh torment these past few days. He deserved her admonishment. "It has," he agreed solemnly.

"So I have taken it upon myself to prepare a suitable introduction for her," she informed him. "I have hired Madame Bernaise to create her wardrobe, and as soon as possible, I shall take her out in public with me, ensuring she is seen by the loosest-tongued gossips in the city."

He rubbed his arm, the ache now pounding down to his fingertips. "How does that stop rumors that I want her for myself?"

"It does not. That is why we will proceed as if she is accepting suitors, whether she wants them or not. That is also why I have asked Thomas Matteson to spread the rumor that she is hunting a husband and that Strathmore is offering a generous dowry."

"Strathmore is, is he?" His lips twitched irritably.

Her brow lifted, daring him to contradict her. "A *very* generous dowry."

He grimaced, knowing that bit of news would bring

a flock of fortune hunters and curiosity seekers to his doorstep. "Thomas agreed to that?"

"He and Nathaniel allowed you to get into that juvenile duel. I consider it only a pittance of what is owed."

He stared at his aunt. She'd always been protective of the family's reputation, but giving Kate the debut season she planned went beyond any familial loyalty he'd ever seen in her before. Perhaps the recent loss of one duke and the near loss of another had shaken her more than he realized. "You're planning a full assault for her season, then."

"Yes." Her lips pressed together distastefully. "I have even secured vouchers for Almack's."

At that, he burst out laughing, then immediately winced at the sharp pain. If the countess was willing to venture into Almack's, a place she despised almost as much as he did, then he wasn't the only one suffering because of Katherine Benton.

"There is one more point to settle," she added. "Miss Benton claims she is innocent of whatever deceit you have accused her."

"She's lying." After all, he'd read the truth with his own eyes.

Augusta looked at him with quiet affection. "Then why did she come here to nurse you?"

"To convince me to give up the guardianship."

"In that case," she pointed out gently, "she would have been wise to let you die."

He stared at her grimly, not having an answer for that. He'd been wondering the same thing himself. Just as he couldn't fathom why she would seduce him into voiding the guardianship when he'd already agreed to give her whatever help she needed with Brambly. There was no gain in that for her. And unlike the letter, which couldn't be denied, she'd protested her innocence in seducing him. Quite strongly. Even now his cheek throbbed at the memory.

But he hadn't been willing to believe her then. He'd been too angry to listen because he'd felt like a fool for wanting yet another woman who deceived him. And *sweet Lucifer* how much he'd wanted her. Even now, his gut still clenched at the thought of being inside her, how tight and warm her body was around his, how sweet to hear his name on her lips when she came beneath him... His little angel had given him the best night of his life, only to betray him in the morning.

Had he been wrong? Was she innocent in that? She'd worn boy's breeches, for God's sake. What kind of temptress would set out to seduce a man while wearing breeches?

A beautiful one, he thought with chagrin.

But was she also an innocent one?

"Think about what I have said." Augusta leaned over him and placed a motherly kiss on his forehead, although he suspected she was also checking for fever. "And rest now."

He watched her leave the room, then gladly closed his eyes.

Bloody hell. Kate was here, staying in his home, sleeping in a bed just a few rooms down the hall. Pandora didn't just open the box. Apparently, she rode a stolen horse right through it.

As far as he was concerned, though, nothing had changed. She'd deceived him by writing to her father, and for that, he couldn't forgive her.

If she had been any other woman, he wouldn't have given her a second thought. He would have let himself enjoy taking his pleasure in her and ridden back to London without a backward glance, content to leave her forgotten in the countryside where she belonged.

But not her. Katherine Benton was proving to be the woman who'd gotten under his skin unlike any other, the one he couldn't get out of his head, even banished all the way to the moors.

And Lord help him, the one he still wanted.

CHAPTER SIXTEEN

The next afternoon, Augusta hurried Kate into the barouche and insisted the driver spend an hour taking them around Hyde Park...around and around...until Kate felt like a ribbon on a Maypole. Augusta forced her to smile and wave at all the well-dressed lords and ladies of the *ton* but ordered the driver not to stop.

"Why not?" Kate asked, since several of the couples warmly returned their waves.

"You are meant to be seen, nothing more," she informed her with conspiratorial glee. She waved to a couple in a stylish phaeton. "Today, we dangle the carrot."

"And tomorrow?"

Augusta smiled wickedly. "We have rabbit stew!"

They repeated the drive every afternoon for the following week, and soon, it seemed that all the *ton* appeared for the promenade, craning their necks to catch a glimpse of the young woman riding with the Countess of Tourney. Every time Kate saw people speaking beneath parasols or behind fans, she wondered if they were gossiping about her.

"Of course, they are!" Augusta assured her happily, which did not put Kate at ease.

Then, the rides through the park stopped, replaced by a week of mornings spent calling on the countess's acquaintances just early enough that they would not be received. Augusta even purchased calling cards embossed with Kate's name so she could purposefully leave one behind as proof that Strathmore's ward existed and was fine enough to engage with the quality, even if no one was awake to receive her.

This week, however, there were no more rides nor craftily failed attempts to call on acquaintances. Instead, they simply stayed home.

"Now," Augusta told her confidently, "they will come to us."

And the women of the *ton* did exactly that. The front bell started ringing just after two o'clock each afternoon and continued late into the day. Various women of all ranks and fortunes appeared at the door, eager to call on Augusta and welcome Kate warmly to London, only to leave their cards in disappointment when Kingsley informed them that the countess and Miss Benton were not receiving visitors.

As Kate surreptitiously watched from the first-floor sitting room window, finely dressed ladies with dainty parasols and grand hats arrived in a stream, only to be turned away. A reverse parade. Instead of moving past them as she had done in the barouche, this time they paraded past her.

"I don't understand," she puzzled as another visitor departed. "Why did we visit everyone last week if we don't want to receive them now?"

"Anticipation." Augusta smiled with satisfaction, like a cat at the cream. "It makes everything sweeter."

Kate thought again about Edward and the inevitable confrontation they would have as soon as he was well enough to leave his room. Anticipating *that* was definitely not sweet. "What happens next?"

"The invitations arrive, then the suitors will follow."

She bit back the urge to remind Augusta—again and repeatedly—that she had no intention of marrying. But gifts from overly confident gentlemen and fortune hunters wanting to make an alliance with the Duke of Strathmore had already started to arrive, and the countess refused to let her send them back.

"Mark my words, Katherine—in two weeks, you will be sought out as this season's incomparable."

A sinking hollow formed in her stomach. She didn't want to be this season's anything. It was all overwhelming, and she wanted none of it. But she also wanted to return to Brambly, and the only way to get there was through the London season.

Augusta smiled warmly at her. "And I hope that you are enjoying your debut."

"I am." A lie, but she didn't want to upset Augusta with the truth.

And not when she beamed at her like a proud mother presenting her own daughter. "You have become a diamond, my dear."

She sighed, "Just like Cinderella."

Augusta looked utterly aghast at the notion. "You will *not* turn into a scullery maid at midnight!"

Kate's hand flew to her lips to cover her surprised laugh, but she couldn't stop the flush coloring her cheeks. In the short time she'd known the countess, she'd come to adore the woman, especially at moments like this.

"My mother would have loved that I had this opportunity for a real London season," she told Augusta affectionately. "And I think she'd be happy to know you're here with me."

She leaned over and kissed the countess on the cheek. Augusta blushed scarlet, too flummoxed by the display of affection to formulate a response.

Kate turned back toward the window under the pretense of watching for more visitors, but she really needed a moment to blink back the tears that threatened at her lashes. When the season was over and she was back at Brambly, she was going to miss Aunt Augusta very much.

"Do not fret. An introduction comes in waves, my dear, like a military campaign." Augusta rose elegantly, misreading Kate's distress. "And this afternoon, we prepare for battle."

Fresh dread swept over her. "How?"

"Shopping on Bond Street!" With a determined air, she glided from the room. "We leave in an hour."

Kate watched her go, then faced the window again just in time to see another carriage pull into the drive, bringing yet another visitor with hat and parasol who would be refused entry.

She shook her head. Military campaigns and battles... when had her life turned into a war?

"The moment you met a tall, handsome army colonel," she mumbled with a defeated roll of her shoulders.

If Augusta was right, and her introduction to society was truly like a military campaign, then Kate was in serious trouble. She was a healer, not a soldier, and she knew nothing about fighting battles or waging wars, certainly not of the social kind, and she seriously doubted she'd be able to tell friend from foe among the ranks of the *ton*.

"If this is to be a military campaign," she sighed with a grimace, "then I might as well wave a white glove of surrender."

"Perhaps you need an experienced soldier to aid you."

She spun around, her lips parting in surprise—

Edward.

He leaned heavily against the doorframe, his dark eyes staring at her coolly. Dressed only in black trousers over bare feet and a jacket draped over his shoulders, with his bare chest and the white bandage clearly visible beneath, he looked disheveled and fatigued, still weak. A growth of beard darkened his face, his thick hair bed-ruffled.

And he'd never looked more breathtaking.

His gaze deliberately moved up and down the length of her. Despite her anger at him, she felt her insides warm at the inviting look his eyes sent her, the familiar tingle rising from her toes all the way up into her blushing cheeks.

She swallowed and forced herself to look away from his bare chest, the same chest she'd covered with kisses the night of the storm. "You should be in bed. I don't think Dr. Brandon wants—"

"Haven't you heard? I'm all better."

With a great physical effort, he pushed himself away from the doorway and stepped into the room, but he swayed unsteadily. She resisted the urge to reach for him, knowing he would refuse. Even wounded and weak, the blasted man was too proud to ask for help.

"So," he drawled, "Augusta is determined to see your introduction through."

"Yes," she replied cautiously. The coldness still existed inside him, she saw it in the way he gazed at her, in the hardness of his face. But his anger seemed to have eased. For the moment. "Your aunt can be quite focused."

"Stubborn, you mean."

Kate sighed her agreement, "Regimented."

At that, a small smile pulled at his lips, and her heart tugged. She remembered how wonderful it felt to have the full force of one of Edward's grins on her, and she desperately wanted that again, despite the biting resentment she still carried toward him for sending her away.

"When it comes to Augusta, I've learned it's best to surrender and do what she wants."

She nodded at the bandage beneath the jacket. "Well, I'm certain she wants you to follow Dr. Brandon's orders and return to bed."

His eyes narrowed. "Worried about me, Kate?"

"Of course," she answered honestly. But of course, she was still hurt and angry, too.

"You shouldn't be." He dismissed her concern with a wave of his hand that set him swaying again, "What concern am I of yours?"

Because I still care about you, you infuriating man! She drew a deep breath to calm herself and bit her lip before answering, "None, I suppose, except that you're still my guardian. My care and protection are still in your hands."

He gave a curt laugh of disbelief. "Is that why you're

here in London—hoping I'll release you from that agreement?"

Her chest squeezed around her heart, but she held her face carefully blank, not wanting him to see the heartrending torment he was capable of inflicting. Her mother had worn her emotions on her face, and her father only despised her more for it. "I'm not naïve enough to think that being in your home when you want nothing to do with me will convince you to tear up that agreement, not when you sent me halfway across the country." She lowered her voice. "For making love to you."

"For deceiving me," he corrected.

His words pierced her. He was hurt and angry, but so was she, yet she knew that arguing back would get her nowhere. "We struck a truce once, do you remember?" she offered. "That first night at dinner."

"I remember," he murmured. His eyes gleamed at the memory.

Her heartbeat skipped. For a moment, she had a glimpse in him of the man she knew before, the kind and charming Edward she'd known, not the cold stranger he'd become. "Then, perhaps we could negotiate another one." When he didn't decline the idea, she drew a deep breath and tried again, "Are you all right?"

"I'm fine." But he swayed, this time reaching for the back of a chair to steady himself.

Oh, he wasn't fine. He was still weak and fatigued, and if he wasn't careful, he could tear open his wound again, especially since his sutures had been removed early against her protests. A hollow pang of homesickness knotted her belly. She missed Brambly, where no one questioned her medical expertise, or lack of it.

"Dr. Brandon said your shoulder was mending quickly." She cleared her throat and gestured toward the bandage. "May I?"

He hesitated, as if deciding whether he could trust her even this little bit. Then he shrugged, as if he didn't care either way. "If you'd like."

Tentatively, she approached him and prayed he couldn't see the trembling in her hands as she reached up to push back the jacket and let it fall to the floor at his feet, to bare his shoulder to her worried eyes. Raising her hand carefully toward the white bandage rolled in thick layers like a mummy's wrap around his shoulder, she hesitated. She wouldn't unwrap it, but she had to touch it, had to touch *him*.

When her fingertips brushed against the bandage, he inhaled sharply though clenched teeth, and she flinched. But she couldn't have hurt him—she'd barely touched him at all.

Her eyes darted up, and she saw a hundred different emotions flash across his face. But not one of them was hatred. Her heart thudded with hope, desperately wanting to believe that Augusta was right. That he did not hate her after all.

He murmured, "Why are you here, Katherine?"

Her breath caught in her throat. She knew what he was asking, and it had nothing to do with society introductions and guardianships. "Because you were hurt," she admitted cautiously, "and I couldn't let you go through that alone, not again."

He frowned, struggling with whether he could believe her. "Augusta was here."

Gently, she shook her head. "That's not the same." She

traced a fingertip cautiously across his shoulder to feel his warm, bare skin.

He shuddered.

She hesitated. "Am I hurting you?"

"Yes," he rasped, but her fingers were nowhere near his wound.

"I never meant to," she whispered. "Please believe me."

His eyes closed briefly, then opened to stare at her with raw honesty. "I don't know what to believe about you."

His words ripped away her breath, and she shuddered as fresh anguish gripped her. She'd confessed everything except loving him, yet he still couldn't bring himself to forgive her. "You can believe that."

He shifted, leaning almost imperceptibly closer, but she felt the movement and the responding heat shivering through her. "Kate..."

"Yes?" Unable to resist, her fingertips traced down his chest to the hard ripples of his abdomen.

His breath hitched at her touch. "You deceived me by writing to your father."

"Yes." She drew closer to him, urged on by the heat of his body and the memory of being in his arms. His muscles twitched thrillingly beneath her fingertips. "I regret it. It was a mistake, and I wish I had never done it. But the other," she whispered, drawing soft circles across his stomach and through the sprinkling of dark hair leading down to the waistband of his trousers, "I could never do something like that." *And never with you.*

His hand covered hers and stilled her fingers against him. His eyes narrowed as they searched her face. "Then why did you give yourself to me?"

Holding her breath, she dared to whisper, "Because I wanted you."

His fingertips caressed along her wrist and found her racing pulse. Proof of her desire for him. "You still do," he murmured heatedly, his eyes flickering.

As if to prove him right, a low ache panged between her thighs. "Edward—"

He swayed unsteadily, and her throat constricted with concern. He was too weak yet to be out of bed, and she didn't want him to hurt himself. Or have to explain to Augusta how a half-naked Edward ended up collapsed at her feet in the drawing room.

"Please," she offered gently, taking his arm, "let me help you to your room."

"I don't need help," he grumbled but didn't pull away, and she leaned into him to bring part of his weight against her as she led him from the room.

His bedchamber was just down the hall, but with each step, he shifted closer to her, leaning more weight against her until she had no choice but to slip her arm around his waist to hold him steady. He was still weak, and in his rush to be out of bed, he'd also fatigued himself.

She nudged open his door with her hip and helped him across the room to the bed. Slipping from her arms, his heavy body slid down to sit on the edge of the mattress. She lifted the covers away and gently helped him back against the pillows.

Immediately, exhaustion swept over him, and he slumped down. But his eyes were still open, despite the heavy lids threatening to close at any moment.

"You should stay in bed," she urged, pulling the sheet up to his waist.

"I am in bed." He lifted an unsteady hand and touched her hip. "And now so are you."

Realizing she sat just inches from him, she scrambled to her feet.

"Damn," he murmured regretfully.

Kate gaped at him, momentarily speechless. He wanted her in bed with him?

She was still furious at him for believing what they'd shared had been manipulated and selfish—

But traitorous heat fluttered low in her belly at the possibility of what might have happened had he been just a bit more rested, and she didn't think she would have had the will to stop him. Not when she still craved him. Even unbathed, unshaved, and half-delirious, he still aroused her. Good heavens, she'd nearly taken off all his clothes just minutes ago in the sitting room!

It was insane, the effect this man had on her. "You're mad!"

"And you're beautiful."

Especially when he said things like that.

Her throat tightened. "Edward—"

"Augusta trusts you. She thinks I should, too."

She turned away under the pretense of reaching toward the bedside table to fix a dose of laudanum so he wouldn't see the anguished expression on her face. "But you never will, will you?"

She stirred the dark liquid into a glass of water, adding a spoonful of sugar to dull the bitterness, then sat next to him on the edge of the bed and held out the glass. Instead of answering, he tossed back the mixture in one swallow, then reached past her to set the glass on the table.

When she started to rise, he grabbed her wrist, tugging

her off-balance and down toward him on the bed. Her arms flailed to catch herself, but she landed sprawled halfway across his solid body, her breasts flattening against his bare chest.

His mouth lowered to her ear. "I know how it feels to be inside you, angel." His breath burned hot across her cheek. "And I know I was the first man to be there."

"Edward," she whispered, closing her eyes against the sweet torture of his words, against the heat of his hand as it swept over her hip to cup her bottom and squeeze.

"I felt you shatter, heard you cry my name..." His warm lips brushed against her earlobe, and she shivered. "That wasn't pretend. You weren't acting that."

And she never could have. Because she'd wanted him as much as he'd wanted her, and she still did.

He tenderly kissed her cheek, to nibble teasingly at the corner of her mouth. "But I also saw your letter, and I can't forget that."

His hand tightened around her arm and lifted her against him as his lips slid fully across hers.

Wrapping her hand behind his neck to pull herself closer, she moaned against his sensuous mouth and drank in his kiss, the kiss she'd longed for during the past weeks without him, the kiss she thought his wrath would keep from her forever. But now, his lips were once again tasting hers, his hands stroking along her curves, and all that mattered was that he not stop.

She craved his touch and whimpered shamelessly for more, and she melted with shivering gratitude when his tongue teased apart her lips and slipped inside to stroke against hers, giving her the intimate contact she desired. She could feel his need for her surging to the surface, just as she could feel his arousal hardening beneath her. Despite his anger and distrust, he still wanted her. And oh, dear Lord, how she still wanted him!

She arched herself against him, to wrap her arms around his shoulders and press herself tight—

With a sharp groan, he drew in a painful breath and reached for his shoulder, his eyes pressing closed as his face paled.

"Oh!" she gasped. "I've hurt you!"

"More than you know," he rasped, his breath panting down the pain. Just as quickly as he'd grabbed her to him, he released her and shifted away.

She sat back in confusion, her body reeling from the sudden rush of desire, from the sudden loss of his heat. His face glowered darkly but his eyes were bright, and she realized he was just as affected by the kiss as she was. Just as confused.

"Why did you do that?" She pressed her hand against her lips, still hot and moist from his.

He stared at her mouth, as if he couldn't bring himself to look into her eyes. "Because I still want you," he admitted.

Her heart sank. How much of that confession was Edward, how much the drug? "But you haven't forgiven me."

"No." He closed his eyes and fatigue pushed him into unconsciousness.

* * *

Phillip Benton watched his daughter and the Countess of Tourney make their way slowly down Bond Street, pausing in front of windows and occasionally entering a shop to re-turn later with piles of boxes and parcels handed over to two liveried footmen to place into the ebony carriage following behind. Oh, Katherine was lovely in her new finery, looking for all the world as if she belonged there among the quality, and in return, the fops and biddies of the *ton* swarmed around her, all of them desiring an introduction to the Duke of Strathmore's new ward.

And to think, just a few weeks ago, she'd sent him a letter begging him to tell her the guardianship was a mistake.

She'd never been a stupid one, but truly, it was laughable for her not to realize the agreement was his insurance in case Strathmore changed his mind and tried to put him into debtor's prison. The public scandal that would erupt if the oh-so-respectable duke tossed his ward's father into prison—the countess would never let that happen.

Then Litchfield had nearly ruined everything. That damned idiot had actually shot Strathmore when all he needed to do was collect the money and walk away, meet him at the café, and split the profits. Now, the baronet had fled the country, taking all the blunt with him and forcing him to start over on a new plan to free himself.

Strathmore would pay for ruining his life. He would make the bastard regret what he'd done to him. And if he had to use his daughter to do so, so be it.

From the looks of her, parading around with the countess and freely spending Strathmore's money, she'd already switched sides. Very likely, she was also sleeping with the enemy according to the gossip of how Strathmore reacted to Litchfield.

He wasn't surprised. She was just like her mother. That scheming bitch had lifted her skirts easily enough, then gotten with child and demanded he marry her, only to turn on him the moment he'd needed a little money. And her daughter had done the same. She'd kept Brambly from him when selling the farm would have secured him for life. He'd felt no guilt in abandoning the mother, and he'd certainly feel none in using the daughter to save himself.

He'd been forced into this, and now, Katherine would make good for all the past wrongs done to him, he'd see to it. Just as he'd make certain that Strathmore would pay.

Oh, how he was going to pay. Very, *very* dearly.

CHAPTER SEVENTEEN

*S*he was going mad. Simply mad!

Pacing in her bedroom, Kate threw up her hands in frustration at yet another sleepless night. And it was all that infuriating man's fault, drat him. Every night since Edward tugged her down into his bed and kissed her, when he'd whispered those words into her ear about how it felt to make love to her, her whirling mind had been unable to think about anything else but him. How wonderfully wanton he made her feel when his hands explored her, when his mouth tasted her. How decadent the feel of his heavy body pushing down into hers. How sweet the ache he bloomed inside her, how even sweeter the release...

Oh, drat him!

Faced with those torturous thoughts, she was once again spending the night pacing barefoot in her night rail, trying to force down by physical exhaustion the hot need for him aching between her thighs and the emotional yearning in her chest, and wondering how many passes a rug could take before it went threadbare.

Lord help her, she still wanted him, and what made the torment worse was knowing that he would welcome her into his bed if she went to him. He'd admitted his desire— she'd *felt* it, for goodness' sake!

Yet nothing had changed. He still believed her capable of seducing him to free herself from the guardianship. And she was still just as angry and hurt that he did.

Taking a deep breath, she stopped and stared at the door. Foolish ninny! She was an absolute cake for still wanting him. Once again pacing, she shook her head, ashamed at her own weakness that had her longing for him to make her shiver with his heat—

She bit her lip, her gaze returning to the door. His bedroom was just down the hall. If she went to him, he would welcome her with hard kisses and soft caresses, not wondering why she came to him but why she'd waited so long.

And truly, why should she wait? Why should she spend her nights pacing, alone in her room, when she could be with him?

Only her pride and his stubbornness stopped them from seeking mutual pleasure. He didn't believe her now, hadn't forgiven her and probably never would, so what would change if she surrendered again to him? When morning came, he would still not believe her, but she would have gained another night in his arms that she would otherwise never have and the satisfaction of being at the center of his desire, if not his love.

They had no future, but they could have tonight. And

when she returned to Brambly, she could take with her the memory of being in his arms one last time, the knowledge that she'd made a man like Edward want her.

Pushing back her shoulders with determination, she hurried across the room and flung open the door.

And caught her breath—

"Edward."

He stood in the doorway, his hand raised as if ready to knock. He wore only his trousers and a much smaller bandage. It was there now more as a reminder not to do something foolish to reopen the wound than as protection, although she knew the pain of the bullet still lingered, just as she knew there was nothing weak or unsteady about him now.

His hand dropped to his side, and the momentary surprise that dashed across his face melted into something hotter as he slowly lingered his gaze over her, taking in the sleeveless night rail with its scooped neckline tied with a bow, and her bare toes peeking out beneath. When his eyes returned to hers, the intensity of his gaze stole her breath away.

"Were you going somewhere, Katherine?" The husky murmur of his voice tickled down her spine, and her bare toes curled beneath her.

"Yes," she breathed, mesmerized by his sudden appearance and her own desire mirrored back in the dark depths of his eyes. He wanted her, and she burned for him.

"Where?"

Her heart skipped, and she whispered, "To your bed."

His eyes flashed with unguarded pleasure at her breathless confession, and her belly began to warm. "Then invite me inside."

She hesitated. Now that he was here, standing before her in oh-so-masculine flesh and blood, her courage faltered, and she bit her bottom lip as she stared up at him. Nothing had changed, nothing at all...Was she a fool to give herself to him?

Sensing her wariness, he shifted closer. "I've been thinking about you," he admitted, "about everything that's happened."

"Have you?" The surprise in her voice emerged as a throaty purr.

But he didn't reach for her, only stared at her with such arousal that she pulsed electric. "Tell me again why you sent that letter to your father."

"Because he's my father." Each word tore at her heart even as it raced furiously, her breath coming shallow. "He's the only family I have left, and that should mean something. We should love each other, shouldn't we? We should care for each other..." Even now the heartbreak of knowing her father would never love her clawed at her, and she inhaled a sharp breath. "I'm so sorry I sent it. Please forgive me."

He lowered his head as if to kiss her but stopped himself, his mouth hovering so close to hers yet without touching that she could feel his heat shadowing her lips. "I already have."

Worry and relief mixed inside her in bittersweet longing. She so desperately wanted him to kiss her and reassure her that he meant what he said, so afraid he wouldn't. "Edward—"

"And tell me again," he whispered, each soft word a feather's tickle against her lips, "why did you give yourself to me?"

"Because I wanted you," she admitted simply, "and no other reason."

His face tightened with tormented remorse. "I'm sorry, Katherine. I was such a damned fool for hurting you like that, for sending you away. I saw the letter and I thought you were no better than..." Inhaling a sharp breath, he shook his head as if not wanting to remember the anguished suffering he'd caused for both of them. "I was wrong, so very wrong, and I will never send you away again, I promise." Then he touched his lips to hers in a kiss that was little more than a hopeful breath. "Forgive me."

In the past few weeks since she arrived in London, she'd come to understand this complicated man and knew why he'd felt compelled to exile her to the moors...not because he didn't want her, but because he wanted her too much. The soft words choked her as she whispered his words back to him. "I already have."

A sigh of relief shuddering through him, he rubbed his thumb across her lower lip. The tiny caress tingled through her in anticipation of what could come, if she let it. "Then invite me inside, Katherine."

She sighed as he looped his thumb up to trace the outline of her mouth, her lips parting delicately beneath his touch, and she whispered, "I'm still furious at you."

His mouth curled into an amused half grin. "Good."

A hot ache sprang up between her legs as that grin wrapped around her, taking her prisoner. Her heart somersaulted, and she stared up at him through lowered lashes, unable to meet his gaze directly in her sudden shyness over the wantonness that had come over her so shamelessly tonight. "Would you..." She swallowed nervously. "Would you like to come inside?"

"Very much," he murmured.

Catching her breath, she raised her eyes to his and slowly backed into the room. Edward followed, step by step, not breaking his gaze from hers even when he reached behind him to close the door and throw the lock.

Her blood ran hot with both nervous excitement and aching arousal, her heart speeding so fast her chest hurt from the pounding of it, and her legs shook as she crossed the dark room toward the bed, one backward step at a time. Even in the dim light from the low fire, she could see the heat shining in his dark eyes, glistening like the devil's own as he stalked after her.

She reached the side of her bed and raised a hand to stop him, just feet from her, and he obeyed. Emboldened by the raw desire she saw on his face, she reached trembling fingers to the bow at the neckline of her nightgown. "Tell me you want me," she ordered softly.

His eyes swept over her, and everywhere he looked, heat prickled her skin. "I want you, Katherine."

She pulled the bow, and the ribbon slipped free, the night rail falling open around her shoulders and revealing just a glimpse of her breasts beneath the billowing white cotton.

"Like this?" she whispered. He watched as she reached up and pushed the loose material from her left shoulder, the white cotton falling down her arm to expose her breast.

"Yes." Beneath his hot gaze, her nipple puckered achingly.

"Or like this?" she tempted again, her hand reaching up to her other shoulder and letting the gown fall away to her waist, baring both breasts to his greedy gaze. And brazenly, she let him look, each ragged breath that tore from him making the need between her legs throb harder.

"God, yes," he groaned, clenching his hands at his sides as he fought his urge to reach for her, knowing to play out his part in her game.

All her uncertainty gone, now replaced by a smoldering desire to make him want her more than he'd wanted any woman, Kate thrilled with her newfound power over him, relishing in the way she both tempted and tantalized him. Already she was wet between her thighs, her body ready to welcome his, but first she wanted to tease him, to torment in deliberate retribution for the way he'd made her want him all those lonely nights in the moors.

She fluttered her hand across her breasts, lightly teasing at her nipples with her fingertips, rewarded by another hungry groan from him. "You like looking at me?"

"Very much," he growled softly.

"Then have a good, long look." She dropped her nightgown to the floor to stand before him, naked and trembling. She heard his breath hitch with a gasp, and with a pulse of excitement, she trailed her hand down her body, fluttering over her breasts and across her belly, until she teased her fingers into the curls between her legs. His hot gaze followed everywhere she so shamelessly touched, and when he wet his lips as she dared to stroke down between her thighs, she gave a throaty laugh at his reaction. "You want your mouth on me, don't you?"

"No," he rasped out. When her fingers paused at his unexpected answer, he took a step toward her, close enough now that she could feel the heat of his body warming her front but not yet touching. It was his turn to tempt and tantalize. He lowered his mouth to her ear and whispered in a hot breath, "I want your wicked little mouth on me."

Her thighs clenched hard, and she surrendered with a breathless plea. "Edward."

He pushed her back onto the bed. She fell onto the mattress with a gentle gasp of surprise, and when he crawled on top of her, his mouth fiercely captured hers. He thrust his tongue between her lips to plunge inside, swirling and sweeping to plunder her mouth, and she eagerly welcomed him, entwining her arms around his neck and arching her breasts against his hard chest.

His weight pressing down on her was delicious, exactly what she'd craved for weeks, and so were his hands as they roamed her body to caress and explore every inch of her. But it was his strength and hardness she'd missed most of all, that wonderful feel of hard male against her feminine softness. And oh, those fingers—those clever fingers that circled, teased, and pinched at her nipples until they ached, until she writhed beneath him, begging for more.

It had been too long since he'd been inside her, simultaneously taking his pleasure and giving it, and her body wanted his. *Now.* With a whimper of need, she spread her legs wide to welcome him.

"Kate," he groaned, tearing his mouth from hers to nip at her throat. "We can't, not like this."

For a heartbeat, she froze. Surely, he didn't mean—he *couldn't* mean that they had to stop! Not now, not when her body wanted this so much that every inch of her quivered with aching need for him, so much that she would burn up and die if she didn't have him. "Edward, please—"

"Like this." He rolled onto his back, bringing her up on top with a surprised gasp as her thighs straddled his hips.

"Oh," she breathed as she looked down at him, and a new excitement pulsed through her. He'd meant that his still-tender shoulder wouldn't tolerate having to brace himself over her to take her as he'd done before. He meant he wanted her sitting on... *Oh!* His erection strained hard beneath the fabric of his breeches, and when she made a taunting little test of his restraint by swirling her bottom against him, he sucked in a mouthful of air between clenched teeth, his entire body shuddering. "Oh my," she whispered wickedly.

Then she leaned over to kiss him, her tongue sliding back and forth across his lips until he opened for her and let her sweep inside to taste his kiss the way he'd tasted hers. He'd surrendered control to her, and she thrilled with it.

Her mouth left his to lick and bite her way down his throat and across his chest, pausing only to worry his flat, male nipples between her teeth before moving lower. His body was amazing, and she couldn't believe any other man could feel this good, so hard the muscles, so soft the bare skin. And every inch of him delicious. Her tongue lapped over the hard ridges of his abdomen, following the thin trail of dark hair until it disappeared beneath the waistband of his trousers.

"These need to go," she whispered, sliding her finger down over his trousers and torturously across the straining bulge. "I want your warm skin against mine tonight."

A soft groan of agreement escaped him, and she gave a playful laugh as she cupped him possessively against her palm through the fabric. Tonight, he was hers, and she refused to let him forget that.

Her fingers trembled as they slid free the buttons in eagerness to have her hands on him. He lifted his hips from the mattress to help her as she peeled the fabric down his legs and off to the floor.

Kate stared, her breath hitching at the naked sight of him. His erection was large and hard with hot arousal for her, simply magnificent in its manliness, and he was all hers, just waiting for her to take what she desired. She touched him gingerly with an exploring brush of her fingertip along his length, fascinated by the feel of his steely hardness beneath wonderfully soft skin even on this part of his body, and he twitched against her fingers.

She gave a soft laugh of wonder and touched him again, and this time when he jumped at her fingertips, Edward rasped out her name in low warning.

But she was too captivated with her power over him to hold back and reached for him again, this time to wrap her entire hand around his hard length and squeeze. His hips bucked beneath her, and with a devilish smile, she began to pump her hand over him, mimicking with her clenched fingers the way her body had stroked around him before.

"That feels...so good," he forced out, his breaths coming in pants, his heart beating so fast she could feel it pulsing through his hard shaft beneath her fingertips. "Don't stop."

But she had no intention of stopping, thrilling with each stroke of her palm along his length and reveling in the way her own body's arousal grew from simply touching him. She shook violently now, the throbbing ache between her legs nearly unbearable, and she was so close to coming just like this, from only having her hands on him while she knelt beside him.

She helplessly whimpered her need, and in answer, he slid his hand between her thighs and slipped his fingers inside her, burying them deep in her wet warmth. A moan tore from her as his fingers plunged in and out of her.

Her folds quivered shamelessly around his fingers, her body taking its own pleasure even as she gave it. "Edward, please," she begged, lost to the wonderful sensation of his manhood in her hands as his clever fingers possessed her sex. Her heart skipped in its fast tattoo with each teasing swirl of his fingertips. "I want—I want... now."

He grabbed her around her hips and lifted her to straddle him. Reaching down between her thighs, he placed her hand back around him, the tip of his erection aimed at her pulsing core.

"Hold me right there, angel," he ordered, his hoarse voice filled with his need to be inside her.

Then, with one large hand clasping her hip, the other reaching between her thighs to spread her open wide with his fingers, he guided her down over him, his length sinking smoothly inside her tight warmth.

He growled as he lifted his hips from the bed to shove up hard inside her until she was fully seated on top of him, his length buried inside her to the hilt. With a soft cry at the sensation of being filled so completely, she grasped for his shoulders to keep her balance.

"Take your pleasure, Katherine," he murmured hotly, circling his hips beneath her in permission for her to let herself go.

Drawing a deep breath, she began to move, rocking herself in gentle, little pulses of her hips. Small, testing movements as she shifted over him—

"Take it," he encouraged her fiercely, his hands clamping around her waist. "Like this."

He lifted her up his length and then dropped her, plunging back into her at such a raw angle that she lost her breath. But, oh, the sensation was amazing! Each time her hips landed against his, he thrust up against her, grinding against the throbbing nub at the top of her folds and sending an electric jolt shooting through her.

But it wasn't enough. With a whimper of need, she instinctively leaned forward onto her knees, the new angle opening her sex against him and rubbing her aching point against his pelvis as she began to move not up and down but forward and back over his body.

Licking her lips, she closed her eyes and grabbed at his shoulders as she thrust over him, each movement grinding against him, rubbing harder at her pulsing bead. Soft whimpers and mewlings escaped from her lips as she rode him hard, her thighs shaking as she galloped toward release.

His hands cupped her bottom to urge her on, and he leaned up to latch his mouth on to her breast. Each hard pull of his sucking mouth shot straight through her, down to the flaming heat where he thrust between her thighs, and she moaned. With a shudder, she tossed back her head as her thighs clenched down hard against his hips, climaxing in a white flash of heat and electricity.

His arms went around her, yanking her down on top of him and capturing her mouth beneath his to smother the passionate cry that tore from her. She was helpless against the waves of pleasure that pulsed through her to do anything more than lie across his chest and whimper softly as he thrust up beneath her, now taking his own pleasure. She felt him jerk between her thighs, followed by the rush of his release deep inside her, and she clung to him, never wanting to let go.

Still holding her tight, he rolled them both gently onto

their sides and slipped from her warmth. He stroked her face as she kept her eyes closed, enjoying the diminishing pulses of pleasure still throbbing dully through her.

He gave a soft laugh and nuzzled her neck. "Good Lord, angel," he panted out as he caught his breath, "if that's what happens when you're angry, I'm going to keep you furious at me forever."

"Don't tease," she chastised gently. "Not about that."

"Apologies," he murmured, his lips caressing her temple. "How about if I keep you happy instead?"

Her heart soared, and unshed tears stung at her eyes. Unable to speak around the tightening of her throat, she tenderly touched his cheek, delighting in the warmth and strength of him beneath her fingertips. He wanted to make her happy, but what more could he do to make her any happier than she was at that moment, at that simply wonderful, perfect moment in his arms?

She felt him hesitate before he added, "As my wife."

Her heart stopped. And when it started again, the painful thud tore her breath away. "Pardon?"

"You can marry me," he explained quietly, carefully, as if he were afraid she might startle and flee like a doe.

Stunned, Kate stared at him in disbelief. *Marriage?* Oh, he was simply *mad*!

"We're meant to be together, Kate. Tonight proves that."

She shook her head, and the happiness humming inside her melted into misery. To be his wife—but she couldn't accept. *Wouldn't* accept. The sacrifices she'd be asked to make would be too great for a man who hadn't admitted to loving her...her home, her medicine, her life. Her heart. He wasn't offering marriage; he was presenting an impossible choice.

He reached to stroke her cheek, but she pulled back, suddenly afraid to let him touch her.

He frowned at her reaction. "Don't you want to be with me, Kate?"

"Yes," she answered honestly, so softly there was no sound.

Of course she wanted to be with him, but at what cost— marriage to him or her freedom? She wouldn't make the same mistake her mother had and marry a man who did not love her. She wouldn't surrender her life, not when she'd already lost her heart.

She pressed her hand against her chest, which burned with the anguish and misery of grief, and she inhaled sharply, knowing his heartbreaking response even as she whispered, "But you don't love me."

"And you don't love me," he countered evenly.

But she did. How could she not love this man, who protected her and promised to keep her safe, who both teased and infuriated her, who made her feel beautiful and wanted? Yet she could never tell him, not as long as he didn't share those feelings. And she wouldn't marry him unless he did. A married woman's life belonged solely to her husband to control, her heart his to wound, her body his to beat or rape, and a man who did not love his wife had little incentive to be kind. Her father had proven that.

Edward wasn't her father, but for all that he'd promised to protect her and made being in his arms so very special, he did not love her.

"Besides, we might not have a choice." He raised a brow. "You might have gotten with child."

With a gasp, she covered her belly with her hands, as if a baby were certainly there. But it wasn't, it couldn't be—

but the panic inside her only grew. "I won't enter a loveless marriage, Edward."

He gave a gentle shake of his head. "If you are carrying the Strathmore heir—"

"I'm not."

"If you are," he repeated, his calm voice only making the emotions churn faster inside her, "we will marry, whether you want to or not."

"I'm *not*," she forced out, somehow finding the strength to boldly meet his dark gaze. "So there is no point in continuing this conversation."

She began to scramble from the bed, but he grabbed her arm and tugged her back to him.

"Kate," he said gently, "I am asking you to be my duchess—"

"I won't give up my medical work." She latched on to the feeble excuse in order to avoid telling him the truth— and oh, how pathetic he would think her if he knew! That she was willing to give up the possibility of a future with him because she foolishly believed in love. Rather, because she knew the devastating consequences of its absence. She pushed against his chest, even now mindful not to hurt his wound. "I can't be both your wife and a doctor, we both know that. No respectable gentleman would let his wife be around diseases and half-dressed male patients, or even be a midwife. Certainly not a duke. There would be gossip and cuts and—"

"No, you can't be both," he agreed solemnly. "A duchess as a doctor would be too scandalous."

She'd put him into an impossible situation, she knew. For all that Edward was nothing like other English peers, he still carried the weight of the Westover reputation on his shoulders, and giving in to her impossible demand to be a doctor was too much, even for him.

"Then I won't be your duchess." She looked away, hoping he wouldn't see in her expression the unbearable anguish and utter desolation tearing at her heart.

But he took her face and forced her to look at him. "It's only because of that, then?" he pressed, his dark eyes flickering as they searched her face for answers. "Because you won't give up your medicine."

She drew a deep breath and lied, "Yes."

He cursed sharply, and she saw the frustration rise instantly in him, the anger smoldering beneath. He shoved himself off the bed and snatched up his trousers, yanked them on, and angrily fastened them.

"I'm so sorry, but I cannot marry you, Edward," she whispered, her heart breaking.

"You will." His quiet words were an order, but she heard the softer pleading underneath. "Because you might not be willing to give up being a doctor, angel." He placed his hands on the mattress and leaned over her, his eyes burning with determination as he lowered his face level with hers. "But I'm not willing to give up *you*."

His mouth captured hers in a fierce kiss. There was no tenderness in him, no persuasion; his kiss was predatory and possessive, making no mistake that he'd branded her with his body and claimed her for his, and now he wanted all of her, body *and* soul.

But what Kate wanted, she could never have, because what she wanted was simply everything—a home, her medical work, and Edward's love.

She would never marry for anything less. Not even to him.

CHAPTER EIGHTEEN

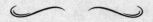

 *Y*ou're certain Benton followed them?" Edward's eyes flicked away from the former sergeant standing before his desk to glance toward Nathaniel Grey as he leaned back against the windowsill. It had been a fortnight since Hedley first saw Benton spying on the two women on Bond Street and reported it to Grey and Edward, and Phillip Benton's activities troubled both of them. Today, he'd been spotted following them through Hyde Park. "Was there any contact between them?"

"No, Colonel, none," Hedley assured him. The man Grey hired to keep watch on Benton's every move had served with them in the Scarlet Scoundrels and was completely trustworthy. "He never got close enough. Don't think they saw 'im at all."

"But he saw them." Unconsciously, he rubbed his hand against his sore shoulder.

Hedley paused, choosing his words carefully. "Can't be certain, sir. If he did, 'e didn't react none."

No—Benton knew Augusta and Kate were there, Edward had no doubt. What he didn't know was what the man hoped to gain.

"Most likely coincidental."

Edward frowned. Too much coincidence for comfort. "Anything else unusual?"

"Nothin', sir."

"If he follows the countess or Miss Benton again, tell me immediately." His eyes flicked to Grey. "And Litchfield?"

"He caught a ship for America." Grey grinned. "With a little help."

Edward grimaced. "Do I want to know the nature of that help?"

"No, sir." Grey's eyes met his, wholly unrepentant. "I don't think you do."

Hedley spoke up, "Anythin' else, then, Colonel?"

"Not for now." Edward stood and handed Hedley his payment. "But keep a close watch. He got by us with Litchfield. I don't trust him not to try something again."

When Hedley nodded, Grey added, "We could help him to America, too."

The thought of Phillip Benton shackled and impressed onto a ship bound for the ends of the earth was appealing. Damnably appealing. And for a moment, as his eyes met Grey's and he saw the man arch a brow in silent suggestion, he considered it strongly, then shook his head. "You can't guarantee he'd stay there."

"Actually, sir." Hedley cleared his throat and lowered his voice. "I think we might could help 'im w' that, too."

Edward knew exactly what kind of help Hedley implied, and he couldn't let that happen, no matter how tempting. "Just keep watching him. He knows we caught him scheming with Litchfield. Perhaps that will be enough to keep him in line."

"Aye, sir. I'll track 'im down right now." Hedley gave him a smart salute.

Edward hesitated before returning it. He was no longer an officer, but he wouldn't deny that he missed army life or the dedication of men like Hedley.

When the ex-sergeant left, Edward crossed to the liquor cabinet to pour two glasses of whiskey and handed one to Grey. It was too early in the evening to start drinking, but he didn't care. The news Hedley had brought of Benton stalking Augusta and Kate rattled him and only reinforced what he knew to be true—Benton was dangerous.

"Tell me the truth, Grey." Edward frowned into his whiskey. "What was Benton doing in Hyde Park?"

"I think he was plotting out what to do next. And he will do something. It's only a matter of time."

"You think I should send him a message, then, to fall in line?"

Grey tossed back half the glass in a single, gasping swallow. "I think you should let him go."

But Edward would never do that. He would never release Benton from his control. "He's already had me shot. What else can he do to me?"

"Next time not miss."

To drive home his point, Grey poked him in his wounded shoulder. Edward sucked in a harsh breath through clenched teeth and somehow kept from punching him.

"That won't happen again." Rubbing his shoulder, Edward shook his head. "But I don't want him anywhere near my family."

"That's the problem, though, isn't it?" Grey studied him over the rim of the glass. "Katherine Benton's not family."

The unintended irony of the comment hit too close to home, almost as sharp as the pain in his shoulder. Kate wasn't family only because she refused to marry him.

He rubbed at his shoulder, the ache lingering, as did his growing frustration. In the week since he'd proposed and she'd refused, the stubborn woman had also refused to open her bedroom door to him at night and never left Augusta's side during the day.

"She's making her debut tonight, and the bachelors will flock around her." Grey shrugged. "Let her settle on one of them and get her off your hands."

Edward gave a bitter but confident laugh. "She won't marry any of those sheep."

"She will if she spots the right ram."

"Not her," he mumbled into his glass, taking a gulp of whiskey and welcoming the burn in his throat. "You don't know what she's like. You've never even met the woman."

A rakish smile pulled at his lips. "But I'd like to."

"*No.*"

The unintended jealousy in the single word surprised even Edward, and instead of having the planned effect of warning his friend away, Grey's smirk blossomed into a full-out grin at Edward's expense.

Grey tossed back the last of his whiskey and set down the glass, then pushed himself to his feet to leave.

"I'll keep close watch on Benton," he assured him. "Count on that."

"And Thomas?"

"He's keeping watch on *you*."

That rankled him. "I don't need to be watched."

"Oh yes, you do." He shot him a glance tinged with worry. "End this, Colonel. Send Benton to the Americas and the girl back to the countryside. No good will come of this."

But it was too late to stop, the events bringing him to this moment having been unfolding for over a year. Benton deserved punishment for Stephen's death, and the thought of sending Kate away again—no.

"Goodness has nothing to do with it," he muttered. "I'll show you out."

Pushing aside all thoughts that Grey might very well be right, Edward walked with him through the house. Although, he was loath to admit, his trip to the front foyer was also to see what new entreaties had arrived for Kate.

She'd taken society by storm, even with her presentation at court just yesterday and her official debut not until tonight at the Countess of St. James's ball. Yet she'd already become the most sought-after lady in London and, thanks to Augusta's well-planned strategies, the talk of the season. The front door never seemed to shut for all the visitors who came by to leave their calling cards and the deliverymen dropping off gifts.

"Good God." Grey stopped suddenly at the sight.

Dozens of floral arrangements filled the entrance, matching the ones already sitting in the morning room, the drawing room, the breakfast room—Edward chased a footman out of his billiards room yesterday when the man tried to place an arrangement of daisies there. There were other gifts, too...chocolates, ribbons, baskets with notes from young men offering to fill them with her favorite foods and take her on a picnic.

Edward grimaced at side table and the silver salver, which was buried under the collective weight of calling cards, and the ones from gentlemen callers stacked separately to the side per Augusta's orders. Those, he snatched up himself.

Grey looked at him and crooked a brow. "Baaaa."

"Get out." Edward shoved his friend outside. The last thing he heard as he shut the door was Grey's laughter.

He scowled. Augusta wanted Kate to be the toast of the season, but this was getting out of hand. Flowers, baskets, books, ribbons—one coxcomb, upon hearing the rumor that Kate missed the countryside, brought her a bird in a cage so she could have a bit of nature with her in the city.

A bird! *Good God.* The next thing he knew, one of them would try to win her heart by buying her a pony—

He froze, then blew out an angry breath at himself and rolled his eyes. *Christ.*

With a scowl, he stomped back into his study and tossed the calling cards into the fire. "Damned fool," he muttered at himself. "Stupid, besotted idiot..."

Although she claimed she wouldn't marry anyone, Kate would have her choice of offers by season's end, and one of those dandies would undoubtedly claim she could continue her medical work. Although it would be a lie—whomever she married would never let her continue to tend to half-dressed male patients and birth babies—Edward would lose her because he wouldn't make the same false claim.

She couldn't be both a duchess and a doctor, and fear tightened in his chest that she was already slipping away.

And now, the house was all aflutter over tonight's event—her debut at the Countess of St. James's annual ball, where she would be introduced to London society as his ward. Already the rumor was circulating among the servants that she resembled an angel in her ball gown.

An angel.

"Damned fool!"

Pacing the study, he shook his head. He didn't know what to do. She wanted to return to Brambly and her medical work, but he wasn't willing to let her go. Medicine! It was ludicrous that she should be so adamant about a profession not even publicly open to women that she was willing to toss over a future with him for it.

True, she'd helped the villagers, and he'd seen with his own eyes how she brought that baby into the world, which made his chest swell with more pride for her than he had a right to feel. But if she married him, she couldn't continue her medical work. As Duchess of Strathmore, she would be one of the most powerful and high-profile women in England, her every move watched and scrutinized. She couldn't seriously expect him to allow her to continue to don breeches and ride off in the middle of the night—

"Edward?" Augusta frowned from the doorway, her burgundy ball gown shimmering as brightly as her diamond tiara. "Are you feeling well?"

"Fine," he lied, forcing a smile for her. "You look stunning."

"Thank you." Her lips curled bemusedly at the obvious flattery. "You look rather terrifying."

"Thank you." He grimaced, saying nothing more. The

last thing he wanted to do was share with his aunt the reasons for his foul mood.

He glanced past her, and she caught his wandering gaze. "If you are hoping to catch a glimpse of Katherine—"

"I'm not." Another lie. Seeing her was exactly what he'd hoped.

"She's still dressing. I wanted a few minutes alone with you before we left."

"Whatever the reason for your visit, you do look lovely." He took her hand as she swept across the room to him and squeezed it briefly. "I hope Isabel Sinclair is ready to accept you as the diamond of her ball."

"That pleasure will belong solely to Katherine," she corrected, "if I have my way."

"You always do."

"Not always." She gave him that regal look of displeasure she'd used on him since he was a boy. "I am not getting my way tonight."

Not bothering to stifle his irritation, he retreated a few feet to lean against his desk, folding his arms. "We've been through this—"

"Lady St. James is expecting you, and Alexander Sinclair has already agreed to give Katherine the second waltz. It is quite a coup for her to have both a duke and an earl reserved for her waltz partners." She smiled, pleased at the filling of Kate's dance card before she even arrived at the ball and oblivious to the jealousy stabbing Edward at the thought of Kate in the arms of that rake Sinclair, earl or not. "So call for Huddleston and change so you can escort us to the ball."

"No."

She arched an imperious brow, not yet weary of fighting this battle, the same one she'd been fighting with him since the invitation arrived. "What excuse do I make for you, then, the guardian who cannot be bothered to introduce his ward?"

"Well, you could remind everyone I've been shot." Her eyes narrowed at his impertinence, but he unrepentantly shrugged, adding, "After all, if fighting a duel can't get a man out of one boring ball, then truly, what good is it?"

"You nearly died." Her voice trembled with emotion as she scolded softly, "Do not jest about such things."

His shoulders sagged. Augusta deserved neither his contempt nor his cynicism, and he felt guilty unleashing them on her. Truly, she was only attempting to repair whatever damage he'd done to the Westover family reputation, however unintentionally.

But she kept pressing, and between her constant assaults and Kate's ever-present temptation, he was reaching the limits of his patience. And sanity.

"My apologies," he said, exhaling deeply. "I simply don't feel up to venturing into society yet."

He rolled his shoulders, failing to ease the tension that had seeped into them during the past week—since the moment when Kate chose her medicine over him.

"Thomas has agreed to escort you tonight," he told her, "and he'll do an excellent job in my stead."

"But he isn't her guardian," she reminded him. "You can leave early if you feel fatigued."

It wouldn't be fatigue that plagued him if he was forced to be with Kate all night, both of them pretending they were nothing but guardian and ward. Worse, he would be expected to waltz with her, and the thought of holding her in his arms, then having to release her to another man—

"No," he refused firmly. He circled behind his desk,

then reached for the stack of reports from his estate agents, wanting to focus his attention anywhere else than on Katherine Benton.

After several moments when Augusta remained standing doggedly before him, not saying anything, not moving, he raised his eyes. The mix of emotions on her face pierced him, a look of maternal love, disappointment, sorrow...all for him.

"Katherine is not Jane," she commented quietly.

For a beat, he froze, every muscle in his body shocked from the jolt of her words. *Jane.* She knew about their affair—somehow, Augusta *knew*!

Dear God. She'd known all along.

He swallowed. "Did Stephen...?"

"No. Your brother went to his grave ignorant of what happened between you two." She shook her head. "He never would have married her if he'd known. Your brother was always loyal to you beyond measure."

He looked away, unable to bring his guilty gaze to meet hers. "I was in the army, and she..."

"She wanted to be a duchess," she finished quietly. "You have a right to be angry at her, but she should not be allowed to continue to hurt you. She is dead, Edward." Her voice softened. "Let her go."

Tenderly, she went to him and brushed his hair from his forehead. There was no exasperated anger in her elegant features now, just deep motherly concern and grief.

"I have." Then he pulled away from her until she couldn't reach him.

Her hand dropped to her side. He knew he'd hurt her, but he couldn't help it.

"Katherine is not Jane," Augusta repeated, more firmly

this time. "Yet you are in love with that girl just the same as you loved Jane, and it terrifies you because you are afraid she will hurt you just as much."

"I am *not* in love with her." His words were raw and unchecked. "I won't love any woman, not even her."

As if in challenge, Augusta stared unflinchingly at him. "If your heart is truly dead, then so be it—but Katherine does not deserve to be persecuted for another woman's sins. She deserves to be happy." Her expression saddened. "If not with you, then with someone else. Either make her yours, or let her go."

All the anger, torment, and humiliation of Kate's rejection surged to the surface in a white-hot pain. "And how exactly do I do that," he forced out through clenched teeth, "when the damned woman has refused to marry me but the guardianship is keeping us together?"

Augusta froze. Then she blinked, incredulous. "Pardon?"

"I asked her to marry me, and she refused," he said quietly, but each word ripped at his heart as he admitted that Kate didn't want him for a husband. The rejection wounded with the same force and pain as the bullet that had pierced his shoulder. "She wants to be let go, but I can't even give her that, because under the law I'm responsible for her until she marries, which she swears never to do. And if I void the guardianship, I'll be leaving her unprotected, which I've sworn never to do." He gave a bitter laugh. "We're damned either way."

His aunt stared at him incredulously, then her face softened with sympathy. "Oh, Edward, I had no idea...," she whispered, her eyes glistening with disappointment. "I thought you two were still furious at each other."

He *was* furious at Kate, and every unbidden thought of

her tore at his chest in equal amounts of futile exasperation and agony. He'd wanted her to be different from other
women, thought that in her he'd finally found someone
he could trust and let into his life, make his wife and the
mother of his children.

But she'd been exactly like Jane—another woman who
did not love him enough to marry him. Except that this time,
when he was able to offer the duchy with the ring, she'd refused precisely because she did not want to be a duchess.

He would have laughed at the irony if his chest wasn't
burning from it.

"But why?" Her brows furrowed in bewilderment. "That
girl loves you. It is clear as day every time she so much as
glances—"

"She loves medicine more." He blew out a harsh breath,
his shoulders sagging, as he explained, "She can't be both
a duchess and a doctor. You know that."

"No, there must be more to it than that. Much more."
She touched his arm and firmly ordered, "You must ask her
again, Edward, and this time, not let her refuse with such a
false excuse."

He shook his head. "Augusta—"

"Ask her again," she urged. Then she closed the distance
between them and lifted onto her tiptoes to kiss his temple.
Despite himself, he obliged by lowering his head. "For me,
my dear boy."

With a last touch to his cheek, her eyes glistening, she
swept from the room.

Blowing out a harsh breath, he poured himself a fresh
glass of whiskey. *Make her yours or let her go.* He laughed
caustically. That's exactly what he'd been trying to do
since the moment he met her.

He ran a frustrated hand through his hair. He never expected Kate to refuse to be his wife, not after the way she rode halfway across the country to nurse him back to life, not after the way she shattered in his arms. And yet…

He frowned. Could Augusta be right? Certainly, the medicine was a part of her refusal. But she hadn't even argued for a compromise, and if there was one thing he'd learned about Katherine Benton, it was that the frustrating woman argued over everything. *Everything.* She should have argued over this, too.

But she hadn't. She'd simply refused. And *that* was nothing like the hellcat he knew.

Setting the glass down untasted, he stalked from the study and through the house, taking the stairs three at a time to reach the family bedrooms in the west wing.

Kate's door was open. When he paused in the doorway, finding her seated at her dressing table while her maid put the last touches on her coiffure, her eyes flickered warily at him in the mirror. He didn't blame her for her suspicions. He wasn't feeling particularly trustworthy himself these days.

"Your Grace." Mary saw him and dropped into a curtsy.

"I need a moment alone with Miss Benton."

Kate lifted her chin defiantly. "Mary, please stay."

The young maid looked uncertainly between mistress and master, biting her bottom lip.

Edward pinned her with a look. "Leave."

"Yes, sir!" Mary fled from the room, still gripping the hairbrush in her hands.

Her eyes glaring at him in disapproval in the mirror, Kate set down the combs she'd been holding. "Edward, you cannot just order her—"

Without moving his eyes from her reflection, he shut the door with a single push of his hand.

She startled, nervousness flashing across her face before she replaced it with an irritated scowl. "Either open that door or call Mary back. We need a chaperone—"

He flipped the lock.

She hesitated just a beat, then slowly rose to her feet in indignation.

He almost smiled at the way she reminded him of Augusta and that imperial bearing of hers, that same look of regal haughtiness...until she faced him and he caught the full impact of how she looked in her silk ball gown of Westover blue, with diamonds and sapphires shining at her neck and ears. For once, she didn't look anything like an angel or a country gel and would-be doctor. Or even the woman who both infuriated and aroused him until he lost his mind.

She looked like a duchess.

She was breathtaking, and not just in that gown. He'd seen her covered with mud and stains, in old dresses that didn't fit properly, and once even in her dressing robe. He'd seen her deliciously sleep-rumpled, too, that dawn after the storm when she awoke in his arms. However much he wanted to deny it, the attraction he felt for her went beyond just beauty. Whenever he was with her, even in the middle of an angry row, he felt alive. And for the first time, he felt as if his life truly mattered, that his existence was more than just being second to Stephen.

He stared at her, his dark eyes not knowing where to look that didn't cause the hairs on his arms to stand on end with desire. *Sweet Lucifer.* He was unprepared for the liquid fire that rippled down his spine at the sight of her, the pulse of longing in his chest to draw her into his arms. His heart thudded with a dull ache, and a heartbreaking image flashed through his mind of all he'd lost by her refusal to marry him.

"Edward," she said tightly, "open the door."

"No."

With a long-suffering sigh, indicating that she knew he wouldn't give in until he had whatever it was he'd come for, she irritably folded her arms. Which was a mistake because it only drew his attention to the low-cut neckline and the tops of her breasts.

"Well," she insisted, "what do you want?"

"You."

Her eyes widened. That wasn't the answer she expected, but it was exactly what he wanted—Kate, body and soul, belonging only to him, pledging her life to him.

He stalked slowly across the room to her, but to her credit, she didn't retreat. Instead, she stood her ground, her eyes narrowing. "Stop playing games, Edward."

"I'm deadly serious."

"I won't—"

"Why, Katherine?" he demanded, jumping right to the heart of the matter.

She knew what he was asking, and her shoulders lowered. "I told you. I won't give up my medicine. They need me at Brambly."

"And I want you with me." Another step closer, and he felt rather than heard her catch her breath at his persistence.

She turned her face away, not daring to look at him. "You cannot change my mind, Edward."

"Is that why you've been keeping me from your bed?" He was close enough now to murmur the quiet accusation in her ear and to feel the resulting shiver fall through her. "Afraid I'll seduce you into agreeing to marry me?"

"No." But her voice lacked conviction, and its trembling completely undercut her reply.

That was exactly it, he knew. It had been a week since they'd last been intimate, and the way she closed her eyes, as if willing her body to shrink away from him even as she leaned closer, told him that she felt the absence of him as intensely as he did her.

"We want each other, Kate." When he placed his hands on her shoulders, then lightly caressed down her bare arms, goose bumps sprang up everywhere he touched... *Amazing.* "There's no reason we can't marry and take that pleasure whenever we want."

"That doesn't signify—"

"But it does." A smile touched his lips at her obstinacy. Another featherlight caress, this time back up her arms, brushing his thumbs along the sides of her breasts as his hands slid upward. She whimpered so softly he almost didn't hear her, and his cock twitched, already beginning to harden with the delicious pleasure-pain of arousal. "A significant part of a marriage, I should think."

"I don't—"

With a groan, he drew her soft body along the length of his and kissed her, urgent and openmouthed, and she melted weakly against him, grabbing for his waistcoat to fist it into her hands and pull him impossibly closer.

At her reaction, a surge of adrenaline coursed through him with each tattoo beat of his pulse. He knew that feeling—the same feeling he always had when he was with her, since the first moment he laid eyes on her. He felt *alive.*

"No other woman has ever done to me what you have." He tore his mouth away from hers to nip his teeth along her jaw. He wanted to devour every inch of her, and the frustration of being kept from her only added to his urgent need to possess her.

"Wh-what have I done?" she stammered, although at that moment he couldn't have said whether her shaking was from hearing him admit his feelings or from the way his tongue plunged into her ear.

"Make me want you this desperately." He sank his teeth into her earlobe, and when he felt her moan shoot through him, he went instantly hard.

She wrapped her arms around his neck, but even as she dug her fingertips into his hard muscles, she was careful to avoid the tender spot on his shoulder where the bullet had torn into him. And her concern made him even more desperate to have her.

He slid his hands up her back and made quick work of undoing the fastenings of her dress. The gown was too tightly fit, too low cut for a shift. With nothing between her skin and the soft silk, he stripped the bodice down to her waist and dipped his head to lick at her nipple. She whimpered, her fingers combing through his hair as she arched toward him and tugged his head harder against her, thrusting her breast deeper into his mouth as he suckled greedily at her.

"I want you for my wife, Kate." He swept his mouth to her other breast as his hands moved down to cup her bottom.

"You want to control me," she corrected in a breathless pant. Despite her words, a soft mewling of need passed her lips, and he smiled devilishly. She wanted him as much as he wanted her.

"Yes." He lifted her against him, pressing his stiff cock into her belly so there would be no mistaking exactly how much he wanted her. How very much he wanted her to surrender to his control.

Kate tensed, her hands releasing his waistcoat, and she pulled away to stare up into his eyes. Sadness darkened her face, and the look pierced straight through him.

"I can't—I can't let you do that," she whispered. "Edward . . . no."

His frustration reached its snapping point, and he shoved himself back with a curse and spun on his heels to move away. He kept half the room between them, not trusting himself at that moment not to charge back to her and seduce her into changing her mind.

Damned woman! Stubborn, obstinate— *Dear God*, winning against the French had been easier than winning against her.

She pulled her dress up to cover herself. "Edward, please understand." She raised her chin, despite the glistening of her eyes. She was just as frustrated and upset as he was, but the little hellcat wouldn't admit it. "I won't give up my medical work."

His eyes narrowed on her as he studied her face, reading her emotions and the guilty flicker in her eyes, the way she bit her bottom lip—Augusta was right. There was more to her refusal than just her medicine.

Well, if she persisted in claiming it was being a doctor that prevented her from marrying him, he'd give her exactly what she wanted. And then force the truth from her when she could no longer give that as an excuse.

"Very well." Stalking slowly toward her, he smiled at her, and apprehension marred her face at the sudden change in him. "If you marry me, you can keep practicing your medicine. You won't have to stop helping the sick."

"Pardon?" She paled.

"As a duchess, you'll be expected to maintain a certain propriety, so there won't be any more rides through storms to birth babies. But there are other ways you can continue your work." Giving in to her demand—within reason— was the right decision anyway because he wanted her to be happy and he wanted her for his wife, yet he chose his words carefully, to be perfectly clear about the terms he was offering. "But you can hire a doctor for the village and oversee his practice, and there's no reason why you can't continue quietly with your experiments in the country. And in the city, you can be a hospital patroness. I won't lie to you—the *ton* won't make life easy for you. But it's the only way for you to have both." When she only stared up at him silently, he arched a brow. "I'm proposing a compromise, Kate—part duchess, part doctor. That was what you wanted, wasn't it? Marriage if you could continue with your medicine."

As her lips parted delicately in stunned disbelief, he could see the thoughts spinning rapidly through her mind, saw her hand raise to press at her heart as a tormented darkness flickered in her eyes...

"So you'll marry me now."

She breathed, "No."

The single word pierced his chest like a knife, so painful it forced him back a step. Fresh pain tore at his gut. "Damn it, Kate! Why not?"

Then she whispered the heartrending truth, her words little more than an anguished breath, "Because you don't love me."

He froze and stared at her. *Love?* Was that what this was about?

Of course, he didn't love her. He cared for her—he would admit that, just as he'd admit that the darkness that had nearly consumed him for the past ten years was gone now, replaced by a peace he'd never known. Yet in his life, he'd told only one woman he loved her, and she'd betrayed him, rejecting not just his love but also who he was as a man and everything he'd worked so hard to become. And he'd nearly died from it. He'd wanted to die. Hell, he'd *tried* his damnedest to die. And nearly did.

Kate wasn't Jane, he knew that. He trusted her, desired her, enjoyed being with her...but he would never again position himself to be wounded the way Jane had hurt him.

He shook his head. He would offer her marriage and a home together, children, and her medical work. He would protect her and care for her, give her every luxury money could buy, and create the best life possible for her.

But he would never love her.

"I care about you, Kate," he said instead and saw the acute disappointment flash across her face. It wasn't what she wanted to hear, but that was as close as he would ever let himself come to loving her. "And I want you with me because you make me happy. I will be a kind husband to you and a good father to our children." He touched her chin and tilted her face up to look into her eyes. "Do you trust me?"

She gave a jerking nod, but the wretched sadness he saw in her green eyes broke his heart.

"Then let that be enough."

She shook her head and repeated, "You don't love me."

Damnation! Why was she demanding love of him, when

she didn't feel the same? He blew out a harsh breath of frustration. "And you don't love me!"

For an agonizing moment, there was only silence... then she whispered breathlessly, "But I do."

He saw the flash of raw grief shudder through her, how her eyes watered with gathering tears, the look of utter abandonment and desolation marring her beautiful face... The air ripped from his lungs.

Christ.

Kate was in love with him.

* * *

For several moments, neither spoke, neither moved. She counted her slow breaths while she waited for him to answer her. To say he loved her, too. Or just say... anything.

When he didn't, she looked away from his incredulous stare, praying she had enough strength not to break down.

She was such a fool! Of course, he didn't love her. Why would he? Simply because she wanted it, like some wish on a starry night... Foolish, foolish! Her entire body pulsed hollow with pain. Excruciating! So hard she lost her breath and each heartbeat came like a hammer blow in her chest. She hadn't imagined anyone could ever wound her this much simply by being silent.

Forcing herself to breathe, she stepped away, and her hands shook as she smoothed them down the front of her dress with the pretense of pressing out the wrinkles. "It's all right if you don't feel the same," she whispered, not daring to look at him. "I know you don't, and I don't expect you to."

"Kate," he finally whispered, but nothing else came from his stunned lips.

She shut her eyes tightly against his silence, but then, what else could he say except to lie and admit to feelings he didn't have for her? He wanted to marry her, give her a family, protect her...Any woman would have been thrilled to receive such an offer.

But it wasn't enough for her. And it never would be.

She drew a shaking breath and confessed, "My parents were forced to marry—my mother was increasing, you see." For a moment, she let her hand rest against her belly, then dropped it away, not daring to wish for the wonderful miracle of having Edward's baby inside her. "She loved my father to her dying breath." She trembled at the painful memories, her voice quivering. "But he never loved her, and he made her life a living hell. He stole from her, said such hateful things, made horrible accusations..." She pressed her fingers against her mouth.

Edward stepped up behind her and touched her arm, and for once, the heat of his fingers didn't sooth or excite but pierced through to her heart. "Katherine, I am not like your father."

She shook her head, not knowing how to make him understand. "A married woman's life is not her own. Everything she has and does is by her husband's leave. If her husband doesn't love her but she loves him—" She choked, a soft sob escaping from her lips. "It nearly destroyed my mother, Edward. I won't live that life."

"I will never hurt you." He slipped his arms around her and gently drew her back against him. "What can I do to reassure you?"

Love me. But he didn't, and she wasn't certain he ever could.

She slowly stepped out of his arms, and thankfully, he let her go without struggle. "If you can't love me, then I won't be your wife, Edward."

"Kate." Her name was an anguished rasp. "Please."

She shook her head, the hot tears stinging at her lashes preventing any more words from coming. But truly, what was left to say, except the admission of love he would never give?

The moment she'd met him, he'd inverted her world until it was impossible to tell up from down, forward from backward, all of it swirling together. He had caused her so much suffering and torment, so much anger, but he'd also revealed the tenderness and vulnerability in himself, the kindness and loyalty that made her fall in love with him. Even when he'd sent her to the moors, he'd exiled her for his own protection, to keep his heart from breaking. She'd forgiven him for that and accepted why he'd done it, knowing he'd never do it again…

But she couldn't accept not being loved.

"I think you should leave now," she said as firmly as her trembling voice allowed.

He nodded slowly, but the firm nod of resolve couldn't hide from her eyes the anguish that flitted across his face, so fleeting that anyone else would have missed it.

But not her. She'd come to know him so well that he could hide none of his feelings from her now behind that carefully stoic face he showed to the world like a mask. The misery inside him was just as great as that swirling through her, but there was no help for it. He couldn't force himself to love her, just as she couldn't force herself to stop loving him.

"Come here," he ordered quietly.

Her lips parted, surprised, and her eyes blinked rapidly to clear her blurry eyes as she stared at him. He wanted to...hold her? "Pardon?"

"I have to fasten up your dress," he explained.

"Oh." Disappointment ripped her breath away that she was denied this final time in his arms, but she somehow found the strength to whisper, "Of course."

He frowned as she turned her back to him, and he began to secure her dress, to hide all traces that he'd just bared her to the waist and had his mouth on her. The heat of his fingers next to her bare skin was torture, but thank God he was careful not to let his fingers accidentally brush against her as he fastened the last of the tiny hooks. She couldn't have borne it.

When he finished straightening her, she wordlessly returned to her dressing table and reached for the combs she'd been holding when he'd barged inside. Once she was seated, he straightened his shoulders, took a deep breath, and opened the door.

Mary waited outside in the hallway, and she hurried over to Kate to finish her coiffure as if they'd never been interrupted, completely ignoring Edward now as she concentrated on Kate's hair, obviously more afraid of Kate's appearing before Augusta with curls out of place than of any lack of propriety that might have occurred between them.

As he stepped into the hall and paused to glance back at her, her eyes found his in the mirror, holding them for just a moment before looking away, unable to bear the anger and pain she saw in him. "Would you close the door, please, Mary?"

"Yes, miss." The maid hesitated as she saw Edward still lingering in the hallway, then bit her lip in silent apology and shut the door.

Mary reached to take the combs from her hands and worked in silence for several minutes to secure the last pins into place. From the way the little maid avoided making eye contact with her, Kate knew she suspected...but she was too kind to make any comment or show any look of pity.

"Perfect." Kate summoned all the strength within her to force a smile as Mary finished her hair and stepped back. "Would you please go downstairs and tell the countess that I'm going to be a few minutes longer?"

"Yes, miss." Mary left quickly, the door closing behind her with a soft click.

Alone, Kate stared at her reflection. For a moment, she didn't recognize herself. The woman in the mirror was dressed so elegantly in silks and jewels, her hair swept into a shining glory on her head. Regal. Beautiful—except that she was crying, tears rolling down her pale cheeks. She looked so sad, filled with so much grief, as if mourning her own death. At least Kate didn't have to look at her for very long, because her own eyes were blurring so much she could no longer see anything.

It was over. All the happiness she'd known with Edward, all the joy she'd felt in his arms, all the wonderful possibilities of a future with him...All of it, gone.

She squeezed her eyes shut against the agonizing pain and somehow found the will to stop the tears, if not the grief. And it *was* grief, because she was grieving over her lost future with Edward with as much wretchedness as when she lost her mother.

Oh, she'd been a fool! To ever hope...but there was no hope now. To love a man who did not love her, even after they'd made themselves so vulnerable to each other—the anguish was excruciating, and to continue on like this would only destroy her the same way it destroyed her mother.

Edward was never going to love her, and she couldn't remain here any longer. She needed to leave. To return to her life at Brambly, to her work caring for the servants and the villagers, and find a way to carry on, as if she'd never met him. And somehow make that life enough.

Tonight she would go to the ball and pretend everything was fine. She owed it to Augusta to put in a proper appearance, and she cared for the woman too much not to give her this one night of showing her off as Edward's ward and restoring the Westover reputation.

And tomorrow, she would return to Brambly, but she would never again be with Edward. Would the compensation be enough—her freedom for her heart?

Behind her, the door opened, and she heard not Mary's soft footsteps but a man's heavy tread. She choked on her tears, fresh pain shattering through her.

Edward. He'd come back, most likely to try to convince her one last time to change her mind, perhaps even to seduce her into surrendering and agreeing to marry him. Despite the anguish burning inside her, a shiver of heat fell through her. Just as it always would for this man. She would always love him, even if he never loved her.

Drawing a deep breath, praying she had the strength to refuse him, she swiped at her eyes and turned. "Edward, please—"

A hand clamped over her mouth as she screamed.

* * *

Edward stormed downstairs and back into his study, seeking out the quiet sanctuary the room usually afforded him but tonight finding no release from the frustration swirling inside him, the clenching of his gut, nor the pounding of his heart, which still beat furiously from his encounter with Kate in her room.

His hand shook as he poured himself a whiskey. Even as he tossed back the drink in one gasping gulp and welcomed the burn down his throat, he couldn't shake the raw emotion eating at him. So he poured a second and found just as little solace in it.

Running a hand through his hair, he struggled to fight down the shaking that gripped him and the overwhelming sense of emptiness aching in his chest, which threatened to consume him. He'd lost her. She was gone forever now, with absolutely no help for it.

He splashed more whiskey into his glass, determined to drink himself into oblivion.

Thomas Matteson had already arrived to escort Augusta and Kate to the ball—he'd glimpsed the marquess's carriage waiting in the drive through the stairwell window when he left Kate's room. All three of them would soon be gathered in the drawing room down the hall, enjoying a bit of quiet conversation and a glass of Madeira before heading off. As duke and host, and as the damned woman's guardian on the night she was being formally introduced, he should have been in there with them. Hell, at the very least he should have greeted Thomas.

But he couldn't make himself join them, couldn't pretend in front of Thomas and Augusta that Kate's rejection of him wasn't tearing at him. Even now, the image burned into his mind of Kate standing there in her ball grown, looking every inch a duchess, with tears at her lashes as she admitted to loving him.

"*Damnation!*" He threw the glass into the fireplace, shattering it in a rain of crystal and fire.

He fisted his hands against the back of his chair. What the hell did she expect? That he'd declare his undying love like some untried green boy who didn't know firsthand the pain and problems that love caused? That he would leave himself vulnerable to wounding by a woman again, and especially by her?

He didn't doubt her feelings. For God's sake, she'd ridden halfway across the country to save his life. And the way she'd given herself to him, so sincerely and with so much vulnerability and passion, how tenderly she'd kissed him afterward... well, she couldn't have faked that. *That* was the one thing about which he was certain.

He'd wanted her desperately that night at the lock-keeper's cottage, the night that started it all—he *still* wanted her, more than he'd wanted any woman in his life. Even more than Jane. But if he cared only about satisfying his lust, he would have become bored with her by now and moved on without a thought.

Of course, it wasn't just lust. It was everything about her, right down to the stubborn way she raised her chin whenever he aggravated her. He wanted the warmth that filled him whenever she smiled and the amusement he felt whenever she frowned in irritation, the way she teased him as if they were old friends and spoke her mind as if they were adversaries—and a thousand other things that had nothing to do with sex.

He wanted a life with her.

But he would never allow himself to love her. The cost was simply too great.

A commotion went up from the entry hall at the bottom of the front stairs, followed by shouts and horse hooves on the gravel drive outside.

Uneasiness flashing through him, Edward hurried from the study.

"What's the matter?" he called to Thomas and Augusta, who were already in the hallway and just as bewildered at the evening's sudden disruption as he.

"No idea," Thomas informed him, falling into step beside him as the two men headed toward the stairs. "I just arrived and was pouring a drink for the countess—"

"Your Grace!" The butler's shout echoed through the front foyer and stairwell. "Come quickly, sir!"

Edward ran down the stairs.

A group of footmen gathered on the portico, their faces grim. The front door stood flung wide open, all the lamps blazing, and Kingsley, the butler, stood in the middle of the confusion, looking extremely put out in his own household.

"Your Grace," Kingsley called out as Edward reached the bottom of the stairs, his brows drawn tightly together. "Here, sir."

The footmen stepped back to reveal a badly beaten Hedley lying on the marble portico, his clothes torn and muddied, his hand pressed against his forehead to stanch the blood dripping from a deep gash on his head.

"Colonel." He tried to pull himself to his feet, but Edward put a hand to his shoulder and kept him down.

"Stay still," he ordered. "What happened?"

"After I left you an' the major, I went out through the

back, an' I saw Benton there i' th' alley behind th' stables. I watched 'im, to see what he would do..."

Edward tore off his cravat to press it against the man's head and stanch the bleeding. "He attacked you?"

Hedley winced. "He had help. Two men."

Edward glanced at Kingsley. "Send for a doctor."

"Go! Fetch Dr. Brandon," the butler ordered one of the footmen who hurried from the house.

"What was he doing, Hedley?"

"Breaking into th' house, sir."

"The house..." He felt the blood drain from his face as fear gripped his chest and dread pulsed through him, inexplicably knowing the worst. "Kate—where is she?"

"They took the lass, sir." Hedley tried to sit up. "They brought 'er down the back stairs and through the garden." Regret tightened his blood-smeared face. "I tried to stop 'em, but they were too many, too big..."

Edward grabbed his shoulders, his heart pounding frantically. "Did they hurt her?"

"No—I don't know."

"Did you see them leave?" A deep voice cut in calmly behind Edward.

Hedley's eyes flicked over Edward's shoulder at Thomas Matteson, and he nodded. "Aye, sir. To the north. Put her into a black carriage with crimson upholstery an' brass trim. Broken right lamp."

"And the horses?" Thomas asked, his face grim.

"Mismatched. A bay with white socks on its front legs and a blaze, the other a gray."

Edward demanded, "And the men?"

Hedley shook his head. "Didn't get a good look, Colonel, 'fore they bashed m' skull."

"You did well, Hedley." Edward clamped the man on the shoulder. "Stay here, wait for the doctor." He glanced at Augusta as she reached the bottom of the stairs. "They've taken Katherine. We're going after her. Send for Grey at his town house."

She nodded calmly despite the ashen paleness of her face.

"Tell him to bring his men. And to head north."

He rushed out the door toward the stables, with Thomas close on his heels.

Not taking the time to rouse the grooms, they quickly saddled their own horses and sprang up onto their backs. With each second that passed, Edward felt the panic grow inside him that he had lost Kate. The same metallic taste of fear that he remembered from the war formed on his tongue when he thought that he might never have the chance to see her again, never have the chance to hold her in his arms and tell her…that he loved her. And just when he'd found her again.

Thomas pulled his prancing gelding into a circle around Edward's big colt. "Don't worry, Colonel, we'll find her."

Edward nodded, his face expressionless, his back and shoulders straight. Unconsciously, he'd assumed the same posture in the saddle that had become second nature in his army years, right before he rode into battle. But that was exactly what he was doing—riding into battle once more, this time to fight for Kate.

He took the pistol Thomas pulled from beneath his formal evening jacket and handed over to him, not blinking an eye that the marquess came armed to a society ball.

"If that bastard hurts her," Edward growled, "I'll kill him."

Then he dug his heels into the horse's sides, and the colt sprang forward.

CHAPTER NINETEEN

"So, lifted your skirts for Strathmore, did you, poppet?" Rough fingers jerked the blindfold from her eyes.

Kate blinked, slowly clearing away the blurriness and bringing her father's face into focus.

He sat back on his haunches in front of her. Early morning sunlight slanted into the abandoned cottage through half-covered windows where she sat on the dirt floor. The two men who helped kidnap her played cards at a small table on the other side of the room and ignored her plight, even as a length of cloth torn from the bottom of her gown bound her hands so tightly at her wrists that her fingertips were numb.

Bruises and scrapes covered her body. They'd jammed a pistol into her side so hard that when she breathed she could still feel the bruise between her ribs. Then they forced her down the back stairs of Strathmore House and shoved her inside a carriage, placing a blindfold around her eyes and a gag in her mouth so she couldn't cry out for help or see where they had taken her.

Her father leered at her. "For your sake, you'd better hope he enjoyed rutting with you."

She knew better than to say anything to that. When her father was angry, there was no reasoning with him. And right now, he was enraged.

Instead, she calmly held up her hands. "Would you untie me, please, Papa?"

"And have you escape?" He shook his head with an amused smile. "You're my treasure, poppet." He pulled at her skirt as she sat in the dirt. "I wouldn't dare risk losing you, now that you're worth so much."

Struggling to keep the shock from registering on her face, knowing that seeing it would only please him and give him more power over her, she forced herself to keep her breathing slow and controlled, her hands from shaking. But cold fear churned inside her, and her heart raced so hard with rising panic that her chest burned.

She still wore her thin gown from last night. No fire blazed inside the cottage, and with her arms and legs bared to the cold morning air, she shivered violently. Her beautiful dress was ruined now, the skirt torn from where he'd cut off a strip of the silk to bind her, the bodice dirt-smeared from the floor of the cottage where they'd tossed her. Her fine shoes and gloves were gone, her stockings ripped, her neck and ears bare.

She fought to keep the shivering from her voice, afraid to let him see how suddenly frightened she was of him. "Where is my jewelry?"

"Where do you think?" he snorted sarcastically.

"But those don't belong to me." Augusta loaned her the beautiful sapphire-and-diamond necklace and earbobs because they matched her dress—Westover blue, the countess told her, so everyone would know she was now part of the family. "I have to return them. You can have anything else if you—"

"Brambly, that's what I want." He grabbed her chin, his fingers digging into her jaw so hard she winced. "Are you willing to give me the farm?"

Never! She'd rather die than surrender Brambly.

When she didn't answer, he shoved her head away, and she gasped softly at the sharp pain. She willed herself not to let him see that he'd hurt her, because she knew he would do it again, that he would take pleasure in causing her pain and making her cry. Just as he had her mother.

"Selfish bitch!" he snarled. "I deserve that property. I could have sold it and made enough money to be set for life. But you refused, and after all I did for you, the way I raised you and took care of you." His voice lowered. "But you'll make it even now. Every last pence."

Dread swelled inside her chest so heavy she could barely breathe. He wasn't the father she knew. He'd changed and become so much worse than he'd ever shown her before. "What do you mean?"

"You're Strathmore's favorite toy these days. I have a feeling he'll pay dearly for your return."

She stared at him in wild disbelief, her stomach roiling. Could it be true? Had he really kidnapped her in order to ransom her? When her father needed money, he grew desperate, but this scheme was mad, even for him.

Edward had been right about him. Her father cared

nothing for her; worse, he truly was dangerous, just as Edward warned her. The truth tore through her chest in a sickening wave of grief and terror. And she knew now as she choked back her distress and looked into his hate-filled eyes that she meant nothing to him except as a way to hurt Edward.

He tightened the binding around her wrists. "He thought he could make me his prisoner. I was innocent, but Strathmore took the law into his own hands."

"You killed his brother," she whispered.

"It was an accident!" The words bellowed from him so fiercely that the two men looked up from their cards to glance at him.

Her voice trembling with fear and cold, she breathed, "You'd been drinking."

"It was dark, the streets were wet—the horses lost their footing and couldn't stop. It was an accident! I was found innocent."

"But the guardianship," she said carefully, trying not to upset him again. It was the last thread of hope she had left to cling to, that he'd given her to Edward in order to protect her. Because in giving her away he'd proved he cared about her, even just a little . . . "You requested that."

A self-pleased sneer pulled at his lips, "Becoming the duke's ward increased your market value."

"Market value?" she repeated numbly. He'd never cared about her, not even enough to give her away. Grief swept over her, pounding through her hollow chest so terribly it felt as if he'd died, so completely had she lost him.

"I'll get my highest payment from Strathmore, but if he doesn't want you after all, then I sell you to the highest bidder." At her look of horror, he shrugged callously. "They sell mares and bitches at auction all the time."

She couldn't breathe as anguish clawed at her heart. When she first saw the guardianship agreement, she'd refused to believe it because she knew her father would never just sign her away like livestock to be bought and sold. But that was exactly how he thought of her. And nothing more.

"Oh, you'll fetch a dear price, even in rags." With a laugh, he pulled at her skirt. "The man who wins you will have a connection to the duke he can use to gain position and a pretty wife in whom to spend himself. That ought to be worth quite a bit to me."

Fighting down the urge to scream, she clenched her hands into fists, digging her fingernails hard into her palms as an icy-cold terror shuddered through her. Because she knew what her father planned, and it was far worse than the forced marriage he openly admitted he would do to her if Edward didn't free her. Looking at the stranger he had always been to her, seeing now the monster he had become and the blackness in his eyes that held no soul, she *knew* . . .

If he didn't get the money for her that he wanted, he would kill her.

"So for your sake, poppet"—he reached out and tapped playfully at her nose, and she recoiled from his touch—"I certainly hope you left Strathmore panting for more."

He stood to join his cronies at the table. Choking back the bile rising in her throat as the fear and anguish sickened her, she closed her eyes tightly and tried to keep breathing, but not before a single tear fell onto the binding around her wrists. The only one she would let herself cry.

"Deliver this to Meacham's office." He handed a folded note to one of the two men.

"What's that?" The man didn't glance up from his cards.

"The ransom note. Drop it off for the attorney, and don't let anyone see you."

Taking the note, the man pushed back his chair and left the cottage without so much as a glance of remorse at her. Through the broken windows, she heard the sound of horse hooves as he mounted and rode away.

Then all was quiet except for the steady slap of cards as her father slid into the man's empty chair, and he and his remaining crony played on.

She huddled helplessly on the floor with her arms wrapped around herself for warmth and comfort that wouldn't come. Oh God, how it hurt! Everything she'd believed in as a child was nothing more than a cruel joke, all the sacrifices she'd made just so her father would love her—it all meant nothing. He had lied, abused her mother, left them both to rot away uncared for except for the money they could give him, and she'd been so foolish, so *stupidly* foolish, to keep giving him money, to let him take Brambly from her one piece at a time. Because she thought she could buy his love. But he'd never wanted her; he'd wanted her money, and he couldn't have cared less what suffering he caused to get it.

Her eyes burned, her heart so broken she pressed her tied hands against her chest to physically ease the pain of each agonizing heartbeat. She had no idea where she was, no idea if Edward was coming after her or how he would be able to find her.

But she knew she *had* to get away.

Crawling to the wall, she pushed herself up to her feet

and leaned unsteadily against it until she found her footing.

"Going somewhere, poppet?" Her father didn't bother to glance away from his cards.

"My legs are stiff," she lied. "I just need to stand for a bit."

"Then stand there."

For several minutes, she leaned against the wall, letting the blood come back into her limbs, feeling the pins and needles as her circulation returned. As the two men played their game, she watched silently and concentrated on pushing down the fear licking at her toes. *Think!* She had to think and find a way to flee.

She had time, she told her frantically pounding heart, because the man delivering the note would be gone for at least two hours. Meacham's office was in the City of London, and based on the lack of street noise outside the cottage, even at the closest they were out beyond the fringes of London. With three of them watching over her, she didn't stand a chance. But perhaps, with only two, and if one of the remaining two was distracted—

She cleared her throat. "I have to use the necessary."

"Piss in the corner," her father answered.

"I will not!"

"Then piss yourself, I don't give a damn."

She gritted her teeth, welcoming the outrage as it overtook her fear. "I don't think that soiling myself will add to my *market value*, do you?"

"I'd be happy to take her outside an' help her up with her skirts," his crony offered. He glanced across the room at her, and as his lecherous gaze traveled down the length of her, he licked his lips.

Stifling a repulsive shudder, she lifted her chin. "Papa, please?"

With a fierce curse, Phillip Benton threw his cards down and shoved back from the table. He grabbed her arm, and jerking her so hard her teeth jarred, he shoved her out the door and around the side of the cottage to the outhouse in the bushes.

She paused.

"Get in there."

She held up her bound wrists. "Untie me?"

"Better not try anything," he warned as he loosened the knots and tore off the binding.

Rubbing the red marks on her wrists, she entered the little building and shut the door.

Frantically, she glanced around. No lock, nothing inside she could use as a weapon. Her shoulders sagged. Not that the thin walls of the little building would have slowed him down if he'd been forced to break in after her, anyway.

But at least the trip outside gave her an excuse she could use every two hours or so to separate the men and get her hands untied, and hopefully, eventually the knots would be retied loosely enough to free herself from the binding. And if that didn't happen and they were still there by nightfall, then she planned on attempting to flee into the darkness, even if her wrists were still bound.

His fist banged on the door. "Long enough."

"Just a moment!" she snapped out.

More pounding, so hard the entire shack shook. "Come out of there!"

Taking a deep breath, she pushed open the door and stepped outside, her hands angrily on her hips as she glared with mutinous resentment. "At least have the decency to give me a few moments for personal cares."

He ignored her. "Give me your hands."

She refused to move her hands from her hips.

He grabbed her arm and twisted it forward, and she bit back a cry. Holding her wrist, he grabbed for the other one, then lashed them together so tightly this time she winced as he cinched down the knots. Her stomach sickened, not at the pain but at knowing her father would physically harm her.

"Back into the house." He shoved her toward the cottage, pushed open the door to drag her inside—and stopped.

The cottage was empty, the other man gone.

"Get over there," he ordered and tossed her toward the corner, slamming the door shut. "Smythe! Where are you?"

He waited, listening for any sound or movement outside.

"Maybe he stepped out to relieve himself—"

"Quiet!" he snarled, then yelled, "Smythe!"

There was no answer. Outside the cottage, the morning was unusually still and silent. No wind, not even the sound of birds chirping from the trees.

She took a deep breath. "Papa, if you—"

"Shut up!"

Her father grabbed her around the neck, jerking her up against him. Cold, hard metal jammed against the small of her back as he pressed the end of his pistol against her. A scream tore from Kate's throat

"I'll kill her!" Benton shouted. "I've got a gun at her back. Come after me, and I'll shoot!"

Terrified, Kate held her breath, straining for any sound of movement from outside but hearing only the rush of blood pounding in her ears. Silence fell again, the morning eerily still. But she sensed unheard movement circling the cottage, unseen men moving carefully along its stone walls.

"Let her walk out, Benton, and you won't be hurt."

"Edward!" she cried.

Her father squeezed his arm against her throat, choking her until she gasped for breath. Her fingernails dug into his arm.

"I'm not letting go of her," he answered, dragging her to the side of the window so he could lean against the wall and look outside, using her body as a shield. Kate could see nothing through the dirty glass, but she felt the tension rising in the air.

"The cottage is surrounded. Let her walk out, and we'll take her and leave."

"You think I'm that stupid?" Benton gave a deranged laugh. "The minute I let her go, you'll kill me."

"I won't, you have my word."

"Worthless!"

"No," Kate protested, her voice raspy, "he means it. Listen to him pl—"

"Shut up!"

He struck her across the temple with the pistol handle. Blackness flashed before her eyes, and a trickle of blood seeped sticky warm down her face.

"I'm leaving here and taking her with me, you hear me?" he shouted out the window.

Kate shuddered, her knees buckling beneath her. But he jerked her roughly against him to hold her propped up on her feet.

"Bring a horse to the door, tie it there, then back away." When there was no answer, he shouted, "Do it! Or I'll kill her right now."

"All right."

The soft sound of hooves moved toward the cottage, then the door was opened slowly from the outside.

Through the doorway, she saw Edward's chestnut colt tied just a few feet away.

"Come on," he ordered, pulling her toward the door and repositioning the pistol at her head.

When they stepped into the sunlight, Kate saw a man from the corner of her eye, crouching behind the rear of the cottage, a brace of pistols in his hands. Beneath the black carriage near the barn lay another, a pistol in each hand and another half dozen laid out on the ground in a semicircle in front of him.

Someone was going to die here, she realized with a terrified shudder. *Please, God, not Edward!*

The subject of her prayers stood fully upright, drawn to his full six feet of height, and fully exposed in plain view just a few yards from the cottage door, his hand gripping a pistol lowered at his side. His black hair glistened brilliantly in the bright sunlight, his face set hard as his dark eyes never left her father, seeing and following every move and shift of his body. His spine was ramrod straight, his shoulders back, and she suddenly had a glimpse of what he must have looked like as a colonel leading his troops into battle. He was magnificent. And deadly.

"We're getting on that horse and riding off." Benton pressed the gun harder into her cheek, and she flinched, terrified tears gathering at her lashes.

"No, you're not," Edward replied as calmly as if he were commenting on the weather. "Let her go, and you'll get to live."

"So you can make me your prisoner again? I'd die before I'd let you do that."

"As you wish," Edward answered quietly.

Keeping Kate as his shield between his body and

Edward's pistol, her father pulled her backward toward the waiting horse. He lowered the gun from her head to wrap his arm around her neck while his free hand reached down to untie the reins. He fumbled with the leather straps as he tried to keep his hold on her and his eyes on Edward.

His arm loosened around her neck, his eyes darted down to the reins—

With a fierce cry, Kate sank her teeth into his right thumb, biting down through the flesh until she hit bone. He screamed, instinctively jerking back his arm, and the pistol dropped from his mutilated hand.

She kicked the pistol away and staggered backward just out of his furious reach.

Edward raised his gun, pointing it at her father's chest.

She screamed, "Edward, no!"

He hesitated. All three of them stood there, frozen in place—Edward with his pistol pointed at her father, her father glaring murderously, and Kate glancing frantically between the two men, holding her breath, waiting for the sound of gunshots and death.

"Edward," she pleaded, "lower the gun and let him go."

His eyes never moved from her father. "He killed Stephen and Jane, and he hurt you."

"I know." Her voice choked in her throat.

"He's a spineless, murdering bastard who deserves to die."

"But he's also my father," she said, desperate to stop the firing of guns and the taking of lives.

"If I kill him, it ends right here, and he can't hurt anyone else I love."

He glanced at her then, his dark eyes leveling on hers for just an instant before flicking back to her father.

She saw the indecision tearing at him as he was forced

to choose...her or her father, the man he hated or the woman he loved. If he pulled the trigger now, he'd secure the ultimate revenge against her father, and he would never be arrested for it, not after all her father had done. But if Edward killed him, and right in front of her...she would lose him forever.

"You're not a murderer, Edward," she said softly. "Don't let him turn you into one."

She took a step toward him, her trembling hands reaching toward his pistol.

* * *

Edward felt his breath catch painfully in his chest, watching as she moved between her father and the end of the pistol. He'd loved and admired Stephen, but his brother was gone now. Nothing would ever bring him back.

But the same hand of fate that had stripped Stephen from his life had also given him Kate, who was alive, warm, and vibrant. When he swore revenge against Phillip Benton at all costs, he'd been wrong—he wasn't willing to lose Kate. He loved her, with every beat of his heart and every breath he took.

"Edward, please."

She stepped slowly toward him. Looking into his eyes, she slid her hands down his arm in a gentle caress and eased the pistol from his hand. "It's all right, darling," she assured him, bending down to place the pistol on the ground at their feet, then rising up into his arms. "You saved me. I'm safe now—"

Benton swung up onto the back of the horse. Matteson and Grey tensed, aimed their guns—

"No!" she screamed.

"Hold fire!" Edward yelled, waving his right arm in the air to get their attention while he grabbed Kate tightly to him with his left, pulling her face down against his chest to shield her eyes. "Hold your fire!"

The horse reared on its hind legs, then surged forward. It bolted into the bushes toward the open fields and woods beyond. In a matter of seconds, Phillip Benton was gone.

Kate swayed.

Edward caught her as she sank, scooping her into his arms and setting her gently across his lap as he sat on the ground, then wrapped his arms around her to hold her pressed tightly against him, his head lowering to bury his face in her hair. His heart thudded painfully, his breathing shallow and fast, as he finally let himself think about the danger she had been in, how close he'd come to losing her.

"Kate, are you all right?" His fingers gently touched the cut at her temple.

"I'm fine—"

He cupped her chin against his palm and tipped up her face to kiss her, all the relief inside him pouring into her. A shudder pulsed through her, then eased into trembling as she sighed against his lips, and when she rose up to lean into his embrace, he knew, finally, that the nightmare was over. She was safe in his arms, and no one would ever take her from him again.

"Colonel?" Nathaniel Grey approached them.

Edward nodded, and Grey sent up two sharp whistles. Two more whistles answered from the woods, followed by the muffled sounds of horses racing away.

"It's done, sir. My men will have him before he reaches the river."

Kate gasped. "You can't kill him!"

"I work for the War Office, my lady." Grey bent down next to her, lightly resting on the balls of his feet as he pulled a knife from his boot and gently slipped the edge beneath the binding around her wrist, cutting her free. "They won't kill him if they don't have to, but they're not letting him go, either." He sheathed the knife. "I'm arresting your father, to make certain he never has the chance to harm either of you again."

From the way her face paled, Edward knew she understood what Grey meant. He and his men wouldn't kill her father, but for kidnapping her and threatening the life of a peer, her father would most likely hang at the gallows for what he'd done. But Edward also knew from the flicker of determination in her green eyes that even now, after all Benton had done, she'd still plead with the magistrates to spare his life.

That was his darling angel, he thought as he raised her freed hands to his lips, merciful even to those who weren't worthy of it. He'd experienced that same mercy himself, and he wanted to spend the rest of his life proving to her that he deserved it.

But there would be time later for that. Now, he just wanted to hold her in his arms, where she belonged.

"Come on." Thomas clamped a hand onto Grey's shoulder. "Help me hitch up the horses so we can get her home."

As the two men retreated toward the carriage, Edward tightened his hold around Kate. He didn't want to let her go and pressed her head against his chest, hoping she could feel the beating of his heart against her cheek and know exactly how terrified he'd been.

"When they took you," he murmured into her hair, "I was afraid I'd lost you forever."

Her arms tightened around him even as she pulled back to gaze silently up at him, her green eyes bright with tears. Words she was unable to speak choked on her parted lips.

"I was a fool." He stroked his finger across her cheek. "I thought I could have a life with you yet keep my heart my own because I was terrified you'd shatter it. I knew I'd never recover if..."

She tangled her hands in his jacket lapels as if afraid he would slip away from her. But he had no intention of ever leaving her side again.

"I'm a soldier, Kate," he told her, "and I always will be, no matter what titles I possess, and I don't know the beautiful words of poets or the pretty phrases of love letters." He took a deep breath, his body shaking as he exhaled. "All I can tell you is how I feel. That you make me warm and alive, that you are everything to me. And I...I love you, angel."

"What?" she breathed, her wide eyes incredulous.

"I love you, Katherine," he repeated, the words coming easier this time. "I know that now. I never realized how much you meant to me, how much I truly loved you, until I thought I'd lost you. I was terrified I'd never be able to tell you." His fingers trembled as he cupped her face in his hands. "And I am never again letting you go."

A tear slipped down her cheek, and she beamed at him, a brilliant smile full of happiness and hope. In that smile, he could see the future stretching out before them, one they would share together of home, children, and love. Lots and lots of love.

"You'd better not," she whispered.

With a laugh, he lowered his head and kissed her.

EPILOGUE

Three Weeks Later
Strathmore House, London

The sapphire-and-diamond ring shined in the firelight. It was official now. She was engaged.

Oh my.

Her heart thudded as she lay on her bed, still wearing her ball gown, and lovingly traced her fingertip over the ring. Edward had placed it on her hand tonight at their engagement ball, which was already being heralded as the event of the season, possibly second only to the upcoming wedding itself scheduled for three weeks from now in St. Paul's Cathedral. Augusta refused to even consider the notion of holding the ceremony anywhere else, just as she'd refused an engagement period of less than six weeks, despite the special license they'd acquired.

Less than six weeks to plan both an engagement ball

and a wedding was simply impossible, Augusta declared. *Impossible!* And so Kate spent the last three weeks in a flurry of plans and arrangements, dress fittings, and shopping outings for her trousseau, as well as entertaining an endless stream of callers. It seemed everyone in England wanted to meet the woman who captured the duke's heart.

Waiting to be married hadn't been all bad, she considered with a smile, as she lay back on the coverlet. Because there had been Edward.

For propriety's sake, he'd moved out of Strathmore House and into Grey's bachelor townhome, but he came by every morning for breakfast, every evening for dinner, and he took her for drives through the city, picnics in the park, boat rides on the Thames, fireworks at Vauxhall... all those wonderful excursions suitors arranged for their ladies. He'd even rented a hot-air balloon and kissed her as they rose above London. A hot-air balloon!

When she complained that he was spoiling her, he looked at her as if she'd gone mad and replied, "Of course I am."

Of course.

And, then, there had been the nights.

He often lingered at Strathmore House after dinner, with the explicit purpose of joining her in her room after Augusta retired. They'd started their honeymoon early, and she was glad, so very glad. Just the thought of him in her bed made her body tingle with anticipation.

That's why she hadn't let Mary undress her. Because she knew he would come to her tonight to make love to her, and she wanted him to take down her hair and peel the silk gown from her skin, the dress of Westover blue that had been specially made to replace the one her father ruined.

She'd been so blind about Papa. Grimacing with mortification and grief, she remembered the way she'd defended him to Edward when he first showed her the guardianship. She'd underestimated the evil that he was capable of committing, but thank God, she'd never underestimated the good in Edward.

It was only when she'd appeared before the magistrates during her father's trial to argue for his exportation rather than his death that she realized exactly how much Edward loved her, because he said not one word to dissuade her from doing so, even though her father's hanging would have finally meant justice for Stephen and Jane's deaths.

But Phillip Benton never reached Australia. He was killed in an attempted break from Newgate, and Edward held her while she cried over the news, not for the man but for the father she'd never had.

"Katherine."

Glancing up at the deep voice, her gaze fell on him as he stood in the doorway. In his formal evening clothes, with his blue brocade waistcoat over a snow-white shirt and cravat, white trousers and black superfine jacket, his hair shining in the firelight, he stole her breath away. She'd always thought him more handsome than other men, with his firm jaw and high cheekbones, the obsidian depths of his eyes... But tonight, he was simply magnificent.

She held out her hand.

Closing the door behind him, he moved to lie down on the bed next to her. He laced his fingers through hers, then raised her hand to his lips to kiss it. For several minutes, they lay together in silence, shoulder to shoulder and eyes on the canopy above, simply enjoying each other's presence.

"So." He rubbed his thumb over her ring. "Did you enjoy your party?"

She squeezed his hand, never having been happier in her life. "Immensely."

She'd truly felt like Cinderella, dancing in the arms of her Prince Charming and changing partners only to offer quadrilles to Grey and Thomas and her second waltz to the Prince Regent, who surprised everyone by appearing at the ball.

"I stepped on Prinny's toes." With a soft giggle, she turned toward him on her side and smiled. "When I apologized, he said it was only fair, since he'd been stepping on your toes for years."

He laughed. Rolling toward her, he wrapped his arms around her and buried his face in her hair. His laughter warmed through her, and the now-familiar ache of desire stirred low in her belly. She sighed and snuggled closer. *Dear God*, how much she loved this man!

"I have your wedding gift with me," he told her. "I want to give it to you tonight."

"But you've already given me so much." And she had him. She didn't need anything more.

Sitting up, he pulled a folded paper from his breast pocket. "I had Meacham write it this morning."

She hesitated as she reached for it, her hand freezing in midair. "Isn't this where we started?" Her heart skipped in warning. "With Meacham drawing up papers."

"Trust me, angel. This one you'll like."

She cautiously took it and unfolded it. As her eyes moved over the page, she froze and read it again. Did it really say— Her heart thumped with happiness. Oh, she'd never dared hope for Edward and this, too. But she was marrying the kindest, most generous man in the world, and what else would he have given her but the most perfect wedding gift of all?

"Brambly," she breathed, finally finding her voice. "You're giving me Brambly."

Her grandparents knew when they established the entailment that her father would never provide her with a dowry and the farm would have to serve, so they stipulated that when she married, Brambly would pass to her husband. It was the only property she brought to the marriage and so pitifully small in comparison to what any other woman who married a duke would have offered.

But he'd agreed to relinquish all rights, to revert the farm's ownership completely and in perpetuity to her... and to their future daughters.

Edward had given Brambly back to her.

He touched her shoulder. "Does it make you happy?"

"Oh, so very much." She took his hand and laced her fingers through his, never wanting to let him go.

"Good." He leaned over to touch his lips tenderly to hers. "Because that's how I plan to spend the rest of my life, Kate. Making you happy."

He pulled her against him as his mouth came down on hers. The sweetest kiss she'd ever known, passionate and possessive, full of love and tenderness. Dear heavens! She could actually taste the happiness on his lips.

He left a trail of hot kisses along her jaw and back to her ear. "Is there anything else I can do to make you happy?"

A thrill pulsed through her, her mind racing with wanton thoughts of all the ways he could make her happy right here in her bed. Instead, she smiled as she ran her fingers through the silky, black hair at his nape, and teased, "Wed me tomorrow so we don't have to wait three more weeks to become husband and wife."

"Why, Miss Benton." He pulled back and raised his brows, feigning shock at her suggestion. "Are you asking me to elope?"

She stared at him, her mind spinning. She'd only been teasing, but ... was that really such an outlandish idea? "We still have the special license," she ventured. "We *could* be married tomorrow!—Oh, Edward." She clenched his waistcoat in her hands. "If we left tonight, we could be married at Brambly in the morning."

He paused, as if truly contemplating the idea, then regretfully shook his head. "Augusta would be devastated if she wasn't there when we married."

"Then we'll bring her with us!"

With a kiss to his cheek and a happy laugh, she slipped from his arms and hurried across the room to her armoire. She reached inside for her travel bag.

He slid off the bed and followed. "Let me see if I understand correctly—we're eloping with my aunt?"

"Yes! Isn't that wonderful?"

"Not exactly the word I would choose," he muttered grimly. When she placed her green day dress into the bag, he picked up the night rail Mary had left out for her on the chair and placed it into the bag for her. "Grey and Thomas are standing up with us. We cannot marry without them."

She rose on tiptoes to kiss his cheek. "Then we'll bring them, too."

"Wonderful," he repeated in a sardonic mumble. "And Mrs. Elston, Arthur, Dorrie—"

"All of them—we'll have all of them with us!" She laughed with happiness and excitement, throwing her arms around his neck. "We'll have a ceremony at Brambly just for us and our family, to start our honeymoon and life together, then we'll marry at St. Paul's in three weeks as planned, for everyone else to witness."

He laughed. "We're doing it backwards, angel."

Yes, she supposed they were. But then, nothing about their romance had been traditional, so why should the wedding? She lovingly touched his cheek. "With us, could it be any other way?"

He swept her up into his arms. "I love you."

"I know." With a sigh, she rested her head against his shoulder. "But don't ever stop telling me."

"Never." He carried her downstairs, over the threshold, and out of the house.

Major Nathaniel Grey will do anything to bring his friend's little sister home. But instead of the gangly girl he remembers, he's greeted by a stunningly beautiful woman holding a loaded musket. And he's utterly captivated by her...

Please see the next page
for a preview of

ALONG CAME A ROGUE.

CHAPTER ONE

London, England
April 1816

*H*idden from sight in the dark shadows at the rear of the private opera box, Nathaniel Grey leaned one hand against the wall for support and with the other raised the glass of whiskey to his lips, then glanced down at the woman kneeling in front of him, her beautifully coiffed head bobbing at his crotch.

Oh, Lady Margaret Roquefort was a lovely woman with a deliciously wicked mouth. He enjoyed her company immensely, more so when in private, and luckily, she shared his own interest in opera, finding far more fun in the activities occurring in the dark boxes than in whatever happened onstage.

The rising notes of the aria drowned her soft moan of pleasure, her lips closing tightly around him. Shutting his eyes, he let himself enjoy the moment.

He wasn't meant to be there, two boxes down from the Prince Regent, dressed in elegant evening clothes, and taking pleasure in one of the most beautiful ladies in English society. Not him. Not the bastard son of God only knew whom and an orphan so inconsequential, so worthless to the world, that the lie he chose to tell about himself—that he was the runaway son of a blacksmith—was a decided improvement over the truth. But even at ten, when he ran away from the squalor and brutality of the orphanage, effectively running away from fate, he knew he was destined for more.

He somehow talked his way into a job as a stable boy at Henley Park, where he had a roof over his head, food in his belly, and pennies each week in pay—but more importantly, he had an education thrust upon him by the old Dowager Viscountess Henley, who forced him to attend her grandsons' tutoring sessions. She had made it her personal mission to ensure that every employee at Henley could read, write, and speak properly, if in varying degrees, including the misfit stable boy who became so adept at lying about his past that he'd almost come to believe his father truly was a blacksmith.

"Grey," Margaret moaned, sensing his distraction, and he reached down to stroke his finger across her cheek.

He smiled at the wry irony of his current situation as arousal throbbed hot through his veins. Would Lady Roquefort be pleasuring him right now if she knew the truth?

He choked back a laugh. Knowing Margaret, the baroness would have been perversely delighted in pleasuring someone so far beneath her station, her lips sucking even more eagerly in rebellious glee.

But she knew nothing of that past, and he fully intended to keep it that way. Because when he turned eighteen, he'd purged even that part of his life by taking the money he'd managed to scrimp together to purchase a commission and joined the cavalry as the lowest ranking officer, somehow ending up as part of the exclusive First Dragoons. Grey suspected the meddling of the dowager viscountess on his behalf, yet the old woman denied it. He knew the truth, however, and he was immeasurably grateful.

In the army, he'd risked his life in order to have one worth living, and through skill and sheer fearlessness, he rose to the rank of captain with the Scarlet Scoundrels, that group of soldiers under Colonel Westover's command who earned their hard-won reputation in saber charges across the battlefields of Spain. The bastard orphan had managed to make a decent life for himself, after all.

But then fate found him again, in the middle of a sunflower field, in the form of a single bullet to his leg.

It hadn't taken his life, but it had snatched away his career, forcing him once again to reinvent himself, this time as a War Office agent. He was often called on to carry out jobs that other men connected to the War Office either didn't have the wherewithal to complete or wouldn't dirty their hands to do. Grey didn't mind. He'd proven himself very good at it, rising quickly in the estimation of the undersecretaries and generals, proudly earning himself a promotion to major.

Now he was here, the last place an orphan should have been. He looked like every other gentleman in the opera house, his cravat elaborately knotted and secured with a ruby pin, his maroon brocade waistcoat from the best tailor on Bond Street. And he had more than earned his right to be there, having killed—and nearly been killed himself—to protect all of them from Napoléon and other enemies within, without a word of thanks.

Yet while he could dress like them, gamble with them, drink their best whiskey, and bed their finest ladies, he would never truly be one of them.

Still, living on the periphery of society was more than an orphan could ever have hoped to achieve, and he certainly never regretted any of the lies. Why would he? Lying had given him a far better life than telling the truth.

The soprano reached her last notes, and pulling a rasping breath through his clenched teeth, Grey shuddered and released himself. He felt Margaret swallow around him as her hot mouth milked his cock, and when she'd finished, he pulled away and handed her the glass.

As she drank the remaining liquor, he fastened up his trousers. Ah, how much he enjoyed the opera! And one of these nights, he fully intended to watch a performance.

"Ugh! Whiskey." Margaret made a disgusted face as he took her elbow and helped her to her feet. "You know I can't stand the stuff, Grey. Why don't you ever drink anything that I enjoy—like port or brandy?"

"I never drink brandy." *Not anymore.* His mind registered the sound of applause around them, followed by the rise of the audience to their feet as they filed from their boxes for the intermission. The mindless chattering among the blue bloods rose nearly as loud as the opera singers.

"Port, then." She set the empty glass aside and smoothed her hands down her skirt to press out any telltale wrinkles around her knees, and his lips twitched in private amusement at her expense. He enjoyed women like Lady

Roquefort, those well-bred ladies of the *ton* who were always so proper and fashionable, even when on their knees. "Next time, bring me port."

He forced a charming smile for her, this woman who meant absolutely nothing to him except as an evening's entertainment, and stifled a contemptuous laugh because she thought she could order him about. But he'd humor her. Only because she'd implied that he'd get to enjoy her again. "Of course, my lady." He reached out to trail his fingertips over the swells of her breasts revealed by the daringly low neckline and felt her breath quicken. "Anything you desire."

She gave a long exhalation and trembled beneath his exploring hands. "You know, all the ladies were gossiping about you tonight in the retiring room."

"Hmm...and what did they say?" She expected him to ask, so he indulged her, yet he couldn't have cared less about those gossipy hens.

"They wondered what the major was like as a lover, if he'd singled out anyone to be his mistress or if he prefers being promiscuous."

"Promiscuous," he murmured with mock solemnity, dipping his head to trace the tip of his tongue down her throat. "Definitely promiscuous."

With a flirtatious laugh, she swatted playfully at his shoulder and forced him to step away as the noise of the milling crowd grew louder around them. With a sigh, she tugged her dress back into place and adjusted her long gloves. "How do I look, then?"

"Stunning." Carefully keeping all sardonic amusement for her from his face, he took her hand and raised it to his lips. "As always."

The flattery was empty, but it pleased her. Which was all that mattered. He needed to keep her happy only so he could enjoy Mozart again with her in the future.

With her eyes shining, she leaned casually against the wall. "Quite a coup by you, securing a private box all to yourself tonight. However did you manage?"

"I've always appreciated the privacy of a reserved box," he said earnestly, expertly deflecting her question.

He'd long ago grown used to the backhanded compliments leveled at him by her kind. They no more bothered him now than getting caught in a warm summer rain. But he wasn't foolish enough to open himself to wounding by admitting that the box belonged to Edward Westover, Duke of Strathmore, and his former colonel.

No doubt Margaret thought she'd been utterly scandalous tonight by having her mouth on him. She was right, of course, although not because of the act itself but because of who he was. As an army officer and the imposter son of a blacksmith, he'd never be able to show his face publicly with any woman of Lady Roquefort's status, he knew that—even the rank of major wasn't enough for that when he had no allowance or family name to accompany it—and he certainly would never be able to marry one of the innocent darlings of the *ton*.

Neither did he care. Hell would freeze over before he leg-shackled himself.

In that, he was superior to the rest of the fop dandies crowding the opera house tonight, despite their wealth and titles, their storied family histories, and their roles in Parliament, in which they agreed to send expendable men like him into battle without so much as a second thought. He had no grand estate, no need for an heir, and so no need to bind himself to a wife and then spend the rest of his life longing for the freedom of bachelorhood and all its delights. He was free to bed whomever he wanted, whenever he wanted—and in the case of Lady Roquefort, *wherever* he wanted—and answer to no one but himself.

He was willing to lay down his life for his country, but as for domestication...He repressed a shudder at just the thought of it. *Good God.* Never!

"Now, be a good girl"—he turned her toward the box entrance, happily done with her for the evening—"and return to your husband before the old baron discovers you're missing."

With a satisfied grin and a playful slap to her arse that made her jump, he was gone, stepping through the curtain into the hallway and blending into the milling crowd, making his way down toward the crush in the lobby and leaving her behind without another thought.

The night was still early. There was time yet for a few hours of cards at one of the clubs since he no longer had any reason to linger at the opera house. After all, he certainly hadn't attended to hear the Mozart.

As he made his way downstairs, he slipped between the groups of operagoers gathered to gossip in the hall and even on the wide stairs, which curved down into the grand two-story lobby below. He nodded his head occasionally at acquaintances among the men and carefully kept all knowing expressions from his face at acquaintances among the women. But none of them gave him a second glance, their attentions oddly rapt on the new bit of juicy *on-dit* floating through the house tonight. Juicy enough that some of the faces held shocked looks from the ladies and bewilderment from the men.

He skirted a group of pastel-donned debutantes at a safe distance but heard the shocked whisper rise from behind a flutter of fans, "...the marquess!"

Lots of marquesses among the quality, Grey dismissed, paying the comment no mind as he slipped down the stairs and past yet another group of gossiping hens with the same shocked expressions, the same frantic waving of their fans in agitated excitement. Just as with the debutantes, he gave the hens a wide berth. The last thing he wanted to sour his mood tonight was those disapproving glances that society matrons were so skilled in sending at rakes like him.

"So terrible...the marquess...dying like that..."

The snippets of conversation wafted up to him as he reached the lobby. Hmm...a dying marquess. So that was what caused such flapping among the hens and dandies tonight. Must have been fresh news about the Marquess of Dunwich. The old man had taken to bed a few days ago with the same fever that claimed both his son and grandson and left the title without an heir apparent, and the entire *ton* buzzed with speculation over what would become of the estate and who would inherent if he died. Without a clear line of inheritance, the title and fortune would be swept up in an aristocratic cockfight as cousins of all kinds emerged from the woodwork to claim it. Based on the titillated anxiousness floating through the crowd, the old goat must have finally given up the ghost.

He nodded at the Earl of St. James and his mother as he passed, doing his best to catch the eye of Lady Sydney Rowland standing next to them, but failing, blast it. The young widow was beautiful and quality—exactly the kind of woman he preferred—but Baroness Rowland showed no interest. Pity. So he grinned at her anyway and moved on toward the door.

"Have you heard?" The quiet question was aimed directly at him as he passed a man whose name Grey couldn't remember, some friend of Thomas Matteson's from university.

Grey paused just a moment to nod at the man. "I've heard. Terrible shame." Then moved on through the crush, ignoring the completely aghast look on the man's face that he should care so little about the marquess.

If he cared anything about tonight's gossip, it was only because Alistair Crenshaw, now-dead Marquess of Dunwich, was distantly related to the Matteson family through the marriage of Thomas's sister Emily. But ironically, Emily's own husband died just a few months ago, and any hope her parents had that the title would be united into the Duke of Chatham's line was now as dead as her husband.

He neared the door, longing for the quiet and coolness outside.

"Such a shock—the marquess was so young."

He stopped instantly, his head snapping up. A *young* marquess?

The man who uttered that news stood only a few feet away at the center of a group of bejeweled ladies and gentlemen, holding their interest with his retelling of the gossip and reveling at being the center of attention. He paused to let the information sink in and parceled out the news bit by bit to greatest effect.

Grey forced a lazy half smile that belied the rising unease inside him as he sauntered over to the group. "What young marquess?"

"Why, Chesney." The man blinked, surprised that anyone in the opera house could possibly not have heard the news by now. "Thomas Matteson. Shot in the avenue tonight, just at sunset. No one knows—"

Thomas. Grey ran for the street.

When he reached Chatham House, the townhome was ablaze with lamps and candles. Two saddle horses stood tied in the front, along with the massive black carriage marked with the Duke of Strathmore's coat of arms.

A cold knot of dread clenched his chest as he raced up the front steps of the stone portico and pounded on the door with his fist.

Jensen, the Chatham butler, opened the door and looked out solemnly, his round face drawn and his gray brows knitted, but he did not move back to let Grey pass.

"The house is closed tonight, Major," Jensen told him grimly. "Please return tomorrow."

When he tried to close the door, Grey shoved his shoulder against it and pushed his way inside, forcing the butler to stumble backward to make way for him.

Had it been any other night, he never would have caused such an uproar, and he would have returned the next day as asked, just to keep peace in Thomas's household. But not tonight. There were few houses in Mayfair where he was allowed admittance through the front door, and he was not going to let some pompous, arrogant butler keep him from this one. Not tonight.

"Where is Chesney?" Grey demanded. "Is he here?"

Jensen's face drew into a troubled scowl. "Major, please! The house is closed, upon order of His Gr—"

"Jensen." A deep voice from the upstairs landing cut through the scuffle. "Let him pass."

The butler glanced up at the Duke of Strathmore, and with an aggravated *humph!* beneath his breath at having his authority undermined, he bowed and backed away to let Grey into the house.

Grey raised his eyes grimly as he raced up the curving marble stairs toward Edward Westover. "Thomas?"

"He's here," Edward informed him solemnly, keeping his voice low so they wouldn't be overheard by Jensen or the other servants. "The surgeons are with him."

Grey's hand gripped the banister tightly to steady himself. "He's still alive?"

"Barely."

"What happened?" he choked out, relief flooding through him.

With a glance down at Jensen, still lingering in the foyer, Edward indicated toward the nearby library with a look.

Grey followed him inside the room and accepted the glass of scotch the duke poured from a bottle on the table just inside the door, the half-filled glass beside it telling him that Edward had already sought out his own liquid strength.

As he raised the glass to his mouth, he tried to hide the shaking of his hands. "Was it the French?" His voice was quiet so that only Edward could hear. "Was he discovered?"

Edward and Grey were two of a handful of people who knew that the young marquess had continued to dedicate himself to his country after the war by signing on to work with the War Office, continuing the country's effort against the French in secret. If the French had discovered he was serving as a spy, they might have attempted an assassination.

Edward shook his head. "A footpad." He splashed more scotch into his glass and took a long swallow. "He'd been visiting me at Strathmore House and was on his way home when a man shot him two streets from here. A groom heard the report and found the man rifling through Thomas's pockets as he lay bleeding on the footpath."

"How badly is he wounded?" Grey steeled himself.

Edward hesitated. "Gut shot."

Christ. Grey leaned against the wall, the air rushing from him, and he squeezed his eyes shut. Not Thomas. Not after they'd stared down death together in Spain, to be killed two streets from his own home.

"The surgeons are operating now." Edward paused, studying the amber liquid in his glass. "But he's lost a lot of blood. Thank God that groom came upon him when he did, or he would have bled out right there."

"The carriage," Grey forced out, trying to clear the swirling fear and fury fogging his mind. "You brought the duchess with you."

Edward nodded. "Jensen sent a messenger to the house. When she heard, she insisted on coming with me to attend the surgeons."

"Is that wise in her condition?"

Edward's lips pressed together grimly at the reminder that his wife was expecting their first child. "You try stopping her when she's set her mind on something."

Taking careful breaths, concentrating on the air filling his lungs, Grey tried to steady himself, but his heart kept pounding harder, his stomach roiling painfully. *Gut shot . . .* Thomas was alive, but he'd be dead by dawn.

"Damnation!" Edward slammed down the crystal tumbler so hard the liquid splashed onto the table. Sucking in a harsh breath, he rubbed at his forehead. "I sent him away tonight. Kate asked him to stay with us for dinner, but I wanted an evening alone with her." Guilt stiffened his shoulders. "If I hadn't—if I had just invited him to stay, or offered another drink..."

"It wasn't your fault, Colonel." Grey knew Edward had kept Thomas alive in Spain, saving his life at least a half dozen times, and as he had then, he felt responsible for him now.

"I know," he agreed quietly, "but it damned well feels like it." He reached for his glass again. "I've sent for his parents. The duke and duchess are at Stonewall Abbey," he continued in that same emotionless, duty-bound way Grey remembered from the Peninsula, when Edward had been responsible for all their lives.

"He has a sister up north, near York...Emily," Grey reminded him, an image flashing through his mind from several years back of a stick of a girl with big ears and blond braids who had adored her brother. "We need to send for her, too."

Edward nodded grimly, both men knowing the harsh reality of the news, which wouldn't reach his sister for days, and by then, Thomas would already be dead and past whatever comfort she could give. "I've hired Bow Street to track down the shooter and ordered Jensen to close the house to visitors. There's nothing else to do but wait."

Grey stared at him. Edward was only three years older than him in age, but at that moment, the former colonel looked as if he'd aged decades under the strain of once again being responsible for Thomas's life.

But since that day in San Cristobal when Thomas saved his wounded leg from the field surgeons, Grey felt just as responsible as Edward for overseeing Thomas's life, and if necessary, his death. And he'd be damned if he did nothing more tonight than pace the floor and wait for his best friend to die.

Downing the rest of the scotch, he shoved himself away from the wall and charged toward the door.

"Where are you going?"

"To find the man who did this." He glanced over his shoulder at Edward as he strode from the room, his calm outward appearance belying the white-hot fury burning inside him.

Edward followed him. "Let Bow Street take care of this. They have access to Mayfair."

"I have better contacts. I'll have my men in the streets within an hour—"

"Grey." Edward put his hand on his arm as they reached the stairs and repeated meaningfully, "Bow Street has access to Mayfair."

Grey clenched his jaw, knowing the unspoken meaning beneath Edward's comment. The Bow Street men would be allowed into any house in Mayfair if they said they were there to investigate the marquess's shooting, allowed complete access to all the household staffs and all the buildings. He and his War Office men wouldn't be allowed past the front door.

It was another reminder that he would never belong to English society. No matter how hard he worked or how far he moved up in rank, he would always be an outsider, and the truth of that had never been more brutal than at that moment, when being an outsider made it impossible to help Thomas.

"I will find that man," Grey repeated, jerking his arm

away from Edward's grasp. "I might not have the same access to Mayfair as a Bow Street runner or a blue blood," he said coldly, noting the narrowing of the duke's eyes, "but I also have nothing to lose. And if Thomas dies, I'll make that bastard regret the day he was born."

Without a backward glance, he charged down the stairs and through the front door, slamming it closed behind him.

Fall in Love with Forever Romance

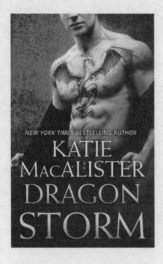

DRAGON STORM
by Katie MacAlister

In *New York Times* bestselling author Katie MacAlister's *Dragon Storm*, Constantine must choose: save his fellow dragons or the mortal woman he's grown to love.

HIS ALL NIGHT
by Elle Wright

In relationships, Calisa Harper has clear rules: no expectations, no commitments, no one gets hurt. She doesn't need a diamond ring to bring her happiness. She just needs Jared. Fine, fit, and ferocious in bed, Jared is Calisa's ideal combination of friend and lover. But the no-strings status they've shared for years is about to get very tangled...

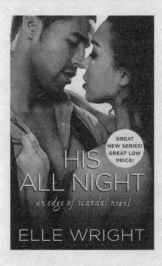

Fall in Love with Forever Romance

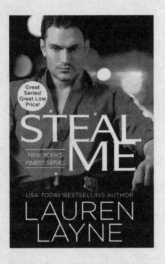

STEAL ME
by Lauren Layne

Faster than a New York minute, homicide detective Anthony Moretti and waitress Maggie Walker find themselves in a perilous pursuit that only gets hotter with each and every rule-breaking kiss.

A BILLIONAIRE
BETWEEN THE SHEETS
by Katie Lane

A commanding presence in the boardroom and the bedroom, Deacon Beaumont has come to save the failing company French Kiss. But one bold and beautiful woman dares to question his authority and everything he knows about love.

Fall in Love with Forever Romance

DUKES ARE FOREVER
by **Anna Harrington**

When Edward Westover takes possession of his rival's estate, everything that villain held dear—even his beautiful daughter—belongs to Edward. Will Kate Benton fall for the man who now owns everything she has come to know and love—including herself? Fans of Elizabeth Hoyt, Grace Burrowes, and Madeline Hunter will love this Regency–era romance.